IN A DISTANT G[illegible],
THE PEACEFUL PLANET LORIEN
WAS DECIMATED BY
THE BRUTAL MOGADORIANS.

The last survivors of Lorien—the Garde—were sent to Earth as children. Scattered across the continents, they developed their extraordinary powers known as Legacies and readied themselves to defend their adopted home world.

The Garde thwarted the Mogadorian invasion of Earth. In the process, they changed the very nature of the planet. Legacies began to manifest in human beings.

These new Garde frighten some people, while others look for ways to manipulate them to their benefit.

And although the Legacies are meant to protect Earth, not every Garde will use their powers for good.

I AM PITTACUS LORE.
RECORDER OF THE FATES,
CHRONICLER OF THE LEGACIES.

I TELL THE TALES OF THOSE
WHO WOULD SHAPE WORLDS.

BY PITTACUS LORE

THE ◇ LORIEN LEGACIES REBORN ◇

Novels

GENERATION ONE

FUGITIVE SIX

RETURN TO ZERO

The Legacy Chronicles Novellas

#1: OUT OF THE ASHES

#2: INTO THE FIRE

#3: UP IN SMOKE

#4: CHASING GHOSTS

#5: RAISING MONSTERS

#6: KILLING GIANTS

The Legacy Chronicles Novella Collections

TRIAL BY FIRE *(Contains novellas #1–#3)*

OUT OF THE SHADOWS *(Contains novellas #4–#6)*

THE LORIEN LEGACIES

Novels

I AM NUMBER FOUR

THE POWER OF SIX

THE RISE OF NINE

THE FALL OF FIVE

THE REVENGE OF SEVEN

THE FATE OF TEN

UNITED AS ONE

The Lost Files Novellas

#1: SIX'S LEGACY

#2: NINE'S LEGACY

#3: THE FALLEN LEGACIES

#4: THE SEARCH FOR SAM

#5: THE LAST DAYS OF LORIEN

#6: THE FORGOTTEN ONES

#7: FIVE'S LEGACY

#8: RETURN TO PARADISE

#9: FIVE'S BETRAYAL

#10: THE FUGITIVE

#11: THE NAVIGATOR

#12: THE GUARD

#13: LEGACIES REBORN

#14: LAST DEFENSE

#15: HUNT FOR THE GARDE

The Lost Files Novella Collections

THE LEGACIES
(Contains novellas #1–#3)

SECRET HISTORIES
(Contains novellas #4–#6)

HIDDEN ENEMY
(Contains novellas #7–#9)

REBEL ALLIES
(Contains novellas #10–#12)

ZERO HOUR
(Contains novellas #13–#15)

THE LEGACY CHRONICLES

OUT OF THE SHADOWS

PITTACUS LORE

HARPER
An Imprint of HarperCollins*Publishers*

 For information address HarperCollins Children's Books, a division of HarperCollins Publishers, 195 Broadway, New York, NY 10007.
www.epicreads.com

ISBN 978-0-06-249408-5
19 20 21 22 23 PC/LSCH 10 9 8 7 6 5 4 3 2 1
❖
First Edition

CONTENTS

THE LEGACY CHRONICLES

CHASING GHOSTS

CHAPTER ONE

SAM
RENO, NEVADA

"ISN'T THIS STEALING?"

Nemo watched as Sam ran his fingers over the keypad on the ATM, pretending to punch in a sequence of numbers in case anyone was looking while actually telepathically telling the computer inside what to do. Or at least *trying* to. His Legacies were still not working right. He had flashes of success, but they were short and unpredictable.

Come on, come on, come on, he thought, hoping he could connect just long enough for the machine to do what he needed it to do.

The ATM chirped, then began spitting out twenty-dollar bills into Sam's hand. He breathed a sigh of relief. "It's not coming out of any specific person's account," he said, responding to Nemo. "This is the money the machine is stocked with. It's the bank's money."

"Totally doesn't answer my question, Robin Hood," Nemo remarked as Sam folded the bills and stuffed them into the pocket of his jeans.

"We'll repay them," Sam said as he turned and walked away from the bank. "Once things are sorted out."

"Mm-hmm," Nemo said vaguely.

"It's going to be fine," said Sam. He checked both ways for traffic on the street, then crossed to the diner on the other side.

"I didn't say I was worried," Nemo replied as Sam opened the door and they went inside. "If anything goes wrong, my plan is to tell everyone you and Six kidnapped me and forced me into a life of crime."

The two of them walked to the back of the diner, where Six was seated in a booth. She had her phone out and was looking at something on the screen. Sam slid in beside her while Nemo sat opposite them.

"Everything go okay?" Six asked without looking up.

Sam patted the fat wad of cash in his pocket. "Great," he said.

"You remembered to turn off the camera, right?" Six asked.

Sam smacked his forehead with his palm. "Damn it!" he said. "I knew I forgot something."

Six glanced at him and started to respond. Then she saw Sam giving her a look that said "Do you think I'm an idiot?"

"Sorry," she said.

"Wow," said Nemo. "An apology. And it isn't even Christmas."

Sam snorted while Six returned to her phone. A moment later, a waitress appeared, carrying the food they'd ordered before Sam made the trip to the bank.

"Pancakes for you," she said, setting down a plate in front of Nemo. "Chili burger with cheese fries for you," she said to Six, who put aside her phone. "And for you, a grilled cheese and bowl of tomato soup. I'll be right back with the drinks."

"So," Sam said as he dunked his sandwich into the soup. "Any luck?"

He was speaking to Six, who had been working on her own assignment.

"Not so far," Six said. "No reply to my message on the board."

It had been a little more than a day since they'd walked out of Nine's office at the Human Garde Academy. This was after Six had announced her decision to no longer be part of Peter McKenna's covert group. She'd been angry at finding out that they were unknowingly working alongside another group called Watchtower that was overseen by former FBI agent Karen Walker. It was Walker who was now in possession of both the Legacy-blocking serum that Sam and Six had been injected with and the scientist who had created it. Six and Sam had been completely left out of that decision.

Sam understood why she was angry and had backed her up, but he wasn't as sure as Six was that they had made the right decision. He'd kept his thoughts to himself, knowing it would do no good to argue with Six. Besides, it wasn't just about them. They had Nemo to worry about. Bringing her along had been a last-second decision, and they'd done it mostly because their current order of business was to find Ghost, Nemo's friend and one of the four teens they'd picked up in New Orleans. Ghost had turned on them, or had at least been brainwashed by her captors into believing that Sam, Six and basically anyone involved with Earth Garde and the Human Garde Academy were her enemies.

The plan was to find out where Ghost was and to try to rescue her. It was a good plan except for one thing—they had no idea how to locate the girl. They'd last seen her teleporting out of Bray's mansion in Argentina along with another teleporter, a boy called Scotty. Where they'd gone, nobody knew.

It was Nemo who'd come up with the idea of posting a message on the online networks for kids with Legacies who wanted to stay off the grid and not report to the authorities, as was required by law. That's how she had originally met Ghost and their friend Max, who was still back at the HGA along with Rena. Although many of the sites—including the one Nemo had used—had been shut down or were heavily monitored and therefore not used by the more militant members of the anti-Garde community, a couple remained, operating on the dark web.

In their hotel room the night before, Six had taken a dive into the murky waters of the dark web and found something promising, a site where kids with Legacies exchanged information. Some were looking for ways to hide or even remove their powers, while others wanted advice on whether to turn themselves in. Six had read through the various posts until one had caught her eye: a message from someone claiming to offer help to those who wanted to disappear and not be found. It had been left by someone using the screen name BeamUUp. Sam thought it might be a reference to the old television show *Star Trek* and the character Scotty, who operated the transporter. And if so, maybe it was the same Scotty who was involved with Bray's organization.

It was a long shot, but it was the only one they had at the moment. As the post had been made six months earlier and BeamUUp hadn't been active since, it also might be a dead end, anyway. But Six had pretended to be a boy who had recently discovered a Legacy. Jack, the name she made up for herself, wrote that his family was freaked out by his power and wanted to send him to the HGA. He didn't want to go, as he didn't trust the government and had heard they were using Human Garde to do things against their will. Six had purposefully made Jack sound a little naïve and scared, as that was the kind of kid the people Scotty was involved with targeted, luring them in with promises of help and then exploiting their Legacies for profit.

Even if BeamUUp was Scotty, they didn't know if his organization was still functioning. Bray was dead, as was his right-hand man, Dennings. Several others were in custody, like Drac, and most of the kids they'd taken were now free. For all anyone knew—and hoped—the entire operation was out of commission. But Ghost and Scotty were out there somewhere, and it was possible they had connected with whatever was left of the group. Or not. Maybe they were on their own. Either way, it was all Sam and Six had to go on for now, and so they'd posted the message with their contact info and waited.

They were still waiting. With no reason to be anywhere in particular, they'd driven east, away from California and into Nevada. They'd stopped in Reno, holed up in a little motel while they figured out their next move. They'd spent the morning buying some warmer clothes, using up the last of their cash in the process. Because they didn't want to leave a paper trail in case Walker or anyone else was tracking them, Sam had talked the ATM into giving him a loan.

If they didn't hear anything from BeamUUp or figure out something else soon, the plan was to stay in Reno one more night. After that? They didn't know. Before signing on with McKenna, they'd been traveling around the world, going wherever they felt like. No one place was home. Taking the job with him and being headquartered in New York seemed like a way to settle down for a while, at least to Sam. Now, that wasn't an option. And going back to California and the HGA was probably out of the question too after the way they'd left things.

There was Nemo to think about as well. Personally, Sam thought she would be better off returning to the Academy. He knew Nine would take her back, and if their search for Ghost went nowhere, it was the best place for her to be. But

Nemo was like Six, stubborn and impossible to reason with until she was ready. And she wasn't ready.

As if sensing that he was thinking about her, Nemo paused with her fork halfway to her mouth and said, "What?"

"Nothing," Sam said, taking a bite of his sandwich and chewing to avoid further conversation.

Nemo turned her attention to Six instead. "What happens if we do hear from this guy, BeamUUp?"

"Well, it's first contact," Six said. "If it is Scotty, he's probably still freaked out. He'd been shot and was in bad shape when Ghost took him out of Bray's mansion. And with all his bosses dead or in custody—at least the ones we know about—he might be on his own."

"'If it is Scotty' being the key part of that sentence," Sam reminded them. "It could be anybody, including someone involved with Earth Garde or the HGA."

Six shrugged. "Could be. We'll just have to see what happens. I posted that the situation is bad, and I need to get out right away," she said. "I said my parents want to ship me off to the HGA tomorrow."

"Dramatic," Nemo said.

"I had to make it sound desperate," said Six. "We want him to respond. If this guy thinks Jack is running out of time, he'll be more likely to agree to help."

"Which is actually a problem," said Sam.

Nemo and Six looked at him.

"Because there is no Jack," Sam said.

"He doesn't know that," Six said. "I'm assuming he's

going to teleport wherever we tell him to meet us. When he shows up, we'll . . ." She realized what she was saying and sighed. "Okay, yeah, we need a Jack."

"We need a *plan*," Sam said. "With or without a Jack, what are we going to do when he shows up? Remember, he's a teleporter. Once he sees us, he'll just disappear again. And even if we catch him, how does that help us get to Ghost?"

"If Jack," Nemo said, putting air quotes around the name, "goes with this guy, we could track him, like you did when you sent us in with Dennings."

"Because that worked out so well," Sam remarked. "Two people died, remember? And anyway, we don't have a Jack."

"Maybe we could get one," Six said.

"What are we going to do, grab someone off the street?" said Sam. "Even if we could find someone, Jack is supposed to have a Legacy."

There was a pause as everybody thought. Their food went untouched. Then Nemo said, "What about Max?"

"Max?" said Sam. He shook his head. "No."

"Why not?" Nemo asked. "He's got a Legacy, and Scotty's never seen him. He wasn't with us in Texas or Montana, remember?"

"She's right," said Six.

"Maybe Scotty has never seen him, but Ghost obviously has," Sam argued. "Once she sees him, she'll know something's up."

"Maybe not," Nemo said. "I mean, obviously she'll recognize him. But she also is way tighter with him than pretty much anyone else. Even me. And Max totally has a thing for her."

"He does?" Sam said.

"Big-time," said Nemo. "Didn't you ever notice how nervous he got around her?"

"We didn't actually see them together for very long, remember?" Six said.

A shadow passed briefly over Nemo's face as she recalled the events in New Orleans that had led to Ghost being taken. "Right," she said. "Well, trust me, he likes her. I think he'd do pretty much anything for her. If he makes her believe he lied about being Jack because he was afraid she wouldn't talk to him, it would actually be the truth. She'd totally buy it."

"Except that she's kind of crazy right now," Sam reminded her. "Besides, Max is back at the Academy."

"Which is less than four hours from here," said Six. She looked at her watch. "We could drive there, get him and be back here tonight."

"Why even come back?" Nemo asked. "If this guy is really Scotty, he can meet Jack anywhere. We could pick up Max and go somewhere close by. Jack's already told him that his parents are trying to force him to go to the HGA. He could write again and say he ran away while they were on the way there."

"Even better," Six said.

"Not better," Sam objected. "Have you both forgotten that we just *left* the Academy? Now you want to drive back, walk in and ask if we can borrow Max for the same kind of mission that ended up getting Kirk and Yo-Yo killed?"

"I wouldn't *ask* anybody," Six retorted. "Except Max. And if he doesn't want to do it, we won't do it."

"Of course he'll want to do it," said Sam. "Ghost is his friend. More than that if Nemo is right. It's unfair to put him in that position."

"It's our best option," said Six. "Besides, he won't be going in alone. We'll go with him. Well, we'll go after him. Once we know where he is."

"And hope Scotty—or whoever this guy turns out to be—doesn't whisk him away to someplace on the other side of the planet," said Sam. "None of us can teleport, remember?"

"You're determined to find every hole in this plan, aren't you?" Nemo said as she pulled out her phone.

"What are you doing?" Sam asked.

"My phone vibrated. I got a text." She swiped at her screen, then looked up. "Forget about Jack," she said. "We don't need him anymore."

"Why?" Six asked.

"The text is from Max," Nemo said. "Ghost contacted him. She wants to talk to him about coming to the Academy."

Sam looked at Six. "That's . . . weird. It's like he knew we were talking about him."

"And we were just getting to the part where you had to admit that my plan was awesome," said Six.

"Whatever," said Nemo. "She wants to meet with him. Tonight." Her fingers flew over the screen of her phone.

"What are you doing?" Sam said.

"Texting Max back," said Nemo. "Telling him we'll be there."

"We haven't even talked about it!" Sam objected.

"What's to talk about?" said Nemo, setting her phone on the table and picking up her fork. She stabbed a piece of pancake, swirled it around in the puddle of syrup on her plate and popped it in her mouth.

"She's right," Six said as she picked up her burger and resumed eating it. Only Sam sat sullenly staring at his sandwich and soup.

"You shouldn't let it get cold," Six said. "Cold soup is the worst."

Sam poked his spoon into the soup. He scooped up some and was bringing it to his mouth when Nemo's phone rattled on the table. She looked at it and grinned. "He said he'll sneak out and meet us."

"Tell him we'll be there around seven," Six said.

"I guess this is happening then," Sam muttered.

Six and Nemo nodded in unison, confirming.

Sam put the spoon in his mouth and made a face. "And the soup's cold."

CHAPTER TWO

SIX
POINT REYES, CALIFORNIA

SIX PULLED THE SUV OFF THE ROAD AND INTO THE parking area above the beach. She left the engine running. A moment later, a shadow detached from the darkness beyond the picnic tables that lined one side of the lot and jogged towards them. Nemo opened the rear door and jumped out.

"Max!" she said, holding her arms open.

Then Six noticed a second shadow emerge from the dark.

"Nemo!" she called out. "Get back in!"

"Relax," Max's voice said as he hugged Nemo. "It's Seamus."

"Seamus?" said Six as the second boy walked up to the car and lifted his hand in a halfhearted greeting. "What are you doing here?"

"I needed help sneaking out," Max said. "Since you guys ran off, they've been supersuspicious. Nobody's allowed outside unsupervised, and the cameras are always on. So, you know, thanks for that."

"And you helped out? How?" Six asked Seamus as he climbed into the back of the SUV and tossed a bag into the rear compartment.

"Bees," Seamus said, shutting the door. "It's amazing how hard it is for cameras to see what's going on when the lenses are covered with swarms of them."

Six chuckled. "Good one," she said. "But this definitely complicates things. Your dad is going to be really pissed off when he finds out you're gone."

Seamus shrugged. "We're not exactly speaking as it is," he said. "Besides, he's got other things to worry about."

"Oh?" said Six. "Like what?"

"I'm not sure. Rumor is, he and that woman who's been around had a big fight after you guys left. She told him he couldn't handle his job or something. I don't know, and I don't really care."

"Woman?" Sam said, shooting a glance at Six. "Do you mean Walker?"

"Maybe," Seamus said. "Red hair? Acts like she owns the place?"

"That's her," Six said. "Looks like we got him in trouble."

"Anyway, I'm here," Seamus said as Max got into the vehicle and Nemo slid in beside him.

Six turned to Max. "So, what did Ghost say?"

"Just that she wanted to talk," Max answered. "Said she's thinking about coming to the Academy."

"Did you tell Nine or anyone else?" Six asked.

Max shook his head. "I was afraid they would do something to her."

"Like what?" Six said.

Max shrugged. "I don't know," he said. "Anyway, I told you guys, didn't I?" He looked sad. "I think she's scared she's in trouble."

Six snorted. "I can't imagine why."

"It's not her fault," Max said, sounding angry. "They did something to her."

Six didn't respond to that. Max wasn't wrong. But he hadn't had the run-ins with Ghost that she and Sam and Nemo had. Jagger Dennings and his gang had indeed done something to Ghost. The question was, could she be fixed? The last time they'd seen her, she'd tried her best to kill them. So why was she suddenly interested in making nice? Did she really want out? Or was she panicking because everyone in charge had been killed or captured?

"Where does she want to meet?" Sam asked.

"San Rafael," Max said. "At a mall."

"A mall?" said Sam.

"It's called Northgate," Max said.

"She's a teleporter," Sam said. "Why not just teleport to where you are instead of making you come to her?"

"Like I said, I think she's scared," said Max. "Maybe she thinks meeting in public is safer."

"The mall it is," Six said, doing a search on the SUV's navigation system and finding the address. It was less than an hour away.

"I'm supposed to come alone," Max said.

"Don't worry," Six assured him. "As far as Ghost will know, you will be."

"And then what?" Seamus asked.

Nobody said anything. This was the question that had been on Six's mind the entire drive back to the Academy, and she hadn't yet thought of a good answer.

"If she really wants to come to the HGA, we could bring her back," Max suggested.

Seamus laughed. "You think they'll be happy to see us?" he said.

"We can explain—," Max began.

"We'll worry about that once Max talks to her," Six interrupted. "If she's scared, she probably just wants to talk to a friend."

"Yeah," Max said. "A friend."

"I don't know," Seamus persisted. "I heard she was pretty messed up when you ran into her at Bray's place."

"At least this is better than waiting for Might Be Scotty to answer us," Nemo said, cutting him off before he could say anything else.

"Scotty?" said Seamus. "The teleporter?"

"Yes, that one," Six said.

"You've talked to him?" Seamus asked, sounding surprised.

"We've communicated with someone we think might be him," Sam explained.

"Huh," Seamus said. "I thought he was dead. I heard he got shot up pretty good."

"You sure do hear a lot," Six remarked. "Who told you that?"

"People talk," Seamus said. "I listen."

Just like your dad, Six thought, but she kept it to herself. Seamus McKenna was still a question mark to her. She wasn't entirely sure he could be trusted, and she wasn't happy that Max had involved him in what they were doing. But getting upset about it wouldn't help. She would wait and hope he didn't become a bigger problem than he already was.

Six could tell it was time to rally the troops and get morale back up. Even though everything Seamus had said mirrored her own fears and doubts about the situation. "Let's go over the plan," she said.

"Great idea," said Nemo. "What is it exactly?"

"We'll go to the mall. Max will meet Ghost and see if she's really ready to come in. If she is, he can break it to her that he didn't come alone. Hopefully, she won't spook and run."

"That's not much of a plan," Nemo said instantly. "I say we drug her so she can't get away. Bring her in. Work it out once she's at the Academy."

"We don't drug and kidnap people," said Sam. "She's got to come on her own."

"You kind of do," Seamus said.

"Do what?" Sam asked.

"Kidnap people. Like all the kids you brought from the ship in Mexico."

"They weren't kidnapped," Six objected. "They were rescued."

"Did you ask them if they wanted to be rescued?" Seamus countered.

"Dennings is the one who was holding them prisoner," said Six.

"So, they can just leave if they want to?" said Seamus. He shook his head and looked out the window.

"No one is kidnapping Ghost," Sam said. "Hopefully she'll want our help."

"I wish we had some of the cool stuff Lexa has in her bat cave," Nemo said. "You know, just in case."

"Actually, we do," Seamus said.

Nemo turned to him. "What are you talking about?"

"I might have borrowed a couple of things," Seamus said coolly. "A communication device or two. Some other stuff."

"What other stuff?" Six asked.

In the rearview mirror she saw Seamus shrug. "A transmitter, I think. Maybe an explosive device. I just kind of grabbed things. I only had like half a minute in there, and it's not like there are displays or anything."

"An explosive device," Sam said. "Fantastic."

"It's in my bag in the back. If you want to see it."

"You're sure you have a communicator?" Six asked.

Seamus nodded. "That one I recognized. I've seen them before."

"That will come in handy," said Six.

"Okay," said Nemo. "That's better. But what if—"

"I can handle it," Max said defensively, interrupting her.

"No offense, but you've kind of been sitting on the bench," Nemo said. "This is like putting you in the game when you've only been to three practices."

"Hey, I know I don't have a cool Legacy like you or Ghost, but I can take care of myself," Max shot back.

"Your Legacy is plenty cool," said Nemo, her voice softer. "I'm just trying to make sure nothing happens to you."

"I'll be fine," Max muttered, but less angrily.

They drove in silence for a while. When Six saw a sign for a 7-Eleven, she pulled in and stopped at the gas pump.

"Hey, Dad," Nemo said, tapping Sam on the shoulder. "Can we have some cash for snacks?"

Sam took out some of the ATM money and gave it to them. "Don't go filling up on junk now, kids," he said, affecting an older man's voice.

As Sam got out to fill up the SUV, Nemo, Max and Seamus went inside the store. Six rolled down her window so she could talk to Sam.

"That was smart of Seamus to think of bringing some things," she said. "Even if he did technically steal them."

"I've been thinking about him," Sam said.

Six raised an eyebrow. "And?"

"What if he isn't running away from his father?" Sam said.

"Meaning what?" Six asked.

"Meaning, what if he just wants us to think he is? What if *McKenna* wants us to think he is?"

"You mean, what if he's working for his dad," Six said. "And McKenna sent him to spy on us."

Sam nodded. "It crossed my mind."

"It would be a great cover," Six said. "But I don't think that's what's happening. He seems too sure of himself. If he wanted us to believe he was running from his dad, I think he would pretend to be less helpful. Bringing all that stuff from Lexa's office would be too convenient."

"Maybe," said Sam. "I don't know." He looked out the window for a moment. When he turned back to Six he said, "Do you really think we should send Max in there alone?"

"No," Six said. "It's a huge risk. But I also know we don't have any other options right now."

Before Sam could reply, the rear doors opened and the three teens piled in. Each of them was carrying a Slurpee, and Max and Nemo both had a second one. Seamus had two bags full of snacks.

Nemo handed Six a Slurpee. "I got you piña colada," she said. "You seemed like you might like something tropical."

"And you get cherry cola," said Max, passing one to Sam in the front seat.

"We also have chips, chocolate bars, beef jerky and something called a Big Mama pickled sausage. Max wanted that." He held up something and wiggled it.

"Hey, they're good," Max said, snatching it away and tearing at the package with his teeth.

Six took a sip of the Slurpee. A blast of sweet, icy liquid hit her throat. Nemo had guessed right.

There wasn't much talking for the rest of the trip. When they reached the mall, Six navigated the SUV through the parking lot and found a spot. "Nemo and Seamus, you wait here," she said.

"What?" Nemo exclaimed, pausing as she reached for the door handle. "Why?"

"Because it will be easier to stay out of view if it's just me and Sam," Six said. "Seamus, get that communicator you brought."

Seamus turned and retrieved his bag. Rummaging through it, he pulled out a pair of what looked like fancy wristwatches and handed them to Six. She pressed a couple of buttons, and the watches lit up for a few seconds and emitted a beep. She handed one to Sam, then spoke into the other one. "Speech-to-text function," Sam said as he read her words on his watch's screen. "Sweet."

Six handed the watch to Max, who put it on. "Does it do anything else?" he asked.

"Knowing Lexa, yes," Six said. "But all we need it to do right now is let us listen in to your conversation with Ghost. Your watch will pick up what you say and relay it to us as text."

Max nodded.

"All right," Six said. She looked at Nemo and Seamus. "You two *stay here.* Got it?"

"Got it," Seamus said.

"Nemo?" said Six.

Nemo grunted.

"I'll take that as a yes. Okay then. Max, you go in first. Head straight for the food court. Sam and I will be nearby, out of the way."

"Got it," Max said. "Let's do this."

Seamus held out his fist. Max bumped it with his. "Good luck," Seamus said.

Max turned to Nemo and held out his fist. Instead of bumping it, she leaned over and hugged him hard. "Don't you dare get hurt," she said. "If you do, I'll kill you."

They held each other for a long while, then Seamus got out and Max exited the SUV. He, Six and Sam walked through the parking lot to the doors. Max was more quiet than usual.

"Are you worried about anything?" Sam asked.

"What if Ghost gets angry when she finds out I told you?"

"She's still your friend," Sam said. "Underneath everything. Your job is to get her to see that you really care about her."

"I do care," Max said. "She, me and Nemo are a family."

"Remember that," Sam said, putting his hand on Max's shoulder.

Looking at a directory of the mall, they located the spot where Ghost had told Max to meet her, near a movie theater. Six checked her watch. It was five minutes to eight. "Max, you'll go in by yourself," she said. "Sam and I will follow in two minutes, then wait inside one of the other stores. If things go okay with Ghost, ask her if she wants to get something to eat. Then we'll take it from there."

Max took a deep breath and nodded.

"You can do this," Six said. "You're just talking to your friend."

Max put his hands in his pockets. "Oh, crap," he said. "I left my phone in the car."

"You've got your watch," Six said. "Don't worry. Your phone will be fine."

Max went into the mall. Six and Sam waited two minutes, then followed him. They passed by several shops until they came to the central courtyard. The movie theater was to their left. They saw Max standing outside it, looking at the posters for what was playing. Sam and Six stayed hidden around the corner.

Six looked at her watch. "Ghost should be showing up any time now."

All of a sudden, the doors to the theater opened, and people streamed into the mall, surrounding Max.

"Shoot. A movie must have just ended," Six said as she tried to keep an eye on Max while also looking for Ghost. But there were a lot of people, and Max had been swallowed up by them. Then she found him. He was standing alone, looking around.

That's when Six noticed the boy walking up behind him. He was wearing sunglasses, and it took her a moment to realize who he was.

"It's Scotty," she said to Sam.

Max, oblivious, was still scanning the crowd as Scotty approached him.

"Something's wrong," Sam said. "We've got to get him out of there."

Six and Sam raced towards the theater just as Scotty reached Max.

"Max!" Six shouted.

Max, startled, looked at her, an expression of confusion on his face. At the same time Scotty placed his hand on Max's shoulder.

They both disappeared.

CHAPTER THREE

MAX
UNKNOWN LOCATION

"WHAT THE HELL IS GOING ON?"

Max stared at the boy who had just whisked him away from the mall. The guy grinned. "Relax, dude," he said. "It's all good."

Max backed away, looking around the room in which they were standing. It was large, with high ceilings and a wall of tall windows that were covered by heavy, red velvet draperies that puddled beneath them. The wood floor was covered by several antique-looking carpets patterned with flowers and birds. A chandelier hung in the middle of the room, its dangling crystals glowing with soft-yellow light that wasn't quite bright enough to illuminate the far corners of the room, which remained in shadow. Several pieces of solid, dark-wood furniture were scattered around: a long couch, two armchairs, a bookcase. The air was warm and damp, and smelled slightly moldy, as if the house had been shut up for a long time.

"Welcome to Rotwood," said a girl's voice.

Max turned and saw behind him a low, round table. A girl sat there, playing with what looked like a deck of cards that she was laying out on the table in front of her. She had short, pink hair and pale skin, and she was wearing a sleeveless white dress that reminded Max of something from an antique photograph. She looked up at Max, and something about her eyes didn't seem quite right. But before Max could get a closer look, she glanced down again and turned over a card.

"The Fool," she said. "That's probably you. Off on a big adventure. I wonder where it will take you? Hopefully nowhere dangerous." She laughed lightly.

"Don't pay any attention to Magdalena's mumbo jumbo," said a male voice from another part of the room. Then a piano began to play, an ominous, rippling song that made Max think of nighttime and the things that hid within in. "And it's Rothwood," he added. "Although Magdalena's name is probably more appropriate."

"What is that you're playing?" the girl asked.

"Chopin," said the young man seated at the piano. Like Magdalena his skin was also pale. Unlike her, his hair was long and black, hanging around his face as he bent over the keyboard.

Magdalena sighed. "Not bad for a human composer," she said.

Max looked from one to the other, searching for answers. Then he realized what the girl had said. "Why did you say that?" he asked.

"What?" said Magdalena.

"You called him 'human composer,'" Max said. "What else would he be?"

Magdalena looked up at him. "Well, I don't know," she said. "He could be an alien. There seem to be a lot of them hanging around these days." Her eyes stared into Max's, and all of a sudden he realized why they looked different. His heart skittered in his chest, and he quickly backed away.

"You're a Mog!"

The girl gasped. "I am?" she said. She ran her hands over her chest, then patted her cheeks. Her eyes widened, and Max noted again how dark they were. "How did that happen?" she said, then laughed, revealing a mouth of sharp teeth.

Max's breath left him. He'd seen pictures and videos of Mogs, of course. Everyone had. But he'd never seen one in person. And there weren't supposed to be any just walking among regular people. They had all been rounded up. Sent to that prison. At first glance Magdalena seemed like an ordinary girl, but if you paid attention you'd notice the distinctive features of a Mog.

Max looked at the young man playing the piano. He hadn't stopped, and the music still floated through the air. Was he one, too? Max couldn't see his face clearly enough to tell. Instead, he looked at the boy who had transported him there. He was definitely human. And he was grinning as if this was the best joke he had ever played on anyone.

Max didn't find it funny at all. He felt his pulse quicken even more as panic started to overwhelm him. If the Mogs were there, he was in serious trouble. He had to get out. Now.

"It's all right, Max."

Max whirled around at the sound of a familiar voice. "Ghost!"

His friend was standing there. She looked much different from the last time he'd seen her. Tired. And she had a scar on her cheek that he didn't remember. But when she smiled, she was the same old Ghost. He'd never been so happy to see someone. He ran over to her and gave her a hug.

"Are you okay? Are the Mogs hurting you?" he whispered.

"We can hear you, you know," Magdalena said.

"It's okay," Ghost said. "Magdalena and Byron are my friends."

The piano playing stopped, and the young man walked towards them. He was dressed in jeans and a black *Star Wars* T-shirt. He was of average human height and build, maybe even a little on the thin side. He came over and dropped into one of the armchairs, placing his hands on the ends. He looked at Max and smiled. Unlike Magdalena, he had normal-looking teeth. And his eyes were blue. If Max had seen him on the street, he would have thought the guy was just another teenager. But he wasn't. *How many of them are out there living among us?* Max wondered.

"That's a very fancy watch you have there," Byron said.

Max felt a stab of panic cut through him. Instinctively, he had been touching his watch, wishing he could call Six and Sam for help. He reached down and pushed the sleeve of his hoodie over his wrist. "It's just a watch," he said.

"May I see it?" Byron asked.

Max started to say no, then worried that if he did, it would seem suspicious. So he reluctantly removed it from his arm, stood and walked over to Byron, holding out the watch. Being this close to a Mog made him more nervous than he'd ever been in his entire life.

Byron took the watch. His fingers touched Max's. Max recoiled. Byron laughed. "Don't worry," he said. "We don't bite."

Max retreated to the relative safety of the couch, where Ghost had taken a seat. He sat close to her, feeling anything but safe. He still didn't understand why she was hanging around the creepy old house with freaking Mogs, and she hadn't explained anything.

Byron examined the watch. "No brand name," he said. "Where did you get it?"

Max felt the worry inside of him threaten to boil over. The watch was his one link to Sam, Six and Nemo. If he lost it, they would have no way to contact him. But he also couldn't let Byron and the others see how upset he was about having it taken from him.

"It's standard issue at the HGA," he said, thinking back to his stint at the military academy his parents had sent him to and how they had all been given standard issue supplies there. Too late, he realized that this might be a mistake.

"Did someone mention the camp for misfit humans?" said a female voice.

A new girl walked into the room. Taller than Byron, she had striking blond hair pulled back into a ponytail that hung to her waist. She wore black leather pants tucked into tall leather boots. A formfitting leather jacket covered her upper half, secured with a complicated system of straps and buckles. She had black designs tattooed on her face, coming out from under her hair and extending down the left side of her face.

The girl stopped in front of the couch and looked at Max, her hands on her hips. "I am Eleni," she said. "And you must be Max. We've heard a lot about you from Ghost."

Max didn't know what to say. He still hadn't wrapped his head around the fact that he was in a room with actual Mogs. It was like waking up and finding himself in bed surrounded by tigers. His instincts told him to run, but there was no way out. Besides, Ghost didn't seem bothered by their presence at all. She was sitting calmly beside him, and that made him feel a little less uneasy. But only a little.

"It's, um, nice to meet you," he said.

"Mmm," Eleni said. She looked at him for another long moment, then turned to Byron. She held out her hand, and he placed Max's watch in it. Eleni examined it closely. She touched the buttons. With every passing moment, the knot in Max's stomach grew larger and larger.

"Human technology is so amusing," Eleni said.

"It's nothing special," Max said.

Eleni didn't say anything as she put the device into her pocket and sat down in the other armchair. "Byron, why don't you go get our guest something to drink. I'm sure he could use some refreshment."

Byron got up and left the room. Eleni turned her attention to Max. "Now, let's talk about why you're here," she said.

The shock of being transported away and ending up in a room with Mogs had completely made Max forget why he was there in the first place. Now he turned to Ghost. "You said you wanted my help."

"I do," Ghost said.

"You said you were thinking about coming to the HGA," said Max.

"Yeah," said Ghost. "That part isn't really true. But I didn't know how else to get you to come talk to me. I was afraid maybe they told you things about me that aren't true."

"I heard about what happened in Mexico," he said. "And Argentina."

Ghost frowned but said nothing.

"I still would have talked to you, though," Max said. "You're my friend, Ghost. You didn't need to kidnap me."

"We weren't sure what they might have done to you," Eleni said before Ghost could speak. "As Ghost said, you've probably been told a lot of things that aren't true. About her. About us. About the so-called Earth Garde."

Max looked at her. His fear was slowly being replaced by

anger. "I know the same thing everybody else does," he said hesitantly.

"About us, you mean," Eleni said.

Max shrugged. "Well, yeah."

"The Garde that took you in New Orleans," Eleni said. "Did she tell you anything about the history between our people?"

"Six, you mean?" Max said. "No. She's never said anything about you. Why?"

Eleni's face hardened. "They involve you in our war. Make us come here to try and claim what they took from us. They make you believe that we're monsters."

Max said nothing. He'd seen enough news reports about the war. Heard stories. He knew they weren't made up.

Just then Byron returned and handed Max a glass filled with a dark beverage. "Root beer," he said. "It's Ghost's favorite, so I thought you might like it too."

Max accepted the drink, avoiding touching Byron's hand. Several cubes of ice clinked as Max tipped the soda into his mouth. He gulped the drink as Eleni continued talking.

"It's true that some of my people—the older generation—went about things in a bad way," she said. "You have to understand that they were only reacting to what was done to them. To us. To our home. But we aren't all like that. Our generation"—she indicated Byron and Magdalena—"is different. We want to help. Share technology and scientific discoveries. Make peace, so that we can all live together. Be friends. The Loric do not want this to happen."

"They don't?" Max said, wiping his mouth with the back of his hand as he set the now-empty glass down.

Eleni shook her head. "They want to keep control for themselves," she said. "See how they are forcing those of you with powers to be rounded up and controlled?"

Max shrugged. "It's for our own good," he said. "They're helping us learn to use our Legacies."

"For now, maybe," Eleni said. "I assure you, soon it will be different. Soon they will want more control. They don't want you to know what you're really capable of."

Max thought about the HGA. Yes, they had a lot of rules. And Eleni was right that kids with Legacies had to report there by law. That didn't seem like such a big deal, though.

Then again, not everything was great. "They've left me out of everything," he said. "I don't think they trust me, on account of I kept sticking up for Ghost and saying we needed to help her."

Eleni nodded. "But the other girl—Nemo—she is Ghost's friend as well, no?"

"She was," Ghost said, her voice thick with anger. "Not anymore."

"Nemo is more like them," Max said. "She and Six have become buddies."

"Of course," Eleni said.

"They're a lot alike," Max said. "She helps Nemo with her Legacies. So does Nine. I guess they think what she does is cool or whatever."

"She breathes underwater, I hear," Eleni said.

"Yeah," Max confirmed. "Which *is* pretty great. But they make a huge deal about her."

"And you?" Eleni asked. "You do not have a cool Legacy?"

"My Legacy?" Max said. "It's all right, I guess."

"He can understand any language," Ghost said, her voice practically a whisper.

"Can he?" Eleni said. "ты хочешь что-нибудь выпить, макс?"

"Maybe another root beer?" Max said.

"Me temo que solo tengo agua," Eleni replied.

"That's okay," said Max, grinning. "Water is fine."

Byron, who had been quietly observing, clapped his hands. "That's a neat trick," he said.

"Om inte han redan visste ryska och spanska," Magdalena said from her place at the table.

"I don't actually know Russian or Spanish," Max said. "Or whatever you were just speaking. Well, maybe a little Spanish, but that's because I took a year of it in school."

"Magdalena was speaking Swedish," Eleni said. "So you don't know what the language is that you're hearing, or how to speak it yourself?"

Max shook his head. "I just know what the person is saying."

"That's unfortunate for you," Eleni said. "Although perhaps we can fix that."

"Fix it?" Max said. "How?"

"The Garde are not the only ones who can help you learn

to use your gifts," Eleni said.

Max was about to reply to her when he realized she'd spoken in another language he didn't know. Unlike the others, though, this one didn't sound like anything he'd ever heard.

"Was that Mogadorian?" he asked excitedly.

"Did you understand it?" said Eleni.

Max nodded. "But how can you help me? Mogs—Mogadorians—don't have Legacies," Max said.

"Well, that's not entirely true," said Eleni. "You may have heard from those Garde you're involved with that our scientists have been doing some experiments."

"They mentioned it," Max said carefully. He thought about how Six and Sam had lost their Legacies because of the serum that man Drac had injected them with. And he'd heard that Bray, the guy behind all of it, had turned into some kind of monster because he'd injected himself with a drug that was supposed to give him Legacies.

"As I said, not everything you've been told is true, Max," Eleni said softly. She looked at him and smiled. "There were mistakes made," she continued. "But the people who made them are no longer working with us."

Max nodded. Everything Eleni was saying made a lot of sense. He looked over at Ghost, who smiled at him. He had the thought that everything was going to be fine now. Why had he been so worried?

"I think we are going to be good friends, Max," Eleni said. "Don't you, Byron?"

Byron nodded and smiled. "Very good friends," Byron said.

"Wonderful friends," Magdalena said.

Eleni looked at Ghost. "Why don't you show Max to his room? I'm sure he's tired."

Max yawned, as if her saying he was tired made him so. But it *had* been a long day. Ghost stood up and he did as well. "Good night," he said. "I'll see you all in the morning."

"Not if we see you first," Magdalena said without looking up.

"Good night, Max," said Eleni. "Sleep well."

Ghost left the room, with Max following her. She passed into a long hallway that was lit by old-fashioned gas lights. The walls were covered with ornately painted paper that was peeling in some places, revealing bare plaster underneath.

"What did Byron say this place is called?" Max said. "Rothwood?"

"Yes," said Ghost. "I think it's the name of the family that built it or something."

"And where exactly are we?" Max asked. "It smells kind of . . . swampy."

"It is," Ghost said, but she didn't give any more information than that. "The house is very old."

They came to a stairway, a set of wide wooden steps leading to the next floor. The boards were well-worn, as if countless feet had gone up and down them. Ghost and Max walked up and were in yet another hallway. This one had doors on either side, all of them closed. The same gas lamps lit the space with a dim, flickering light.

"Doesn't this place have electricity?" he asked.

"It does," Ghost said. "But the old gas pipes are still here, too." She walked almost to the end and opened a door on the right-hand side. They stepped into a bedroom.

"This is your room," she said as Max looked around. "Mine is across the hall."

Like the rest of the house, the room was filled with heavy, dark furniture. The huge bed had curtains on it that were tied back. Through an open door, Max could see a bathroom. He sat down on the bed and sank into the mattress. He had a lot of questions. But he was suddenly exhausted, and all he could think about was going to sleep. He vaguely thought about Six and Sam, and wondered how they would find him now, but that seemed unimportant. He could worry about it later.

"I'm glad you're here, Max," Ghost said. "I missed you a lot."

"I missed you, too," Max said.

"And I'm sorry I lied about wanting to go to the Academy and sending Scotty when I said I would come. That was Eleni's idea. He's still a better teleporter, and she knew he wouldn't have a problem getting you out if there was trouble. She can be a little suspicious."

"I can tell," Max said. "And it's okay. I get it."

"Then you're not mad?"

Max shook his head. "You know I could never be mad at you," he said. "I—"

Ghost leaned forward and kissed him. Just for a second, and then laughed. "Sorry," she said, looking away. "I missed you. I didn't mean to—"

"No, it's okay," Max said quickly.

Ghost looked at him. "Really?"

Max nodded. "Yeah," he said. Despite his happiness, he found himself suddenly yawning.

"Wow, am I that bad?" Ghost asked.

"No! You're great! I'm just—I'm exhausted."

"I was just teasing," said Ghost. "You should go to sleep. We can talk tomorrow."

Max nodded. Ghost went to the door. "Good night," she said, and slipped out, closing the door behind her.

Max went into the bathroom, where he found a toothbrush and other things sitting on the sink counter. He brushed his teeth, then went back to the bedroom. Undressing, he got into bed, turned off the lamp on the bedside table and snuggled into the softness of the blankets. He couldn't believe that Ghost had kissed him. His stomach still felt funny. Best of all, he wasn't afraid anymore. Everything was going to be fine, he thought as he closed his eyes.

He was so tired that he drifted into sleep within a minute and didn't hear the click of the door. Someone was locking it from the other side.

CHAPTER FOUR

SAM

SAN FRANCISCO, CALIFORNIA

"ALABAMA?" SIX SAID.

Sam looked at the readings on the computer screen again. "That's what it says," he told Six.

They were still in the mall. Max and Scotty had disappeared only a few minutes before. Fortunately, Max's watch also had a tracking function on it. It had transmitted its location not long after.

"What the hell is over there?" Six asked.

"Scotty and Max, apparently," said Sam.

"And no Ghost," Six said. "We were set up."

Sam nodded. Something about the whole thing was definitely off. "What now?" he asked.

Six shrugged. "We go to Alabama. Where exactly are they?"

Sam communicated with his phone, asking it to perform the necessary calculations. It stubbornly refused. "No, I don't want a recipe for chicken parmigiana." He groaned. "I guess I'll have to do this the hard way," he said, typing.

"I'll be so glad when our Legacies are working reliably." Six held up her hand and watched it slowly go translucent but stop just before becoming completely invisible. "Or at all," she added.

"He's about an hour northeast of Mobile," Sam said. He did some more searching. "That's weird. It looks like it's right in the middle of swampland."

Six made a noise of disgust. "All right," she said. "This isn't good, but I guess it could be a lot worse. How far away is that?"

Sam searched. "Thirty-four hours if we drive," he said. "Or we can get on a flight just after midnight tonight and be there a little after nine o'clock tomorrow morning."

"That's as good as it's going to get," Six said. "Book two tickets."

"Four," Sam said, holding up that many fingers.

Six groaned. "I forgot about those two. That complicates things. They're really going to slow us down."

"Well, we can't just leave them somewhere," said Sam. "And we can't take them back to the Academy. For one thing, they wouldn't go. For another . . ." He left the thought unfinished.

"I know," Six said. "It's my fault."

"I didn't say that," Sam countered. "And it's not your

fault. Well, it's a little your fault. But neither of them wants to be there, so it doesn't really matter."

Six looked at her watch. "That flight leaves in four hours," she said. "We've got to go. Order four tickets."

"If I use a credit card, they'll be able to track us," Sam reminded her.

"Shoot. Then we go to the airport. Buy them with cash. We did it all the time when we were traveling."

"Yeah, but there were only two of us," said Sam. "Four teenagers traveling together at the last minute? That's going to look weird." He thought for a moment. "But I have an idea," he said. "Come on."

They returned to the parking lot, where Nemo started peppering them with questions the second they got into the SUV.

"Everything is fine," Six said. "I'll explain everything when we're at the airport."

"Airport?" said Nemo. "I thought Ghost was coming back to the Academy."

"There's been a little change in the plan," Six told her. "Right now I need to know if you both have ID. With your real names on it," she added, looking at Nemo meaningfully.

"I have ID with *a* name on it," Nemo answered.

"Good enough," Six said. "Seamus?"

Seamus nodded. "Why?"

"Because you're going to need it to get on the plane we're taking," Six said as she started the car.

Sam brought up the airport in San Francisco with the

SUV's onboard navigation system, and Six drove. When they arrived, they grabbed their backpacks and went into the terminal.

"Will you tell me your brilliant plan now?" Six asked as they approached the ticket counters.

Sam walked up to one of the self-check-in machines. "Simple," he said. "I'm going to access the reservation system and print us four boarding passes."

Six grinned. "Brilliant," she said. "If it actually works."

"Only one way to find out," said Sam with a smile. "Give me your IDs."

Nemo and Seamus handed over their cards. Sam looked at them. "Eula-Mae Butterfield?" he said, looking at Nemo.

"What do you expect for twenty bucks?" she said.

Sam placed his hand on the touch screen, pretending to be checking in. Linking into the computer inside, he directed it to look for the flight to Mobile, then for four seats. As it had when he'd interfaced with the ATM, his Legacy worked in fits and starts.

"No, not Moline," he muttered to the machine. He concentrated harder. "Alabama! Not Alaska."

He feared his Legacy was on the fritz again. But finally, the machine responded correctly. Sam breathed a sigh of relief.

"You want a window or an aisle?" he asked Six. "Quick, before it decides to give me tickets to Argentina."

"Exit row," she said. "More legroom."

The computer filled in the information as Sam

telegraphed it from the identification cards. A moment later, the machine began printing out boarding passes. Sam picked them up, checked the names and handed them to the others.

"If I had your Legacy, I'd have front-row seats to every concert I ever wanted to go to," Nemo said. "Have you ever thought about being a scalper?"

"I only use my powers for good, *Eula-Mae*," Sam said. "Everybody ready?"

"Wait a minute," Six said. She looked at Seamus. "All that stuff you have in that backpack is going to set off the scanners at security."

"Can't Sam magic them like he did here?" Seamus asked.

"I don't know that I like the idea of trying to bring an *explosive* onto a plane," Sam said.

"Although you never know when one will come in handy," Six pointed out. "It would be a shame to leave it behind."

"I'll see what I can do," Sam said.

The line going through security was short, as not many flights were leaving so late in the evening. Sam was nervous that the woman checking IDs against boarding passes might be suspicious of Nemo's unlikely name, but she barely glanced at her before handing her documents back and saying, "Have a nice flight, Miss Butterfield." Then they were at the scanners, and he got nervous again. As Seamus put his bag on the conveyor belt, Sam reached out to the machine. This was going to be trickier than booking tickets. He had to fool the person looking at the scanner images, not just block them out or make the scanner malfunction. And with his Legacy still refusing to cooperate reliably, it was going to take a whole lot of luck as well.

Since Seamus's backpack was similar to one that was ahead of it in line, Sam told the machine to reverse their images on the screen. A moment later he saw the TSA agent working the scanner look at the screen with a puzzled expression. She moved the conveyor belt forward, looked at the backpack that came out, then reversed the belt.

"Something's wrong with my machine," she said. "It's showing a laptop case, not a backpack."

The agent at another station asked the others, "Does one of your scanners show a backpack on it?"

"Mine does," the female agent overseeing Sam's line called back. "You got a laptop bag?"

"Nope."

"I've got a laptop bag over here," a third TSA agent called. "Who's got the carry-on with scuba diving gear in it, because that's what's on my screen right now."

Sam panicked. Instead of just one, he'd messed up all the machines. Now the agents would be extra cautious. They might even decide to search all the bags, and then he and the others would be done for. *Why had he thought this would be a good idea with his Legacies on the fritz?*

As the agents bustled around trying to sort out what was happening, he quickly reached out to the machines again, trying to fix the mix-up. But before he could, Sam saw a security guard had picked up the backpack sitting on the conveyor belt.

Sam readied himself. If the guard discovered the bomb in Seamus's bag, he'd use his telekinesis to knock all the agents down so he, Six and the others could make a run for it. But then the guard waved to a girl ahead of Seamus. "Miss, will you step over here?" he said.

Miraculously, Seamus's bag had gone right through, untouched in the confusion. Seamus collected it and joined Six and Nemo, who were already done and waiting. Sam refocused, telling the machines to go back to working like normal. The agent for his line looked at her screen, doubled-checked that Sam's bag matched what she saw, then nodded. "They're working right again," she said to the agents. "Must have been a glitch."

"Machines," Sam said, smiling at her. "They're so temperamental."

The woman grunted and nodded. Sam grabbed his things and went over to the others. As he put on his shoes, he heard the security guard say to the girl he'd pulled aside, "This is a what?"

"A bath bomb," the girl said.

"I'm afraid you're going to have to come with me," the agent said sternly.

"Not a *bomb* bomb," the frustrated girl said. "It makes *bubbles.*"

"That's all your fault you know," Nemo said to Sam.

Sam, feeling guilty for the trouble he'd caused the girl, gave her a sympathetic glance as their group walked to the gate. They had a little time before boarding, so he and Six went to get coffee, while Nemo and Seamus stayed behind, watching their bags.

"I used to love being in airports," Sam said as they sat at a café, drinking. "It always meant we were off to somewhere new and exciting."

"Alabama is new," Six said.

"But not exciting," said Sam. He hesitated before continuing. He was thinking about how long it would be before they got to Max. "A lot can happen in the next twelve hours."

"He'll be fine," Six assured him.

"He's not Nemo," Sam said. "Or Rena. He hasn't been through what they have."

"Neither had you when you got involved in all this," Six reminded him. "And you rose to the occasion. Max will, too."

Sam sighed. "Do you think we should call in reinforcements?"

Six set down her coffee. "Like who?" she said. "Nine? McKenna?" She shook her head. "No. Not yet."

"Not yet?" said Sam.

"What are they going to do that we aren't?" Six asked.

"Get there more quickly," said Sam. "Have somewhere to keep Nemo and Seamus out of the way. Have equipment and backup."

Six picked up her coffee and took a long swallow. "We have equipment," she said.

"Seamus's bo—bath bubbles?" Sam said.

"We have our Legacies," Six said. "That's usually all we need."

"Except they aren't all the way back yet," said Sam, thinking about the fiasco they just had going through security.

"They're getting there," Six said.

Sam knew better than to continue the discussion. Besides, talking about it endlessly wasn't going to change anything. He sat, silently drinking his coffee and wondering what they were going to find in Alabama the next day. Hopefully, just Scotty hiding out somewhere. Ghost too if they were lucky. If it was more than that, he might have to resurrect the idea of calling in Nine or McKenna.

They finished their drinks, then headed back to the gate just as the attendants were announcing boarding. There were fewer than two dozen people on the flight, so the entire process went quickly; and soon the four of them were seated, Six and Sam on one side of the aisle and Nemo and Seamus on the other. Fifteen minutes later they were in the air. Nemo, who had picked up a Stephen King novel at the airport, began reading. Seamus slipped in earbuds and leaned back, closing his eyes.

Six, seated by the window, went to sleep. Sam envied her ability to do that. He knew he should get some rest too, but he couldn't get comfortable. Also, he was still worried. Six seemed confident that everything was going to be fine, but he couldn't shake the feeling that they might be walking into something that was more complicated than they expected.

Eventually, exhaustion won out over worry and he passed out. But after what felt like only a few minutes, the pilot announced their descent into George Bush Intercontinental Airport in Houston, where they would change planes. Sam shook Six awake, while across the aisle Nemo, who appeared never to have gone to sleep at all, folded over the page of her book and tucked it away in her backpack before not so gently nudging Seamus awake.

It was just after six in the morning local time, although to Sam it still felt like the middle of the night. He sat in the waiting area while the others went in search of breakfast, resuming his fretting over their next steps. The first thing he did was check to see if Max's watch was still transmitting its location. He was relieved to see it was, and that it hadn't moved. That was one major concern crossed off his list. When Six returned with a bagel and orange juice for him, he gratefully accepted it.

"You're still worrying," Six said.

"It's my job," Sam replied. "Your job is to tell me everything will be fine."

"Everything *will* be fine," said Six.

"Thanks," Sam said. "Now make me believe it."

A moment later, Nemo and Seamus appeared. And not long after that came the announcement that their second flight was boarding. Sam got up quickly and grabbed his bag. Six followed him.

This flight was shorter than the first, and ninety minutes later they touched down in Mobile. Once they were off the plane, Nemo said, "Where to now?"

"We need a car," Sam said. "You guys wait down at baggage claim. Hopefully, I'll be back shortly."

He got onto a car rental shuttle bus, taking it to the lot where the cars were parked. But instead of going inside, he walked quickly down the rows until he came to a white Ford Explorer. He opened the door and slipped inside. As he'd hoped, the key was already in the ignition.

The difficult part was supposed to be getting the car out without a pass code. But, thankfully, when he told the computer what it wanted to hear, the gate slid open without any hassle. Sam was out and driving back to the airport in no time. When he reached the others at baggage claim, he rolled down the window and called out to Six, "Need a lift?"

As they drove away from the airport, the towns they passed through grew smaller and smaller, until just before noon they were passing by little collections of what could only generously be called shacks. They were far out in the country now, and Sam was starting to wonder if they were on a wild-goose chase. According to the coordinates being sent out by Max's watch, they were within five miles of where it was. But all that seemed to be around them was swampland. When Sam saw a tiny gas station along the side of the road, he pulled off and went inside. Behind the counter, an old man in faded overalls and a blue work shirt stood as if he'd been waiting for a hundred years for someone to come in.

"Need to fill up?" he asked Sam.

"Yes," Sam said, taking some money out of his pocket.

"But I also have a question. Are there any houses around here?"

"Houses?" the man said. He seemed to think about the question, as if nobody had ever asked it before. "Well, there are a couple of old plantation houses down some of the little side roads. But they've been abandoned for years. Mostly."

"Mostly?" Sam said.

The man nodded. "Sometimes you get people squatting in them. Nobody would live in them proper-like. Not anymore. They're mostly falling down. Only one still has its roof and all its walls is the Rothwood place."

"Oh?" Sam said. "Where's that?"

The man stared at him suspiciously, as if maybe Sam was looking to move in and live there rent-free.

"I'm a photographer," Sam said. "I like to photograph old places."

The man seemed to find this a satisfactory answer. "You go down the road about a mile, turn off on the dirt road there. Follow that all the way back. Might have to get out and walk if any trees have fallen down. Keep your eyes open for copperheads. Not usually out this time of year, but it's been warm."

"Thanks," Sam said. He handed the man some bills. "I'll just fill up and be on my way."

He went outside, started fueling up the Explorer and leaned in the window to talk to Six. "I think I might know where we're headed," he told her. He filled her in on what the old man had told him.

"A plantation house?" Six said. "In a swamp?"

"There are probably ghosts there," Seamus remarked as he did something on his phone. When this was met with silence, he looked up. "Oh. Sorry. I didn't mean—"

"We know what you meant," Nemo interrupted. "And there's only one Ghost we're looking for."

Sam heard the pump click off. He removed the nozzle from the gas tank, shut the door and got back in. Pulling onto the road, he followed the old man's instructions. He almost missed the turnoff, as it was overgrown with tall grass, but at the last minute he saw it and pulled the Explorer onto the rutted dirt road.

"We're not just going to drive up to the place, are we?" Nemo asked from the backseat.

"No," Sam said. "We'll stop somewhere up here and walk in. How close are we?" he asked Six, who was monitoring their position on the laptop.

"About a quarter of a mile," she said. "If this is right."

Sam brought the car to a stop. Looking through the windshield, he saw nothing but swampland. The dirt road ran right into it, disappearing beneath the shadows of some trees from which moss hung like curtains.

"Well," he said. "We're about to find out."

CHAPTER FIVE

MAX

PENSACOLA, FLORIDA

"DO YOU HAVE ANY TATTOOS?"

Max looked at Byron and shook his head. "No. I'm not old enough. Don't you have to be eighteen?"

Byron laughed. "Not if you know the right people. Ghost, show him your ink."

Ghost pulled up the sleeve of her shirt. On her left forearm, just below the crook of her elbow, there was a circle with five dots inside of it placed at equal distances around the circumference. A line ran from one dot diagonally across the circle to connect with a dot on the opposite side.

"What is it?" Max asked.

"A star," Ghost said. "Well, the first part of one. I'll add the other lines later, when I—"

"When she achieves certain goals," Byron said. He looked

at Ghost, who looked down.

"What does it mean?" Max asked.

"It's a symbol," Byron said. "Of our group. Our family."

"Oh," Max said. He wasn't really sure what Byron was getting at, but he liked the idea that the tattoo meant that Ghost was part of something. "It's cool."

"Would you like to get one?" Byron asked.

"Me?" Max said. "Oh no. My parents would kill me."

"I don't see your parents here. Do you?" Byron pretended to look around.

Max laughed. "Right," he said. "Sometimes I forget that I don't have to worry about them anymore."

Thinking about his parents made Max feel down. He looked out at the ocean. Byron and Ghost had brought him to Pensacola for the day. Byron said he wanted to show Max the beach. Max had seen beaches before, so he didn't really know what the big deal was. But the thought of spending the day with Ghost was appealing. Eleni and Magdalena said they had things to do at the house, so they hadn't come.

With Ghost by his side, Max had strangely enough been getting used to being around the Mogs. It helped that Byron and the others didn't look all that different from the people who crowded the beach. It was too chilly for swimming, but that wasn't stopping people from doing other things. They walked. Dogs chased balls and Frisbees. Down the beach, a volleyball game was taking place, while at some picnic tables a raucous group was laughing and singing along to music blasting from a radio.

"Don't think about your parents." Ghost's voice crept into his thoughts as she leaned against him and slipped her hand into his. "You've got me now."

Max looked down at their entwined arms and saw her tattoo again. He squeezed her hand. "I think I do want one," he said. "A tattoo, I mean."

"That's the spirit," Byron said, jumping up from the bench on which they were seated. "Come on."

"Now?" Max asked.

"Why wait? We'll go see my friend," said Byron as Ghost stood and pulled Max up with her.

They walked down the sidewalk, passing shops and restaurants. Max's thoughts swirled as he contemplated what he was about to do. When they came to a place called Skwid Ink and Byron pulled open the door, Max hesitated.

"Don't worry. You'll be fine," Ghost said, putting her hand on Max's shoulder.

They went inside. As Max looked at all the tattoo designs displayed on the walls, Byron walked up to the desk where a huge man with short, snow-white hair stood. He wore a black T-shirt with the Skwid Ink logo—a cephalopod holding tattoo machines in each of its eight arms—and every square inch of him seemed to be covered with colorful artwork. He also had icy-blue eyes and a goatee the same white color as his hair.

"Byron!" the man boomed. "Here for another piece?"

"Not for me," Byron said. "For my friend Max here."

He beckoned for Max to come over. "This is Hoth."

The huge man held out a fist, and Max saw that his knuckles were tattooed with the letters *S-I-N-K*. He glanced down at Hoth's other hand, which was resting on the counter, and saw that the knuckles there were inked with *S-W-I-M*. He bumped Hoth's fist with his own, which felt like hitting a pebble against a boulder. "Hey," Max said, trying to sound casual and not at all worried about the pain.

"Max is here to get his circle," Byron told Hoth.

Hoth grinned. "Another brother for the tribe." He turned his left arm over, and Max saw that he had a tattoo like Ghost's, except that all the lines of the star were filled in.

"I guess," Max said uncertainly, looking over at Ghost.

"Come on back," said Hoth.

They all walked into the rear of the shop where there were several barber-style chairs scattered around. Hoth led them to one, patted it and said, "Have a seat, bro."

Max got into the chair while Byron and Ghost pulled up two regular folding chairs and sat down. Max fidgeted as he watched the artist set up his equipment and squirt black ink into several tiny plastic cups. Then Hoth had him hold out his left arm, which he wiped down with an alcohol rub before applying a stencil.

"How's it look?" Hoth asked.

"Great," Max said. "How about we just leave it like this?" He chuckled nervously.

Ghost pulled her seat up next to Max and held on to his other hand, giving him an encouraging smile. "It doesn't hurt too bad."

Hoth turned on the tattoo machine, which buzzed like a swarm of angry bees. "Try to relax," he said. "It will be over before you know it."

Max closed his eyes as Hoth lowered the needle. When it touched his skin, Max forced himself not to cry out or jump. Ghost was right. It didn't exactly hurt, but it felt like a thousand little claws scratching at him. He kept his eyes closed and focused on his breathing as Hoth worked. And when the man finally said, "Okay. We're done," Max opened his eyes with relief.

There was now a black circle with five small dots inside of it on his arm. The area around it was a little red and puffy, and it felt like a sunburn. Hoth squirted water onto a paper towel and wiped away stray bits of ink.

"What do you think?" he asked.

Max grinned. "It's cool," he said.

"Just like mine," said Ghost, who had come over to stand beside Max.

"Not quite," Max reminded her. "You have one arm of your star."

"And so will you soon," Byron assured him.

Hoth bandaged Max's arm. Then they all walked out to the front of the shop, where Max suddenly panicked. "I—I don't know if I have enough money to pay for this."

Hoth laughed. "Don't worry about it, brother," he said. "It's taken care of."

"You're sure?" said Max.

"Totally," Hoth answered. "We're family now, remember?

Family takes care of each other."

Max held out his fist. "Thanks," he said.

Hoth bumped his massive hand against Max's again. "You come back when it's time for the next part," he said.

They left the shop and went out into the bright afternoon sun. "Are either of you hungry?" Byron asked.

"Starving," Max said.

They headed to a nearby restaurant, where they ate burgers and drank milk shakes. Max kept glancing at his forearm. He wanted to take off the bandage and look at his star, but Hoth had said to leave it on until they got home. Max couldn't wait to see his tattoo again. Having it made him feel special. Like he was connected to Ghost. And also part of a select group. He wondered what Nemo would say when she saw it.

Thinking about Nemo made him think about Six and Sam, and all of a sudden he didn't feel quite so happy. He'd practically forgotten about them since arriving at the house the night before. How was that possible? The whole point of him being there was so that they could locate him and help get Ghost out of there. But it was like they were a memory from another time.

Byron pushed his plate away. "So," he said. "How would you like to get to work earning your first star line?"

The question brought Max back to the moment. "Now?" he said. "How?"

"I have some business to conduct while we're here in

Florida," Byron said. "I want you to come with me and be my ears."

"What do you mean?" Max asked.

"The people I will be meeting speak a language I don't," Byron explained. "I need you to listen to what they're saying and tell me if they're being honest. Can you do that?"

Max shrugged. "I guess so," he said. "What kind of business is it?"

"A sales transaction," Byron said. "That's not important right now. What is important is that you remain cool. You sat for your tattoo with no problem, so I think you can do this."

"Sure," Max said. He looked at Ghost. "Are you coming?"

"Ghost will wait for us at the beach. I want to make sure you can handle this on your own," Byron said. "But we won't be long."

"Okay," Max said. "I think."

"Great," Byron said, putting down some money on the table. "Let's go then. I need to get something from the car first."

They left the restaurant and walked back to where they'd parked. Byron popped open the trunk and removed a small black leather bag from it. Then they said good-bye to Ghost, who walked back towards the beach while Byron and Max left in the other direction. Max wanted to ask where they were going, but he thought playing it cool would show he was down for whatever it was they were doing, so he kept quiet.

After about ten minutes they came to a skate park. The concrete hills and valleys were swarming with people on skateboards. Max watched as the riders flew up the slopes and into the air, sometimes turning flips before coming back down. The sound of wheels against cement filled the air.

Byron paused at the edge of the park. He lifted his hand, and a moment later a young man came whizzing up the side of the bowl they were standing near and neatly landed right in front of them. He unbuckled his helmet and removed it.

"Tanet," Byron said. "Nice to see you, as always."

The man—he was probably seventeen or eighteen, Max estimated—nodded. "You, too. You bring me some goodies?"

Byron nodded. "Why don't we go to your place and do our transaction there?"

"Sure thing," Tanet said. He looked at Max. "Who's the kid?"

"Max," Byron said. "And he's older than he looks." He winked at Max, who straightened up.

Tanet nodded at Max, who nodded back. Tanet held his skateboard under his arm as they walked. Max looked at it. "Is that a Flip deck?" he asked.

"Sure is," Tanet said. "You ride?"

"I've got a Toy Machine board," Max told him. "But I left it at home when I— It's at home."

"Cool," Tanet said. "Bring it next time, and we'll hit the park."

They arrived at an apartment complex made up of several two-story stucco buildings painted light pink. Tanet walked up the stairs of one of the buildings to the second floor, where he rapped on the door. A moment later someone said, "Who is it?" Only it was said in a language that wasn't English. Max thought is sounded Asian, but he didn't know where it was from.

"It's Tanet," the guy replied in the same language. "I'm with the vampire."

Max laughed, then turned the laugh into a cough when Tanet looked at him with a puzzled expression. Max assumed he was talking about Byron, who did sort of resemble a movie vampire with his pale skin, black clothes and hair, and dark glasses.

The door opened, and Tanet stepped inside. He motioned for Byron and Max to follow. They entered into a living room. The windows all had the shades pulled, and the room was illuminated mainly by a huge television mounted on one wall. The TV was playing what appeared to be a martial arts film, but the sound was turned down so that it just looked like a whole bunch of people fighting each other for no reason. There were two couches in the room with a coffee table between them. On the table was an assortment of small plastic bags, a bowl filled with white powder and several plastic bottles. A handful of pills of various shapes and colors were scattered across the tabletop.

"Are those drugs?" Max asked, forgetting himself.

Byron put his hand on Max's shoulder and squeezed hard. He leaned over. "I said, be cool," he whispered.

Thankfully, Tanet and the other man were busy discussing

something in their own language and hadn't heard Max speak.

"Can you understand them?" Byron asked softly.

Max nodded. The guys were arguing. The one whose name Max didn't know was saying that he didn't want to do business with Byron anymore. "But he makes us a lot of money," Tanet argued. "More than the other stuff combined."

The man shook his head, but Tanet turned to Max and Byron. "Please forgive my brother's mood," he said. "He is not feeling well."

"Maybe this will make him feel better," Byron said. He walked over to the couch and sat down. Clearing some space on the table, he set down the black leather bag and opened it. From inside he took out a small jar filled with what looked like black powder. He unscrewed the top of the jar, tipped it and poured a small amount of the powder onto the table. It trickled out like very fine sand. He picked up a razor blade that was sitting on the table and used it to scrape the powder into two short, thin lines. Then he beckoned to Tanet and his brother.

The brother frowned. In their language he said, "I don't want any of the vampire's blood."

Tanet said, "Don't offend him. Do it."

Reluctantly, the man came over to the couch, where he sat as far from Byron as he could while still being on the same piece of furniture. Leaning over the coffee table, he placed one finger on the side of his nose and snorted. The black powder disappeared up his nose. He repeated the process with the other line. When he was done, he leaned back on the couch with his eyes closed.

Max had never seen anyone take drugs before, and he was almost shaking with fear. This was not at all what he had expected when Byron said they were going to make a business transaction. But Byron seemed cool as could be, and Max wanted the Mog to like him, so he stayed cool, too.

Tanet's brother opened his eyes. Even in the dim light of the room, Max could see that the man's pupils were huge and the centers of his eyes were like black moons. *He kind of looks like he has Mog eyes,* he thought. It was unsettling.

"How do you feel?" Byron asked.

The man didn't answer for a moment. Then he said, "Like I can do anything." His voice was different somehow. More confident. He grinned. "It's good."

Byron looked at Tanet. "We're improving it every time. You'll have no trouble selling this."

Tanet smiled. "We'll take all you have," he said. "Wait here." He disappeared into another room, leaving Byron and Max alone with his brother, who suddenly jumped up and started performing martial arts moves like the people in the movie playing on the television.

"What's wrong with him?" Max asked.

"Nothing," said Byron. "Nothing at all. He just hasn't learned how to focus the power of the drug."

"What kind of drug is it?"

"We'll talk about that later," Byron said as Tanet walked back into the room. He was carrying several thick wads of cash, which he handed to Byron. Byron thumbed through them, then deposited the money in the leather bag. "As always, Tanet, it's nice doing business with you. I'll see you soon."

Tanet showed them to the door while, behind them, his brother kicked and punched at the air. As Max and Byron walked back down the stairs, Max said, "What language were they speaking?"

"Thai," Byron said. "What did they say?"

Max hesitated. He didn't want to offend Byron. "They called you a vampire," he finally admitted. "The brother said he didn't want any of your blood. What did he mean?"

Byron laughed. "I suppose that's one way of looking at it," he said.

Max didn't understand, but he didn't say anything. Byron turned and looked at him. "You did a great job," he said. "A couple more transactions and we'll see about getting you that star line."

Max nodded. He was still shaken by what they'd just done, but he was also excited about the idea of getting a star like the one Hoth had. Then he and Ghost would be the same.

"But right now," Byron said brightly, "how about we find Ghost and get some ice cream?"

CHAPTER SIX

SIX AND SAM
OUTSIDE OF MOBILE, ALABAMA

"IT REALLY DOES LOOK LIKE A HAUNTED HOUSE," Six said.

They were in the trees, peering out at the dilapidated old plantation home. They'd been watching it for twenty minutes, and so far no one had come out and no movement had been detected inside. Sam looked at his phone, to which he was relaying the signal from Max's watch. "It still says the watch is in there."

"Maybe a raccoon found it and carried it in," Six suggested. "Or an alligator. Or whatever lives in this swamp."

They'd left Nemo and Seamus back in the Explorer with strict instructions to get out of sight and alert them if anyone came by. They'd heard nothing.

"We might as well go in," Six said.

"Are you feeling up to it?" Sam asked. "I mean, you know, if anything happens?"

"If you mean are my Legacies back, no. Not a hundred percent, anyway," Six said. "But I'm ready. I'm always ready."

Together, they walked out of the trees and through the tall cogon grass that surrounded the house. The sound of insects enveloped them, and the afternoon sun high overhead bathed the house in light. Even so, it looked forgotten and tired. The paint had peeled away, leaving the wood to fade. Vines twined around the pillars that lined the front. Several of the windows were smashed. Six could tell it had been beautiful once.

They went around to the rear, where they found an overgrown garden. A henhouse, the chickens that occupied it long gone, listed to one side as if something had tried to push it over. Farther out, three small cottages sagged under their own weight, the roofs mostly gone. Nearer the house, a set of rickety-looking steps rose out of the tangle of trumpet vine that was slowly consuming the lower part of the porch. Six hoped these led to a kitchen.

They did. Six pushed open a screen door whose screen had long ago rotted away, and she and Sam stepped into the kitchen. Surprisingly, it was clean. And when she opened the antique-looking refrigerator, there was food inside. Someone had obviously been using it recently. But who? And were they still in the house?

They walked out of the kitchen and into a narrow hallway that led to a dining room. Again, the furniture was old but clean. A cracked china plate sat on the table with a setting of silverware on a cloth napkin beside it and a crystal goblet above it. The goblet was filled with what looked like red wine.

"That's not weird at all," Sam said in a low voice.

They moved into a large living room, which was populated with a couch, some chairs, a piano and a small round table on which were spread out a series of cards.

"Tarot?" Six said, picking up one that had an image of a devil on it.

"Again, not at all weird or creepy," said Sam. "If someone *was* here, they left in a hurry."

Six was thinking the same thing, and it worried her. If Max was in the house, they should have heard something, some kind of noise, by now. But the place was as silent as a tomb.

"Let's check upstairs," she suggested.

They found the stairs, climbed them. On the second floor they found a line of closed doors. Most were locked, but Sam's application of a little telekinesis easily unlocked the simple mechanisms. Opened, the doors revealed a series of bedrooms, each one neat and tidy but seemingly unlived in. The whole thing was unsettling. Why would someone bother to clean the rooms and not actually live there?

The fourth door they opened was to a library or office. One wall was covered with shelves of dusty old books, the smell of which filled the stuffy room. Against another wall stood a desk. There were various items scattered across the desktop: a pen, a letter opener, a pair of scissors.

Sam hurried to the desk, picked up a watch, and examined it closely.

"It's his," he told Six.

"Good, I guess," Six said. "But where is he?"

A noise coming from downstairs interrupted their conversation, a loud bang and the sound of feet running. Six and Sam looked at each other, then bolted out of the room and down the hallway. As they reached the bottom of the stairs, they saw a figure in a dress disappearing into the dining room. At the same time, a loud crash came from the living room, and a boy's voice yelled, "Help!"

"Go after the girl," Six said. "I'll look in there. It could be Max."

Sam took off after the fleeing figure, while Six went into the living room. "Max?" she called out.

A low moan answered her, coming from the shadows behind the piano. "Help," a voice said, but more faintly than before.

Six ran over to the piano. A figure was lying on the floor. She knelt down. "Max?"

A hand flew out and gripped her wrist. The figure turned its head to look at her. "Afraid not," he said.

"Scotty," Six said, trying to pull away. But then she felt the peculiar sensation that came with being teleported. Her vision blurred, and there was a push. Then everything came back together. She was standing outside, in snow. The air was cold and the bright sun overhead blinded her. The change in atmosphere was disorienting, but she focused on Scotty, who was standing a few feet away, grinning.

She charged at him, swinging her fist at his face. He laughed and ducked. His hand caught her leg, and then everything shifted again. She felt the momentum of her attack continue to propel her forward even as they teleported, and when they reappeared she stumbled. They were at the top of a tall building, and she found herself teetering on the edge of the roof. Below her was a street filled with people and cars. She tried to stop herself but was too late. She tumbled over the side and began to fall.

She heard laughter, and once again she was shoved through space. She couldn't breathe. Then she was back in open air, still hurtling downward to her death. But Scotty was holding on to her ankle, so she kicked at him. He let go just as they plunged into water.

It was warm, salty. Six continued to descend through the clear blue. She fanned her arms and legs, trying to slow herself. She twisted around, looking for Scotty and trying to get her bearings. She felt a heavy current tug at her, drawing her deeper. She fought against it, but it was stronger. Already breathless from teleporting, her lungs burned. She was going to drown.

Six fought with the last of her strength. She felt herself beginning to pass out. And then she was moving again, pulled out of the water as Scotty once again transported them. She gasped for air. She inhaled gratefully as her head spun around looking for the teleporter.

"Having fun?"

She heard Scotty's voice, but couldn't see him. They were in complete darkness. She didn't even know if they were indoors or outdoors.

She struck out, and her fist connected with flesh. She heard Scotty swear.

"Now I am," Six said.

Her eyes were adjusting. She saw Scotty on the ground, holding his nose. She pounced on him, raising her fist to hit him again. As his hand touched her, she realized her mistake.

Another jump. Another room. She was barely able to look around before she was grabbed roughly by several sets of hands and a bag of some kind was pulled over her head and secured around her throat. She fought back, but the series of teleportations had sapped her strength. Metal cuffs were slipped around her wrists and she heard the sound of a chain rattling. A moment later, her hands were forcibly lifted up and over her head. In just a couple of minutes she'd gone from thinking she had found Max to being a prisoner. But whose?

"Does somebody want to tell me what's going on?" she snarled, her voice muffled by the sack over her head.

"All in good time," said a female voice.

Six heard the sound of a door slamming shut, followed by the grinding of metal. Wherever she was, she was locked in. She immediately tried reaching out with her telekinesis to work on her restraints, but it did no good. She couldn't even move the bag away from her face, as whatever secured it around her neck wouldn't break. For the moment she was stuck the way she was.

Unable to do anything about her own situation, she thought about Sam. Obviously they had been set up. Scotty had been waiting for them, and his call for help was meant to make them think he was Max and split them up. But who was the other person, the one they'd seen running away? Was it Ghost? Maybe, but then where was Max?

She thought about the various pieces of the puzzle. She didn't know Max's whereabouts. She didn't know if the mystery girl Sam had run after really was Ghost. So she focused on the *why*. Why had they wanted to separate Six and Sam? Yes, they were less powerful apart. But she had a sinking feeling there was another reason. She just didn't know what it was.

Then she thought about Seamus and Nemo. Were they all right? What if Sam couldn't get back to them? Or what if he, like her, had been transported somewhere else?

Sam was right, she thought miserably. *Involving all of them had been a mistake.*

Sam burst into the kitchen just as his quarry disappeared out the screen doorway. He ran after her and saw her rushing through the grass, heading for the trio of tumbledown shacks at the rear of the property. It was a girl. She had short, pink hair.

He ran after her. The girl was surprisingly quick, passing

through the cogon grass and leaving the fuzzy white tips swaying behind her. She laughed, which was strangely unnerving. She looked back for a moment, and Sam saw that it wasn't Ghost. There was something off about her face. Then the girl turned and ran faster, as if they were merely playing a game of tag. She got to the center house and skipped inside. Sam reached the door not long after and paused. The house's roof had collapsed in the middle, and the girl was standing on the dirt floor inside a ring of sunlight. Dust motes floated in the air all around her as she spun in a slow circle.

"Who are you?" Sam asked.

The girl stopped spinning and tilted her head to one side, looking at him. Seeing her full-on for the first time, Sam realized what it was about her that had seemed out of place earlier. She was Mogadorian.

"Magdalena," she said, smiling slightly. "And you're Sam. I've heard a lot about you." Her smile turned into a frown. "You've hurt some of my friends."

"Funny how that happens in a war," Sam said.

Magdalena said nothing but continued to stare at him. Then she closed her eyes, seeming to bathe in the light streaming over her body. She didn't appear to be at all afraid of him, which made Sam nervous.

"Where's Max?" he asked. "We found his watch."

"Not here," Magdalena said, beginning to turn again. "He's out. With the others."

"Others?" Sam asked. "And what do you mean 'out'?"

"Out," Magdalena repeated. "I don't know where, exactly. But they'll be back."

"Who was that back in the house then?"

"Scotty," Magdalena said. "But he's probably gone by now. With your friend."

Realizing what the girl meant, Sam panicked. Scotty had taken Six somewhere? Had that been the plan all along?

"Eleni will be disappointed," Magdalena said. "She was hoping to test herself against Six. I suppose you'll have to do as a warm-up."

"Eleni?" Sam said.

"She'll be back," said Magdalena. "She just went to collect the two you left in the car."

Sam swore and turned, his instincts telling him to forget the girl and make sure that Seamus and Nemo were all right.

"You really shouldn't have left them alone," Magdalena said. "Not out here. It isn't safe."

Sam turned back to her. He lifted his hands. "I think we're done here."

Nothing happened. His telekinesis stalled.

"Seriously?" Sam said, looking at his hands. "You're going to crap out on me now?"

Something suddenly struck him in the back. He fell onto the dirt floor, hitting his chin and biting his lip. He tasted blood. A few feet away, Magdalena clapped her hands together happily, as if he had just performed the world's best magic trick for her.

Sam rolled over. Standing in the doorway was an imposing figure dressed all in black leather. Like Magdalena, she was a Mogadorian. Who were they? How had they not been caught and taken to Mog prison? And what did they want?

He would have to worry about those questions later. Right now, the Mog was coming at him. Sam went into hand-to-hand combat mode, crouching and waiting until she was closer before springing at her. The Mog deflected him with one arm, sweeping him aside and tumbling him into the dirt. He got up and went after her again. They exchanged blows and kicks. For every punch Sam landed, he got one in return. After all his time with Six, Sam had gotten in shape and was strong. The Mog was stronger.

She swept her leg, tripping him, and he went down. Then she was on top of him, pinning him to the ground. Sam tried to catch his breath, but she barely seemed tired. A second later, he saw Magdalena peering down at him over the other Mog's shoulder.

"This is Eleni," she said. "I told him you were hoping for Six," she added to the other Mog.

"I think maybe she would have put up more of a fight," Eleni said. "Then again, I don't want to hurt you."

"What do you want?" Sam asked. "Where's Six?"

"So many questions," Eleni said. "Where is this one? Where is that one? Why do the Mogadorians want to invade Earth? Humans are always asking questions. How about I ask you one? What are you willing to do to keep those two Human Garde you brought with you alive?"

Sam felt his heart stop for a moment. Nemo and Seamus.

"What have you done with them?"

Eleni sighed. "Again with the questions. Nothing yet," she said. "But if you decide to be uncooperative, I will not hesitate to kill them. So, will you cooperate?"

Sam had no doubt the Mog would do as she said. But what did she want from him, from them? Every atom of him wanted to fight her more, to hurt her and make her tell him where Six was, where Max and Ghost were, where Nemo and Seamus were, and what she was doing here at all. He pushed down those instincts, though. If he wanted to see them again, he had to let her think she had won. For now.

He looked into her eyes. "Yes," he said.

CHAPTER SEVEN

NEMO

OUTSIDE OF MOBILE, ALABAMA

NEMO, SUBMERGED IN THE BRACKISH WATERS OF the swamp, tried not to think about what else might be waiting beneath the surface. It was bad enough that she could barely see her hand in front of her face. Every time something bumped into her she was sure it was a snake or an alligator. She didn't even really know what kind of animals lived in swamps, but she was pretty sure most of them were poisonous or deadly.

But not as deadly as the Mog who was probably waiting for her to emerge from hiding.

Thank the gods she'd had to pee a couple of minutes ago. Otherwise, she would have been in the SUV with Seamus when the Mog showed up. As it was, Nemo had barely had time to get her pants pulled up and find a hiding place in the trees. She'd watched as the Mog had approached the car and pulled Seamus out. Her friend hadn't even had time to shout out a warning or use his Legacy to try and defend himself.

Nemo had thought about trying to fight the Mog, but she could tell the woman was way stronger than she was. She just *looked* dangerous. And while Nemo wasn't normally one to back down from a fight, her control of her telekinesis wasn't yet up to the level of that kind of confrontation. At least being able to breathe underwater was coming in handy. Although she wasn't sure how long she could stay submerged. It wasn't exactly warm, and she was already shivering. She thought about her bag back in the Explorer and wondered if the Mog had taken it. If so, she wouldn't have anything to change into, and once night came, the temperature would drop a lot.

She was going to have to emerge from the water eventually. Would the Mog be waiting for her? Maybe she didn't even know Nemo was there. Maybe Seamus hadn't said anything. She was miles from anything like civilization. Fortunately, she'd had the presence of mind to hide her phone before going into the water. That might help, if she could get a signal. But who would she call? 911? The HGA?

She wondered where Sam and Six were. Did the Mog showing up mean she had done something to them? Or maybe the Mog didn't even know about them. That would be the best-case scenario. Maybe right now Six and Sam were taking care of her or had already done so and were looking for Nemo so they could all get out of there.

There were so many things going through Nemo's brain. Should she keep hiding or get out of the water? Should she go looking for her friends or just call for help? And why was there a Mog there in the first place? She realized it was the first time she'd ever seen one up close. She'd been so startled at the time that she hadn't paused to think about that. Now it hit her. A Mog had taken Seamus. A real live *Mog.* As in the things that had attacked Earth.

Mogs had lurked in her nightmares since their attack on the planet. And like most humans, she'd wondered what she would do if she ever came face-to-face with one. Now she knew. She would run and hide, leaving her friend to try and defend himself.

She was momentarily overwhelmed by guilt and shame. She should have stayed. She should have fought, even if she would almost certainly have lost. She knew Mogs were trained killers. That made her more worried for Seamus, Six, Sam and whoever else might have gotten in the Mog woman's way.

Something slithered across her arm. Instinctively, she rose to the surface to get away from it. Her head broke the water and she could see again. Behind her, a harmless black swamp snake glided sinuously through the brown water.

Nemo looked around for any sign of the Mog. She saw nothing. Which didn't mean she wasn't out there. She could be hiding, waiting. But Nemo wasn't going back underwater again. Although the air was warm, she was shaking. It was nothing like the icy lake in Montana that she and Sam had fallen into, but the water didn't have to be all that cold for hypothermia to kick in. Nemo needed to get out of the swamp, even if it was risky.

She climbed out and went to the spot where she'd hidden her phone beneath a log. She checked it for a signal, found none. Then she walked back through the woods. She tried to stay in the shadows of the trees in case the Mog was looking for her, but she saw and heard nothing. Water dripped from her clothes, and her feet squished inside her boots, but slowly she began to dry out.

When she reached the spot where she had been peeing, she crouched down and surveyed the area. The Explorer was gone. But then she heard the noise of an engine. She squatted even lower, with just her head above the grass so that she could see what was coming.

A moment later a car came slowly down the road. The windows were tinted, and she couldn't see who was inside of the vehicle. It passed the spot where the Explorer had been parked and continued on. When it was out of sight, Nemo began to follow it. She stayed in the trees as much as possible, following the edge of the dirt road. The car disappeared ahead of her, but there was only one place it could be going.

Finally, the plantation house came into view. The car was parked outside. The Explorer was also there. Nemo stopped, trying to come up with a plan. There was already one Mog she knew about. Had the car brought even more of them? If she couldn't take on one, how would she ever handle a whole group?

She looked up at the sky. In a couple of hours it would be dark. While it would also be colder then, it would be easier to sneak around without being seen. And that would give her time to get her head together. She retraced her steps, heading back for the cover of the woods, although this time she went even deeper, until she found a small clearing where she could rest. She quickly stripped down to her underwear, hanging her damp clothes over some branches to finish drying in the sun. She was particularly happy to get off her boots and socks and to let her feet breathe.

She wished she could build a fire, but she had no matches or anything else helpful, and her Legacies were of no use for that. Still, she was warmer, and the sunshine felt good on her bare skin. She sat down on a fallen pine tree and once again looked at her phone. No signal, and the power was down to less than fifty percent. She turned it off to conserve what was left.

A second later, she felt something sting her on the leg. She swatted at it, squashing the deerfly that had bitten her. A splash of blood colored her skin. Then she felt another fly land on her arm. She shooed it away. The fly's sting already itched.

Soon there was a small army of flies circling around her. She flapped her hands at them, sending them buzzing away, but only for a moment. As soon as she stopped, they came in for another attack. *I wish I could control them like Seamus can,* she thought.

Now that this had occurred to her, she wondered why

Seamus hadn't done something similar when the Mog came for him. He could easily have called up an entire swarm of the tiny, biting monsters. But he hadn't. Had he been too surprised to think of it? Not had enough time? Maybe. But it still seemed odd. As aloof as he acted, Seamus was smart on his feet. It was one of the things she liked about him.

She smacked another fly, leaving the blood on her skin as a reminder to the others that she meant business. After a while they seemed to grow tired of trying and left her alone. But the bites itched fiercely, and the question about why Seamus hadn't used his Legacy itched, too.

Her stomach rumbled. She wished she had some of the chips or candy bars that Max had bought the day before. She wished she had a lot of things. But she didn't. She got up and checked her clothes. They were mostly dry now, so she put her shirt and pants back on. Her socks she left for a little longer while she sat down again and thought through her next steps.

She had to get inside the house. At the very least, Seamus was in there. Maybe Six and Sam, too. *Hopefully* Six and Sam, because if they weren't it meant something bad had happened to them. And that's where Max's watch was supposed to be, so maybe he was there, too. And Ghost.

Nemo got up and walked around the clearing. She scanned the area for anything she could use as a weapon. All she found were branches and sticks. "I never thought I'd say this," she muttered. "But a gun bush would come in really handy right about now. Maybe a grenade tree." She thought about Seamus's bag in the Explorer and wished she had that, too.

She picked up several short sticks. Then she found a razor-edged rock. Taking them back to the log, she sat down and started chipping away at the end of the sticks. Pieces flew off, and when Nemo was done each stick had a sharp point. She held one out and stabbed the air with it. These weren't much, but they were better than nothing. *Besides,* she thought. *If our ancestors could bring down mammoths with pointed sticks, I should be able to take care of a Mog.*

Dusk was settling over the swamp now, the sky darkening as the early-winter night crept in between the trees. Nemo put on her socks, then her boots, lacing them up tightly. Her thoughts flashed back to Montana and being tracked through the snow by the husband and wife who had paid money to hunt down her and Rena. Had that happened just a week or so ago? And now here she was in another forest, preparing for another hunt. This time she didn't know if she was the hunter or the hunted. Maybe both. One thing she did know was that she wasn't the same girl from that night. She was tougher. And she was angrier.

She stood up. It was time.

She moved as silently as she could through the forest, what little noise she did make covered up by the sounds of insects, birds and frogs. The moon was only a sliver, providing little light, but it was all she needed.

When she reached the house, she saw no lights in the windows, and for a moment she thought maybe everyone had left. But the two cars were still there. She hunched over and ran to the Explorer. Opening the door on the side away from the house, she looked inside. Everything had been taken. This was not a surprise, but she was still disappointed.

She ignored the other car and moved closer to the house. When she reached the side, she saw that the windows were covered by curtains, which is why it had looked like no one was home. Now she could see faint lines of light. She also heard voices, muffled and indistinct.

She hefted a stick in her hand. She had another two tucked into the side pockets of her cargo pants. She tried not to think about what she might have to do with them as she traversed the length of the house and slid around the side. She made her way to the back of the house, but when she turned the corner, she froze. In the backyard she saw a spark of fire.

Someone was standing there. And whoever it was was smoking. The smell of burning tobacco floated to her on the air, and she again saw the glow of the cigarette as the smoker inhaled. Was it the Mog woman? The shadow didn't look like her. It was thinner. Smaller. Was it another Mog or a human? She had no way of telling. But whoever it was was an enemy.

"Where is he now?" she heard an unfamiliar male voice ask.

"Somewhere he can't cause any trouble," said a female voice.

So, there were two of them. The second, Nemo thought,

must be standing right next to the first one.

"Not with Six, I hope," said the male voice. "Keeping them apart makes them less dangerous."

A second shadow detached from the first one and walked a little way off. A second glow appeared in the air. "Of course not," the female voice said. "Eleni knows what she's doing."

"I hope so," said the male voice. "My part of the plan is working just the way I said it would."

"With some help from Eleni," the female voice said.

"Yes, yes," the male voice said. He sounded irritable. "It's always with Eleni's help. Thank you for reminding me."

"You're just jealous because she's always been the favorite," the female voice said.

The man snorted. "Jealous? Eleni is far too interested in acquiring Loric magic tricks for herself," he said.

The woman giggled. The glow of her cigarette suddenly spun in circles, as if she herself was spinning. "Magic tricks!" she said. "I wish I knew some!"

"Brains and training are all I've ever needed," the man said defensively. "Getting the humans hooked on the black powder was my idea, don't forget. Eleni had nothing to do with that."

"Of course," the female voice said. The orange glow of a cigarette butt flew through the air towards Nemo, landing not far off. It lay in the grass, still burning.

"Are you trying to start a fire?" the male voice said as the shadow moved towards Nemo.

She pressed herself against the side of the house. As the

shadow drew nearer, the person behind it came into view. It was a man. A Mog. Nemo gripped her spike in her hand, ready to use it if he saw her.

He didn't. He ground out the cigarette and went back to where the woman was waiting. Then the two of them went through a rear doorway and into the house.

Nemo, her heart pounding, took several breaths to steady herself. Now she knew there were more Mogs in the house. The man had said the name Eleni. Was that the female Mog who had taken Seamus? And again, where had all these Mogs come from? There weren't supposed to be any of them just wandering around free. They were supposed to be contained in that camp in Alaska. But here they were. Why? And what were they doing? The male Mog had said something about humans and black powder. What was that all about?

More important right now were Six and Sam. They'd clearly been captured, which was disheartening. But it also meant they were alive. She couldn't lose all hope. And she still didn't know where Ghost, Max and Seamus were.

She weighed her options. She could leave now, walk back to the gas station they'd stopped at earlier in the day and call for help. Or she could go into the house and see if any of her friends were in there. The smart thing to do would be to go for help.

She decided to go into the house.

She walked slowly towards the doorway that the two Mogs had gone through. She knew it was a stupid thing to do. But her friends were possibly inside, and with Six and

Sam unable to help them, she was the only one who could. *Me and my pointy sticks,* she thought, trying to forget how outnumbered and overpowered she was.

She reached for the handle when the door opened towards her. Someone came out, pushing her down the steps. She stumbled, caught herself and lifted her stick high in the air, ready to bring it down on her attacker.

"Nemo?" a voice whispered.

Nemo, startled, looked hard at the person in front of her. "Seamus?"

She didn't know what to say. She had been sneaking into the house to try to rescue him, and here he was walking out as if nothing at all was going on. "How'd you get out?"

"Oh," Seamus said. "I, uh—"

"Are Max and Ghost in there?" Nemo asked before he could answer. "We have to get them, too." She started to push past him.

"No," Seamus said, stopping her. "I mean, they're not in there. It was just me. I don't know where they are."

"Let's go then," Nemo said. "Come on. Before they realize you're gone."

She took Seamus's hand and tugged. He came down the steps but didn't seem to be in much of a hurry. Something was wrong. Nemo stopped. Seamus looked back at the house.

"What?" Nemo said.

"I . . . um," Seamus said.

"Seamus," said Nemo. "We've got to go. Now."

Behind Seamus, someone else came out the door. Nemo

looked up and saw the Mog man.

"Run!" Nemo shouted.

Seamus looked at her. "I'm sorry, Nemo."

The Mog leaped down the steps, his long hair flying. Before she could even think about what she was doing, Nemo raised her hands. She sent out a blast of telekinetic energy, and the stick in her hand flew. It hit the oncoming Mog in the stomach, where it buried itself deep. The Mog screamed in rage and pain and fell to his knees, clutching the end of the stick. He slumped over sideways.

Nemo went to grab Seamus's hand again, but she saw him kneel beside the Mog. Was Seamus helping him? She didn't understand.

"Seamus?"

He didn't look at her. Then Nemo heard voices. Someone else was coming.

Nemo turned and ran harder than she had ever run in her life.

CHAPTER EIGHT

SAM AND SIX
UNKNOWN LOCATIONS

SAM OPENED HIS EYES.

He was in the dark, although a faint, greenish light emanated from somewhere in front of him. He was lying on something hard. He reached out and almost immediately felt cold walls all around him. He tried to sit up, bumped his head and lay down again. He slowly extended his hands up and felt the wall a foot above him.

He was in some kind of metal cocoon.

He tried to figure out how he might have gotten here. He remembered fighting a Mog and her telling him that if he didn't cooperate, she would hurt Nemo and Seamus. He remembered wanting to kill her but wanting more to make sure that everyone was okay. He remembered saying yes. After that it was blank. At some point, obviously, he had been knocked out. And now he was here. Wherever that was.

Suddenly the light intensified as a screen near his feet came to life. He was looking at the face of the Mog. She smiled coldly.

"Hello, Sam. I apologize for not being able to greet you in person, but as you're buried twenty feet below the surface, that would be a little difficult. I hope you understand."

"Where are Nemo and Seamus?" Sam asked.

"Still worried about them more than yourself?" the Mog said. "How human of you."

"You said you wouldn't hurt them if I cooperated."

"They're alive and well. For now."

"Then why am I here?"

The Mog sighed. "Because while you've been compliant, your friend has not."

"Six?" Sam said.

"I've tried being reasonable with her," the woman said. "She might say I've also tried being unreasonable with her. That didn't work either. I'm afraid you're my last resort."

"Meaning what?" said Sam. "You're going to kill me?"

"Only if she continues to refuse to help us," the woman answered. "She has twelve hours. If she still insists on being difficult, the capsule you're in will fill with sand."

Somewhere above Sam's head, something made a grinding sound. A moment later, sand began to trickle onto his face. He coughed, turned his head and spit out the bits that had gone into his mouth. Then it stopped.

"That was so you know I'm not kidding," the Mog said. "I

considered using water, but drowning is relatively painless. Suffocating from sand isn't."

She let Sam think about that for a moment before continuing.

"As I said, your capsule is buried twenty feet down. I suppose you could try to use your Legacies to break out of it, but I wouldn't advise it. Unless you can dig up through hard-packed red clay, that is. Can you do that?"

Sam said nothing. The Mog pretended to wait for his answer, then said, "I'll take that as a no. In which case, let's hope Six decides to adjust her attitude."

The screen went blank, but the greenish light remained. Sam closed his eyes and calmed the panic that was growing inside him. He tried not to think about the fact that he was basically in a coffin and that it would be *his* coffin if it actually filled with sand. Unless Six did whatever it was they wanted her to do.

He'd been in situations like this before, also thanks to the Mogadorians. And he knew that the best way to deal with it was to focus on figuring out what was happening and why. Worrying about what Six would do, or whether or not the Mog was even telling the truth, would only lead to more panic. But if he worked on looking at all the clues and trying to organize them into a clearer picture, it would occupy his thoughts and keep them from going to places he didn't want to go.

The Mog woman was the key. Obviously, she was involved in whatever had happened to Max. Seamus and Nemo, too, of course. And Six. But luring Max away was most likely the first part of her plan. Did that mean Ghost was working with her? It seemed likely given the girl's connection to Bray, and the madman's involvement with Drac and the black ooze. Drac had mentioned something about making a deal with Mogs in his interrogation. Now it looked like maybe he'd been telling the truth.

Did that mean the Mogs were the real power behind Bray's organization? It seemed unlikely. The majority of them remaining on Earth were imprisoned. The Garde had always known that a few Mogadorians could still be running loose, but so far they hadn't caused any noticeable trouble. Maybe that was changing. Maybe with Bray out of the picture now, the Mogs he'd been involved with were taking over what was left of his operation. Or maybe that had been their plan all along: use Bray for his money and connections, then let him destroy himself so that they could assume power. That was classic Mog mentality.

The question then was, what was their ultimate goal? They'd already lost the battle for Earth, and it was highly unlikely there were enough of them to try again, or that they would succeed if they did. So what did they want?

Sam had enough firsthand experience with Mogs and their way of thinking to know that what they couldn't control, they would destroy rather than let someone else have. They were single-minded in their lust for domination and their hatred of anything they couldn't possess for themselves. They had been unable to conquer Earth, although they had left it badly damaged. What else did humanity have that they didn't?

Legacies.

Before the Garde stopped Setrákus Ra, they had a run-in with a handful of Mogs who had been given powers of their own—thanks to the Mogadorian leader's experiments. Sam and the others refused to call their new abilities Legacies. They were just augmentations. Thankfully the Garde had managed to take them all out.

Maybe these Mogs wanted the very same thing. After all they'd been through to get here, Sam knew it must have been infuriating to see the Entity choosing to bestow Legacies on humans. Those in the camps must have watched with growing rage as thankless human teenagers became increasingly powerful. Mogs considered themselves superior to humans, and many of them were physically bigger and stronger. First to be beaten by humans in combat and now to see them developing these gifts was the worst kind of humiliation.

Sam knew that occasionally a Mog prisoner or two must have gone missing at the camp. That was to be expected. This, though. This was something else. Something bigger. The Mog woman who had attacked him was an experienced fighter, probably a veteran of the battle for Earth. Had she escaped capture in the first place, gone underground and waited for an opportunity, for someone like Bray or Jagger Dennings to come along and provide what she needed? Or had she somehow escaped from the prison?

There was no way to know. There were files on all the

incarcerated Mogs, of course, but accessing them would mean getting out of his current predicament. Again, he pushed this worry aside and focused on what he could deal with, namely what was going on with the kids. Even though they were all teenagers, he still thought of the new Garde as children sometimes. Particularly Nemo, Max and Rena, as he was closest to them. Ghost too, although she was in a different category now after what had happened to her during her time with Dennings. Still, he felt some responsibility for that as well. She had been taken under his watch, and that was never far from his mind.

Plus, he and Six had brought them into the middle of whatever was going on now. They hadn't forced them, but they also hadn't tried hard to dissuade them from coming. Maybe that had been a mistake. Maybe they had assumed too much, thinking they could protect the newcomers from danger. Or that they were strong enough to protect themselves. True, all of them except Max had been in fights for their lives before. All of them had been tested. But that didn't mean they were ready.

Again, he told himself to set aside these thoughts for another time. Second-guessing his actions wasn't going to help anyone. He returned to the question of the Mogs' master plan. The woman had said that he was being used to incentivize Six. But what did they want her to cooperate with? If the Mog thought gaining Six's cooperation was going to be as easy as threatening her, she clearly hadn't done her homework.

Thinking about this actually made him laugh. The sound echoed through the tiny space, reminding him of how small the capsule was. Then he realized that although it was a tiny area, it wasn't getting hot. The temperature had remained the same. The air too was clearly being circulated somehow. And the camera was being powered by something. He closed his eyes, stilled his breathing and concentrated. His mind reached out, searching for any technology. Maybe, he thought, he could use the screen and camera to communicate with someone. He prodded but got nothing. And then he found something else. Somewhere outside the capsule but still connected to it. Power. A circulating fan. He wondered if he could somehow use these to his advantage.

As he was considering the possibilities, he looked at the screen at the end of the capsule again. Even though the monitor was black, a green light was still on. He sensed the camera inside working. Someone was watching him.

Six looked up at the television screen through the one eye that wasn't swollen shut. The Mog woman—Eleni—stood beside it, looking furious. She'd just subjected Six to another half-hour beating, each hit harder than the last. After the last punch, Six had looked her in the eye and said, "Could you do my back again? I've got a cramp that just won't go away."

Things would be different if her hands weren't still shackled over her head and her legs weren't restrained by chains running through eyebolts in the floor. Then she would have happily taken on the Mog in a fair fight. Picturing the woman lying on the floor, her face rearranged a little, made Six happy. And she would get her chance to make that happen. She just needed to stay focused.

The problem was, she couldn't give the Mog what she wanted. Of course, figuring out what that *was* had taken some time. Like most of her kind, this Mog had a sadistic streak a mile wide, and she had refused to say anything at all, preferring instead to use Six as her personal punching bag.

Finally, though, the question had been asked: Where were the samples and technology that were taken from the ship in Mexico and the underground laboratory in Argentina?

Six had answered truthfully: she didn't know.

This was the wrong answer. The Mog had resumed her brutal and unrefined methods of persuasion. Six's split lip, which was still bleeding, was an early casualty. The now-swollen eye came later. In between there were dozens of hits to every exposed part of her body. Then the question had been asked again. The answer remained the same, as was Eleni's response. And so it had continued, over and over, with no change.

It probably hadn't helped that Six had asked at one point, "Should I use smaller words? Or are you just too stupid to understand what I'm telling you?" That had earned her a punch to the jaw that had loosened a tooth.

Now, she looked up at the screen. "Are we going to watch an instructional video?" she asked.

Eleni hit a button. All of a sudden, Six was looking at

Sam's face. The camera was at his feet, apparently, giving her a view of his prone body. He seemed to be aware that he was being watched, as he looked right into the camera.

"Six?" she heard him say. "Six? Can you see me?"

"Sam!" she shouted.

The Mog grinned. "He can't hear you," she said. "But please, scream all you like."

"What have you done to him?" Six snarled.

"Nothing yet," said the Mog. She said something in Mogadorian, apparently speaking to someone located elsewhere. A moment later Sam turned his head, coughing as something fell onto his face.

"It's sand," the Mog told Six. "Answer my question and it will stop."

The sand continued to pour. Sam scraped it away from his face, pushing it to other parts of the capsule.

"I've told you already; I don't know where the materials that were seized are," Six said.

The Mog woman nodded. "That is unfortunate. If you don't know, it means your superiors don't trust you with the information. Which means their faith in you is low. Which means I have no use for you."

Six didn't argue with her. This was, in fact, the very thing she had been thinking herself ever since McKenna had informed them that Agent Walker was now in charge of the serum, the technology and the scientists involved with it. She wasn't about to tell the Mog this, however.

"If you believe me, then why do any of this?" she said,

spitting a mouthful of blood at Eleni.

The Mog ignored her, watching the screen with a satisfied smile on her face. "It must be a terrible thing knowing that you're going to die and that your fate is completely out of your hands," she said.

"Why don't you let me know," Six said.

The Mog laughed. "Threats?" she said. "You're hardly in a position to threaten me."

"Only because I'm chained up," Six said. "How about you let me go and we settle this hand-to-hand? That's what a real warrior would do."

The Mog frowned. Six had touched a nerve. She looked at the woman more closely. Although she was bigger than an average human, she wasn't nearly as imposing as some of the vatborn Mogs who were bred for battle. She was a trueborn. They enjoyed greater social status than their manufactured counterparts, but the vatborn were always more physically impressive. Perhaps this was why she had dyed her hair. She was trying to distinguish herself in other ways, which to Six indicated that she had some insecurities. She was trying to prove something. To who, Six wondered. She seemed to be in charge of whatever was going on here. But maybe she wasn't. Maybe there was someone above her, someone whose approval she was trying to win.

The Mog spoke some more words, and the sand stopped falling onto Sam's face. He sputtered, clearing the bits that had gotten into his mouth. Six watched him, knowing that he must be afraid and wishing he could hear her. Then the screen went dark and she was staring at nothing.

"I'll let you think for a little while," the Mog said. "See if you can remember anything you might have forgotten. But if you tell me no again, the sand will continue to fall until he's dead." Then she left the room, turning off the light and leaving Six alone in the darkness.

"How can I tell you what I don't know?!" Six screamed.

She rattled the chains in frustration, sending new pain down her aching arms. She had long ago lost feeling in her wrists, but her shoulder muscles burned with the stress of her arms being stretched over her head.

She needed a plan. She couldn't give the Mog what she wanted. But could she fake it? She could give her an answer—any answer. Send her off looking for the things she wanted. Inevitably, though, she would figure out that Six had lied. And then she would have no reason to let Sam or Six live.

The only solution was to give her what she wanted. And since Six couldn't do that, she had to find someone who could. The only people with that information were Walker herself and maybe Peter McKenna, although Six wasn't even sure about that. She knew enough about Walker to know that the former FBI agent would never reveal the information, not even to save the lives of Six and Sam.

No, she was going to have to handle this herself. And she had no idea how.

CHAPTER NINE

NEMO
OUTSIDE OF MOBILE, ALABAMA

AS NEMO BURST THROUGH THE DOOR OF THE GAS station, she thought her heart would explode. She'd run the entire way from the plantation house, never looking back as her feet pounded on the pavement. She could feel the blisters that had formed, and she was dripping with sweat. But she had made it, and no one had followed her. So far.

The old man behind the counter stared at her as she tried to catch her breath.

"My friends," she said. "We were here earlier today . . . for gas . . . and directions."

"I remember. What's wrong? There been an accident?"

Nemo shook her head. "Someone . . . at the house."

"At the Rothwood place? Someone there is hurt?" There

was a phone attached to the wall behind the counter. He picked it up. "I'll call 911."

"No!" Nemo shouted.

The man hesitated, the phone in his hand. "No one's hurt?"

Nemo shook her head again. Someone *was* hurt. The Mog she'd stabbed with her improvised spear-arrow thing. But she wasn't about to call for help for him.

"I don't understand," the man said.

An old woman came down the stairs that led to the next floor. She saw Nemo and gasped. "What's happened?"

"Don't know," the man said. "Think someone might be hurt."

"No one is hurt," Nemo said. She was getting her breath back. And now that she wasn't running, she actually wasn't really sure what she wanted the man to do. She reached in her pocket for her own phone. It was gone. "Shit," she muttered. "I must have dropped it."

"No need for that kind of language, young lady," the old woman said disapprovingly. "Now, can you tell us what's going on?"

"I need to call someone. Can I use your phone?"

"Of course," the woman said. "But why don't you come upstairs and use the one there. You can sit down, and I'll get you some water."

Nemo nodded and went to the stairs. As she walked up, she didn't see the woman turn to her husband and whisper, "Call Alvin."

Upstairs, she showed Nemo to a small but comfortable living room. Nemo sank onto the couch, relieved just to be sitting down, while the woman went into the kitchen and returned with a glass of water. "Thank you," Nemo said, accepting it from her and draining the entire thing. When she was done she said, "I don't think I've run that much since soccer camp when I was ten."

"What were you running from, dear?"

Nemo didn't know what to tell her. Saying "Well, see, there are these alien killing machines living in that house down the road" seemed a little bit hysterical, even if it was true. Besides, she didn't want the woman to know everything. Things were bad enough as it was without getting the whole county in an uproar.

"Nothing," she said. "I wasn't running from anything. It's just that, um, my friends . . . they . . . Can I just use the phone? It will only take a minute."

"Of course," the woman said. "It's right over there." She indicated an old-fashioned rotary phone sitting on the table beside the couch.

"Wow," Nemo said. "I haven't seen one of those outside of a movie."

"Yes, well, things move more slowly in these parts. Haven't even got color television yet."

Nemo started to say something, but the old woman laughed. "That's a joke, dear. Anyway, you go on and use the telephone."

Nemo picked up the receiver. Then she realized she

had no idea how to actually call the HGA. Was there even a number for the Academy? There must be. She just hadn't memorized it. "I don't suppose you have a computer?" she asked, thinking it would be easy enough to look up.

"I'm afraid not," the woman answered.

Nemo hung up. She had to get in touch with Nine or Lexa. They were the only people who might possibly be able to help. But it was not like Nine would have ever given her his number. And she'd never tried to find one without just looking it up. Would the Academy's number be in the phone book?

She was about to ask the woman for help, but voices interrupted from downstairs.

"What's this about, Claude?" a man said. "Molly called me from the station, said you needed me to stop by. Good thing I was making my rounds and was just about to pass by here."

"Who's that?" Nemo asked.

"That's just Alvin," the old woman said. "You don't worry about a thing. He'll know what to do."

Footsteps sounded on the stairs, ponderous and heavy. A moment later, a large man entered the room. He was wearing a policeman's uniform and a faded tan cowboy hat. He nodded at the old woman. "Agnes," he said.

"Sheriff Radley." She emphasized his title, and Nemo got the point. The law was here now, and was taking over.

The man's eyes turned to Nemo. He took in her disheveled appearance, her turquoise-colored hair, her dirty boots.

His expression didn't change, but Nemo could tell he wasn't impressed.

"What seems to be the trouble, miss?" he asked.

"This young lady and her friends ran into some difficulty over at the Rothwood house," Agnes said. "Isn't that right?" she added to Nemo.

"Sort of," Nemo said vaguely. She didn't like the police, and this one was staring hard at her. She also didn't like that he was standing between her and the only door.

"Sort of?" the sheriff said. "Exactly what kind of difficulty?"

Nemo thought quickly. "We just went to look at the house," she said. "You know, because it's historic or whatever. Turns out there are some people living in it."

"Living in it?" Radley repeated. "Why? The place is falling apart."

"Probably homeless," Agnes said. "Or, you know"—she dropped her voice to a whisper—"drugs."

The sheriff snorted. "Got that kind all over the place now. So, what happened? Your friends get into a fight with them?"

"Yeah," Nemo said. It wasn't the truth, exactly, but it also wasn't a lie.

"All right," Radley said. "Let's take a ride over there. See what's going on."

Nemo hesitated. "Is that a good idea?" she said. "I mean, I think they had guns."

The sheriff put his hand on the grip of his own holstered pistol. "I think I can handle it," he said. "You come with me."

"Me?" Nemo asked. "Why?"

"In case I need you to show me what happened or help your friends."

Nemo nodded. "Sure," she said. "Sure. I can do that."

She hated leaving without calling someone to let them know what was going on. But now she could hardly insist on using the phone with the officer there. She thanked Agnes for the water and went back downstairs. The two men exchanged good-byes, and then the sheriff was opening the rear door of his car. Nemo got in and he shut it, getting into the front.

"Where y'all come here from?" Radley asked as he drove onto the road and back towards the old plantation house.

"Uh, New Orleans," she said, naming the first place she could think of.

"Road trip? School break?"

"Something like that."

She saw the sheriff watching her in his rearview mirror. What did he think was really going on? He didn't seem all that concerned. He wasn't turning on the lights or siren, or even driving all that fast. They might as well be out for a Sunday drive.

"My friends could be in trouble," she said. "Maybe we should hurry."

"It's right up here," he said.

As they turned onto the dirt road leading to the plantation house, Nemo felt herself get tense. What was waiting for them there? The sheriff had a gun, but would that be enough? She suddenly wished she'd told him everything about the Mogs. But he already thought she was making up stories. He'd never believe her.

The police cruiser bounced over the rutted road and passed through the grove of trees that surrounded the house. When it emerged from the trees, the headlights swept across the lawn in front of the house. The Explorer was there, but the other car was gone.

"There were two cars here," Nemo said. "Ours and theirs. That one is ours."

"Then your friends are probably still here," the sheriff said as he parked. He got out, then opened the door for Nemo. Together, they walked around the house, the sheriff shining his flashlight all around the grassy field and the outbuildings.

"We should check the house," Nemo said.

The sheriff chuckled. "I hadn't thought of that."

"This isn't a joke," Nemo snapped, and immediately regretted it.

The sheriff laughed again. "Come on," he said.

They went to the front door. It swung open easily. Inside, he shone the flashlight around the foyer. Then they went into the living room. There was nobody there. Nemo walked around, looking for any evidence that someone *had* been there. She came to a round table and found a card on it. She picked it up. It had a picture of a castle-like tower being struck by lightning. Two figures were falling from the tower, their arms outstretched.

The sheriff came over and shone his light on the card. "Looks like one of those Ouija cards," he said.

"Tarot," Nemo said. "It's a tarot card. See. Someone was here."

The sheriff sighed. "Lots of people break into these old houses," he said. "They use them to party in. Dare each other to stay and wait for the ghosts to show up. Probably some kids came and tried to conjure up the devil with those." He laughed. "Maybe he showed up. Scared them off."

Nemo was getting frustrated. "My friends are missing," she said. "Don't you take that seriously?"

"How old are you?" the sheriff asked.

"Eighteen," Nemo answered automatically.

"Look more like fifteen or sixteen to me. Know what I think?"

Nemo didn't reply.

"What I think is, you and your friends interrupted a party. Got into a little fight. You ran off. Your friends and whoever they ran into got scared, thought they'd get in trouble and they left. Maybe they're looking for you right now."

"It wasn't teenagers we ran into," Nemo snapped. "It was Mogs."

"Mogs?" the sheriff said. "What's a Mog?"

Nemo hesitated. Did he really not know what a Mog was? Surely every human who had lived through the battle for Earth knew.

Suddenly, the sheriff roared with laughter. "You mean one of those alien things? You expect me to believe you found a couple of them shacking up here in an Alabama swamp?"

Nemo wanted to say that yes, that was exactly what she expected him to believe. But he started laughing again, and it enraged her. Also, she wished she'd never brought up the Mogadorians. Of course he wasn't going to believe her. Everybody wanted to think that the Mogs had been taken care of, that they weren't a threat anymore. Nobody wanted to hear that they were living in their own backyard.

"Come on," the sheriff said. "Let's check upstairs. Stay behind me, though. I don't want any aliens taking you up in one of their spaceships."

He kept laughing as they went to the second floor, and as they looked from room to room. They did find evidence that people had been sleeping in the beds there, but that was it. There were no other clues. And there were no people.

Finally, they went back outside and looked around in the rear. Nemo found the place where the Mog had fallen after she'd impaled him. There were dark spots on the grass, but nothing else. She also found the crushed cigarette butt but didn't bother mentioning it to Sheriff Radley. He'd already made up his mind about what had happened here. To him it was a simple case of some kids getting into a fight, and one of them—her—making way too big a deal about it.

They went back to the car. When the sheriff opened the back door, Nemo reluctantly got in. He got in the front. Only then did Nemo realize that she was now trapped.

In the front seat, the sheriff was doing something on a screen attached to his dashboard. Nemo couldn't tell what it was. A minute later, he turned and looked at her.

"You got any ID on you?"

Nemo shook her head. "I lost my wallet—just like my phone," she lied, hoping he wouldn't check her pockets.

The sheriff stared for a long moment in the rearview mirror, then started up the engine.

"Where are we going?" Nemo asked.

"Mobile," the man answered.

"Mobile? Why?"

"Because I ran the plate on that Explorer, and it was reported stolen from a car rental place at the airport this morning. I don't suppose you can explain how you and your friends happened to end up with it?"

Nemo's heart skipped a beat. How could she have forgotten that detail?

"Is there anything you'd like to tell me?" the sheriff asked as they drove away from the plantation house.

Nemo shook her head. "No, sir," she said.

"Usually when people in the backseat start calling me 'sir' it means they're trying to get on my good side. I'll ask you again, is there anything you want to tell me?"

"No," Nemo said.

He waited. "No 'sir' this time? Guess we're not going to be friends then. Well, we've got a little while before we get to Mobile. I'll let you think about it and see if you suddenly remember anything you might be forgetting right now. I know it's been an eventful evening."

Nemo sat in silence as the car moved through the night.

She looked out the window, thinking. If she walked into the police station in Mobile, it probably wouldn't take long before they figured out she was a runaway. Then her parents would be notified, and she'd be in a whole lot more trouble than she was right now.

She needed to get out.

The door could only be opened from the outside, but she could do that with her telekinesis. The problem was, she was in a moving vehicle. So she needed Radley to stop the car, and he had no reason to do that.

Unless being inside the car was more dangerous than being outside it, she thought.

She waited, letting the sheriff relax a little and think that she was giving in. She even sniffled a little, to make him believe she was upset enough to cry, before settling back into silence. Outside, the road began to pass along water. They were on a causeway that seemed to go on for miles. The moonlight glinted off the surface of the water, which stretched out for a long way in both directions. Nemo had no idea what body of water it was, but it gave her another idea.

She began to moan.

"What's wrong?" Ridley asked.

"I don't know," Nemo said. "It's my stomach. I think I'm going to be sick." She moaned louder and began to heave.

"Aw, crap," the sheriff said. "Don't toss your cookies in my car, kid. The smell will follow us all the way to Mobile."

"Pull over," Nemo said, moaning some more. "I'm serious. It's coming up."

The sheriff swore under his breath. She could tell the last thing he wanted to do was stop on the causeway. But there was very little traffic, and room to pull over. She let out a loud, retching sound.

"All right. All right," Radley said. "Hold on."

He swerved to the right, bringing the car to a stop on the shoulder and turning on the lights. He got out and opened the back door, practically pulling Nemo out. She ran to the side and leaned over the railing. The water was less than a dozen feet below them. She could easily make it.

The sheriff had his back to her, watching for traffic. He had no reason to think she would try to run, as there was nowhere to go. He would never expect her to go into the water. She waited until a tractor-trailer passed on the opposite side of the road, providing cover with its passing roar. She scrambled over the railing and jumped, landing with a heavy splash.

When Radley turned around, he was alone.

CHAPTER TEN

MAX
UNKNOWN LOCATION

MAX STARED AT THE STAKE PROTRUDING FROM Byron's stomach. The Mog was lying on top of a table. Scotty and Seamus were holding him down as he struggled. He was moaning in pain. Then he screamed.

"Get it out!" he wailed.

"Where's Chiron?" asked Magdalena. She sounded afraid, which made Max afraid.

He had no idea where they even were. He'd been sitting in the living room with Ghost and Magdalena at Rothwood when Seamus had run in, shouting that Byron was hurt and needed help. Everything after that was a blur. First, Scotty had teleported away with Byron and Magdalena. Then Ghost had done the same with him and Seamus. They'd ended up in the room they were in now.

Max looked around. It was small, windowless, nondescript. Apart from the table, there was no other furniture. The overhead light was fluorescent, harsh, and the air smelled like the inside of a plane, as if it was being filtered or pumped in. Oddest of all, the walls seemed to be made of smooth concrete. The sound of machinery humming vibrated through him.

Max had once gone on a school trip to see the Hoover Dam in Nevada. Part of the visit involved taking an elevator underground to the generator room and tunnels. Walking through the massive stone passageways and hearing the machinery that operated the dam rumbling around them had been both a little scary and very exciting. Max was feeling similarly now.

Except he was a lot more scared. Something bad had happened to Byron. He didn't know what, but he was afraid the Mog might die. Just a couple of days ago, a Mog dying wouldn't have bothered him at all. But now Byron was his friend, and Max was worried.

The door to the room burst open, and a boy came running in. Short and wiry, he had curly black hair and olive skin. His brown eyes took in the sight of Byron writhing on the table, and he frowned. "What happened?"

"What does it look like?" Magdalena said, her voice tight with fear.

The boy went over to Byron and examined the area of the wound. He reached down, took Byron's shirt in his hands and ripped. It pulled apart, separating around the stake. The boy pulled it aside, revealing Byron's abdomen. There was a lot of blood, and the area around the piece of wood was a purplish-black color.

"That's not good," the boy said.

"Of course it's not good, Chiron," Magdalena snapped. "But you're a healer. So heal him."

"We're going to have to pull out the stake first," the boy said. "I can't do it with that thing in there."

"Then pull it out," said Magdalena.

Byron had grown quiet. His skin had become gray. His eyes were closed.

"And hurry," Magdalena said. "I'm going to go get Eleni. Have that stake out by the time I'm back."

She left. As soon as she was gone, the boy turned to Max. "Who are you?"

"Max."

"Max, I'm Chiron," the boy said. "I need your help."

"What can I do?"

"Pull the stake out while these two hold him down," Chiron said.

Max shook his head. "I can't do that!" He looked helplessly at Ghost.

"You're stronger than I am," Ghost said.

"She's right," Chiron said. "Come on. I'll tell you what to do."

Max hesitated a moment, then went over to the table. Chiron placed his hands on Byron's stomach. The Mog moaned, but his eyes didn't open.

"Grab the stake with both hands," Chiron instructed. "I'm going to start healing him. When I tell you to, pull straight up. And keep pulling, even if he screams."

He looked at Seamus and Scotty. "And you two hold him down, no matter what."

Max reached out and wrapped his hands around the stake a few inches above Byron's body. Chiron closed his eyes. A look of concentration furrowed his brow. Then the area around his hands began to glow with a golden light.

"Okay," Chiron said in a low voice. "Pull. Slowly."

Max pulled. He felt the stake move a little bit. Byron cried out and bucked. Seamus and Scotty pressed down on his shoulders and feet, steadying him.

"Keep going," Chiron urged.

Very slowly, the stake emerged from Byron's body. As more and more of the wood appeared, more blood flowed from the wound. Chiron pressed his hands hard against the wounded area. The light flowed over Byron's skin, seeming to sink into it.

"Is it working?" Seamus asked.

"He's hurt pretty bad," said Chiron. "It's not like it's just a scratch. I'm trying."

"I thought you guys could heal anything," Scotty remarked.

Chiron grunted. "Like I said, I'm trying."

"Well, try really hard," said Scotty. "If he dies, we're all in deep—"

The door banged open again. This time Eleni stormed

in. Magdalena was behind her. Eleni came to the table and looked at what they were doing. Max tried to ignore her presence as he continued to lift up the stake.

"Will my brother live, healer?" Eleni asked.

"Working on it," said Chiron.

Nobody spoke as they continued. Max had pulled almost six inches of the stake out of Byron. There couldn't be much more left. Maybe, he thought, everything would be all right. He gave a last pull. The stake came out, the pointed end covered in blood and tissue.

Chiron put his hands directly over the opening in Byron's abdomen. He sent out more light. The skin around the wound began to pull together, closing the wound. Max breathed a sigh of relief and started to smile.

Then Byron's eyes flew open. He gasped, and blood trickled from between his lips. He turned his head, looking right at Eleni. "Sister," he said in Mogadorian, the words translating in Max's head without him even thinking about it. "Destroy every last one of them."

A moment later, parts of Byron's body had disintegrated, covering the table in a horrifying mix of flesh, blood, and ash. Chiron groaned and collapsed onto the floor. Nobody moved to help him.

All eyes turned to Eleni. She stood silently, her face a mask of fury and pain. She reached down, touching Byron's face, and closed his eyes. Then she gave Chiron a brutal kick that made him scream in pain, and stormed out of the room. Magdalena followed her.

Max dropped the stake onto the table, then knelt to check on Chiron. The boy was groaning and holding his side where Eleni had hit him.

"Are you okay?" Max asked.

"I think she broke a couple of ribs," Chiron replied. "I can fix that. At least she didn't kill me."

"Only because you're the last healer we've got," Scotty said.

Max helped Chiron stand. "Hey, I healed *your* butt when you were shot up," Chiron reminded Scotty. "It's not my fault the guy was too far gone. Who did this to him, anyway?"

"Nemo," Seamus said.

Max looked at him, then at Ghost. "Nemo?"

"Who's Nemo?" said Chiron.

"Our friend," Max said.

"Your friend better not be within a hundred miles of here then," Chiron said. "Eleni is going to want his head."

"Her head," Max corrected him.

"Her head then," said Chiron. He had his hand on his side, and Max saw the golden light seeping out into his skin. Chiron sighed. "That's better."

Max turned to Seamus. "Nemo did this?"

Seamus nodded but didn't elaborate.

"We need to clean up this mess," Scotty said. "I'm going to go get something to put the body in. Chiron, you might want to make yourself scarce in case Eleni decides this *is* your fault."

"Already thought of that," Chiron said, heading for the

door. "Hey, don't suppose you want to teleport me back to Crete until this all blows over?"

"You three stay here," Scotty said, following Chiron out. "I'll be back in a few minutes."

Once they were alone Max asked Seamus, "What happened?"

"Byron and Magdalena were in the backyard," Seamus said. "Nemo just showed up out of nowhere and attacked him. Then she ran off."

Max had been shocked to see Seamus at Rothwood when he had returned with Ghost and Byron from their day at the beach. He'd been even more surprised *not* to see Six, Sam or Nemo. Seamus had told him about being in touch with Ghost all along and coming to find her so they could figure out what to do next, and even though it hadn't made much sense to Max at the time, he'd still been so excited about his tattoo and the mission he'd completed that he hadn't really cared. And then all hell had broken loose, and there had been no time to ask questions.

Now he did.

"You weren't there alone, were you?" he said to Seamus. "Nemo was with you. Six and Sam, too. Weren't they?"

Seamus looked at Ghost.

"It's complicated, Max," Ghost said.

"Stop telling me how complicated everything is!" Max yelled. "Tell me the truth!"

"All right," Seamus said. "Just calm down. You don't want to make anyone mad."

"I don't care if they're mad!" said Max. "*I'm* mad. Now what's going on? Where are Sam and Six?"

"We don't know," Ghost admitted. "But they're okay."

"How do you know that if you don't know where they are?"

"You have to trust us, Max," said Ghost. "We're your friends."

"So are Six and Sam! And what about Nemo?" He looked at Seamus. "If she came to the house with you, why did she attack Byron?"

"She freaked out when she saw a Mo—saw Eleni," Seamus answered. "She ran off before I could explain. It's not her fault. She thought we were being attacked. She must have hidden somewhere and come back to try and help us."

That actually sounded exactly like something Nemo would do. But it didn't explain where Six and Sam were. Or why Seamus had known all along what was happening with Ghost and not said anything.

"I don't understand," he said.

"It's compl—," Ghost began, stopping when she saw Max's face. "It's a long story. We weren't sure you were ready to hear it all. You know, because of the things you'd been told about Mogs and everything."

Max wished there was someplace he could sit down and think, but the only thing in the room was the table, and that was covered with what was left of Byron. The best he could do was lean against the wall and slide to the floor, where he sat with his face in his hands. Ghost came over and sat next to him, but when she put her hand on his knee, he jerked away.

"Leave me alone."

Instead of doing that, Seamus came and sat down on his other side. Max felt his friends—or the people he'd thought were his friends—beside him. Part of him wanted to get up and run away from them. But where would he go? He didn't know where he was. He didn't know where Six or Sam or Nemo were. He didn't have a phone or his watch or any money.

"I know this is a lot," Ghost said. "And I know you're probably really confused. I'm not even sure where to start to explain everything. First, yeah, Seamus and I have been in touch."

"Why did you even come to the HGA?" Max muttered, not looking at Seamus. "Why not just stay with your *real* friends."

"I wanted to see what people there were saying," Seamus answered. "And I wanted to see my dad. See if I could maybe talk to him about all of this. Only he didn't want to listen."

"Then why not just leave?"

"I was going to," Seamus said. "Then Ghost said she wanted to see if we could get you to talk to us. Well, to her. She thought it would be best if she contacted you, since you both have a connection and I barely know you."

"And then she just happened to suggest that I ask for your help getting out," said Max.

"Yeah," said Seamus. "And hey, it worked, right? Those bees were pretty awesome."

"But why did you let Sam, Six and Nemo think you were on their side? Why did you lie?"

"I didn't lie, exactly," Seamus answered. "Just like you needed my help to get out of the HGA, I needed a little help getting to Alabama."

"Scotty could have just teleported you," Max said. "Or Ghost." Then something occurred to him. "But you needed to get Sam and Six there, too. Right?"

Neither Ghost nor Seamus said anything. Max looked up. "The Mogs wanted Sam and Six, didn't they? That was all part of their plan? And don't tell me it's complicated. Just yes or no."

"Yes," Seamus said.

"So you used me as bait," Max said. "Thanks. Thanks a lot."

"Don't be so dramatic. You're only freaking out now because the drug is probably wearing off." Seamus's eyes flashed as soon as he said it, realizing his mistake.

"Drug? What the hell is he talking about?" Max asked Ghost.

"We—they—put something in your drink," Ghost said. "It was just something to help calm you down a little and—"

"The root beer," Max said. "That's why I didn't freak out about the Mogs and why I didn't care what was happening with Nemo and the others."

Then a thought suddenly occurred to him and a look of utter betrayal came over his face. "Was everything a lie? Were you pretending with me this whole time?" Before Ghost could answer, he jumped to his feet and walked towards the door.

"It's not like that, Max," she said. "Where are you going?"

"Away from you two," Max said. "I'll figure it out."

Ghost scrambled to her feet, with Seamus behind her. "Max, you can't," she said, reaching out to grab his arm.

Max whirled. "Don't tell me what I can and can't do!" he shouted. "And don't even think about touching me!" At the same time, he held up his hands. He watched in wonder and shock as Ghost and Seamus were flung backwards with astonishing force. He only had time to register the looks of surprise on their faces before they slammed into the far wall hard enough to be knocked unconscious. They crumpled to the floor.

Max ignored his instinct to make sure they were okay. He didn't care if they were or not. They weren't really his friends. He put his hand on the door and opened it. He stepped out into an empty hallway going in both directions. With no idea where it went, he picked the left-hand side and started running.

EPILOGUE

SIX
UNKNOWN LOCATION

SIX TASTED BLOOD.

Eleni had stormed in a few minutes earlier and began pummeling her without saying a word. Six hung helplessly from her chains as the Mog hit her again and again. She had stopped momentarily and walked over to the monitor, turning it back on.

"Change of plans," Eleni said, her voice quivering with barely concealed rage. She spoke some words in the Mog language. As before, a moment later sand hit Sam in the face.

"This time it won't stop," Eleni said. She walked over to stand directly in front of Six. "You've taken something from me. Now I am taking something from you. And you're going to watch."

Six had no idea what the Mog was talking about, but there

was a fury in her eyes that Six was all too familiar with. And she knew it: Sam was going to die, and there was nothing she could do about it.

"How does it feel?" Eleni asked.

Six said nothing. She kept her eyes on the monitor, where Sam was jerking his head back and forth, trying to keep the sand out of his mouth.

"If you like I can turn on the sound so you can tell him good-bye," Eleni teased.

Six shut her eyes. She concentrated, willing her Legacies to come back. She sent up a silent entreaty to the Entity. *Just long enough,* she said.

Something within her sparked to life. She reached out with her telepathy, testing the chains around her ankles and wrists. She felt the metal shift. She tried going invisible, but nothing happened.

"That's okay," she said aloud, causing Eleni to look over at her. "I can make do with this."

A surge of telepathy poured from her. The chains shattered. Her arms fell to her sides, burning as blood poured back into them. She ignored the pain as she leaned back and delivered a roundhouse kick to Eleni's face. The Mog stumbled. Before she could recover Six attacked again. This time she used her fists. She could barely feel them as she pounded Eleni's face over and over again. The Mog fell to her knees. Six took Eleni's chin in her hand and twisted her face up. "Where is he?" she said. "Tell me right now or I'll kill you."

"Then you'll have to kill me," Eleni said.

Six was ready to do just that, but the door to the room opened and someone came in. It was Scotty. He took one look at Six and Eleni and reached out for the Mog. Six let go just in time. A moment later, both Scotty and Eleni were gone.

Six looked at the monitor, where sand was still pouring out over Sam's face.

"Hang on," she said. "I'm coming to get you."

THE LEGACY CHRONICLES

RAISING MONSTERS

CHAPTER ONE

SIX
UNKNOWN LOCATION

SIX RAN.

The Mog, Eleni, was gone, whisked away by the teleporter Scotty. Six still had unfinished business with her. But it could wait. Her immediate concern was finding Sam and getting him out of the chamber he was being held in before it filled up with sand and his time ran out.

The problem was, she had no idea where it was. Or where she was. Or if she and Sam were even in the same place. For all she knew, he was being held hundreds of miles away, in which case she'd never get to him in time. She pushed that terrible possibility out of her mind. She *had* to find him. And something told her that he wasn't far away. She hated it when people talked about following their hearts, but that's what she was doing now.

Her footsteps echoed through the corridor as she ran, and she wondered vaguely if she was underground. Something about the windowless hallway, the smell of the air circulating through the building, the way sound moved, all made her think that she was below the surface of the earth. That too could wait. Right now, she needed some kind of direction.

The corridor was oddly empty. There were cameras mounted on the walls at regular intervals, so she assumed she was being watched by someone. She also assumed that there were probably other Mogs around. Why had none of them come to confront her? They must know her Legacies weren't working, at least not to full capacity. The brief return of her telekinesis had come at just the right time, allowing her to break her chains and get away from Eleni. But she worried that it was temporary, maybe only revived by her urgent need to rescue Sam.

She wished her invisibility would return, too. She hated that her moves were almost certainly being tracked. Not that she could really go anywhere but forward at the moment. There were doors lining the corridor, but the ones she tried were all locked. It was as if she was being herded in one direction.

When she came to the end of the hallway, it split in two directions, left and right. More empty stretches of nothing with no discernible ends. Her frustration grew. And then she heard a sound. To her left, a door opened and a girl walked out. She was looking at something she held in her hand, and didn't see Six.

Six concentrated hard. She looked down and saw her body flickering in and out of visibility. *Come on*, she thought, trying to force her Legacy to work through sheer determination. She could almost feel her powers trying to respond. And then they did. She disappeared.

The girl was now walking away from her. Six darted forward and grabbed her, putting her arm around the girl's throat from behind and clamping one hand over her mouth.

"Don't scream," she whispered in the girl's ear. "Not a word. Understand?"

The girl nodded. Six couldn't see her face, but she noted the girl's hair, which was cut very short and dyed pink. For a moment it reminded her of Nemo's turquoise-colored hair, and she hoped the young Garde was okay.

"Good," Six said. "Now I'm going to ask you a question. I think my friend is being held here in a room or chamber or something that is filling up with sand. Do you have any idea what I'm talking about?"

She held her breath, hoping the girl would nod again. She did.

"Do you know where it is?"

Another nod.

"You're going to take me there," Six said. "As quickly as you can. We don't have much time. Is it far?"

The girl shook her head. Six's heart filled with hope.

"Start walking," she told the girl. "I'm going to remove my hand. If you scream, you'll regret it."

She took her hand away from the girl's mouth. They

started walking, Six keeping one hand on the girl's arm to remind her she was there.

"I know who you are," the girl said in a soft voice. "You're Six."

Six didn't respond.

"I heard you were here," the girl continued. She sounded excited. "Everyone has been talking about it. And the friend you're looking for, that's Sam."

The girl stopped in front of what looked like three sets of elevator doors.

"We have to go down another level," she said, pressing some buttons on a keypad beside one of the doors.

Six didn't like the idea of being trapped in an elevator, but she had no choice but to believe the girl was telling the truth.

"My name is Maggie," the girl said as they waited.

"What are you doing here, Maggie?" Six asked her. "What is this place?"

The elevator doors opened, and they stepped inside. Six maintained her position at Maggie's back.

"I'm not sure, exactly," Maggie said as the elevator descended. "They brought us here after what happened in Mexico."

"You were on the ship?" Six asked.

"No," Maggie said. "I was somewhere else. But they transferred us here. I don't even really know where here is."

Six had a lot of questions. She also briefly worried that the girl might have a Legacy that would pose a problem. Then the elevator stopped, the doors opened, and they stepped out into another corridor. It was narrower than the previous one, and darker. There were no doors lining it.

"What is this?" Six asked.

"A maintenance area," Maggie said. "Engine rooms and stuff. Almost nobody comes down here except the work crew."

Six felt something inside of her shift, like a current of electricity shorting out. She was visible again. She glanced around, saw no cameras. Not that it mattered much. If she was being tracked, she would just have to deal with whatever happened.

"There you are," Maggie said.

"Where's Sam?" said Six. She didn't know if she could even trust this girl, but she really had no choice. Sam was running out of time.

"Down here," the girl answered. "Through that door at the end."

Six hurried her along. While she was relieved not to have confronted any resistance, it also worried her. Sam was too important to leave unattended, especially when Eleni surely knew that finding him would be Six's number one priority. She kept waiting for the Mog to appear out of thin air, teleported by Scotty.

They came to the door Maggie had indicated. Six pushed on it. It didn't budge.

"There's a scanner," Maggie said, pointing to a keypad on the wall. She placed her hand against it. "Guess you're lucky I had janitor duty this month, huh?" She giggled. It was a strange sound, childlike, and Six wondered why the girl would have been given access to a room requiring such sophisticated clearance. She started to ask.

Then the door slid open and the question was forgotten as Six practically pushed Maggie inside. The door shut behind them. Six looked around. The room was not very large. One wall was lined with monitors and a bank of controls of various kinds. In the center was a large metal box about eight feet long, four feet wide and four feet high.

"He's in there," Maggie said, indicating the box.

"How do I get him out?" asked Six. She ran her hands over the surface of the box. There was no obvious way to open it.

Behind her, Maggie sighed. "Do I have to do everything?"

Something about the girl's voice had changed. Six swung around, suddenly alert. Maggie was looking at her and smiling. For the first time, Six had a chance to look directly at her face. She couldn't believe she hadn't noticed earlier. This girl wasn't a Human Garde.

"You're a Mog."

Maggie laughed. "You sound just like Max!" she said. "Well, I thought Maggie sounded more . . . human. But my name is actually Magdalena."

Six didn't know what to do. Had she been trapped? It certainly felt that way. And yet, the Mogadorian seemed totally relaxed. She walked over to the control panel and started pushing buttons.

"What are you doing?" Six said, rushing over and grabbing her, pulling her away from the buttons and switches.

"Do you want to save Sam or not?" Magdalena asked her. "Because I'm your only chance, and I'd say you have about thirty seconds left before that chamber is completely filled and he won't be able to breathe."

Six had no choice. She let the Mog go.

Magdalena went back to work. "There," she said after pressing one final button.

Six went over to the metal box. "It's not opening," she said.

"I didn't open it yet," said Magdalena. "I just stopped the sand."

"How do I know you did anything?" Six asked.

"You don't," said Magdalena. "But I promise you I did."

"Why would I believe a Mog?"

"Because you don't have any choice," Magdalena said. "Don't you think if I wanted you dead, you would be?"

"So why are you helping me?"

Magdalena leaned against the instrument panel. "I mostly let Eleni decide how to handle situations like this," she said. "In this instance, though, I think she's letting her personal feelings get in the way. Also, the cards told me you would be important."

"Cards? What cards?"

"It doesn't matter," said the Mog. "The important thing is, I need something from you, and I can't get it if you're dead. To tell the truth, I don't care what happens to your boyfriend. You're the one I really want. But I thought you'd be more likely to help me if you were reunited with him. Right?"

Six didn't answer. The Mog was playing a game of some kind, and Six knew all too well that Mog games had rules that worked only in their favor.

"Is that a no?" Magdalena asked. She put her hand over one of the buttons on the console. "Should I start the sand flowing again?"

"What is it you want?" Six snapped.

Magdalena frowned. "Your tone could be a little nicer," she said. "But I get it. You're under a lot of stress right now. As for what I want, it's not a big deal. We'll get to that later. I think we need to hurry things along. Scotty is only going to be able to distract Eleni for so long."

"Wait," Six said. "You set that up?"

"I needed to get you alone," Magdalena said. "I admit I didn't count on you breaking your chains. That was a coincidence. But it made the whole thing look totally believable, so thanks for that."

Six had no idea what was going on. What did she want? And why did she have to do it away from Eleni? Nothing was making sense.

"Did I mention that in addition to turning off the sand, I might also have stopped air from filling the chamber?" Magdalena said. She covered her mouth with her fingertips. "Oops. My bad."

"Turn the air back on," Six ordered.

"No," Magdalena said. "Either he comes out or he dies. And that's up to you. Do we have a deal?"

Six was studying the console as she spoke, wondering whether she could use it without the Mog's help.

"You could probably get the air back on, sure," Magdalena said. "But then there's the little problem of actually opening the chamber. Only Eleni and I know the codes for that."

Anger flared up in Six, and she made a step towards the Mog.

"Scotty," Magdalena said. "I may need you to get me out of here."

Six stopped. She should have known the Mog would have some kind of communication device. She stood still, glaring at Magdalena.

"This is starting to feel awkward," the Mog said. "Maybe it was a bad idea."

The girl was really starting to get on Six's nerves. She wanted nothing more than to get her hands on her, force her to let Sam out of the metal box. *If he's even in there*, she thought. For all she knew, this whole thing was a ruse.

"What exactly do you want from me?" she said, trying to keep her voice even.

The Mog harrumphed. "Okay, fine. I'll tell you," she said. "See, the thing is, there's this parasite."

"What parasite?"

"The one inside you," Magdalena said. "I put it in while you were knocked out."

"You put something inside me?" Six said.

The girl nodded. "It's kind of what I do," she said. "Experimenting, I mean. Eleni is the fighter. Byron is the planner. Well, was. Before that girl you had with you killed him. That wasn't very nice, by the way. And it really pissed off Eleni, which is another reason I needed to get you away from her. She isn't taking the whole thing very well."

Six tried to process a lot of things at once, but settled on one. "What the hell did you put in me?"

"Right," Magdalena said. "Well, like I said, it's a parasite. I haven't given it an official name yet. Not that you probably care what it's called. Anyway, it attaches to the brain. You know how your Legacies have been blocked?"

Six hesitated. Then she decided there was no point in denying it. "Because of what Drac injected us with."

"At first, yes," Magdalena said. "The serum. That was one of our early projects. We've since moved on, and now I think this works perfectly. Well, maybe that's not the right word. There's still the issue of the parasite maybe killing you."

Six didn't know whether to believe anything the Mog was saying. Her Legacies felt like they might actually be coming back. And this girl seemed more than a little bit crazy.

"There's a chance it *won't* kill you," Magdalena continued, seemingly oblivious to Six's growing rage. "But it did kill the humans I tried it out on. I feel a little bad about that." She paused, giggled. "Actually, no, I don't feel bad. I mean, they're only *humans*, right? They were perfectly happy to kill us during that whole battle-for-Earth thing. Of course, so were you, so . . ." Her voice trailed off as she looked at the watch on her wrist. "Hey, you know Sam is probably on his last breaths."

Six's heart was pounding as the anger inside of her boiled over. She was sure now that the Mog girl was insane. If there was something in her head, surely she should be feeling it. But if what she said about a parasite was true, Six needed to know what she was dealing with. "What does it do?"

"Oh, it feeds on your brain," Magdalena said. "And I'm pretty sure that's why your Legacies are affected, although I don't entirely know why because, well, nobody is really sure how they work in the first place, are they? But that's how we learn, by experimenting!"

"You said you wanted something from me," Six reminded her.

Magdalena sighed. "Here's the thing," she said. "I need the parasite to finish growing. That takes a while. Like, a couple of weeks. So you have to stay alive until then."

"That's it?" Six said. "You need me to stay alive?"

"For a couple of weeks," Magdalena said. "And then I have to take the parasite out, so that I can see if it did what I hope it will do."

"Which is what?"

"I can't tell you that! It's a secret. Besides, if I don't take it out, then you'll definitely die," said Magdalena. "Sam, too. And Max."

"You put one of these things in Max?"

The Mog nodded. "Don't worry, though. He was asleep and didn't feel a thing. But like I said, these things definitely kill humans. So that's part of the deal. If you let me take the one out of you, I'll throw in Sam and Max, too."

The girl had to be joking. She couldn't really expect Six to agree to be part of her twisted science experiment. If she was even telling the truth.

"Nobody else will be able to take it out," Magdalena said. "Trust me. If I don't, it will have to come out by itself. That's the part where you all die."

Six was still not convinced anything the Mog said was true. But there was no time to argue with her. "Get Sam out," she said. "Now."

"So I'm taking that as a yes," Magdalena said. She clapped her hands together like a little kid. "Okay. Let's do this."

She turned to the console and started typing on a keyboard. A low hum filled the room. Six looked at the metal box, expecting it to open. When it didn't, she turned back to Magdalena.

"It's not responding," the Mog said.

"What do you mean, it's not responding?" said Six. "Did you type in the code?"

Magdalena nodded. She typed again. "Eleni must have changed it."

"Can't you override it?"

Magdalena shook her head. "That's kind of the point," she said.

"You need to get him out," Six said.

"Technically, I don't," said the girl. "He's just my backup. You know, in case something happens to you. But I only need one of you alive for my experi—"

The word was cut off as Six grabbed the Mog by the throat and squeezed. Magdalena looked at her, eyes wide as she gasped for breath.

"Try calling Scotty now," Six said.

Magdalena's hands beat uselessly at Six's arms. Six maintained her grip and lifted the small girl off the ground.

"Get Eleni in here," she said.

"She. Won't. Do. It," Magdalena squeaked.

Six looked back at the box. She knew that this time at least the Mog was telling the truth. She released Magdalena, who slumped to the floor, sucking in air. Six ran to the box and banged on it with her fists.

"Sam!" she shouted. "Sam! If you can hear me, you need to tell the machine to open!"

She knew she sounded desperate. But she was. Their only chance was if Sam's technopathy Legacy had returned. Whether it had or not, she had no idea.

She banged again on the cold metal of the box. Suddenly, it felt like a coffin.

"Sam!" she shouted. "Sam!"

There was no answer.

CHAPTER TWO

NEMO

OUTSIDE MOBILE, ALABAMA

WHEN NEMO SAW THE SHARKS, SHE DECIDED SHE'D been underwater long enough.

She'd been swimming for what felt like hours, but probably it had been only twenty or thirty minutes. After diving off the causeway and into Mobile Bay, she had just started swimming as fast as she could to get away from Sheriff Radley, trying to stay close to the bottom so she would remain invisible to anyone searching for her. The murkiness of the water helped in that regard. Unfortunately, it also made it almost impossible to see. Often, things weren't visible until they were right in front of her.

Like the sharks. She'd sensed them swimming in the water with her, but she'd been more concerned about getting away from the sheriff, and had pushed all other worries out of her mind. Now that she was pretty sure she'd managed to avoid being followed, she had time to think about it.

She didn't even know exactly where she was. The water tasted brackish, which made her suspect there was fresh water emptying into the ocean, so she was probably in the bay she recalled seeing on the map in the gas station. But that wasn't much to go on. She didn't know what direction she was heading in, only that the shore was somewhere to her left.

And now there were sharks. Three of them. They weren't very big, maybe three or four feet long, but they were still sharks. They had pointed snouts and long, narrow fins. Years of watching Shark Week programs on television made her suspect that these were bull sharks. She remembered learning that they were often found where seawater and fresh water mixed, frequently attacked swimmers in shallow water, and that they fed at dusk. She was currently three for three on the potential-victim scorecard.

It was time to get out.

She made for shore, trying not to splash around too much and look like prey. The sharks followed her, then disappeared into the murky water. This didn't make her feel any better. She swam faster. Her legs started to cramp.

She gave one more kick and found her head breaking the surface. Ahead of her was a beach. She swam towards it until she felt sand beneath her. Exhausted, she sank to her knees and started to crawl. When she was out of the water, she allowed herself to collapse on the sand. She rested a moment, then rolled onto her back. Two faces were staring down at her, a boy and a girl, both about Nemo's age.

"Whoa. Are you okay?" the girl asked.

Before Nemo could answer, the boy said, "Where the hell did you come from?"

"Swimming," Nemo said. Her legs were cramping again, and now she started to shiver.

The girl knelt beside her. "Here," she said, helping Nemo sit up and wrapping a towel around her.

"Thanks," said Nemo.

"We've been sitting here for over an hour," the guy said. "We didn't see you get into the water. And why are you wearing street clothes?"

"Leave her alone, Dwayne," the girl said. "Can't you see she's freezing?"

"I just want to know where she came from, Jackie," Dwayne shot back. "I mean what is she, a mermaid?"

"Does she look like she has a tail?" said Jackie. "Back off already." She looked at Nemo. "You're bleeding." She pointed to Nemo's leg. There was a rip in her jeans at the calf, and blood was seeping out.

"I must have cut it on something," Nemo said. "I didn't even feel it."

"We need to get you out of these wet things and get that fixed up," Jackie said. "Do you live near here? Are you staying at one of the hotels?"

Nemo started to lie and say that she was. But then she shook her head. "No."

"Maybe she fell off a ship," Dwayne suggested. "That

would maybe explain the clothes."

Nemo began shivering again. "So cold," she muttered. "Just need to get warm."

"Help me get her up," Jackie said to Dwayne. "I'm taking her to my house."

Dwayne started to argue, but Jackie shot him a look. He took one of Nemo's arms while Jackie took the other. Together, they lifted her up. Nemo was able to stand, but she needed their assistance to walk. Luckily, Jackie's car was only a short walk away. They helped her into the front passenger seat. Jackie gave her another towel to hold against her leg.

"I don't live far from here," Jackie said as she started the car. "As soon as we get there, you can hop into the shower. That will warm you up. And we'll put a bandage on that leg. Hopefully, you won't need stitches. It doesn't look too bad."

"Can you at least tell us your name?" Dwayne asked from the backseat.

"Nemo."

"That explains it," he said. "She must have gotten shot out of her submarine by accident."

"Ignore Dwayne," Jackie said to Nemo. "In case you can't tell, he's a smart-ass."

"So . . . so . . . am . . . I," Nemo said, her teeth banging together.

Dwayne laughed. Jackie turned up the heat in the car, and Nemo felt warm air flow over her hands. She closed her eyes and relaxed a little.

When they got to Jackie's house, Jackie and Dwayne

helped her inside and upstairs to Jackie's room. Dwayne left them alone, and Jackie showed Nemo into the attached bathroom. "I'll put something out for you to wear when you get out," Jackie said. She opened the medicine cabinet. "I've got hydrogen peroxide, antibiotic ointment and some bandages. If you need more than that, I'll have to run to the store. Will you be okay on your own?"

Nemo nodded. "And thanks," she said.

"No problem," said Jackie. "Take as long as you want. I'll be downstairs."

When she was alone, Nemo got out of her wet clothes. As she was taking her pants off, she realized that both her wallet and her phone were gone. Everything was gone. They must have fallen out during her jump into the water. She felt herself begin to panic. Then she reminded herself that she was safe, at least for the moment. She just had to take one thing at a time.

First she attended to the cut on her leg. Fortunately, it wasn't bad. The bleeding had stopped, and it wasn't deep. She cleaned it off with some hydrogen peroxide, gritting her teeth against the pain, and decided to wait until after her shower to do anything else.

Nemo turned on the water in the shower. The hot water felt wonderful on her cold skin, and within a few minutes she was in much better spirits. She used some of the orange-scented soap that was on the shelf, then washed her hair, removing the smell of the ocean. When she was done, she dried herself off. Then she rubbed some antibiotic ointment on her leg and covered it with a bandage.

She put on the clothes that Jackie had left her, grateful for the warmth. Then she went downstairs and found Jackie in the kitchen, pouring cocoa into two mugs. She handed one to Nemo.

"I sent Dwayne home," she said. "I didn't want him pestering you with a million questions."

"What about the rest of your family?" Nemo asked.

"It's just me and my parents, and they're away visiting some friends. They won't be back for a couple of days."

Nemo sipped the cocoa. It was delicious, and it warmed her up from the inside out. Jackie sat down at the table in the kitchen, and Nemo joined her.

"Thanks for helping me," she said.

"Hey, it's not every day a girl walks out of the ocean," Jackie said.

"More like flopped out," said Nemo.

Jackie laughed. "Yeah, it wasn't maybe the most graceful entrance. Or would it be *exit*?"

Nemo could tell the girl *really* wanted to ask her what was going on. But she didn't. And that earned her big points with Nemo.

"Can I ask for another favor?" Nemo said. "Can I borrow your phone? I need to call someone."

"Sure," Jackie said without hesitation. "Here." She placed her cell phone on the table, then stood up. "I'll be back in a few."

Alone again, Nemo dialed. She hoped she remembered

the number correctly. Nine had given it to her, telling her to use it in an emergency. This definitely qualified.

The phone didn't even ring once before she heard Nine's voice. "Who is this?"

"It's Nemo."

"Why are you calling me from a phone belonging to someone called Jacqueline Portnoy?"

"That's a long story," Nemo said.

She filled him in on everything that had happened since they'd left the Academy, or as much of it as she knew. She told him about the plan to meet up with Ghost, and how instead Max had been taken. She told him about the Mogs, and about the house where they had been staying with Ghost. She told him about Seamus McKenna, and about how she thought he might actually be helping the Mogs. She told him about Six and Sam going missing, and about how she'd escaped from the sheriff.

"I was afraid something like this was happening," Nine said. "And I think you're right about Seamus. When he left the Academy, he took something very valuable."

"The bomb?" Nemo asked.

"What bomb?"

Nemo told him about the explosive device Seamus had brought.

"That was no explosive device," Nine said. "It was something much more dangerous. But that's not our immediate worry. We need to figure out where Six and Sam are."

"How?" Nemo asked.

"I'm going to go talk to Lexa," Nine said. "You just sit tight. I'll be there in the morning."

"Here?" Nemo said.

"Yes," said Nine. "It sounds like you're safe for now. The best thing is for me to come there. I've already pulled the address. I should arrive around noon."

"Um, okay, then," Nemo said. "I guess I'll see you tomorrow."

"We're going to find them, Nemo," Nine said. "And one more thing."

"Yeah?"

"You did a good job."

Nemo felt herself blush. "I didn't do anything," she said. "I didn't even fight the Mogs, really. I ran away."

"Which is exactly what you should have done," Nine assured her. "You got away safe, and now we're going to find our friends. That's a good job in my book."

Nemo felt a catch in her throat. "Thanks," she said.

Nine hung up. Nemo set the phone down, then went looking for Jackie. She was on the deck outside, reclining on a lounge chair. A gas firepit was going, providing warmth in the cool night air.

"Everything okay?" Jackie asked as Nemo took a chair beside her.

"I think so," Nemo said, stretching out her sore legs. "I mean, it will be."

"Good," Jackie said. She paused a moment. "Can I ask you something personal?"

Nemo instinctively hesitated. She was conditioned not to talk to people about herself. But the girl had been so kind, and seemed like a genuinely good person, so she said, "Sure."

"Were you using black dust?"

"Black dust?" Nemo said. "I don't even know what that is."

"It's got other names," said Jackie. "Some people call it Instant Legacy."

"Instant Legacy? No, what is it?" Nemo asked.

"A drug," said Jackie. "Don't take it the wrong way. I don't mean you look like someone who's into drugs or anything. Not that there's a special look. But it might have explained the whole swimming thing."

Nemo was starting to understand. "There's a drug that gives people Legacies?" She had never heard of anything like that. If it was true, it was totally a game changer. "You're kidding, right?"

"Well, sort of," Jackie answered. "Supposedly, it makes you *feel* like you have them. At least, that's what Cubby says."

"Who's Cubby?"

"Dwayne's brother," said Jackie. "He's tried it a couple of times. Or says he has. You never know with Cubby. Anyway, it's kind of a thing around here with some people. I just thought maybe you might have used it and thought you could breathe underwater or something." She laughed. "Sorry. I know that's crazy."

Nemo laughed, too, but not comfortably. Jackie had helped her out big-time, but she wondered how much she could trust the girl. Or *should* trust her. It wasn't like having a Legacy was a crime or anything. She'd just never talked about it with someone she didn't know. Maybe, she thought, it was time she did.

"I actually can," she said. "Breathe underwater, I mean."

Jackie looked at her. "Seriously?"

"Seriously."

"That's awesome," Jackie said. "What a cool superpower."

"I don't know if I'd call it a superpower. It's not as flashy or impressive as some of the others I've seen," Nemo said. "I mean, don't get me wrong. . . . It definitely comes in handy from time to time."

"So what were you trying to get away from? I'm assuming you weren't just swimming for fun."

"It's a long story," Nemo said. "The short version is, I'm here with some friends looking for another friend who's missing, and we ran into some trouble. But it will be okay. Someone is coming to help me. Which reminds me. I have one more favor to ask."

"You need a sidekick?" Jackie said. "Like, someone to be your Robin or whatever? Because I'm totally down with that."

Nemo laughed. "Nothing that exciting," she said. "I just need somewhere to stay tonight."

"No problem," said Jackie. "Like I said, my parents won't be back for a while."

"Thanks," Nemo said. "It's really cool of you to help me out with, well, everything."

Jackie laughed. "It's kind of a thing I do," she said. "People.

Animals. Anyone or anything that needs helping. Dwayne says I'm too nice."

"I don't think anyone can be too nice," said Nemo. "And Dwayne doesn't know everything."

Jackie laughed. "You're right about that," she said.

"So, are you and him like a thing?" Nemo asked.

"Dwayne?" Jackie said. She snorted. "He wishes. No, we're just friends. He's actually really nice when he's not being, you know, all Dwayne-y. How about you? Seeing anyone? Is that who's coming tomorrow?"

Nemo shook her head. "Life is kind of crazy right now," she said. "Well, kind of ever since I developed a Legacy."

"I bet," Jackie said. "Hey, do you go to that school? The one kids like you—I mean, people with Legacies—go to?"

"Sort of," said Nemo. "I'm kind of on a little break right now, though."

"A guy I know goes there," Jackie said. "Trevor. His power has something to do with electricity. To be honest, he was kind of a jerk before he got a Legacy and so he's probably even worse now. His sister walks around like she's some kind of royalty because he got this thing. It's ridiculous." She reached over and put her hand on Nemo's arm. "Sorry. I don't want to sound like I'm dissing people with Legacies."

"I was totally shocked when I developed mine," Nemo said. "There doesn't seem to be any reason for why some people get them and some don't. At least, that's what Nine says."

"Nine?" said Jackie. "As in *Number Nine*, the alien? You know him?"

"Yeah," Nemo said. "He runs the Academy."

Jackie sighed. "He's gorgeous," she said. "I think if I ever met him in person I'd turn into a stuttering idiot."

"Well, you'd better practice what you'll say, because he'll be here tomorrow."

"What?" Jackie yelped, practically jumping out of her chair. "Nine? Here?"

"He's the friend who's coming," Nemo said, gently prying Jackie's hand away from her arm, which the girl was clutching so tightly that her nails were digging into Nemo's skin.

"Sorry," Jackie said. "But seriously, Nine is going to be in my house tomorrow? I don't even know what I should wear."

Nemo wanted to tell her she didn't think Nine would care. But Jackie was so excited that Nemo let her ramble on for a few minutes. When she finally calmed down, Nemo said, "I think you need to tell him about this drug you mentioned. It could be important."

"Way to put the pressure on," Jackie said. "I'll be lucky if I can remember my *name*."

"You'll be fine," Nemo assured her. "He's really nice."

She let Jackie gush about Nine for a little while longer; then they went inside and made dinner. After washing up, they watched a little television before heading for bed. Jackie showed Nemo to the guest room, where she lay thinking about everything that happened and worrying about how they were going to sort it all out. But eventually exhaustion won, and she slept.

The next day, as promised, Nine arrived just before

lunchtime, pulling up to the house in a nondescript rental car. When Nemo opened the door and brought Nine in, Jackie just stood there, staring at him.

"Nine, this is *Jackie*," Nemo said, reminding her new friend of her own name.

"Right," Jackie said. "This is Jackie. I mean, I'm me. I mean, hi."

"It's nice to meet you, Jackie," Nine said, extending his hand. "I hear you've taken good care of Nemo."

"I did?" Jackie said. "Great. Super. Glad I could help."

"Why don't we get something to drink?" Nemo suggested, herding Jackie towards the kitchen and giving her a task to distract her. Nine followed, and they all sat down around the table.

"Jackie told me something interesting last night," Nemo said. "I think you should hear this."

Jackie, still nervous, told Nine about the drug. "It's supposed to contain some of the—stuff—that makes Legacies. At least, that's what Cubby says."

"Cubby?" said Nine.

"Dwayne's brother," Nemo explained. "Jackie's friend."

"Ah," Nine said. "So, people are taking this stuff because they think it gives them Legacies?"

Jackie shook her head. "Not really *gives* them Legacies. More like it makes them feel like they would if they *had* them."

"Where is Cubby getting this drug from?" Nine asked.

"There's this guy," Jackie said. "I've never met him. Supposedly, he has some connection to those Mogs. But Cubby makes a lot of things up, too, so I don't really know."

At the mention of Mogs, Nemo looked at Nine. His expression was, as usual, unreadable.

"Well, that's really helpful info, Jackie," he said. "Thank you. Now, I think Nemo and I need to hit the road."

"Already?" Jackie said, sounding disappointed.

"I'm afraid so," said Nine.

Nemo stood up. Jackie did, too, holding out her arms. Nemo stepped into them and allowed herself to be hugged, even though it wasn't her favorite thing to do.

"Thanks for everything," Nemo said. "I really appreciate it."

"Anytime," Jackie said, letting her go. "Oh." She took a piece of paper from a pad on the kitchen counter and scribbled something on it. "Here's my email and my cell." She folded the paper up and handed it to Nemo. "Stay in touch, okay?"

"I will," Nemo promised. "Maybe you can come visit us at the Academy sometime."

"As long as I don't have to be nice to Trevor," Jackie said, making a face.

"Trevor?" said Nine. "The electricity kid?" He also made a face.

Jackie and Nemo laughed. Then Jackie walked them to the front door, where she gave Nemo another hug before Nemo and Nine escaped to the safety of the car.

"She likes to hug, doesn't she?" Nine remarked as he started the car.

"You're lucky she didn't try to give you one," Nemo told him. "She's got a major crush on you."

"Smart girl," Nine joked.

"Do you think we need to be worried about that drug stuff?" Nemo asked.

"We'll have to look into it later. Right now we have something more important to do."

"Where are we going?" Nemo asked.

"To get Six and Sam and Max," Nine said.

"You know where they are?" Nemo asked excitedly.

"No," Nine admitted.

Nemo's hopes fell.

Nine looked over at her and grinned. "But when has that ever stopped me?"

CHAPTER THREE

MAX
UNKNOWN LOCATION

"MAX! COME ON! I JUST WANT TO TALK TO YOU!"

Ghost's voice chased Max as he stumbled through the hallways of the bunker. His heart pounded as he searched frantically for a way out. But every turn he took seemed to reveal another identical corridor, each one a tunnel of cold, polished concrete lined with locked doors.

He tried not to think about what had happened back in the room. The blood and pieces of the dead Mog. The revelation that he had been drugged by people he'd thought were his friends. The Mogs and Ghost had used him to lure Sam and Six to that house in the swamp. They'd pretended to care about him. But they didn't.

Seamus's betrayal was bad—he was apparently working

with the Mogs—but it didn't hurt him as much as Ghost's did. She and Max had been through a lot together. He'd thought that he was rescuing her, helping her get away from people who had done terrible things to her. In reality, she was trying to trap him.

He rubbed the fresh tattoo on his arm. It had started to itch, and the skin was tender. He'd been so excited to get it, to feel like he was part of something along with Ghost. Now he felt like a fool. Knowing that he'd been under the influence of some kind of drug didn't help. It made him feel even more stupid.

"Max!"

Ghost was right behind him. He had to do something. Although he was furious with her, he still felt a little bad about hurting her earlier. He clenched his hands. His telekinesis had never worked like that before. Never been so strong. He figured it probably had to do with him being angry. He didn't know if he could do it again, and he didn't really want to find out. Seeing Seamus and Ghost hit the wall after he blasted them with his telekinesis had shocked him.

He wished he'd never developed Legacies. It had brought him nothing but trouble. Now he was in even more. He had no idea where he was. He had no one to help him. He was just blindly running, hoping something would happen to make everything okay.

Again, he came to the end of a hallway. This time, there were no other corridors, only a door. And like all the others, it was locked. He rattled the handle, but nothing happened.

He closed his eyes and concentrated, trying to will it open. Nothing.

Ghost entered the corridor.

"Max!" she called. She sounded relieved, and for a moment he thought maybe he had made a mistake. Maybe she really was his friend. Max turned and leaned against the door, looking at Ghost. She smiled.

Then Seamus staggered into the hallway behind her. He was limping, and he held a hand to his head. Blood spotted his cheek. He turned and looked at Max.

"You're going to be sorry you did that," he said.

Ghost held her hand up. "Let me handle this."

Max bristled. "I'm not sorry!" he shouted. "And I'll do it again!"

He held his hands up. He saw Ghost and Seamus pause for a moment. Then Seamus laughed. "Oh yeah?" he said. "I think that was a lucky shot. And don't forget, we have Legacies, too."

Max tried to use his telekinesis. He felt a little bit of something flow through his hands, but nothing like the blast he'd managed to produce before. He shook his hands, as if this might somehow clear whatever was blocking the energy he was trying to call up.

Seamus grinned. "Like I said, you got a lucky shot."

"Max, no one wants to hurt you," Ghost said.

She was still advancing. Max stared at her hands, as if they were weapons that could go off at any moment.

"It's going to be okay," she said, and Max saw her fingers

twitch as if she was preparing to attack him.

Behind him, something else moved. It was the door he was leaning against. For a second he thought he had somehow managed to make it open. Then he realized that somebody was pushing against it from the other side. This set off a new feeling of panic. He was surrounded.

The door rattled again. There was no way of seeing who was pushing on it, and Max had only moments to decide what was worse—waiting for Ghost and Seamus to nab him or finding out who was trying to come through from the other side.

He stepped forward, taking his weight off the door. It opened a crack.

"This way!" a voice said as a hand reached out and tugged at his shirt.

Max hesitated. He had no idea who the voice belonged to, or what was waiting for him behind the door. But he knew what was waiting if he stayed, so he pulled the door open, looked at Ghost and Seamus just long enough to see their expressions change to ones of surprise, then slipped through.

"Get back," said the boy who was standing there.

Max stepped away from the door. The boy's hands began to glow, and a moment later the metal push bar started to melt, twisting into a steaming knot.

"That should keep them out," he said.

"Until Ghost teleports them through it," said Max.

The boy was wearing glasses. He pushed them up on the

bridge of his nose and frowned. "Good point," he said. "I guess we need to go to plan B."

"What's plan B?"

"We run," the boy said.

Behind him was a flight of stairs. He took off down them, his sneakers slapping on the steps as he went. Max followed. As they went down, Max got a better look at him. Short and skinny, he had dark brown skin and black hair. He was dressed in shorts and an Aquaman T-shirt.

"What's your name?" Max said, trying to keep up with the boy, who was practically jumping from landing to landing as they descended. Each floor had another door on it, but the boy didn't go through any of them.

"Kona," the boy called back. "But everyone calls me Lava."

"I'm Max."

"I know," Lava said. "We've been watching you."

"We?" said Max.

"You'll see," Lava said as they came to another landing and another door. This one, he finally shoved open.

They were in another hallway. Lava walked quickly, looking back over his shoulder from time to time.

"Where are we going?" Max asked.

"Somewhere safe," said Lava. "Well, safe-ish. Safer than being back up there, anyway."

All around them, Max heard the thrumming of machinery.

"It's the pumps," Lava said, noticing him looking around. "For the lake."

"Lake?" said Max.

"Do you have any idea where we are?" Lava asked.

Max shook his head. "None. We teleported here. The last place I was in was Alabama."

"You're a long way from Alabama now," Lava said.

Max noticed now that the hallway was lined with framed photographs. They showed what looked to be a big construction project of some kind. There were bulldozers, and piles of rock. In one, a group of smiling men stood on top of a case with *DYNAMITE* stenciled on the side. The landscape in all of the photos was similar—a mountain covered with scrubby pine trees—so the pictures had all obviously been taken in the same place.

Lava stopped in front of another picture. Only this one wasn't a photo. It was a map. And it was made of a copper-colored metal, with the various features of the landscape in relief.

"We're in Utah," he said. He placed his finger in the northeast corner of the map, on top of a large raised area that seemed to be a mountain. "Here. In a place called Shilo."

He pressed his finger against the mountain. A moment later, a panel in the wall opened inward. Lava grinned. "After you," he said to Max.

Max stepped through and into a narrow corridor. Lava followed, pushing the hidden door closed. The hallway they were in was wood paneled. Globe-shaped fixtures at regular intervals along the wall glowed with soft yellow light. The air was cool.

The corridor went on for about a hundred feet, then opened into a much larger room. Max stood, dumbfounded, as he looked around at what seemed to be the library from an old manor house. The walls were lined with bookcases, each one filled with leather-bound volumes. Oil paintings hung on the walls. Leather couches and armchairs provided numerous spots to sit, and thick carpets covered the floors.

"How did this get here?" Max asked.

"They built it when they built the rest of this place," Lava said. He pointed to one of the armchairs. "Have a seat, we'll be safe here. And I'll tell you the story."

Max sat down, and Lava sat in another chair across from him. "Like I said, we're in Shilo, Utah. Specifically, we're inside a bunker built by a dude named Digby Klumber-Bach."

"Bunker?" said Max. "Like a place people hid in during wars?"

"Exactly," Lava said. "This Digby guy was megarich. His family owned steel companies, pharmaceutical companies, weapons manufacturing, all sorts of stuff. They made a ton of money during World War One, and they used it to build a mansion way out in the middle of nowhere."

"You mean here?" said Max.

Lava pointed towards the ceiling. "I mean up there. Way up there, like three hundred feet up."

"We're that far down?"

"Yep," said Lava. "See, the mansion was just the tip of the iceberg. The real reason for building way out here was to build this bunker."

"Why?"

Lava grinned. "The Klumber-Bachs had a feeling that World War One wouldn't be the last, and they were pretty sure the next one would be even deadlier. They decided to build a place where they could hide out when it happened. And what could be safer than being inside a mountain?"

"Not having a war," Max suggested.

"Actually, it's a mountain in a lake," Lava said. "Which I guess technically makes it an island. But the lake is man-made."

"How do you know all of this?" Max asked.

"Some of old Digby's great-great-whatevers are still around," said Lava. "The family still owns this place, but the bunker part is a big secret. Anyway, one of the family got mixed up with the Mogs somehow. I don't know all the details. She's apparently kind of nuts."

Max thought about the woman who had supposedly paid to hunt Rena, Nemo and the others in Montana. Helena something. He'd heard that she was involved with the group that was responsible for taking kids with Legacies. "How did you end up in this place?" he asked.

"Some of us were brought here," Lava answered. "Maybe a dozen or so."

"Why?"

Lava shrugged. "Don't really know," he said. "We got moved around a lot."

Max had the feeling Lava wasn't telling him everything. Or maybe he really didn't know. He guessed it didn't matter.

The important thing was that he had gotten away from Ghost and Seamus.

"How did you find this place?" he asked, indicating the room they were in.

Lava grinned. "Cool, isn't it? It's Digby's private hideaway. The place he came when he really wanted to get away from everybody. He didn't tell anybody about it, not even his family. Bats is the one who found it."

"Bats?"

"My friend," said Lava. "She sees through walls and stuff. Sort of. Her Legacy is a kind of echolocation. Like bats use to navigate. She figured out there was something behind the wall in the hallway. It took us a little longer to find out how to get in here. That map trick is pretty cool, huh?"

Max nodded. It was cool. "So, are you and Bats hiding in here?"

Lava's grin faded away. "That's complicated," he said. "I am. Mostly. I come out sometimes when I need stuff. Bats still lives out there with the others. She's not one of them, though. She's only doing it because of Kalea. My twin sister."

He sounded sad. Max waited for him to say more.

"Kalea has a Legacy, too," Lava continued after a moment. "She's an earth mover. Basically, she causes earthquakes. That's why we call her Shaky. Which she hates, by the way." His grin returned, but only for a moment. "She tried to get everyone to call her Pele, after the Hawaiian goddess of fire and volcanoes, but I already have the lava thing going on, so she got stuck with Shaky."

"And she's here?" Max asked.

"Yeah," Lava said. "I tried to get her to leave with me, but she wouldn't. They've got her convinced that the world is going to be a bad place for people like us soon."

"Like us?" said Max. "You mean people with Legacies?"

"Right," Lava said. "They keep saying that things are going to change, and that pretty soon people with Legacies will be rounded up. They say we'll only be safe if we stay here. Stay together. It's this whole conspiracy theory thing. Kalea's always been a little paranoid, which is how she and I ended up going underground in the first place."

Max thought about Nemo. "Sounds like a friend of mine," he said.

"You were on the run, too?"

"For a while," Max said. "Then we went to the Human Garde Academy. It's a long story. Short version is, they're really great. Only . . ." His voice trailed off as he thought about the events of the past few days.

"Only what?"

Max sighed. "Only now we're in trouble again."

"Obviously," Lava said. "I mean, you're here and those two were after you. Heard a Mog got killed, too." He shook his head. "They're not going to like that. Especially if a human kid killed him."

"You keep saying 'they,'" Max said. "Are you talking about the Mogs?"

"Them and the humans who are working with them."

"How many are there?"

"Not many Mogs," Lava said. "Maybe half a dozen or so. About twice that many humans. It's hard to say. They come and go."

"And how many kids are here?"

"Seven," said Lava. "Not counting your two buddies. There's me, Bats and Shaky. Scotty you probably already know."

Max nodded. "Who else?"

"Boomer and Spike," Lava said. "Boomer makes things explode, and Spike causes temperature fluctuations. Oh, then there's Freakshow." He shuddered visibly.

"Wait," said Max. "I know that name. That's the girl Rena met at Dennings's camp. The one who makes you experience your biggest fear."

"That's her," Lava confirmed. "She's the worst. She did it to me once."

"What did you see?"

"Nothing good," Lava said. "If you ever run into her, turn right around and get out of there."

"I thought Rena said that guy Drac took her Legacy away," Max said, recalling the story.

"Just temporarily," Lava said. "As punishment. That's what they were using to keep people in line. Making us afraid they could take our Legacies."

Max thought about Six and Sam, and how something was interfering with their Legacies now. He didn't say anything about it to Lava, though, as he didn't want to worry him even more. Instead, he tried to get him to say more about himself.

"When did you decide you wanted to leave?"

"Couple of weeks ago," Lava said. "When I found out the Mogs are planning something. Something big."

"What kind of something?"

Lava shrugged. "That's the problem. We don't know. Bats overheard a couple of the humans talking about it, but they didn't say anything specific. We think it might be some kind of an attack. But the Mogs only speak their own language to each other, so it's hard to say. None of us can understand them."

"I can," Max said.

Lava looked surprised. "You know Mog?"

"I know every language," Max said.

"Piha‘u¯ o‘u mokukauaheahe i na¯ puhi," Lava said.

"Your hovercraft is full of eels?" said Max. "I don't have any idea what that means."

"You need to watch more *Monty Python*," Lava said. "Anyway, that's really cool. And useful. Now all we have to do is get you near the Mogs so you can figure out what they're saying."

Max stiffened. The thought of going anywhere near the Mogs made him uneasy. "Can't we just get out of here?" he suggested. "Then we could call someone who can really help."

"There are two problems with that," said Lava. "One, I'm not leaving here without Kalea."

"You could show *me* the way out," Max suggested. "And I could contact the HGA."

"And two," Lava continued, ignoring him, "it's pretty much impossible to get out. This place is locked up tight. Monitors everywhere. Believe me, we've looked into it. We know the way up to the mansion up there, of course, but actually getting into it is something else."

"You mean we're trapped down here?"

"Basically," said Lava. "There are a handful of people who come and go, bringing in food and supplies and whatever. But the rest of us are trapped in the hive until they decide to let us out."

Max didn't like the sound of this. But, he reminded himself, he was safe for the moment.

Lava stood up. "We should go," he said.

"Go? Why? Is someone coming?"

"No," Lava said. "But we're not doing any good hanging around here. We might as well put that Legacy of yours to use and spy on the Mogs."

"How?" Max asked. "We can't just walk around. People will see us."

"I've got that covered," said Lava, his mischievous grin making another appearance. "This room isn't the only secret Digby kept from his family."

CHAPTER FOUR

SAM

SHILO, UTAH

THE SOUND ECHOED IN HIS HEAD—A DULL THUDding, like the pounding of fists on a far-off door.

Sam couldn't move. His body was surrounded by sand, imprisoning him in a gritty cocoon that weighed heavily on his chest and kept his arms and legs pinned. Now his face was almost completely covered as well. He gasped, forcing himself to keep his mouth closed so that he wouldn't choke. But along with the tiny amount of air he breathed in came grains of sand that scoured his nasal passages, leaving them raw. He tasted blood in his throat.

This was how he was going to die.

The pounding came again. And now he also heard a voice, faint and distorted. Someone calling his name. It occurred to him that he might be hallucinating, imagining in his last moments that someone was attempting to save him. Then the voice grew louder, and the pounding increased.

"Sam!"

He held his breath, trying to hear more clearly.

"Sam!"

Somehow, he knew that it was Six, and that she was there. Really there. Not only in his head. He willed himself to calm down and listen.

"Sam! Try to use your Legacy! Tell the machinery to stop!"

He had already tried that. Of course he had. It hadn't worked. That was before he knew Six was there, though—when he thought he was alone, buried who knew how far underground. But if Six was there, he wasn't underground, and maybe he had a chance. Maybe he could do it for her.

The sand was up to his nose. He was almost out of time.

He took a final breath before he was completely buried. The sand trickled over the tip of his nose. He clamped his lips shut and waited. He didn't have long.

As he had before, he concentrated on linking his mind with the machinery around him. And as before, he met a wall of silence. He could feel the various pieces of his prison, the wiring and gears, the chips emitting electronic signals to the heavy metal components that kept him entombed. But they remained just out of reach.

"Sam!"

The thudding increased, and he realized that Six was hitting her hands against the walls of the thing he was trapped in. They were separated by sand and metal. More than anything, he wanted to see her again, to touch her and look into her eyes.

He cried out silently in a frenzy of frustration and rage. And something clicked. Somewhere inside the machinery, something answered him. He had its attention.

He thought quickly, before the connection could be severed. He considered telling the machine to close the pipe delivering sand to the box, but since his face was now covered, that served no useful purpose. Instead, he targeted the locking mechanisms. He didn't know how the box was constructed, but there had to be some way to open it.

The air in his chest was being used up. He felt a burning sensation begin to spread through him.

A code. That's what the machine wanted. Numbers. Its language was numbers.

Sam's head pounded. Numbers rushed around in his brain, a cacophony of digits all fighting to be heard. He needed them to be quiet, to arrange themselves in an orderly fashion. Only one sequence would grant him exit from what was quickly becoming his tomb.

"Sam!"

Six's voice was growing faint. He felt himself floating away, sinking deeper into the embrace of the sand. All he could do was shut his eyes.

The first number fell into place, startling him awake again. Sam pushed. The machine responded. Sam swam up through the fog surrounding him, bombarding the mechanism with numbers. His heart pounded in his ears. He had no idea if he was accomplishing anything or if this was his last desperate attempt at reaching the surface.

Then he felt it, the sliding of metal rods, the release of tension. Above him, something clicked. He felt the box shudder. There was a grinding, a shifting of weight as the sand around him began to slip.

"Sam!"

Six's voice was louder, closer. Then he felt movement. The sand was brushed away from his face. He inhaled, and air filled his lungs. He coughed. Opened his eyes, then closed them again as he was blinded by bright light.

Hands were on his cheeks; then a mouth was pressed against his. He opened his eyes again, and this time he saw Six looking down at him.

"I guess you heard me, huh?" Six said.

"It was kind of hard not to, what with all the pounding you were doing," said Sam as Six helped him sit up. "You interrupted my nap."

As if remembering something important, Six whirled around. "Damn it," she muttered.

"Lose something?" Sam asked.

"A Mog," said Six. "I should have known she'd slip out of here."

Sam brushed the remaining sand away from his legs. Now that the box he'd been trapped in was opened, the sand it had contained was all over the floor of the room. He looked around. "Where are we?"

"I have no idea," Six said. "But we need to get out of here. I have a feeling we're going to have company any second now."

Sam got off the table. He moved shakily. His body ached all over. "Do we have any weapons? Comms? Anything?"

Six shook her head.

Sam sighed. "Is there *any* good news?"

"Uh, you're not in a sand coffin anymore," said Six.

"Point taken," Sam said. "So, this Mog. What did she look like?"

"Pink hair," said Six. "Kind of manic-pixie-girl type."

"Magdalena."

"You've met?"

"Briefly," Sam said. "Right before her bigger, meaner friend came along and told me she would hurt Seamus and Nemo if I didn't cooperate."

"That would probably be Eleni," said Six. "She's a whole lot of fun, isn't she?" She touched her face where the Mog had hit her.

"I was wondering about the black eye," Sam said.

"I paid her back," Six assured him. "A little, anyway. We'll settle up later, I'm sure."

"I assume she's the reason we need to get out of here?"

Six nodded. "One of the reasons." She paused. "Wait. Did you actually tell her you'd cooperate with her?"

"You've seen her," Sam said. "She's tough. And she said she had Seamus and Nemo? Was that a lie?"

"I don't know where any of them are anymore," Six said.

"Although Magdalena said something about Nemo killing another Mog. Which hasn't improved Eleni's mood, apparently."

"Nemo killed a Mog?" Sam said. "Wow. Yeah, I can see how that might piss Eleni off. Any other problems I should know about?"

"Just the parasite," said Six.

Sam raised an eyebrow.

"Magdalena claims she put parasites in us," said Six.

"And you believe her?"

Six hesitated a moment before replying. "Maybe she did, maybe she didn't. I think she's a little crazy, so she might be making it all up."

"Okay," Sam said. "So, there might be parasites in us. Any idea what kind? What they do?"

Six shook her head. "Don't know what kind, exactly. Supposedly, it attaches to the brain. So I assume some kind of brain-eating one. We didn't get that far. You know, because you were suffocating and all."

"I'm starting to think maybe I should have stayed in the box," Sam said.

"It'll be fine," said Six. "But we should probably go."

"Which brings us back to the question of, where?"

"Again, don't know exactly," Six said. "Or even vaguely. Just . . . out."

Sam went to the control console that ran across one of the walls and began looking at it.

"Do you know what any of that does?" Six asked.

"Not really, no," Sam replied. "But maybe I can make it work for us anyway."

He placed his hands on the controls and reached out with his technopathy. It had worked when he needed it before, maybe it would work again. He sensed Six watching him. "No, it's not back," he said, answering the unspoken question. "Not totally, anyway."

"Did I mention that Magdalena said that the parasite would make that problem worse?" said Six.

Sam looked at her. "Can we not talk about the parasite for the next couple of minutes?"

"Sure," said Six. "I'll just be quiet now."

"Thanks," Sam said, returning to the controls. He had no idea what anything on the panel was for, but electronics were electronics. If he could find some way of sending a message or signal, he was going to try to reach out to Nine, Lexa and anyone else who might be able to help. But first he had to get the equipment to respond to him at all.

"Getting anything?" Six asked after a moment.

"I thought you were going to be quiet," Sam reminded her. "And no."

He could tell that Six wanted to leave. But he feared this might be their only chance to try and communicate with people outside wherever it was he and Six currently were. He focused his energy, trying to connect. As before, at first all he heard were a lot of electronic voices, all murmuring to one another and ignoring him. The console was alive with activity, like a beehive or ant colony. Only he was an outsider trying to integrate himself with them, and they weren't letting him in.

His head hurt, and he thought for a moment about the parasite Six had mentioned. Had the Mog really put something inside of them? It wouldn't surprise him in the least. The idea that something—some *thing*—might be living inside of him right now, maybe feeding on him, was horrifying. That it might be adding to the problems he was having with his Legacy made it even more infuriating.

"Sam?" Six said. A note of worry had crept into her voice, and Sam knew it wasn't because she was anxious to be on the move. She'd noticed something.

"I'm fine," he said. "I'm trying to hook into the network."

"If you can't, it's okay," said Six. "We can work on it later."

"We might not get another chance," Sam said. "Give me another minute."

Six nodded, saying nothing. Sam went back to work. He pictured his Legacy as tendrils of golden, glowing light working their way inside the machinery. He pushed deeper, seeking a connection. The strands of light swirled around the innards of the console. And then there was a spark, a momentary flash as Sam linked into the electronic pathways. He felt himself swept into an information stream. His mind filled with data, overwhelming him.

He fought against the wave, which threatened to pull him under. He'd never felt like this when interacting with a machine. Something was different. It was almost as if the console was trying to control him, and not the other way around.

He could feel himself breathing more heavily. His heart was racing. He had to get out before something got in that he didn't want there. But he hadn't sent any messages. He forced himself to concentrate, to navigate to the part of the network's brain responsible for sending out communications. A telephone line. Email. Anything.

He found it, a phone line of some kind. He dredged up the first phone number he could remember, not even sure who it belonged to. Mentally, he composed a text, directing the computer to transmit it. The machine started to respond. Then Sam felt a violent jerk, as if the connection between him and the computer had been severed by an unseen hand yanking a plug from its socket. He stumbled backwards, his hands going to his temples and pressing hard against his head.

Six was there in a moment, holding him up. "What happened?"

Sam shook his head. "I don't know. It's like someone sensed what I was doing and kicked me out."

"Maybe your Legacy just went out again."

"It wasn't that," Sam said. "This was a lot worse." The pain in his head still lingered, like the effects of an electrical shock. He looked at Six, worried. "Do you think this has anything to do with the parasite?"

"I'm not even sure there *is* a parasite," Six said. She

sounded confident, but Sam could tell that part of her was thinking the same thing. Then she said, "Were you able to send a message?"

"No," said Sam. "Whatever happened, it happened right when I was trying to send it. I can try again."

"No," Six said, and this time the worry in her voice was palpable.

"Do I look that bad?"

"I don't want you pushing yourself right now," Six said. "We'll figure something out." She looked around the room.

"Why don't you seem like you're in a hurry to get out of here?" Sam asked. "A few minutes ago you said we should hurry up."

"I've been thinking about that," Six said. "If anyone was monitoring this room, they would have been here by now, probably with backup. But we've been in here alone a good ten minutes and nobody has shown up. Why?"

Sam considered the question. The throbbing in his head was dying down, but it still ached enough to be distracting. He tried to ignore it. "Because Magdalena made sure no one could see what's happening in here? Because she doesn't want Eleni to catch us?" he suggested.

"She said as much to me earlier," Six said. "But why wouldn't she want us captured?"

Sam thought some more. "She wants to catch us herself?"

"She already had us," Six said. "Or could have. I assume she could have locked the door somehow and trapped us in here."

"She doesn't want Eleni to know she talked to us?"

Six shook her head. "I think it's because she knows we can't get out. Or at least thinks we can't."

"But the door's open," Sam reminded her, pointing.

"Not out of here. Out of this whole place," said Six.

Now Sam understood. "There's always a way out. Maybe not an easy way, but there's always a way."

Six didn't respond. She was obviously thinking.

"What?" Sam asked.

"I don't know," Six said. "This whole thing feels weird. Like we're rats in a maze, being tested or something.

"So, what now?" said Sam. "If we're rats, what's the end-game? Looking for the cheese? Finding our way out?"

Six shook her head. "Not out," she said.

"Not out?" Sam repeated.

"If that's what they *want* us to do, then no," said Six. "We do the opposite."

"We go in?" said Sam.

"Exactly," Six said. "We find out exactly what this place is and what they're doing here. Then we worry about out. Besides, we don't even know where the hell we are."

"Good point," said Sam. "So, where do we start?"

Six pointed to the door. "There," she said. "Ready?"

"No weapons. Spotty Legacies. Possible brain-eating parasites. No idea where we are or what we're up against. Sounds like a blast. Sure, I'm ready. But I've got to tell you, after being buried alive in a sandbox, I'm not sure it can get any better."

"That's the spirit," Six said, heading for the door.

The hallway was empty, which only added to the eeriness of the situation. Sam wondered how many Mogs and humans were running around in this place, and where they all were.

"Where are we headed?" he asked Six.

"The worst things are always hiding in the basement, right?"

Sam shrugged. "In horror movies, yeah."

"I figure we'll go there," Six said. "Figuratively, anyway. Down. They'll be expecting us to go up, I think. Maybe it will buy us some time."

"At least until we run into someone," said Sam.

No sooner were the words out of his mouth than they heard footsteps. Somebody was running. And whoever it was, they were coming towards Six and Sam. Instinctively, Sam stopped and crouched, watching the end of the hallway, hoping he was ready for whatever came around the corner. Six too had assumed a fighting stance.

A moment later, two figures rounded the corner. When they saw Six and Sam, there was a shout of joy.

"Max?" Sam said.

Max darted forward and gripped Sam in a bear hug. Then he let go and did the same to Six. "You're here!" he said. "Lava was right."

"Lava?" said Sam.

The other boy who was with Sam raised a hand. "That would be me," he said. "Hi."

"What are you doing here?" Sam asked Max.

"Looking for you," said Max. "We heard you guys were here."

"Heard from who?" Six asked.

"That's a long story," Max answered. "And we should probably talk about it later. Come on. We have someplace we can go."

"Wait a second," Sam said as the others started to move. "I don't suppose you have a phone?"

Max shook his head. But Lava reached into his pocket. "I do," he said. "Although it doesn't do any good way down here. There's no signal."

"Let me see it," Sam said, holding out his hand.

The boy walked over and handed him an iPhone. Sam turned back to the room he and Six had just left. The others followed him as he went inside.

"What are you doing?" Six asked as Sam went to the console and placed one hand on it while he held the phone in his other.

"Seeing if I can patch the phone into the system," he said. "Then maybe I can send a message with it."

Six put her hand on his arm. "Are you sure this is a good idea?"

"No," Sam said. "But I'm doing it anyway."

Six left her hand where it was as Sam focused on connecting the iPhone to the console. As before, he was met with a chorus of electronic voices, all chattering away. He focused on the phone, which was a simpler machine. When he felt it responding to him, he drew it into the larger network, urging it to slip into the data stream rushing through his mind like a raging river. To his relief, it complied.

He once again recalled a phone number, telling the iPhone to send a message and attach its GPS coordinates. He had no idea if it would work, but the iPhone did as it was told. When it was done, Sam gratefully disconnected himself.

"Your nose is bleeding," Max said.

Sam reached up and touched his lip. When he pulled his fingers away, the tips were covered in a red stain. He looked at Six, whose face was shadowed with worry. Sam felt something in his head lurch. Six's face blurred.

"It went through," Sam said as he fell to the floor.

CHAPTER FIVE

NEMO

IN THE AIR

"CAN YOU DO A BARREL ROLL IN THIS THING?" Nemo asked Nine.

Seated at the controls of the Beechcraft Baron G58, Nine looked over at her. "It's probably not a good idea," he said. "Could be dangerous."

Nemo nodded. "Yeah, yeah. But *can* you?"

"Only one way to find out," Nine said, gripping the yoke and turning it. "Hang on."

The view outside was spectacular, blue and clear with a handful of fluffy white clouds. As they rose up and the plane turned over onto its back, Nemo felt almost like she was swimming. Instinctively, she lifted her arms and pretended she was flying. Nine laughed.

“I wish I had a flying Legacy,” Nemo said as the plane leveled out again.

“Five does,” Nine told her. “So did Lexa’s younger brother, Zane. It was common on Lorien, although it hasn’t shown up nearly as frequently in Human Garde. Your Legacy is much rarer. As far as we know, only Marina has it.”

“I’d like to meet her and talk about it,” Nemo said. “Maybe when this is all over.”

“Maybe,” Nine agreed. He sounded a little sad, and Nemo wondered if he was missing his friend. She wanted to ask him more about the other Garde and their lives, but before she could, he said, “Call up the schematic Lexa sent us. Let’s see how we’re going to get into this mystery mansion.”

The mansion in question was in Utah, which is where they were currently flying. They’d been driving around, trying to decide where to go next, when a text message had come through on Nine’s phone. The number it came from was unfamiliar, but it had contained coordinates, and Lexa had been able to quickly pinpoint the location. Another bit of digging had revealed that the property belonged to Helena Armbruster’s family. That, combined with the fact that only a select few had Nine’s personal number, were enough to convince him that the message had come from Six or Sam, and he’d turned the car in the direction of the nearest private airport.

Nemo opened the laptop she’d stowed under her seat and pulled up the blueprints Lexa had sent. Really, it was a scan of some very old architectural drawings. Not much more than sketches. But it was all they had to go on. Nemo handed the computer to Nine, who balanced it on his lap while he let the plane fly itself for a while.

"This place is actually really cool," he said. "If we weren't breaking into it, I'd be excited about getting to see it."

Nemo snorted. "Right," she said. "You're excited *because* we're going to break into it."

"I do like a challenge," Nine said. "And this place is a major one."

"How can you tell?" Nemo asked.

"For one thing, if it was easy to escape from, whoever sent us the coordinates would already be free," Nine said. "That makes me think that either Six, Sam or both of them are either incapacitated or this place is secured so tightly they can't get out on their own. And if those two can't break out of a place, that's a problem."

"Or maybe someone wants us to *think* they can't," Nemo suggested. "So that we go in and get caught."

"Always a possibility," Nine admitted as he examined the sketches. "But we're not going to get caught, so they'd be wasting their time."

"If this place is owned by the Armbruster woman," Nemo said, "why aren't you just asking her about it?"

Nine sighed. "That's complicated," he said. "She's under Karen Walker's jurisdiction now, and we would have to go through her."

"Which is a problem why? Aren't you on the same side?"

"We are," Nine agreed. "Mostly."

"Mostly?" said Nemo.

"We are," Nine said. "But she doesn't always have to know everything that's going on."

"You mean you don't want her to know that Six and Sam took off and are missing now," Nemo deduced. "Or that Max and Seamus are gone. Or basically that this megahuge thing has happened that could turn out to be a disaster."

"It's not going to be a disaster," Nine said. "But yes, that's more or less it."

"Got it," said Nemo. "Because she would totally rub your nose in this."

"And that," Nine said. "Anyway, we don't need Helena Armbruster when we have Lexa. She's our best secret weapon. You see these?" He held out the laptop. "Those things that look like tunnels running under the rock the mansion is built on?"

Nemo looked. "They're not tunnels?"

"Kind of," Nine said. "But they're way cooler. You see how this whole compound is built in a lake? Well, it's man-made. According to Lexa's research, the guy who built it was really into the ocean. His family had originally made their money in whaling, and I guess he thought he missed out on that kind of life and wanted to pretend he was living on an island in the middle of the sea, complete with storms. So he had engineers build this system of tunnels and engines that would pull the water in and out, creating waves. He even had a boat he would take out so he could pretend he was caught in a storm."

"That's so weird," said Nemo.

"Rich people are weird," Nine said. "It's kind of cool, though. And it's going to help us get inside."

"We're going in through those tunnels? What if someone decides they want to call up a storm?"

"I don't think they've been used in years," Nine said. "Not since the old guy's ship went down in one of the storms and he drowned. And yes, that's how we're going to get in. Now aren't you glad you have your Legacy, instead of a boring old flying one?"

"What about you?" Nemo asked.

"I'm stuck with scuba gear, like a normal person," Nine said, sounding disappointed. "Which is why there are tanks and gear stowed in the back."

"Does anything live in this lake?" Nemo asked.

"Probably some fish," said Nine. "Nothing weird."

"So, old rich dude didn't have them throw a huge white whale in he could hunt or anything? You know, to make the experience even more authentic?"

Nine laughed. "That would be cool," he said. "But unless his ghost is swimming around down there, I think our biggest worry will be lake trout."

"This Armbruster woman sure has been a pain in the ass," Nemo said. "What's with her, anyway?"

"Lexa found out she also owns that house the Mogs were using in Alabama," Nine said. "She has houses all over the place."

"Probably hiding Mogs in all of them," said Nemo. "I hope she never gets out of prison. I don't understand why any human would want to get mixed up with them."

"Like I said before, rich people are weird," said Nine. "Also, greedy and selfish. People like Helena Armbruster and Bray and Dennings are only interested in what they can get for themselves. In every war there are traitors who side with the enemy against their own people."

He went quiet, and Nemo wondered if he was thinking about anyone in particular from his own life. She tried to imagine if there was any reason why she would ever side with the Mogs against other humans. This made her think about Seamus, and once again she wondered if he was really helping the Mogs, and if so, why. What could have made him turn? More importantly, what would they do with him if he has betrayed them?

It felt weird to be thinking these kinds of things. At her age, she should be worrying about school, and going to concerts with her friends and talking about movies and other inconsequential things. Having a Legacy had changed all that. It had forced her to grow up far sooner than she should have. She couldn't even remember what it felt like to have a normal life, or the last time she'd woken up in the morning with nothing to do and nothing to worry about.

Actually, she did remember it. It was the day she'd discovered for sure that she had Legacies. For a week or two before, she'd had some strange experiences—like things seeming to move on their own when she reached for them—which she now knew was her awakening telekinesis. But back then she'd assumed it was just her imagination. And so one morning, Nemo had woken up with plans to go swimming at the lake with her friends and then have a cookout. Summer things. Fun things. Easy things. But while swimming, she'd gone underwater to play a joke on her friends, to swim out to where they were and pull on their legs from below. She'd swum out, then hung in the water beneath them watching the light filter through the brownish-green water. Only after a long time had passed had she realized that she hadn't run out of air.

The rest of the day was a blur. At first, she'd been delighted. Then terrified. She'd tested herself over and over, all while trying not to draw attention to herself. Part of her wanted to tell her friends, but a bigger part was afraid they would start treating her differently, and so she hadn't said a word. Not then.

Life had been different for her ever since. Her family had been horrified. Her friends had been a little more enthusiastic, but also jealous. And so she had ended up running away. Luckily for her, she'd found Max and Ghost. Although now both of them were in trouble because of their Legacies, too, so maybe none of it was for the better.

"Do you ever wish you weren't one of the ten?" she blurted out.

Nine took a moment to respond. "There's not much point to wishing that," he said. "If I wasn't, I'd be dead, like the rest of Lorien."

"I'm sorry. That's—that's not what I meant," said Nemo. "Do you ever wish you weren't a Garde. Like, if someone could take away your Legacies, would you say yes?"

"No," Nine answered immediately. "Not now, anyway. When I was younger and it all felt too hard and overwhelming sometimes, I might have said yes. But not now. Would you?"

Nemo started to answer, then stopped. She looked out the window. "I don't know," she admitted. "It's not like it would make me *normal*. I was never normal. Whatever that means. And it's not just me that's changed anyway. It's the whole world. There would still be other people with Legacies, and I think I'd rather be someone who has one than someone who doesn't."

"Just in case," Nine said.

"Yeah," Nemo said, laughing. "Just in case."

"You have one advantage the ten of us didn't," Nine said. "You're not alone. You've got friends. People to talk to about it."

Nemo nodded. "Sure. When they're not getting killed, or kidnapped by Mogs, or brainwashed by crazy people," she said.

"Trust me," said Nine. "I know how it is."

"Sorry," Nemo said. "I didn't mean to sound like I have it worse than anyone else."

"It's okay," said Nine. "I know. Just remember, you've got a lot of people on your side. And right now, some of them are waiting for us to help them, so let's focus on that."

They arrived in Utah after dark had fallen. Flying through the stars in the small plane was a spectacular experience, the twinkling points of light seemingly right outside the plane's windows. Yet Nemo was worried about what would happen after they landed. Once again, she felt like a character in a fairy tale, an ordinary girl sent on a trial against overwhelming odds. She tried to remind herself that she wasn't ordinary, and that she wasn't alone, but still she couldn't help but wonder what awaited them beneath the blanket of stars.

"There's no airport here, obviously," Nine said as the plane began its descent. "But we're in open desert, so there shouldn't be any problems. It might be a little bumpy, though."

Nemo's stomach tightened up as the plane broke through the cloud layer and continued down. When they were close enough for the lights of the plane to illuminate the ground, she looked for any obstacles that might be in the way. But Nine was correct. There was nothing but flat, dusty landscape.

"Where's the lake and the island?" Nemo asked.

"About a mile north of here," said Nine as the wheels touched down. The plane bounced once, then settled. It shuddered as it rolled over the rocky ground, but otherwise the landing was unremarkable. When the plane came to a stop, Nine shut it off and said, "Thank you for flying Nine Air. We know you have a choice in carriers, and hope you will fly with us again."

Fifteen minutes later, they were walking through the desert on foot. Nemo was shouldering a pack containing a wet suit and other diving gear, while Nine had a similar bag with the addition of an air cylinder strapped to his back.

"This will be a lot like when we swam out to the ship in Mexico," Nine told Nemo. "Easier, because there aren't any sharks to deal with."

"And once we get inside those tunnels?" Nemo asked. "How do we actually get into the bunker from there?"

"There should be air locks," said Nine.

"Should?"

"The sketches aren't totally detailed," Nine said. "But that's how it looks. And assuming they work—"

"Assuming?" Nemo interrupted.

"Hey," said Nine. "What fun would it be if we knew everything?"

Nemo kept walking, trying to convince herself that it would all go smoothly. Half an hour later, they came to the edge of the lake. In the center, the island rose up, topped by what Nemo assumed was the mansion. She couldn't see it through the darkness, although lights were shining here and there.

"The intake tunnels are on the west side of the island," Nine said as he opened his pack and started getting suited up. "We can swim right up to them. As I said, there shouldn't be any problems getting inside them."

"What if they're on?" Nemo asked as she pulled on her wet suit. "Or if they get turned on while we're in them?"

"They're not," said Nine. "And they won't. Once we're in the tunnels, we'll swim to the end. That's where the air locks should be. *Will* be."

"And then?"

"Then we get inside the bunker, look for Six and Sam and Max and whoever else needs to get out, and get out."

"Oh, okay," Nemo said sarcastically. "I didn't realize it was going to be so easy. You know, without scuba gear for them, or a boat to get them off that island, or basically *any kind of plan at all.*"

"You shouldn't worry so much," said Nine as he handed her a mask. "Here. This will let us talk to each other, just like before. Oh, and the pack I'm bringing has something for us to put on when we get out of our wet suits. We wouldn't want to catch colds down in the bunker."

"Does your pack have anything else useful, like a weapon?"

Nine held up his hand and wiggled his fingers. "I *am* a weapon," he said.

"Right," Nemo said, rolling her eyes. "Faster than a speeding bullet and all that."

"Well, I kind of am," Nine said.

Nemo snorted.

"Would you rather have a gun or me?" Nine asked. "Seriously."

"Right now I would rather have a boat," Nemo said.

Nine shook his head. "No sense of adventure," he said. "You ready?"

Nemo was not ready. But she walked into the water anyway. She tried to ignore the cold as she put the mask over her face and waded out until she could float on her back and put her fins on. The mask also had a built-in light, which she turned on. Then she and Nine synchronized the compasses affixed to their wrists and sank beneath the surface.

Being in a lake was far less scary than the open ocean. Even in the dark. The light on Nemo's mask illuminated an area about five or six feet ahead of her. Even so, there wasn't much to see. At first she was looking at the rocky bottom of the lake, but as they went deeper, all there was to see was empty water. Occasionally a small fish darted into the light, then swam off.

"Are you calling to them?" Nemo asked Nine, curious if he was using his ability to communicate with animals.

"Just sending out a hello." Nine's voice crackled in her ear. "But don't worry. I think we've got the place to ourselves."

They kept swimming. After a while Nemo asked, "How deep is this lake, anyway? You said a ship sank in it."

"A hundred and twenty feet at the deepest," Nine said.

Nemo thought about the shipwreck, which presumably was somewhere beneath them. The thought of an entire boat being swallowed by the lake was creepy, so she forced herself to concentrate on what was ahead of them. When, finally, something began to emerge out of the gloom, she was relieved.

"There are the pipes," Nine said. "Am I good, or what?"

The pipes were much larger than Nemo had expected.

There were three of them, each with an opening that was at least fifteen feet wide. She tried to imagine what it would be like when water was flowing in and out of them, creating waves. It would be amazing to see, but not something she wanted to be this close to while it was happening. She hoped Nine was right, and that they were unused.

They swam into the right-hand opening. The pipe was wide enough that they could swim side by side, and the combined light from their masks lit up most of the interior. Nemo reached out and touched the steel wall. The solidness of it was reassuring somehow, even though the thought of millions of gallons of water rushing through it was hovering in the back of her mind. Still, she felt like maybe this wasn't going to be so hard after all.

"The air locks should be coming up," Nine said. "See? I told you it would be—"

His words were cut off. At the same time, his light disappeared. Rather, it retreated, as Nine was pulled backwards and away from Nemo at an impossibly quick speed. Nemo turned in the water, looking for him. His face was visible for a moment through his mask—his eyes wide with surprise—and then he was pulled out of the range of her light.

"Nine!" she called out. "Where are you?"

"Something. Here." Nine's words were ragged, as if he was struggling.

Nemo could see his light. It was retreating farther, but Nine was obviously thrashing around in the water. Nemo kicked hard, swimming towards him.

"What is it?"

Nine didn't respond, although she could hear his breathing. She also saw something moving in the water around him. Something alive. Before she could process what it was, something long and thick and pale shot out of the darkness and closed around her wrist. She felt it tighten.

She looked down. It was a tentacle. This seemed impossible. But there it was, curled around her arm. The tip flailed in the water, rows of suckers visible. Nemo tried to pull away, and the creature the tentacle belonged to tightened its hold.

"Nine!" she said. "Tell it to let go!"

"I did!" Nine answered. "It's not responding! It's like it's not biological."

Nemo pulled again. The tentacle stayed where it was. She wasn't being dragged away, but she also couldn't get free. It was like the creature, whatever it was, was holding her there to deal with when it was done with Nine.

Something flashed in the water, and the tentacle suddenly let go. It fell away, floating down through the water. Nine had somehow severed it. But there was no blood.

"Go!" Nine shouted. "Swim to the air lock. I'll catch up with you."

"No!" Nemo said, starting to swim towards him to help.

Another tentacle snaked towards her. She dodged it.

"Go!" Nine said again. "I've got this."

Nemo hesitated a moment. Then the tentacle returned, searching for her. She flailed in the water, turning around. Then she kicked as hard as she could. She swam away, guilt dragging at her as if the creature had latched on to her leg. She felt horrible leaving Nine to deal with the thing that had attacked them.

She swam until his light was no longer visible. "Nine?" she said. "Are you okay?"

The only response was crackling. She knew she was probably too far away for the transmitter to work well. Still, she feared it meant something worse.

Then the air lock door was in front of her. A round handle was on one side. She worried that it was rusted shut, but when she gripped it with both hands and twisted, she felt it move. She kept turning, until eventually it stopped moving. Then she pulled. The door swung open. She looked inside and saw a small, water-filled chamber. She swam inside and pulled the door shut behind her. Another handle like the one on the outside sealed it closed again.

She looked around and saw a lever on the wall of the chamber. She pulled it. At first, nothing seemed to happen. Then she heard the sound of machinery coming from somewhere behind the walls. There was a grinding sound, and at her feet a grate slid open. Water poured out.

In a couple of minutes, the chamber was empty. Nemo turned and saw another door set in the far wall, with the same kind of wheel-like handle. She slipped her fins off and walked over to it. This one required more effort to turn, but slowly it did. She pulled, opening it, and looked out into a narrow, low-ceilinged corridor.

She was inside.

She looked back at the door leading to the tunnel. Should she wait for Nine? If he was coming, he would be there soon. But what if he didn't come? Or what if someone inside had been alerted to the air lock being opened? It might not be safe to stay there.

The decision was made for her when, a moment later, water started filling up the air lock again. It rose up through the grate in the floor. Nemo quickly shut the second door and locked it from inside the bunker. Now she had no choice.

She turned and looked down the hallway. She had no idea where she was going or what she would find. Nine had the bag with the dry clothes in it, so she kept her wet suit on. She left the mask and fins, not wanting to carry them with her. Barefoot, dripping wet, and without any weapons, she started walking down the hall.

CHAPTER SIX

MAX

SHILO, UTAH

"WHAT'S THE MATTER WITH HIM?"

Max looked at Sam, who was lying on a couch in Digby Klumber-Bach's hidden library. Max, Lava and Six had carried him back there. Sam didn't look good.

"He's been through a lot," said Six. She told them about the sand-filled chamber. "Then he wore himself out trying to interact with the machines. He needs to rest."

Max suspected there was something else that Six wasn't telling them. She sounded less confident than usual. "Is this about the stuff they injected you with?" he asked. "That hasn't worn off yet?"

"Not quite," Six said. She didn't elaborate. Instead, she looked at Lava. "I don't suppose you have a map of this place?"

"Sort of," Lava said. He went to a desk, opened a drawer and took out a notebook. "Bats and I drew a rough map based on what we know and what she's been able to see behind the walls. That's how we found the secret passageways."

The passageways had allowed them to get Sam back to the room undetected. They were a series of corridors running behind some of the walls of the bunker. "I guess Digby wanted to be able to sneak into the kitchen at night for milk and cookies without being seen," Lava joked as Six looked over the drawings.

"This is an elevator to the surface?" Six asked, pointing to part of the drawing.

"Yeah," Lava confirmed. "It's the only way up or down. That we know of."

"There must be another exit," Six said. "Nobody would be stupid enough to build a place like this and have only one way in and out. It would be too easy to compromise."

"Maybe that's the idea," Lava said. "I don't think old Digby cared all that much about people being able to get in or out once he was down here. In his journal he talked about living down here for years if a war started up."

"You have his journals?" said Six.

"A bunch of them," Lava said. "That guy liked to write about himself. A lot. They're all in the desk."

"Those could be useful," said Six. "We might find something to help us."

"Only if you've got a speed-reading Legacy," Lava joked. "There must be fifty of them. Bats and I have only gotten through a couple. They're super boring."

A light blinked overhead. Lava looked up. "And speaking of Bats, here she comes."

"A warning light?" Max said. "Cool!"

A moment later, a girl walked into the room. At first, Max was startled by her appearance. She was tall, even taller than Six, and she was completely bald. She was wearing jeans and a black tank top, and her pale white skin was covered in tattoos of bloodred roses with black leaves, thorns and twisting vines that wound all around her arms and extended onto her hands. More vines and roses rose up from the neck of her tank top and encircled her neck. She had startlingly blue eyes, which surveyed the scene warily.

The girl reached up and pressed a finger to a rose at the base of her throat. "You found some friends," she said to Lava. Her voice was slightly scratchy.

"You never know who you'll find wandering around this place," Lava said. Then he asked, "How's Kalea?"

Bats shrugged. Again, she placed her finger on her throat. "Okay," she said. "Something's going on. There's a lot of buzz up in the labs."

"What's wrong with your voice?" Max asked, his curiosity getting the best of him.

"Dude!" Lava said. "Rude much?"

"It's okay," Bats said. She came closer to Max, so that he could see what she was doing as she lifted her hand and placed a finger over what he now realized was a small plastic valve in the center of the rose on her throat. "I had cancer," she said. "Of the esophagus. They had to remove my voice box. This is how I talk now."

"Oh," Max said, embarrassed now that he had said anything. "I'm sorry."

"They think maybe getting a Legacy helped me fight the cancer," Bats said. "I don't know." She turned and pointed to Sam. "Is he okay?"

"No," Lava said.

"He will be," Six added quickly. "He just needs to rest. So what's this about a lab? And what are they excited about? And who are '*they*'?"

Again, Max thought maybe Six was trying to distract them from what was going on with Sam. But these were also great questions.

"The Mogs," Bats explained. "Magdalena, mostly. She's the one in charge of the experiments."

"What experiments is she doing?" Six asked.

"A bunch of different things," said Bats.

"That girl is like a mad scientist," Lava remarked.

"She *is* a mad scientist," Bats said. "She just looks like a little girl. Anyway, we don't really know what she's doing because she only speaks Mogadorian when she's working. I don't think she trusts any of the humans."

"How many humans are working with her?" Six asked.

"Besides the kids? Maybe a dozen," said Bats.

"And you can spy on them through these tunnels?"

Bats nodded. "There's one that goes close to the lab. Then you have to crawl up into an air shaft, but it's not hard. You just have to be quiet. But like I said, unless you understand Mog—"

"Max does," Lava interrupted.

Bats looked at Max, an eyebrow raised.

"How many people can fit into that air shaft?" asked Six.

"One," said Bats.

Max knew what was coming next. An excited feeling grew inside of him. "When do we go?" he said, grinning.

Fifteen minutes later, he was standing in a corridor with Bats and Six. They were using hand signals to communicate, although they had gone over the plan a dozen times, so Max knew exactly what to do. Not that it was complicated. There was an opening in the corridor ceiling, which led to the system of air vents that ran throughout the bunker. All he had to do was get up there, crawl through the right vent until he was above the lab and see what he could find out. All without making noise or getting caught.

Six pointed to the ceiling. Max nodded. Six crouched and made a step with her hands. Max put one foot on it and balanced with his hand on Six's head until he was standing straight. Then Six lifted him. He gripped the edge of the opening and pulled himself in while Six pushed from below.

Once he was inside, he moved slowly, being as quiet as he could. He had written Bats's directions on his hand so he wouldn't forget where he was going. Now he followed the mini palm map: straight, right, straight, left. The air vent was narrow, and the deeper he went, the more claustrophobic it felt. But at least the air flowing through was cool, which helped keep him calm. Also, he was excited to actually be doing something to help instead of running away or waiting for someone else to take charge.

He heard voices, and paused. It sounded like kids talking. And they were speaking English. He heard a girl's voice. Then someone laughed. But he couldn't make out what they were saying. The voices stopped, and he guessed whoever had been speaking had walked away. He continued on until the shaft ended in a grate. He peered through it and saw below him a big room filled with equipment of various kinds.

Only there was nobody walking around. His hopes fell. Maybe he was somehow in the wrong place? Or maybe whatever Bats had heard going on, it was over now. He wondered if he should go back to Six and Bats and tell them, or if he should wait to see if something happened.

Then something did. Max felt something crawling on his leg. He turned his head and looked. The lower half of his body was covered with cockroaches. They swarmed over his feet and legs, heading for his torso. Some had gone under his pants and were walking over his skin.

Instinctively, he tried to crawl away. This put him right on top of the grate that opened to the room below. Too late, he realized what he had done. The thin metal screen bent under his weight, then gave way. He tumbled out of the ceiling in a cloud of roaches.

He had no time to think as he fell. Then he hit the hard concrete floor, and the air was knocked out of him. He lay on his back, unable to breathe. Pain radiated throughout his whole body, and he wondered if he had broken anything.

"You could have used your telekinesis to slow his fall," a voice said.

"I could have," said another. "But this was more fun."

Max moved his head, trying to ignore the roaches that were now scurrying away from him in all directions. Things were a little blurry, but slowly his eyes focused as his breath returned. Then he saw the kids standing a little distance away, watching him. He recognized Seamus, but the others were unfamiliar: a girl who resembled Lava enough that he guessed it was his sister, Shaky; a girl whose blond hair was in pigtails; a boy wearing a black knit hat and all black clothes who scowled at the world from beneath thick eyebrows that matched the goatee on his chin.

The blond girl came over to him and leaned down. "I hope you didn't get hurt," she said, looking concerned.

"I'm okay," Max said, although he felt anything but.

The girl grinned, and now she didn't look at all pleasant. "Good. Because by the time I'm done with you, you won't be."

She started to reach for him, and Max put his hands up.

"Freakshow," a voice said.

The girl retreated, looking irritated. "I was just going to play with him a little, Spike."

"Magdalena wants him in one piece," said the same voice. "His body *and* his mind."

A new face now hovered over Max. It was another boy. This one was short and slight, barely looking old enough to have a Legacy. His brown hair was a little long, flopping over his eyes, and he wore thick glasses that he pushed up the bridge of his nose with one finger. Then he reached out his hand.

Max put his hand up again, instinctively preparing to fight.

"Whoa," the boy said. "Take it easy. I'm just helping you up. My name is Spike."

Max hesitated. Spike was acting like they were friends. But they weren't. He was the enemy. Still, it probably wouldn't be a good idea to get into a fight. Not now, anyway. He was outnumbered. He wondered if Six and Bats realized that he was in trouble, and if they would come help him. Until they did, he decided, it was best to play it cool.

"Thanks," he said, taking Spike's hand.

Spike helped him up. "Sorry about that," he said, looking at the busted vent in the ceiling. "That must have hurt."

"You sure made a lot of noise," the girl Spike had called Freakshow said. "We thought you were a giant *rat*." She emphasized the last word, giving Max a hard stare. "How'd you get in there anyway?"

Max eyed her warily. He remembered her name from Rena's stories about being in Dennings's camp. He knew what she could do. "I was looking for a way out," he lied. "I crawled into a vent in one of the other rooms and just kept going. I figured eventually I'd find something."

Freakshow snorted. "Sure," she said. "And I bet Lava and the Bride of Dracula had *nothing* to do with it, right?"

"Who?" said Max, hoping he sounded believable.

"Kona and Bats got out," said the girl Max had pegged as Lava's sister.

Freakshow rolled her eyes. "You know that's not true," she said. "You know no one gets out of this place. And Lava helped this guy get away from Seamus and Ghost, so we know he's here. Bats probably is, too. And when I find them—"

"You talk too much," Spike snapped. "Come on. Magdalena is waiting. We can worry about Lava and Bats another time."

"You going to tie his hands?" Seamus asked.

Max peered at his former friend. Seamus still looked banged-up from their encounter earlier in the day. Still, Max was surprised to hear a note of fear in his voice. It actually gave him a little thrill. He narrowed his eyes and started to lift his hand. Seamus backed away, putting his own hands up.

Max scratched his nose slowly, as if that was what he'd intended to do all along. Behind him, someone laughed. It was the boy in the black hat. He pointed at Seamus. "Dude must have roughed you up pretty good."

"It was a lucky shot," Seamus said. "I don't think he could do it again."

"Then I guess you've got nothing to worry about," said the boy.

"Whatever," Seamus muttered, walking away.

"You two used to be tight, huh?" the boy in the hat said to Max.

Max nodded. "Until he turned out to be a traitor."

The boy reached out and grabbed Max's arm. Lifting it up, he pointed to the tattoo that was there. "Looks like you wanted to be part of the gang, too," he said.

Max pulled his arm away. "I didn't know what the gang was really doing," he said.

The boy shrugged. "And maybe you still don't," he said. Then he walked off, following Seamus along with Freakshow and Shaky.

"What's he mean by that?" Max asked Spike.

"He means maybe things aren't what they look like," he said. "Or what you've been told."

"I've heard that before," Max said, thinking about how Ghost had tried to convince him of the same thing. This time, he wasn't buying it.

"Come on," Spike said, but not meanly. "And seriously, don't try anything. Not everyone is as cool as I am. Just go with it and everything will be fine."

Max allowed himself to be led out of the room. He didn't for a minute believe that everything would be fine. Spike and the others might believe that the Mogs weren't up to no good. He knew a lot of the kids who'd become involved with Jagger Dennings had basically been brainwashed into believing they were doing the right thing. And some of them probably did know the truth and just didn't care. Like Freakshow. She seemed like she might be as bad as the Mogs, ready to use her Legacy to hurt people for fun. Others, though, he couldn't understand. Spike seemed like a nice enough guy, and Lava's sister didn't seem like she belonged there either. So why was she? He hadn't gotten the story from Lava. But something had happened to make her stay while her brother tried to get away. What was it?

He would have to wait for an answer. Right now he was being taken into a different room. He expected it to be another lab of some kind. Instead, it was a small office. There was a desk in it, and behind the desk was Magdalena. She was typing on a keyboard while looking at a computer screen. When Max walked in with Spike, she looked up.

"Oh good. You found him," she said. "You can leave us alone now, Spike."

Spike nodded and left the room, shutting the door behind him. Magdalena pointed to a chair. "Sit," she said.

Max sat. Magdalena continued to type, saying nothing to him for several minutes. Then she stopped, pushed the keyboard away and turned to him.

"Are you hungry?" she asked.

"What?"

"Hungry?" Magdalena said. "Are you? I would think you would be. Or did Lava feed you?"

"No," Max said. He realized he had just given Magdalena information he shouldn't have, and tried to backtrack. "I mean, I haven't found any food and—"

"You don't have to pretend," Magdalena said, waving a hand in the air. "I know all about Bats and Lava's little hideout."

Max didn't know what to say, so he said nothing.

"You're wondering why I haven't captured them," Magdalena said. She giggled. "It's because it amuses me to have them running around, thinking they're getting away with something. Although now that Six and Sam are mixed up with them, I might have to rethink that." She sighed and frowned. "Eleni *really* wants to get her hands on those two. Especially Six. I'll probably have to let her at some point. But, like I told her, I only need her *or* Sam for my experiment." She looked at Max. "How are you feeling, by the way? Any headaches? Anything weird happening with your abilities?"

Max was confused. She was talking to him as if they were having a normal conversation.

"I guess I feel okay," he said.

"Hmm," Magdalena said, biting her lip. "I should probably do a scan anyway. *Something* should be going on in there by now. But let's eat first. Can't have you passing out from hunger or anything."

She picked up a phone on her desk. "Bring something to eat," she said and hung up. Only then did Max realize she had spoken in her own language.

"It will be a few minutes," she said. "While we wait, how about we do a reading?"

"A reading?" Max said.

Magdalena reached into a drawer and pulled something out. Max recognized the deck of cards he'd seen her using before in the house in Alabama. Magdalena started shuffling them in her hand.

"Byron and Eleni think I'm crazy using these," she said.

"They say it's all human superstition."

"What are they?" Max asked, curious despite his worry.

"Tarot cards," said Magdalena. "Some people call them fortune-telling cards, but that's not what they are at all. They're really a kind of mirror."

"Mirror?" said Max.

Magdalena nodded. "Of our psyches," she said. "Or whatever you want to call it. Of what's going on in our lives, I guess. See, you concentrate on a question and focus on the cards giving you an answer to it. The pictures on the cards tell you what's going on. I don't see why that's any weirder than, let's say, an invisible entity giving certain people superpowers. Right?"

Max shrugged. "I don't really know."

Magdalena laid out three cards, facedown. She set the rest of the cards aside. "Want to know what my question is?"

"Sure," Max said, even though he didn't. The Mog girl weirded him out.

"I asked how my plan is going to work out."

"What plan?" Max asked.

Magdalena shook her head. "I can't tell you *everything*," she said. "That would ruin the surprise." She turned over the first card. "The Seven of Rods. Someone who is outnumbered by enemies. I suppose that would be me. But the person will be victorious if he—or she—sticks to the plan. Which I will."

She flipped the second card over. "The Page of Swords." She frowned. "That usually represents someone who is spying or looking to cause trouble." She looked up at Max. "Like you," she said. "Or Six. Or Sam. Or your friend who killed Byron. There are lots of *pages* running around right now. It could be anyone."

She looked at the remaining card. "Shall we see what the final outcome is?" Without waiting for an answer, she turned the card over and held it up. It depicted a full moon hanging over a city. Beneath it, dogs looked up, barking.

"What does it mean?" Max asked.

"Unforeseen dangers," said Magdalena. "Secrets. Things coming out into the open."

"Okay," Max said. "But what does it *mean*?"

"For my plan?" said Magdalena, sweeping up the cards. "I don't know."

"Then what was the point of this?"

"The cards reflect what's happening now," Magdalena said. "And what might happen if things stay as they are. I'm considering this a warning to be careful. But I like the part about secrets." She put the cards away, then rested her elbows on the desktop and placed her chin in her hands. "I have a lot of secrets, Max. Would you like to know one?"

Before Max could answer, there was a tapping on the door.

"Come in," Magdalena called.

The door opened and a Mog walked in. He was carrying a tray, which he placed on the desk. It contained a plate with a cheeseburger, fries and what looked like a chocolate milkshake. Max's mouth began to water from the smell.

"The egg that the human boy brought here with him from

the school has hatched," the Mog said to Magdalena.

Magdalena frowned at him, glancing at Max. "I'll be right there," she said sharply.

The other Mog scurried out. Magdalena turned her attention to Max. "I know you understood what he said."

"He's talking about Seamus, right?" said Max.

"Yes," Magdalena admitted.

"He brought an egg here?" He thought for a moment. "Is that what that thing was? The thing he said was a bomb?"

"It was an incubator," Magdalena explained. "I suppose there's no harm in telling you that. It won't change anything."

"What kind of an egg is it?"

"I said I would tell you *one* secret," Magdalena said, standing up. "Now, eat your dinner like a good boy."

She walked to the door. "You won't be able to get out," she said. "And if you did manage it, Freakshow would make you regret it. I'll be back shortly. Try not to get into any trouble."

She left. Max heard the door lock behind her. He had no doubt that she wasn't lying. For a moment he looked around, wondering if he could use anything in the room to his advantage. He got up and looked at the computer, but it was protected with a fingerprint scanner. The drawers were also locked.

He returned to his seat. He looked at the food on the tray, and his stomach growled. Was it drugged?

There was only one way to find out.

CHAPTER SEVEN

SIX

SHILO, UTAH

"WE HAVE TO GET HIM OUT OF THERE."

Standing in the hidden corridor, Bats looked at Six, her eyes filled with worry. Six shook her head. "That's exactly what they want us to try," she said, knowing what the girl's reaction would be.

"No!" Bats said. "We can't leave him with Magdalena." She started to tremble, and tears formed in her eyes. Six wondered what experiences she'd had with the Mogs to make her so afraid.

"I know how you feel," Six said. "Believe me. But you have to trust me on this. Max is better off waiting this out. If we rush in there trying to rescue him, it's the two of us against however many of them are in there. And right now, my Legacies aren't reliable, which means you'd be doing most of the fighting."

"I can do it!" Bats insisted, her already-rusty voice sounding even more anxious.

Six could feel her intensity. She was practically vibrating with telekinetic powers waiting to be unleashed. And part of her wanted to do what Bats suggested. But it was true—Max was safer being held by their enemies than he was on the run from them. Six was pretty confident that Magdalena wouldn't harm him, at least no more than she might already have by infecting him with a parasite. If that was even true. Plus, there was Sam to worry about. Six was concerned about what was happening with him.

"We need to get back to the safe room," she said. "Then we'll make a plan. Okay?"

Bats looked away, then nodded.

"All right," Six said. "I promise, we'll come for Max. We need to do it in an organized way, though. That's our best chance of getting him out with nobody getting hurt."

Bats led the way back through the passageways. They moved silently, not speaking, but Six's mind was racing with thoughts about how to proceed. It would be easier if she knew that Sam's message to Nine had gotten through, but there was no way of telling. Enough time had passed that if he *had* gotten it, he should have shown up. Or at least be on his way. She hoped that he was.

In addition to Max being captured, they were also now

without any source of information about what Magdalena and the other Mogs were up to. Six had been depending on Max to find out—or at least get a clue to—what was going on in the labs. Now Magdalena would be even more suspicious and on the alert for their presence.

She suddenly felt exhausted. Part of it was being physically tired. She couldn't remember the last time she'd really slept or ate. She didn't even really have a clue what time of day it was, as there were no windows—and being underground was like being trapped in a never-ending twilight. If she could just rest for a moment, she might feel better.

A jolt of pain shot through her head. She gasped, bringing her hands to her temples. She thought she might be sick. Then she was. A trickle of something sticky and acidic dribbled from her mouth and onto the floor. She gagged, bringing up more.

"Are you okay?"

Bats was bent down, her hand on Six's shoulder.

Six couldn't answer. Her head was swimming. Her vision blurred, and her stomach lurched again. This time, nothing came up. And a moment later, the pain was gone, as if it had never been there.

"What's happening?" Bats asked her.

Six wiped her mouth with her hand. "I'm okay," she said. "Let's keep moving."

She stood up. She was very much not okay, but she didn't want the girl to worry. Bats once again took the lead, and

Six kept up with her. She waited for the feelings of pain and nausea to return, but they didn't. Whatever was happening inside of her, she could no longer deny that *something* was wrong. Whether it was really a parasite or a drug or something else Magdalena had done to her, she didn't know. She couldn't deny that she was feeling weaker, though, and Sam seemed to have been feeling the same effects.

They reached the secret room, and for a moment Six felt a sense of relief. She could rest, if only for a little while, and make a plan. But when she and Bats entered the library, they found Lava in a state of panic.

"Sam's gone!" he said as soon as he saw them.

"Where did he go?" Six asked.

Lava shook his head, spinning around as if maybe Sam was somewhere in the room and he just couldn't see him. "I don't know. He said he was hungry, and we were out of food, so I snuck out to get something from the pantry." He pointed to a table, where some bags of potato chips sat beside some cans of soda.

"And Sam was gone when you got back?"

Lava nodded. "He was acting kind of weird," he said. "Before I left. He said his head hurt. Then he threw up."

Six felt Bats look at her. She ignored the glance, focusing on Lava. "Do you have any idea where he might have gone?"

"No," the boy said. "Like I said, he was sitting right there when I left. And he wasn't here when I got back." He paused and looked around. "Wait. Where's Max?"

"He got captured," Bats told him.

Lava sank onto a nearby chair. "No," he said. "No, no, no, no, no."

Bats sat next to him and put an arm around his shoulder. "It's okay," she said, her finger pressed against her throat while she hugged her friend. "We won't let her do it to him. I promise."

Her wording caught Six's attention. "Do what?" she asked. "What is it Magdalena does that you're so scared of?"

Bats continued to keep her arm around Lava as he started to cry silently. "She does something to their brains," she said. "We don't really know what it is. Something that makes them . . . obedient. She did it to Shaky. Kalea."

"But not to the two of you?"

Bats shook her head. "It's why we decided to leave. Well, one of the reasons. To get out before she did."

Lava had stopped crying. He wiped his eyes. "She's evil," he said. "She experiments on people and doesn't care what it does to them." He looked at Six. "Is that what's wrong with Sam? Did she do something to him? Did she do something to you?"

Six was tempted to lie. She didn't want Bats and Lava to worry any more than they already did. But they deserved to know the truth. Also, she might need their help.

"Magdalena claims she infected me and Sam with some kind of parasite."

Lava put his head in his hands. Bats looked as if she'd been given the worst news of her life.

"I don't know if she really did or not," Six continued. "We

were already having trouble with our Legacies because of the serum her doctor pal Drac injected us with. That was wearing off, though."

"That's why you got sick," Bats said. "And why Sam was acting weird."

"Maybe," Six admitted.

She sat down on a chair. "Like I said, I don't know if she's telling the truth or not."

"She is," Lava said. "I know she is."

Six didn't know what to say. Bats and Lava had obviously been counting on her and Sam to help them. Now they seemed defeated. Worse, they were looking at her as if she had some kind of monster inside of her that might burst through her head at any second.

"You've seen this before, haven't you?" she said softly.

Bats nodded. "There was a girl called Firefly," she said. "She did something the Mogs didn't like. Tried to get the rest of us to leave. Magdalena punished her by putting something inside of her. The same thing happened to her that's happening to you."

"I just thought Sam was sick," Lava said. "If I'd known . . ."

"There's nothing you could have done," Bats assured him. "You know that."

"What happened to Firefly?" Six asked. "Where is she now?"

Bats looked as if she didn't want to answer.

"She's dead," Lava said. "She started having headaches. Then she was throwing up this—stuff. Then she said something was trying to eat its way out of her head. Said she could feel it. One night we had to stop her from trying to get it out of herself with a—"

"Lava," Bats said gently, and the boy stopped talking. Bats looked at Six. "She started bleeding from her nose," she said. "Hallucinating. She said she was being attacked by something. We had to restrain her. Magdalena just laughed." She paused. "The weird thing is, for a while Firefly's powers got even more powerful."

"What was her Legacy?" Six asked. "I'm guessing she made light?"

Bats nodded. "It was like the parasite or whatever made her stronger. For a while. But then it killed her."

"How long?" Six asked.

"Once she started throwing up, about three days," said Bats.

Six took in this news, not letting on how alarming it was. Three days was nothing, especially when she was trapped underground with no escape plan. And now Sam was missing and Max was captured. Her odds were not good. She allowed herself a minute to feel the weight of the situation, then pushed those worries to the back of her mind.

"I'm going to need the two of you to help me," she told Lava and Bats.

"What can we do?" Lava asked. "We're screwed."

"No, we're not," said Six sharply. "I've been in worse situations than this, and yet here I am. We can get through this. If we work together. My Legacies might not be working right, but yours are. Between the three of us, we're going to get this done. Got it?"

"Got it," Bats said, although her enthusiasm was obviously forced.

"Lava?" said Six.

"Got it," the boy said, much less convincingly.

"What do we do?" Bats asked.

"Find Sam," Six said. "We can't have him stumbling around this place on his own."

"It might already be too late," said Lava. "Magdalena and the others have probably found him, especially if he's running around like a crazy person."

"Then let's hope we find him first," Six said.

"We're just going to go out there?" said Lava. "We don't even know where he went."

"How many places could he go?" Six said. "Come on."

She hoped she sounded confident. In reality, she was anything but. If Sam had run out of the safe room on his own, it meant he obviously wasn't thinking clearly. And if he was wandering around the halls of the bunker, it was only a matter of time before he ran into someone. Lava was right—it might already be too late.

"We can use the corridors," Bats said. "They don't run everywhere, but they run enough places that it's worth staying hidden until we don't have a choice."

"It doesn't make sense for us all to go the same direction," Six said. "I need one of you with me, since you know where the corridors run and are familiar with this place. Lava, you come with me. Bats, you go on your own."

"What if I find Sam?" Bats asked.

"Try to get him somewhere safe. Back to the library, if you can. If you can't, then come find us and we'll figure it out. But don't put yourself in danger. If the risk is too much, get back to the safe room and stay there. We'll meet back there in an hour. By then, we should have found him, or figured out if someone else has."

"Okay," Bats said. She looked at Lava. "I'll take the lower floors. You and Six take the upper three."

Lava nodded, but looked worried.

"You can do it," Bats assured him, giving him a hug.

She entered one of the corridors that led off of the main hall, the one they had used to reach the laboratories. Lava showed Six the opening to one on the other side. "We go through here," he said.

"How many floors are there in this place?" Six asked as they walked, with Lava leading the way ahead of her.

"At least five," Lava said. "The top one is where they store supplies. The second floor is living quarters and kitchen. The third is where you were held and where Max and I found you. The labs are on the fourth floor. And this is the fifth floor, which is mostly systems and machinery for things like air and water. We think there may be a sixth level, because there's something drawn on one of the maps in Digby's diaries, but we've never found a way to get to it, so it might be something he was planning and never built."

"It's like an entire hotel underground," Six remarked.

"If we're lucky, Sam will still be on this floor," said Lava. "People come down here, but it's not as busy as the other floors."

"Is the maintenance staff Mogs or humans?" Six asked.

"Both," said Lava. "There aren't a ton of Mogs here, but they don't trust humans to be totally in charge, so there are always some Mogs on the crews. The other thing is that to get off the elevators on this floor, you need a crew key. Otherwise, you have to use the stairs. I messed up the doors when Max and I were running from Ghost and Seamus, so they're probably not working right. Unless Sam managed to break through them or get into an elevator somehow, he should be here."

They walked for a while longer; then Lava stopped. "This is the electrical room," he said, pushing on a panel in the wall. It slid aside, opening onto a small area behind some kind of large machinery. "The entrances are all in out-of-the-way places," Lava explained. "We're behind one of the generators."

They walked around the massive machine, which hummed loudly. Peering out from behind it, Six looked into a large room filled with several more generators and rows of other machines she didn't know the purpose of. She saw two men looking at something and talking, but no Sam.

She and Lava retreated into the passageway and continued on. Six could feel a vibration coming through the walls and floor.

"The water room," Lava told her. "The pumps make a

lot of noise when they're running. We won't be able to hear much besides that, so be ready."

When he opened the panel into that room, they were met by the thunderous sound of turbines and pumps. The air practically vibrated with the sounds, and Six could sense the rush of water being pulled through the pipes. Again, they entered in an inconspicuous area in a dark corner of the room, and she had to walk around a massive piece of equipment to get a better look.

She saw Sam immediately. He was lying on the floor, facedown and unmoving. Instinctively, she ran over to him. A small pool of blood had spread out from beneath his nose. She knelt down and turned him over.

"Sam!" she said, forgetting that he wouldn't be able to hear her because of the noise.

She shook him, then slapped the side of his face lightly. Sam opened his eyes. They were glassy and unfocused, moving from side to side. Then, unexpectedly, he pushed Six roughly away, a look of horror on his face. He scrambled to his hands and knees, then stood, looking around wildly.

Six got up, reaching for him. Sam lifted his hands in a protective gesture, and she felt a weak wave of telekinesis hit her. It was enough to make her fall back a step, but not strong enough to do any real damage. Still, Sam was trying to fight her, and that was disturbing.

She felt someone behind her, and whirled to see Lava grabbing at her arm and pointing. She looked, and across the room she saw three teenagers standing, watching the scene between her and Sam. She recognized Seamus immediately. Another one—a blond girl who regarded her with a smirk—looked familiar, and Six realized she'd seen her before. She was one of the girls from Dennings's compound in Texas. Freakshow, they'd called her. The girl who could make people see their biggest fears.

Standing with her and Seamus was a smaller boy with shaggy brown hair and glasses. Six eyed them warily while keeping a watch on Sam. She knew what Freakshow and Seamus could do, but she didn't know what the other boy's power was. She glanced at Lava, hoping he would give her a clue, but he was looking elsewhere. She followed his gaze and saw a fourth person—a girl—standing apart from the others and looking at Lava. It was immediately obvious from their resemblance that she was his sister.

They needed to get Sam and get out. Not only were they outnumbered, but Six feared her Legacies wouldn't work. She also sensed that the group watching them knew this, and were waiting to see what she would do.

She decided she didn't have time to be patient. Grabbing Sam by the wrist, she pulled him to her and wrapped her arms around him. He immediately began to struggle, fighting hard. Although his Legacies were compromised, he was still strong. But she was ready for him. She gripped him more tightly and began to drag him back towards the hidden passageway. The others would see them disappear, but she had no choice.

She'd walked a few feet when the bugs appeared. Spiders

and roaches, swarming out from under the machines. This was Seamus's trick, she knew, and she wasn't frightened by it. She stomped on the hapless insects, even as they started to climb her legs. Sam, seeing them, reacted violently. He jerked away from Six, slipping out of her grip and stumbling away, running blindly in the direction of the group of teenagers watching the proceedings.

Six noticed that Lava was still standing as if in a daze, looking at his sister. As she ran by him, Six hit him hard in the back, jarring him to attention. He shook himself and joined her as she chased after Sam, who was now turning in circles and trying to wipe the bugs off his body.

As Six reached him, she felt the air around her change. The boy with the glasses was holding up his hands. All around Six, the air suddenly sparkled with cold as snowflakes formed. She found herself in the middle of a miniblizzard. Her breath froze, and she started to shake.

Legacies or not, she wasn't about to be trapped by a temperature-shifter. She forced herself to break through the chilly air, even as her body started to shake uncontrollably. The boy attempted to move the area of cold to keep her contained within it, but Six ordered her stiffening muscles to respond and ran from him. She got about a dozen feet before she was hit with a blast of fiery heat that sucked all the air from her lungs, as if she had stepped into a blast furnace.

Waves of heat radiated around her, and through them she saw the boy in the glasses watching her, his hands held up. She grew faint as the temperature soared. Then she saw the boy fly backwards, hit by a wave of telekinetic energy sent out from Lava, who had finally come to her aid. The wall of heat around her collapsed instantly.

Lava continued to use his telekinesis, sending the others scurrying as they fought back. This gave Six time to resume her search for Sam. Only she couldn't see him. He had disappeared. She ran around the room, looking, finding nothing.

Something closed around her wrist. The blond girl had grabbed her. She was grinning at Six with a malevolent smile. Six went to shake her off, but as she did, she suddenly found herself somewhere unexpected. She was inside the Mog prison in West Virginia. Her Cêpan, Katarina, hung before her in chains. Her face was bruised and bloodied. Beside her stood a Mog. He held a dagger in his hand.

"How weak you are," he said. "How unworthy to stand beside the others."

Six felt herself tremble. She looked into Katarina's eyes. She wanted to save her, but knew she couldn't.

"I'm sorry," she heard herself whisper as the Mog placed his dagger on Katarina's chest and pressed it into her heart.

Six cried out as her beloved teacher and friend died in front of her. Her heart broke. She had failed. The Mog laughed at her torment, and his voice echoed in her ears.

The room began to shake. The Mog disappeared, as did the room itself. Six was once more standing in the underground bunker. The girl, Freakshow, had let go of her and was looking around in surprise. Six, still affected by the lingering feeling of reliving her greatest fear, had no idea what was happening.

The noise in the room had grown louder. Six turned, trying to figure out what had changed. Then she saw Sam. He was standing near a control panel of some kind, his hands on it and a strange look on his face. She had no idea what he was doing. All around the room, machinery was creaking and groaning.

Then Six understood. Sam had opened some pipes or told the pumps to do something. Whatever it was, he was overloading the system. A moaning sound began as water rushed through pipes that had not been used in years. Six saw Freakshow and the others gather together in the center of the room. Seamus grabbed Sam and pulled him away from the controls.

It was too late. At the far end of the room, a wall exploded inward. Water poured through in a torrent, shooting across the floor and hitting the teenagers standing there. They were sent sprawling. Six, standing farther away, avoided the blast, but she saw Lava get slammed into a wall by the force of the water and collapse. He didn't move.

The water kept coming. Then there was another explosion and a second river joined the first. The room was flooding.

They needed to get to a higher floor. And fast.

She looked for Sam. She saw him across the room, splashing in the water like a little kid, kicking it up with his feet and laughing. Whatever was happening in his brain, it was getting worse.

She waded towards him, ignoring the others, who were now themselves trying to get out of the room. They were no longer her biggest worry. But as she neared Sam, Freakshow came for her, thrashing through the water. This time, Six was ready for her. As the girl reached out to grab her, Six punched her as hard as she could in the face. The girl's head flew back, and she fell into the water, blood streaming from what Six hoped was a broken nose.

Six got to Sam and took his hand. This time, he didn't fight her. She turned and made her way over to Lava, Sam in tow. The water was to her knees now, and it was cold.

The water grew colder. Then it began to freeze. Six looked down as it began to solidify around her legs. Even as she lifted one foot, she felt the water around it harden, imprisoning her. She turned her head and saw the boy with the glasses. He was transforming the room into ice. His friends had gotten out of the way, standing on machinery that was above the water level. Only Six, Sam and Lava were trapped in the grip of the ice.

Six saw Freakshow jump down onto the ice. She slid across the frozen surface, her hands reaching out. Six could only stand and wait.

CHAPTER EIGHT

NEMO
SHILO, UTAH

NEMO FELT THE WATER BEFORE SHE SAW IT.

She was walking down a long corridor, looking for any way out, when the shaking started, a low rumbling that she first felt through the bottoms of her bare feet. It grew more intense as she started to hurry. There had to be stairs somewhere, or another way to the upper levels.

She heard a groaning sound, like long-unused pipes coming to life and filling with water. She thought immediately of the three huge pipes under the lake. Had someone activated the massive machinery to get them working again? There was still no sign of Nine. Was he in there, battling the thing that had attacked them? Nemo had no idea. All she knew was that she had to find a way out of where she was.

That was when the water came.

It surged around a corner ahead of her, a swirling brown wave several feet high. It rolled down the corridor, hitting Nemo in the legs and knocking her backwards. As water rushed over her face, she clamped her mouth shut so that she wouldn't swallow any. For a moment she panicked, the natural fear of drowning kicking in, but then her Legacy took over and she relaxed a little bit. She could breathe. But she was still being propelled backwards.

She managed to flip herself over into a swimming position, but the water was moving too quickly for her to turn around. She put her arms out in front of her, waiting to crash into a wall. When the impact came, it jarred her shoulders, but at least she was not moving. The water pinned her to the concrete wall as it veered off to the left down the next corridor. She huddled there as the water continued to rise, filling the hallway. Eventually, the current slowed as the pressure equaled out.

Now she could swim. She wished she still had her mask and fins, but they were by the air lock where she'd left them. The water was murky, but she did the best she could, swimming back in the direction she'd been going before the flood. She had no idea where it had come from, but the water had gotten in somehow, and that meant that there was probably a way up.

She traversed the length of the corridor. The water was cold, and she guessed that it was from the lake. She thought momentarily of the thing with the tentacles, and shuddered. Hopefully, there would be no surprises like that awaiting her.

She kept going after reaching the spot where she first got hit with the wave. At the corner, she turned and found what she'd been searching for. A stairwell that went up. It was filled with water now, and she half swam and half walked up it. At the top she found a closed door with a wire screen set into the top. The water had forced the screen out, and it hung to one side. The door itself was still firmly shut.

Nemo placed her hands on the edge of the opening and pulled herself up. She was able to squeeze through and swim to the other side, where she found more stairs. These too were flooded, but only halfway up. When she reached the midway point, she found something even more peculiar. The water was frozen over her head. She put her hands against it and pushed, expecting nothing to happen. But she felt it crack into pieces, opening up a hole.

She pushed her head through and saw that the stairs were a frozen waterfall, as if the water had crystalized instantly in midflow. It was beautiful in an eerie way. She crawled out of the hole and onto the first step, holding on to a railing affixed to the wall for balance as she climbed the remaining steps. At the top she found another door. Thankfully, this one had been pushed open by the flood of water, and she slipped through into another hallway.

She was in a winter wonderland. Or something like it. Ice was everywhere. Her bare feet burned as she walked across it, but she was distracted from the pain by the weirdness of the sight. The water had been several feet deep when it froze, and so she walked through the hallway with the ceiling just overhead. And the ice wasn't entirely solid. Nemo felt water move beneath the surface. The hall was filled with the sound of cracking, shifting ice. It was like walking on a river.

There were other sounds, too. Voices. Somewhere ahead of her. And they sounded upset.

She hurried. She rounded a corner and passed into another hallway. This one had open doorways lining it. And there were people in it. The lights lining the hall were flickering on and off. Then they went out completely. A moment later, pale green safety lights came on. They were mounted at floor level, and glowed beneath the ice, creating an aquarium effect. Nemo was thankful for the lack of light, as it helped her stay hidden in the shadows as she crept down the hall.

"Get up to the labs!" a female voice shouted. "Get them all out! Take them to the teleporters. They know what to do."

Nemo came to the first open door and looked inside. A pink-haired girl was standing in a room full of machinery. She was directing a small group of people and Mogs, who were carrying various pieces of equipment through another door.

"We don't have long!" the girl shouted. "The water system has been compromised, as well as the electrical grid. The backup generators will only work for a little while."

"Calm down, Magdalena," said another voice. Then the Mog Nemo had first seen back at the house in Alabama came into view, the tall blond one. "We'll get your precious creatures out."

"They don't tolerate the cold, Eleni," Magdalena snapped. "They won't survive long."

"Then get Spike to warm it up in here," said the blond Mog.

"That will just make the flooding worse," Magdalena said. "He should have been more careful."

"He's not the one who caused the intake pipes to burst," said Eleni. "The Garde did that."

Nemo's heart lurched. She had to be talking about Six or Sam. Why they would do something to cause a flood, she didn't know. But it meant one or both of them were around somewhere.

"And who let them escape, I wonder?" Eleni asked. Her tone sounded accusatory.

"Six got away on her own," said Magdalena. "You were supposed to be in control of her, remember?"

"Her powers returned unexpectedly," Eleni argued. "I thought your beasts were supposed to take care of that."

"They do," said Magdalena. "Mostly."

"Yes," Eleni said. "Mostly. But not completely, apparently."

"You know that their use is experimental," Magdalena said. "And anyway, we don't have time to argue about this. We need to finish the evacuation. Where are Six and Sam now?"

"Secured," Eleni said.

"Have they been transferred?"

"Not as yet," said Eleni. "I did not have time to prepare

adequate quarters for them in the new location. But soon."

Nemo's spirits, which had fallen when she heard that Sam and Six had been captured, lifted. Six and Sam were still in the bunker somewhere. All she had to do was find them. She decided to focus on that instead of wasting time listening to the Mogs talk. But then Magdalena said something that made her pause.

"The parasite I implanted in Sam is growing. I will need to remove it or it will kill him."

"Let it," said Eleni. "It will save me the trouble."

"He could be of use in the next phase," Magdalena said.

"We have the other one," said Eleni. "And the boy. Max. They will be sufficient."

Magdalena didn't say anything. Nemo wished she would. What creature was she talking about? Why had she put it in Sam? And why would it kill him?

"The parasite has already done enough," Eleni continued. "Isn't that what made him behave the way he has and cause our current problem?" She didn't wait for an answer from Magdalena. "I've indulged your little experiments too long, I fear. Now we do things my way."

"My experiments could be the key to giving you a Legacy," Magdalena said quietly.

"By implanting one of your beasts in me?" said Eleni. "I don't believe it's worth the risk. We've seen what it's done to the humans you tried it with."

"Human minds aren't strong enough," Magdalena said. "Your Mog mind is."

Eleni laughed. "Perhaps," she said. "We can discuss it later. I have the evacuation to oversee."

The blond Mog left the room. Nemo observed Magdalena watching her go. When Eleni was gone, Magdalena returned to what she'd been doing, going to a desk that had floated to the surface and frozen there and taking things out of a drawer. She seemed agitated. Nemo was pretty sure that she'd just witnessed a showdown of some kind between the two Mogs. She wondered what was going on. She also wondered about the Mog she had stabbed back in Alabama. Was he here, too?

All of these questions would have to wait to be answered. She needed to figure out where Six and Sam were. Max, too, as he was obviously here as well. Unless he had been transferred to the evacuation location. She hoped not. She had no idea where that was. And with Nine still missing, she had no backup.

She slipped down the hall, looking for something that would help her find where Six and Sam were being held. Magdalena had mentioned teleporters. That probably meant Scotty and Ghost. If she found them, she might find a lot more than she was looking for.

She kept walking until she located a group of people carrying things up a flight of stairs. In the dim light, she was able to keep herself hidden in the shadows. She grabbed a box from a room as she passed by, joined the back of the line and followed them to the next floor. Here there was no flooding, but still only the emergency lighting was on. She let the people she'd tailed get ahead of her, then peered into the nearest doorway. These were obviously the laboratories that Magdalena had been talking about. There were more people here, both Mogs and humans, but nobody took any notice of her.

The people carrying things continued up to the next floor. There they walked until they came to a room, disappearing through a doorway. Nemo slipped away from the group, still unnoticed, and set the box she'd carried upstairs on the floor. She stayed in the shadows, watching as some of the people who had entered the room left it, apparently making a return journey to the lower levels for more items. Nemo counted, and when the last person had departed, she went back to the doorway and looked inside.

The room was some kind of staging area. Stacks of boxes waited next to piles of equipment. On the tables were large glass jars, half a dozen or so. Nemo could see small things moving around in them. She looked around the room and, seeing nobody, walked over to the jars.

Inside each one was some kind of animal. They were crablike, about three inches wide, with pincerlike claws and multiple legs. Their shells glittered wetly. Something about them made Nemo afraid, although she wasn't sure why. Bugs didn't bother her, and crabs were nothing to be frightened of. But there was something about the things that made her want to get away from them.

Hearing a noise, she thought that someone was coming, and looked for a place to hide. Fortunately, the piles of boxes and other things made this easy. She ducked behind a stack of equipment and crouched down.

"More stuff?" a boy's voice said. He sounded annoyed. "When did we become Magdalena's personal moving company?"

"It's not like it's hard," a girl's voice answered. A familiar voice. It was Ghost.

"I know it's not *hard,*" the boy retorted, and Nemo realized it must be the other teleporter, Scotty. "I just don't like doing it, is all."

"You don't like anything that's work," Ghost teased. "Would you rather be at the Academy, learning how to be a good little soldier?"

Scotty snorted. "No way," he said. "That place is for losers."

Ghost laughed. To Nemo, it felt like being punched in the stomach.

"I guess we should move these next," Scotty said.

From her hiding place, Nemo could see him standing near the table of jars. He was looking at the creatures inside.

"These things give me the creeps," he said. "Can you even imagine having one inside of you? Gross." He looked at the various jars. "I wonder which one was inside Firefly? Think if I let it get inside me it would give me her Legacy?"

"Magdalena thinks so," Ghost said.

"What?" said Scotty. "You don't think it's true?"

"It hasn't worked so far," Ghost said.

"That we *know* of," said Scotty. "Like the Mogs are going to tell us everything."

"Shh!" Ghost said, sounding scared.

"Relax," said Scotty. "There's nobody up here."

"Still," Ghost said. "Let's just take these and get back."

Scotty picked up one of the jars. "Have you seen some of the other stuff Magdalena has created?" he asked. "I don't know if they're animals or robots or what. Anyway, if you think these are badass, wait until you see what she's cooked up for the show."

"Can't wait," Ghost said. "Hey, I've got to go to the restroom. You go ahead and I'll be there in a few minutes, okay?"

"Sure," said Scotty. "See ya on the other side."

He disappeared. Ghost remained behind. She stood, looking at the jars but not moving. Nemo watched her, wondering what was going on.

"If I knew which one of you had been inside Firefly, I'd take you out and stomp on you," she said. Her voice dripped with anger. "I should stomp on *all* of you."

To Nemo's surprise, Ghost started to cry. She hunched over the table of jars, her face in her hands as she sobbed. Her shoulders shook with every breath. Before she knew what she was doing, Nemo stood up.

"Ghost."

Ghost, startled, stepped back from the table. Her eyes found Nemo in the dimly lit room. "Nemo?"

Nemo stepped out and came closer, holding her hands up. "It's okay."

"What are you doing here?" said Ghost. She looked

around, as if there might be other unexpected visitors.

"It's just me," Nemo said, keeping her voice low. "I came to find Max."

This was only partially true, but she worried that mentioning any of the Garde would make Ghost upset.

"You couldn't get in here by yourself," Ghost said. "Who's with you?"

Nemo considered lying again, but Ghost was right. She couldn't have gotten into the bunker alone. "Nine," she admitted. "But he didn't get in. Something in the lake came after us. I don't know where he is. It really is just me."

"You have to go," Ghost said. "If they catch you—"

"Come with me," Nemo interrupted. "Please. Let's find Max and get out of here."

Ghost shook her head. "Max isn't here," she said. "He's been transferred to . . . He's not here."

"Where?" said Nemo. "To the place where all this stuff is going? Where's that?"

Ghost shook her head. "I'm not telling you, Nemo."

"Ghost, please. It can be the way it was again."

Ghost laughed, but angrily. "Can it, Nemo? I don't think so."

"Why not?" Nemo asked. "Why can't you come back to us?"

"Why can't *you* come with me?" Ghost replied.

"Because," Nemo said. "You're with—them."

"Them," Ghost repeated. "And you're better than them, right? You and your Garde and your Academy?"

"Ghost, you've seen what the Mogs do!" Nemo protested. "You've seen what the people associated with them do.

They *hunt* us, Ghost. They use us. They're using you!" She stopped, forcing herself to calm down. "I heard what you said about your friend Firefly. They killed her, right? Magdalena? Whatever she did to her with those things in the jars, it killed her, didn't it?"

Ghost didn't say anything, but Nemo saw her glance at the jars.

"How can someone who would do that be your friend?" Nemo pressed.

Ghost turned her face away. "Just go, Nemo. I won't say anything about you being here. But I'm not going with you. Just leave."

Nemo went to Ghost. She grabbed her hands. "Look, Ghost," she said. "I'm not afraid of you. You could teleport me anywhere, and I'd go with you. Please."

Ghost looked into Nemo's face. "I can't," she said. "Please, Nemo. If we're really friends, then do what I said. Get out of here. There's nothing you can do now anyway."

"What's that supposed to mean?" Nemo said. "There's always something you can do. There's always a way out."

"Not of this," said Ghost. "Not of what's coming."

Before Nemo could ask Ghost what she meant, she heard voices in the hallway.

"Go," Ghost said again. "Once they come in here, I won't stop them. I swear, Nemo. This is your last chance."

Nemo felt Ghost trembling beneath her fingers. She wanted to drag her friend with her, out of the room, out of the bunker. She wanted them to be together again.

"I'll do what I can to help Max," Ghost said. "That's all I can promise."

Nemo let go.

"I'll leave," she said. "But I'm taking one of these things with me."

She picked up one of the jars. Ghost didn't try to stop her. Nemo hesitated a moment longer. She gave Ghost a last long look, then ran for the door. Outside, she saw figures coming towards the room through the glow of the emergency lights. She turned and ran the other way, the jar clutched to her chest.

CHAPTER NINE

SAM

UNKNOWN LOCATION

"I HAVE A LITTLE PROBLEM."

Sam, strapped to a metal table, his wrists and ankles bound with leather straps, looked up at the face of the pink-haired Mog girl. He couldn't quite remember her name, although he knew that he knew what it was. Meg? Maggie?

Magdalena. That was it. He was having trouble remembering a lot of things. Like how he'd come to be tied down. And where he was. And what had happened during the past couple of days. He recalled moments here and there, but it was like looking at the pieces of a puzzle scattered across a tabletop. If he could put them together, he could see the whole picture. At the moment, though, nothing was making sense.

"What's the problem?" he asked, thinking maybe he could

get some answers if he played along.

Magdalena sighed. "I guess it's really your problem, too," she said. "Since it involves the thing in your head."

"There's something in my head?"

"Mmm," the Mog said. She went away for a moment. When she came back, she held up a glass jar so that Sam could see it. Inside, something was crawling around. "One of these. Well, not as big as this one, but it will get to this size."

"One of those is inside my head?" said Sam. He looked at the disgusting bug-like thing. "Get it out!"

"Yeah, well, that's kind of the problem," said the Mog. She disappeared, and he heard her set the jar down somewhere. She kept talking to him. "If I take it out . . ."

Her voice trailed off, and Sam wondered if she had left the room. Then her face reappeared, looking down at him with an expression of concern. "If I take it out, you'll probably die."

Sam didn't know how to respond. Was she serious? Or was this some kind of a joke? He wished he could remember anything.

"That's not one hundred percent for sure," Magdalena continued. "Probably ninety, ninety-five, percent. So there's a chance you wouldn't. But every subject I've taken one out of has, so I don't want you to get your hopes up."

"What happens if you leave it there?" Sam asked.

"It gets bigger," said the Mog. "Like the one in the jar. And then—I'm not sure if I should tell you this part or not."

"Tell me," Sam insisted.

"Okay, well, it's kind of gross. It eats its way out."

"Out of my head?"

Magdalena shook her head. "Oh no. Your skull is too hard. It travels down to your stomach. It's a lot easier to chew a way out through your abdomen. There's no bone to get through."

Sam didn't want to think about that. "How did it get in me?"

"I put it there," Magdalena said. "It's kind of this thing I've been working on. A theory."

Sam pulled against the restraints that were holding him down. The straps cut into his wrists, but didn't budge. He felt weak, drained. Whatever the thing in his head was, it was depleting his energy. He swore in frustration.

"That won't help," Magdalena scolded.

An image flashed in Sam's mind. A room filled with ice. Six was there. And some other people. "Six," he said aloud.

"Six?" Magdalena said. "She's not here. She and Eleni are having a little chat. She's probably not enjoying it very much. Six, I mean. I'm sure Eleni is. But don't worry. Eleni won't kill her. She needs her for the plan."

"Plan?"

Magdalena rolled her eyes. "It's this whole thing," she said. "Personally, I think it's a waste of time. But she lets me do my thing, so I have to let her do hers." She paused, then grinned happily. "Besides, it will give everyone a chance to see my beasties in action."

"Beasties?" Sam said. "What are you talking about?"

Magdalena shook her head. "That's a surprise," she said.

"You'll have to wait to find out." Her smile changed to a frown. "I just hope you live long enough. Eleni only needs one of you, but two would be way better."

Nothing the Mog was saying made any sense to Sam. He wanted to ask more questions, but he knew he wouldn't get anything useful out of Magdalena. Besides, he was really tired. He shut his eyes. Maybe if he could sleep some more . . .

He heard a door open. Then another face appeared next to Magdalena's. This one he recognized right away. It was another Mog. He remembered fighting her at some point. He remembered losing.

"Well?" she said, her voice harsh. "Have you decided what to do with him?"

"I don't think I should take the parasite out," Magdalena said. "Not yet."

"Why not?" Eleni said impatiently.

"It's not fully developed," Magdalena answered. "Besides, the one inside of Six may have more interesting properties."

Eleni grunted. "We just need to see if it works," she said. "I don't care what powers it transfers." She looked at the other Mog. "If it even works."

"I think it will," Magdalena said.

"It hasn't so far," said Eleni.

"Because we've only tried it in humans," Magdalena said. "They aren't as strong as we are."

Eleni glanced at Sam, then said, "If you're not going to operate on him, put him in the cell with the other one. I'm done with her. For now." She turned and walked away.

"Her problem is she always has to be in charge," Magdalena told Sam in a whisper. "She doesn't want anyone else to get a Legacy before she has one. I'm surprised she hasn't tried to pair with one of the parasites when I'm not looking. Which is why I haven't told her how it works."

She held up a syringe. "I'm going to put you out for a while," she said. "It will keep the parasite from developing any further and give us a little more time."

Sam felt a pinch in his neck. Then something burned in his veins and a sour taste filled his mouth. His vision blurred, and a moment later he was unconscious.

When he awoke, he was lying on a cot in a small room. His head ached. The lights were turned off, and he was in the dark.

"Sam?"

"Six?" he said. "You're here?"

A shadow moved, and then a light came on overhead. Sam blinked. His vision was blurry, and the lights hurt his eyes.

"Sorry," Six said, and turned the light off again.

He felt her sit down on the cot beside him. She brushed his hair away from his face with her hand. "How do you feel?" she asked.

"Terrible."

"Do you remember anything? About what happened in the bunker?"

Sam shook his head, then realized Six probably couldn't see the gesture. "No," he said. "Tell me."

"You went a little crazy," Six said. Then she actually

laughed. "Sorry. I know it's not funny. But, man, you did a number on that place."

"I did? What did I do?"

"Turned it into a skating rink," said Six. "Well, you didn't do that part. That kid Spike did. But the water was all you."

She told him about interacting with the machinery that drove the water pipes in the bunker, about making the pipes fill up and explode, about flooding the bunker and forcing the evacuation of everyone in it.

"At least you got us out of there," she said.

"Where are we now?"

"I don't know," Six told him. "Another secret location. Could be anywhere. I was unconscious when they teleported us out. I guess you were, too."

"They drugged you as well?"

Six didn't answer for a moment. "Not exactly," she said.

Something in her voice made Sam worried. He reached out, searching for Six's hand. He found it and laced his fingers through hers. "What did they do to you?"

"Nothing," said Six. She squeezed his hand. "I'm fine."

"You're not fine," said Sam. "Did they hurt you?"

"It was that girl," Six said. "Freakshow. She made me see some things I've spent a long time trying to forget."

Sam forced himself to sit up, even though it made him feel sick to his stomach. Six helped him. He sat next to her and put an arm around her, pulling her close. He didn't ask her to say anything else. He had a feeling he knew what Freakshow had made her see, what her darkest fear was. He sat beside her in the dark, just holding her. After a minute, Six leaned her head against him.

"We'll get out of here," Sam whispered. "It will be okay."

"They have Max," Six said. "And Lava."

It took Sam a moment to remember who Lava was. Then it came to him. "What about Bats?" he asked, recalling the girl who had been helping them.

"I don't think they got her," Six said. "But I don't know for sure. Everything happened really quickly. One minute we were frozen in the ice, and the next I was seeing . . ." Her words trailed off, and she breathed deeply. "I was somewhere else." She sounded exhausted, worn out, almost defeated. It wasn't a Six Sam was accustomed to hearing, and it both frightened him and made him very sad.

"Well, we're together now," he said. "And like I said, it will be okay."

They sat together in silence for a while. Sam could feel Six breathing. The rise and fall of her chest was comforting. He closed his eyes and imagined that they were somewhere else. He tried to remember the last time they were relaxed and happy. Where had they been? His memories were still hazy, flitting around in his head like bats swooping through dusk. They circled around, revealing flashes of themselves as he tried to get them to come into focus, then darting off again before he could hold them in his mind. He recalled a beach, but not where it was. He saw the two of them holding hands as they walked along a street in a city he couldn't name. He heard Six laugh, but didn't remember the joke he'd told her to elicit the reaction.

He cleared his throat. "Magdalena says she put a parasite in me," he said.

Six lifted her head and looked at him. "I know," she said. "She says there's one in me, too. And in Max. I was going to tell you, but then you disappeared."

"I feel different," Sam told her. "Like I'm not alone in here. And I can't think clearly. Do you feel anything?"

"Sometimes," Six answered. "Nothing horrible. Yet. But my Legacies aren't working right. Or at all."

Sam felt more afraid than he had in a very long time. "She says it will probably kill us if she removes it. And if she doesn't, it will kill us getting out itself."

"She says a lot of things. I also think she's more than a little crazy."

"What if it is true?" Sam said. "What if this—thing—really does what she seems to think it does? Absorbs our Legacies somehow? Transfers them to whoever she puts it into once it's out of us?"

"I don't see how that's possible," said Six. "Legacies aren't things that live in a certain organ, or in our blood. They're not things you can swap from person to person."

"How do we know that?" Sam argued. "I mean, Nine can transfer his to other people. John can copy someone else's Legacy. How does that work? They have to come from *something.* What if she's figured it out? We don't even know what these things inside us are. Parasites and other things transfer diseases. Why not Legacies?"

"They don't work that way," Six insisted.

"They *haven't* worked that way. Maybe they do now. The black ooze drained Legacies, and Setrákus figured out ways to block them. Maybe Magdalena really did discover—or make—some creature that can do what she says they do. Like mosquitos that feed on Legacies and pass them on to the next person they bite. The rules about who gets Legacies have changed, Six. Maybe everything about them has."

Six took both of his hands in hers. "The Mogs are obsessed with getting Legacies. I get it. So are some humans. And they're going to try all kinds of insane things to try to get them. This is just another one of those things."

"Yeah, but it's working," Sam said. "You said it yourself. Our Legacies are disappearing. They might even be gone. Have you tried to do anything recently? Anything?"

Six didn't answer, which Sam knew was an answer in itself.

"There's a reason they haven't bothered to separate us," Sam continued. "It's because they're not afraid of us anymore. They know we're drained." Another thought came to him. "Magdalena said something about Eleni needing you for some kind of plan. Do you have any idea what she was talking about?"

Six snorted. "No. But I suspect Eleni always has a plan. She's basically a comic-book supervillain. Wants to destroy us, the world, whatever. She kept telling me how she was going to enjoy watching our time come to an end. I told her she needs a better scriptwriter."

Sam laughed despite himself. "I'm sure she took that well."

"Yeah, well, Mogs aren't generally known for their sense of humor."

They again settled into silence. Sam's thoughts raced, jumping from one thing to another. It made him angry. He hated that whatever was in him had hijacked his brain. He hated that he couldn't remember things.

"Did I really flood the place back there?" he asked Six.

"Big-time," Six confirmed. "If that kid hadn't frozen it, you probably would have turned the whole place into an aquarium."

Sam laughed. "It would have made a great playground for Nemo."

At the mention of Nemo, he got thoughtful again. He wondered where she was, and if she was okay. He wondered too if his message to Nine had gotten through. Not that it mattered now. They were in yet another place, and he had no idea where.

The light snapped on, making him blink. Eleni stood in the doorway. She pointed at Sam.

"You," she said. "Come with me."

"Why?" said Six.

Eleni ignored her. When Sam didn't get up, she walked over and grabbed him by the arm, pulling him up. Six leaped up and pushed her away. Eleni came back, her arm cocked, and punched Six hard in the stomach. Six gasped and collapsed to her knees.

"Leave her alone!" Sam shouted, trying to get between them.

Six got up and rushed at the Mog. But Sam was between them, and he grabbed her, hugging her to him. "Don't," he whispered in her ear. "It won't help."

Behind him, Eleni laughed. Then she took Sam by the collar and pulled him away from Six. Sam continued to hold Six's hand as long as he could. Then Eleni yanked him and their fingers parted. Sam saw the anger and frustration on Six's face as he was taken from the room. Then the door was slammed shut.

"It seems Magdalena's little pets are working," Eleni said as she marched Sam down a hallway. "Perhaps too well. You're both weakening quickly."

Sam knew she wanted him to react, and so he didn't. He wanted to remind Eleni that on a normal day Six would have beaten her easily. He would have as well. She had never encountered them at their strongest. *And you'd better hope you never do*, he thought.

He tried to pay attention to where they were going, storing clues in his mind that might be helpful later. But his thoughts were still all over the place. Also, the hallway they were walking through was nondescript: dingy white walls, fluorescent lights overhead, closed doors with no markings. They could be anywhere.

Then one of the doors opened and a strange creature walked out. Humanoid in shape, its skin was blue and its face was covered in purple and gold markings. Spikes stuck out from its head, and around its neck was a frill. It was laughing, but when it saw Eleni, its expression changed to one of worry.

"Get back inside!" Eleni barked.

The creature retreated, but as Sam moved past the door he glanced inside and saw that the room was filled with similar-looking beings of different colors. He looked into the face of the one in the doorway and saw that one of its eyes was stippled with gold and green dots, while the other stared at him with a distinctly human look. Then the creature turned away and shut the door.

Eleni herded him along, saying nothing about what had just happened. Sam knew asking was probably useless, but he said, "What was that?"

Eleni laughed. "Don't worry," she said. "You'll find out soon enough."

CHAPTER TEN

MAX

SHILO, UTAH

MAX WAS LISTENING TO THE MOGS TALK ABOUT what should be done with him.

"We should just leave him here," said one, a male with a nasty scar that sliced across the left side of his face. "What use is he?"

"Magdalena said to make sure he was transferred," argued the other, a girl.

The male Mog grunted. "I guess he's another one of her pets. I don't know what she sees in these humans. They should all be left here to drown, like rats."

Max wanted to shout, "I can understand everything you're saying!" But he kept quiet, seated in the small office where Magdalena had left him. The cheeseburger and fries he'd eaten hadn't been drugged or poisoned after all, and he actually felt a lot better than he had earlier. Or he would have if the power hadn't apparently gone out, leaving him sitting in a mostly dark room. The emergency lighting that had come on made the whole place glow a faint green.

He wondered what was going on. Clearly, something had happened. He'd expected Magdalena to come back for him, but she hadn't. He'd only seen the two Mogs, and they hadn't explained anything to him or discussed it with each other, apart from their comments about transferring him somewhere. Transfer him where? He had no idea.

Someone shouted from outside the room, and the two Mogs who had been talking about him left. He waited for them to come back. When they didn't, he stood up and went to the door. He tried the handle. To his surprise, it turned. He realized then that the lock must have been controlled electronically, and with the power off, it was no longer closed. He pushed the door open and stepped outside.

There was nobody in the hallway. He heard voices somewhere farther away and decided it would probably be best if he went the other way. He retreated down the corridor, walking quickly. He didn't know where he was going, but he was happy not to be locked in the office anymore.

The floor seemed to be deserted, which was weird. It was as if everybody had simply disappeared. And there was a lot of water. He recalled what the male Mog had said about leaving him there to drown. Something major had happened, and Max had no idea what it was. But if it could make the Mogs evacuate, it was probably not something he wanted to stick around for.

He needed to find Six and Sam, or at least Lava and Bats. Anyone, really. On his own, he had no idea what to do or where to go. But what if they had all left, too? Or worse, what if they had been captured?

He heard voices behind him, turned and saw the shadows of two figures standing outside the room he had recently vacated. It was the Mogs, probably coming back for him. Any moment they would realize that he wasn't in there and come after him.

He ran.

He felt like he was always running, always trying to get away from someone. He wished he felt strong enough to stand and fight. He remembered how it had felt to knock Ghost and Seamus back with his telekinesis. It was both empowering and horrible. He hated hurting people, even ones who might want to hurt him. He especially hated having to hurt people who were supposed to be his friends.

He turned a corner and collided with someone coming the other way. He fell backwards and landed on his butt. He looked up and saw something falling towards him.

"Catch it!" a voice said.

Instinctively, Max lifted his hands. Something landed in them, and he closed his hands around it. It was smooth and cool to the touch.

"Nice one," the voice said.

"Nemo?" asked Max.

His friend materialized out of the gloomy light. Max was so excited to see her that he almost dropped the thing in his hands, which he now realized was a jar. He looked at it, then almost dropped it again when he saw something scrabbling against the side.

"Careful!" Nemo said.

She reached down and took the jar from him, setting it on the floor. Then she offered him her hand and pulled him to his feet. She gave him a hug. It felt so good that Max almost cried. When Nemo let him go, he looked down.

"What is that thing?" Max asked, taking a step away from the jar by their feet.

Nemo bent and retrieved the jar. "I have no idea," she said. "But whatever it is, it's important, so I thought I should take one to show—someone."

"What are you doing here? How did you get in?" Max asked her.

"Long story," said Nemo. "I'll tell you later. The big question is, do you know how to get out?"

Max shook his head. "I was hoping I'd find someone who did."

"What about Sam and Six?"

"I don't know where they are," Max said. "We got separated. Then I got caught."

Nemo sighed. "I lost Nine, too," she said. "Looks like the buddy system didn't work for either of us."

"Hey, we found each other," Max said.

Nemo grinned. "Yeah," she said. Then she added, "I saw Ghost, too. Tried to get her to come with me. She wouldn't. And she said something big was going to happen soon."

"Magdalena said something like that, too," Max said. "One of the Mogs," he added, not knowing if Nemo would know who he meant.

"A lot of weird stuff has happened in the last few days," said Nemo. "Are you okay?"

Max shrugged. "Like you said, a lot of weird stuff has happened."

"You can tell me all about it when we're out of here," Nemo said. "Right now, we need to find ourselves an exit."

"Lava said there's only one way out," Max told her.

"Lava?"

"A guy I met here," Max explained. "He and this girl named Bats were helping us. Before I got caught by Freakshow."

"Freakshow's here?" Nemo said. "Great. Who else?"

Max told her about the others.

"I'd like to get my hands on Seamus," Nemo said angrily. "I can't believe he turned traitor."

"There's something else," Max told her. "That explosive device he supposedly brought from the Academy?"

"What about it?" Nemo said warily.

"It's not a bomb," Max said. "It's an egg. Well, there's an egg *in* it."

"What kind of egg?"

"I don't know. Magdalena didn't say. Just that that's what was in it."

"What the hell is that Mog up to?" Nemo muttered. "Freaky bugs in jars. A mystery egg. The thing in the lake."

"What thing in the lake?" Max asked.

"That's part of the long story," Nemo replied. "Nine and I got attacked by an octopus or something. Only it wasn't a real animal. Not biological," Nine said.

"So, like a mechanical squid?" said Max.

"It didn't feel mechanical," Nemo said, thinking about the tentacles that had wrapped around her arm. "Felt pretty real to me."

"Did it . . . get Nine?" Max asked.

"He was still fighting it when I had to get inside," Nemo said. "I don't know. I waited for him, but the air lock started to fill up with water again and I had to shut it."

She sounded angry, and also ashamed. Max understood that feeling all too well. "It's not your fault," he assured her. "And it's *Nine.* I bet he's fine. He's just been . . . held up for some reason."

Nemo nodded, but Max knew she probably still felt bad. He decided to try to distract her by being brave himself. "We could go look," he said. "For the egg thing, I mean."

"Where?" Nemo said. "They probably took it to wherever they took everything else."

"Maybe," Max agreed. "But it can't hurt to look, right? Then we can try to get out of here. You've already got that thing in the jar. Maybe if we find the egg, we can take both of them back to the Academy and they can figure out what they are. It might help." He didn't know how, exactly, but it sounded good. He tried not to think about the part where, even if they found the egg, they still had to somehow get out of the bunker without being caught. And he especially tried not to think about the part where all of this seemed completely impossible.

"You're right," Nemo said. "Let's do it."

They made their way back to the laboratories. The Mogs seemed to have gone, and the rooms they looked into were deserted. They searched each one for anything useful, but came up empty-handed. Almost everything had been taken, and what had been left behind was useless.

"Well, it was worth looking," Nemo said as she and Max stood in the middle of the last room.

"I guess," Max said, disappointed.

He was about to suggest that they start looking for a way out when there were noises from the hallway. Then he heard Mogs talking in their language.

"Hide!" he said to Nemo.

They found spots behind large pieces of equipment and hunkered down. Moments later, the Mogs entered the room.

"We have everything," one said.

"We still haven't found the human boy," another replied. "And there are the beasts in the cages below. Eleni said to destroy them, since there's nowhere to house them safely in the other location."

The first Mog laughed. "Perhaps we can solve both problems," he said. "Let them out and they can hunt down the human."

The second Mog joined in the laughter. "The creatures will never get out of here anyway. Let them die down here after cleaning up."

They left the room, still laughing. Nemo turned to Max. "What did they say?"

"They said we'd better find that way out, and fast," Max said. Then he translated the rest of the conversation for her.

"I don't even want to know what these beasts are," Nemo said. "If they're anything like that thing in the lake, they're bad news. And we don't have any weapons. I say we get the hell out of here."

They left the lab, but not before Nemo located a discarded bag that she put the jar containing the mysterious bug thing into, making it easier to carry. The Mogs were nowhere to be seen and she and Max crept down the hallway, alert for any signs that they weren't alone.

"Lava said there's one elevator that goes all the way to the top," Max told Nemo. "Maybe we can get in it and just ride out of here."

"If we're lucky," Nemo said.

They weren't. When they located the elevator doors and pressed the button, nothing happened. Whether it was because the power was mostly out or because the elevator had been disabled was impossible to tell. Not that it mattered. The end result was the same.

"I guess it's the stairs, then," Nemo said.

They went in search of the stairway. The door to it was wide open, and they began the ascent to the next floor. They were halfway there when they heard a roar.

"What was that?" Max said.

"Nothing good," said Nemo. "Come on!"

They hurried. Below them, the roaring continued.

Nemo reached the next floor first. She slammed her hands against the door. It didn't move.

"Is it locked?" Max asked. He tried pushing with her. The door rattled, but stayed closed.

"Forget it," said Nemo. "Let's go to the next floor."

They went up. At the next landing, they hit the door hard. Again, it didn't move. Max beat on it with his fists, as if this might help. "Now what?" he wailed.

"Try telekinesis," Nemo said.

They put their hands up. A moment later, the door rattled.

"Push harder," Nemo said.

The door rattled again, and this time it buckled. But only a little. The lock was holding.

"Keep trying!" Max urged.

As if they were mocking him, the things coming after them bellowed.

Nemo shook her head. "There's no time. These doors are too strong. If we can't get one open, we're trapped in this stairwell with whatever is coming up behind us," she said. "I don't like our odds."

"What other choice do we have?" Max asked.

“We go back down,” said Nemo.

“What? Those things are down there!” Max cast a glance down the stairs.

“If they haven’t gotten to the floor we were on yet, we still have a chance,” said Nemo. “Once they get us in here, we don’t.”

Before Max could argue, she turned and started back down the stairs. Max gave the door one more hard shove, then kicked it angrily before following her. Going down was at least easier, but every step also brought them closer to whatever the Mogs had unleashed.

When they reached the floor they had started on, Nemo was first into the hallway. Max was right behind her, but ran into her when she came to a halt in the middle of the hallway.

“What?” Max said.

“We need to go back,” Nemo said. Her voice sounded strange.

“Back where?”

“Down,” said Nemo. “We have to go down. Now.”

Max looked around her. When he saw what was in front of them, his heart nearly stopped.

The creature was difficult to make out in the dim light, but what he could see was enough. It looked like a massive snake. Its lower body was coiled, and the top part rose up with three rows of appendages on either side, arms that ended in clawed hands. The body was topped with a grotesque head that could only be described as dragon-like. Its jaws were open, revealing long sharp teeth. Its eyes glittered a greenish yellow.

The thing roared.

Max wheeled around and ran back through the stairwell door. Nemo was right behind him. Their feet pounded on the stairs as they went down.

"I know this door is open," Nemo said breathlessly. "I came through it earlier."

They came to the door and Max went through with a sense of relief. Then his feet slipped on ice that covered the stairs. He slid down the rest of them and landed on the floor. Nemo was beside him a moment later, helping him up. He didn't have time to ask her what had happened there before the sound of the monster following them filled the air.

Nemo held his hand, steadying him as they ran down the ice-slicked hallway. When they came to the first open doorway they went inside. They were in a large room filled with various kinds of mechanical equipment, all of it encased in skins of ice.

Nemo walked around, looking for something, and Max noticed that she was limping. He also saw that she was leaving dark footprints on the ice.

"You cut yourself," he said.

Nemo looked down. "Great."

"What if those things can smell blood?" Max asked. "Or are smart enough to follow footprints?"

As if in answer, the now-familiar roaring came from behind them. Even more disturbing, it was answered by another roar, this one coming from somewhere else. The creature was calling a companion.

"Could this get any worse?" Max wailed.

A roar answered him as a creature rose up from behind one of the frozen machines.

"Apparently," Nemo said as the thing slithered over the machine, its claws snapping in the air.

Max and Nemo turned to run out of the room, only to find the doorway blocked by one of the other beasts. They stood back-to-back as the two creatures began to circle them. Somewhere in the hallway, the third roared its approach.

The eyes of the monstrous things glowed, as if finally cornering their prey excited them. Their mouths opened and closed as their scaly snake bodies scraped across the ice in the frozen room, filling the air with a sound like rustling leaves. Max felt the jar in Nemo's backpack pressing against him, and shuddered. There were horrible things everywhere.

One of the creatures suddenly darted towards them, its jaws open. Max lifted his hands and hit it with a blast of telekinetic energy. It was a weak attempt, but enough to startle the oncoming monster and stop it. It stayed where it was, rising up in the air and hissing.

"That's right!" Max shouted at it. "Get back!"

In answer, the thing struck at them again. This time Nemo and Max both held up their hands and blasted it. It fell back, then resisted and started coming at them again. The other monster began to roar, as if urging it on.

"You take that one!" Nemo shouted.

Max whirled, facing the beast. It was fewer than fifteen feet away, and its body was easily that long. If he couldn't hold it off, it would be on him in a matter of seconds. Max tried to focus his energy, imagining a wall of power between him and the thing.

"It's not working." Nemo gasped. She sounded exhausted.

"Keep trying!" Max said.

The beasts surged forward. Max pressed back against them. But his energy was faltering. The monster was getting closer and closer. He heard Nemo grunting as she attempted to keep the one she was fighting from reaching them. He wondered how much longer they could continue.

All of a sudden, a scream pierced the air, a roar of pain and agony. The two creatures in the room hesitated, turning their heads. There was another roar, then silence.

"What was that?" Max said.

"You need to speak to them in their language," a voice said.

Nine entered the room. He stood behind the monster that Max was facing. Now the thing turned its huge body and stared at him. Nine held up his hand. "Attack your friend over there," he said. "Kill him."

The snake thing turned and looked at its companion. It opened its mouth and roared. Spittle flew from the jaws.

"You two might want to get out of the way," Nine called out.

Max and Nemo didn't hesitate, scurrying away from the monsters as the one Nine had ordered to attack obeyed the command. They stood beside Nine and watched as the thing slithered forward and sank its teeth into the other creature's neck.

"I'm guessing they're poisonous," Nine said. "The one I told to bite itself died pretty quickly."

The two creatures were writhing around, their tails wrapped around each other and their claws ripping and tearing at one another. Thick, dark liquid spurted from the wounds, and where it touched the ice, steam rose up in acrid puffs. Max covered his nose.

"Let's go," Nine said. "I don't think breathing that is the best idea."

They left the monsters to finish their battle, walking down the outside corridor. Nine seemed to know where he was going, and Max followed eagerly, relieved both to be away from the horrible creatures and to see Nine.

"How did you get away from the thing in the lake?" Nemo asked, sounding as relieved as Max felt to see Nine alive.

"Easy," Nine said. "I tore its heart out. From the inside."

"Wait," Nemo said. "You mean it swallowed you?"

"Just for a minute," Nine said. "Watch out for the blood."

"What bloo—," Nemo said, the word cut off as they turned the corner and she sidestepped to avoid the thick puddle on the floor. One of the snake things lay dead in the hallway. Its teeth were embedded in its own tail.

Nine pushed past it, with Nemo and Max behind him. When Max's hand touched the scaly skin, he recoiled.

"Where are we going?" Nemo asked.

"Out," Nine said.

"Back through the lake?" said Max, suddenly very worried.

"No," Nine answered. "There's another way. A friend told me about it."

"What friend?" Nemo asked him.

Nine stopped and pointed. In the hallway ahead of them was another body. It was a Mog.

"Him," Nine said. "He had a lot of useful information, actually, including where everyone who was here has gone."

"Where's that?" Max asked.

"Later," Nine said, kneeling down beside the Mog. "You're going to have to help me carry him."

"He's not dead?" said Nemo.

"No, he's not dead," Nine answered. He sounded offended. "What kind of monster do you think I am?"

"I didn't mean—," Nemo began.

"I'm kidding," Nine interrupted. "I totally would have killed him. But he might have more information. Now, come on, before he wakes up."

Max and Nemo helped lift the Mog, taking his top half while Nine wrapped his one arm around the Mog's feet. Nine started walking, with the two of them struggling to keep up.

"I thought you said we weren't going back in the water," Nemo said as they headed towards the stairs that led to the air locks.

"We're not," Nine said. "Well, not exactly. We're not *swimming*."

"Then what *are* we doing?" Nemo pressed.

Nine stopped. He dropped the Mog's feet, then touched something on the wall. A panel slid open. Nine looked in. "Good," he said. "The Mog was telling the truth. Take a look."

Nemo and Max set their end of the Mog down and walked to the doorway. Peering inside, they saw a small room. In the center was a round metal ball about six feet in diameter. A single glass window was set into the side.

"What is it?" Max asked.

"That," Nine said, "is our way out. Now hurry up and get in. We have some friends to rescue."

THE LEGACY CHRONICLES

KILLING GIANTS

CHAPTER ONE

SIX
UNKNOWN LOCATION

SIX GLARED AT THE CLOSED DOOR. SHE HAD BEEN doing so for about fifteen minutes—ever since Eleni had dragged Sam out of the room—hoping to jump-start her telekinesis and force it open.

It hadn't worked.

Furious, she sat down on the cot that stood against one wall. Her head throbbed from the effort of trying to get her Legacies to cooperate. *Or maybe that thing Magdalena put inside you is crawling around doing its job*, she thought.

The idea that some kind of parasite was in her head, doing who knew what, made her even angrier. She'd been hoping that the Mog's story about implanting her and Sam and Max with some kind of parasites was a lie, something Magdalena had told her to throw her off. But given how her and Sam's

Legacies weren't cooperating, how weak Sam seemed and how easily Eleni had pushed her aside earlier and prevented her from helping Sam, when normally she would have been able to take the Mog out with a couple of hits, she now had to assume it was true. And that pissed her off.

Thinking about Max, she wondered how he was doing. She and Sam had been teleported from the bunker in Utah to a new location. But what about the others? Where were Max and Bats and Lava now? And the other kids who had attacked them back at the bunker? She wished she could get her hands on those delinquents. Especially that girl, Freakshow, the one who had used her fear-inducing Legacy to make Six relive one of the worst moments of her life. What she wouldn't give for a chance to repay her for that torture.

Pain ricocheted through Six's head. She pictured a rat, gnawing away at wiring, disrupting the electrical signals and causing lights to flicker on and off.

"I swear, if I had a knife I'd try to cut it out myself," she muttered, hitting the side of her head with her fist.

She winced as another jolt of pain throbbed through her, as if the thing inside her head could understand and was telling her she didn't have a chance against it. She lay down, closing her eyes and trying to calm herself. How much longer could the parasite keep doing what it was doing? Days? Or did she have only hours left? Was Magdalena going to remove it, or was the plan to let it kill her?

That was not going to happen. She was not going to allow herself to be a Mog experiment. If it came down to it, she really would try to get the parasite out herself. And if that didn't work, well, she'd die before she let the Mogs steal her Legacies.

She opened her eyes and stared up at the ceiling, trying to channel her anger in a purposeful way and figure out how to get herself out of the room. The door wouldn't open, and there were no windows. There wasn't even an air duct to try to get into. And any second now, she suspected, Eleni would come back for her.

Six didn't intend to be there when that happened.

Her gaze focused on the light fixture in the center of the ceiling. It was the only other thing in the room besides the cot she was lying on. Six concentrated on the wall switch that operated it, trying to make it turn on and off with her telekinesis. Again, nothing happened. She was going to have to find a way out of the room that didn't involve using a Legacy.

The image of the rat chewing on wires flashed in her head again, and an idea began to form. She got up and dragged the cot so that it was directly underneath the light. Standing on it, she was able to reach up and remove the glass globe that covered the two bulbs inside. She placed the globe on the floor, then got back up and examined the inside of the fixture. It was a basic light, nothing fancy, and it was easy enough to twist the base and remove it from the mounting pins, revealing the electrical wires that snaked out from the ceiling. There was a black one and a white one.

Six yanked the white wire out from where it connected

to the fixture. The bulbs in the fixture winked out as the circuit was broken. Now the room was dark except for a thin line of light that seeped in under the door from the hallway outside. But Six didn't need light for what she did next. She took hold of the black wire and pulled it free, being careful not to let it touch the bare end of the white wire.

Getting down, she picked up the glass cover, wrapped it in the thin blanket that had been on the cot, then smacked it against the floor. It shattered. She unwrapped the blanket and carefully examined the shards with her fingers. There were several large ones. These she took out and set aside. She shook the others out onto the floor, then tore several long strips from the blanket. Holding a couple of the biggest pieces of glass together, she wrapped one of the strips around them, forming a grip. She repeated this with a second strip so that she had a handle she could grasp without cutting herself.

Standing on the cot again, she found the black and white wires. "Here goes nothing," she said as she touched the exposed ends of the wires together. There was a loud pop and some sparks. Glancing at the door, she saw that there was no longer any light coming in.

Six let go of the wires and got down from the cot. Picking up her makeshift knife and what was left of the blanket, she positioned herself in the corner where she would be hidden from view if someone opened the door.

Then she waited.

A few seconds later, she heard voices in the hallway.

"Is it out everywhere?" a woman asked.

"I think so," someone answered.

"I'm sure it will be back on in a minute," a third voice, a man's, said. "Let's just stay put."

The voices retreated. Six heard doors opening and shutting. She reached out and tried the handle of the door to the room she was in, but it remained locked. She started to fear that maybe nothing was going to happen after all. But then she heard the sound of someone rattling the handle from the other side.

"The main panel sensor shows the short came from in here," a man's voice said.

The handle turned again. Then Six heard the sound of a key being inserted into the lock. She readied herself. She had no idea who might come through the door, whether they were Mog or human. Whoever they were, though, she wasn't going to wait and ask questions. A moment later, the door opened. A flashlight beam cut through the darkness. The pieces of glass on the floor sparkled.

"Whoa," said a second male voice. "What the hell happened in here?"

"Looks like the fixture fell somehow," said the first man. "Well, it's easy enough to fix. Come on."

The men stepped into the room, leaving the door open. As soon as they weren't blocking it, Six slipped out from behind the door.

"What the—" one of the men exclaimed, jumping back.

Six didn't stop to offer an explanation, pushing past the

men and darting out into the hallway. She saw a flashlight scan the hall behind her as she ran, but nobody followed her. Whoever the men were, they didn't seem to be interested in finding out who she was, which puzzled her. Had Magdalena just left her there without a guard? If they were in yet another Mog stronghold, why had the men come into the room so casually, as if they expected it to be empty?

She reached the end of the hall, which went off to both the left and right. As she stood there in the dark trying to decide which way to go, the lights came back on. All of a sudden, Six was looking at a giant poster depicting a woman who looked strangely familiar. Then she realized why—the woman resembled her. Not enough that anyone would confuse them, but enough that it was an obvious likeness.

The woman was standing with a group of other people, all of them dressed in what looked like black leather uniforms. Several of them had their hands raised, and they looked like they were holding glowing blue stones. At the top of the poster was written *CIRQUE DES ÉTOILES PRESENTS: BATTLE FOR EARTH.*

Six had no idea what this was. She scanned the poster, looking for more clues, but there were none. Now she was even more confused. If she wasn't in some kind of Mog facility, where the hell was she?

"Are you here for a fitting?"

Six whirled, the weapon in her hand held at her side and out of sight, at least for the moment. Looking at her was a young, slight woman with blond hair pulled into a ponytail.

She was holding a clipboard. She didn't seem at all shocked or worried to see Six running loose in the hallway.

"Sorry about the lights," the girl said. "Something went wrong with the electricity. But it's back on now." She laughed. "Obviously. Anyway, you're probably looking for the costuming room, right?" The girl's gaze moved past Six to the poster, and she laughed again. "You look a lot like Camilla," she said. "Are you her understudy? They said a new girl was coming in. I can't believe Lara left right before we open, but a lead on Broadway doesn't happen every day, right? Anyway, she'd probably never get a chance to go on. Camilla is never out." She put her hand to her mouth. "Sorry. I shouldn't have said that. I mean, maybe she'll let you play a matinee once the initial excitement wears off and the crowds slow down. Which will probably be never once people see how amazing this show is. I mean, wait until you see the monsters."

"Monsters?" Six said. She was getting more confused by the moment. She'd expected to encounter Eleni, some other Mogs or even humans who were working for them. But nobody seemed to find her presence there at all alarming.

The girl shook her head. "They're flipping fantastic. Bigger than anything we've ever had. People are going to lose their minds."

Nothing the girl said made any sense to Six. "Who are you?" she asked.

"Oh, sorry. I'm Allison, the assistant to the assistant to the assistant costuming coordinator."

"Okay," Six said, even though she still had no idea what

the girl was talking about. "Well, Allison, I need to make a call. Do you have a phone I could use?"

Allison shook her head. "We don't get reception down here. But there's a phone in the lobby."

"Lobby," Six repeated. "Now we're getting somewhere. If you could just show me how to get there, that would be great."

"Um, you had to walk through it to get down here," Allison said. "You just take the elevator back up."

"Thanks," Six said, and started to walk away.

"What about the fitting?" Allison asked.

Six was going to ignore the question. But then she thought about it. She still had no idea where, exactly, she was. It obviously wasn't a Mog base, but there had to be some reason why she and Sam had been brought here instead of to a more secure facility. She needed to call Nine and find Sam, but she didn't know where Sam might be and she had nothing to actually tell Nine at the moment. While she was anxious to be taking action, it might help if she took a few minutes to see what she could find out. Reluctantly, she turned around.

"Right," she said. "The fitting."

Allison beamed. "Come with me, and I'll get you set up."

Six followed Allison down the hallway.

"What other Cirque des Étoiles shows have you been in?" Allison asked.

"None," Six answered.

Allison looked shocked. "Wow. You must be really good. They usually only let people understudy the principal roles if they've done at least a couple of the touring shows. What's your primary skill set? No. Wait. Let me guess. If you're understudying for Camilla, it's probably aerial."

Six didn't know what that meant, but she nodded.

"Yes," Allison said. "I'm getting really good at guessing just by looking at people. I mean, some of them are obvious. Like, if you're under five feet tall, chances are you're a tumbler. And the clowns are always easy to spot, usually because they look sad. You're graceful and obviously really fit, so aerial makes sense."

They came to a door, which Allison opened. "Welcome to Wonderland," she said as they walked into a room bursting with color.

Everywhere Six looked there were costumes. And not ordinary costumes. These were covered in feathers and sequins, jewels and ribbons. Several people were trying on various things, while a team of people with scissors and tape measures swirled around them, pinning things and making alterations. Things were getting stranger and stranger, and making less and less sense.

Allison led Six over to where a group of three people were examining the bluish-purple scales on a bodysuit worn by a muscular man.

"He still looks too much like a dragon," one of the men said with a sigh. "We need less dragon and more terrifying space lizard. Or whatever. Just make it work."

"Devin," Allison said. "This is . . ." She looked at Six.

"Jess," Six said, pulling a name out of thin air.

"Jess is understudying Camilla," Allison said.

Devin turned, gave Six a sweeping glance from head to toe and back again and said, "Did you fall in a mud puddle?"

Six looked down at herself. She'd been through a lot over the past couple of days, and did look pretty awful. But that was the last thing on her mind at the moment.

"I, uh, kind of got caught in the rain," she fumbled.

Devin arched an eyebrow. "In Vegas?" he said. "It hasn't rained here in like three months. You look like you not only fell into the fountain at the Bellagio, but then rolled in the street afterwards."

"It's been a long couple of days," Six snapped.

"I'll just leave you two to get to know each other," Allison said briskly. "Good luck," she whispered as she passed by Six.

Devin walked around Six, making vague noises. When he came back to stand in front of her, he said, "You look more like her than Camilla does. She's not going to like that. And you have a better body. She *really* isn't going to like that."

"More like who?" said Six.

"Number Six," Devin said. "You know, the role you're understudying for? I know we don't call her that, but everyone knows that's who she's supposed to be."

"Six," said Six. What the hell was going on? she wondered. Then she remembered the poster in the hallway. "Right. Battle for Earth and all of that."

"Mmm," Devin murmured as he walked over to a rack of clothes. He selected some things and returned. "Here," he said, thrusting a pair of hangers at Six. "Try these on. I'll be back in a minute."

Six looked around. "Right here?" she said.

Devin rolled his eyes. "Dressing rooms are for *stars*," he said as he walked away.

Six moved to a corner of the room with fewer people in it, and undressed as quickly as she could. She pulled on the clothing that Devin had given her, which consisted of a pair of leather pants and a leather jacket. They fit Six almost perfectly. The pants also had a convenient pocket for stowing her homemade knife. She looked at herself in the mirror and was surprised to see that she looked great despite everything she'd been through.

"Oh yeah," Devin said, appearing behind her. "Camilla is going to *hate* you. Here. Put these on." He handed her a pair of leather boots.

Six pulled the boots on. They came up almost to the knee, sliding over the legs of the pants. With the costume on, she felt oddly powerful. Almost like her old self. *Maybe it was worth taking this little detour,* she thought.

"We just have to do something about that hair," Devin said. "The color is a little boring. Why don't you take that stuff off and then head down to hair and makeup. Tell Selena I said to make your hair Firefox."

"Firefox," Six said. "Got it."

"You can hang your costume on the rack," Devin said, leaving her alone.

"Or I could just wear it," Six said under her breath,

making sure he was out of sight before leaving the room still in her outfit.

She strode down the hall feeling more confident than she had fifteen minutes earlier. Sure, her Legacies continued to be on the fritz and there was a parasite in her head that wanted to eat her alive, but she did manage to get some information. Now she just had to figure out exactly where she was, find Sam, take care of the Mogs and get the hell out of there.

"First things first," she said as she came to an elevator and hit the button.

As she waited, she half expected Eleni or Magdalena to show up. But there was no sign of the Mogs anywhere, nor of anyone else who had been in the bunker with them. Wherever they were now, it obviously wasn't a Mog stronghold like the last place. They had to have some connection to it, but what? Six added that to the list of questions she had.

When the elevator arrived, Six got in. The rear of the car had another poster like the one she'd seen in the hallway. This one had an additional line of text, though: *EXCLUSIVE TO THE SATURN HOTEL*. Six noticed the same name etched into the metal panel above the buttons on the elevator wall. *Well, now at least I know where I am*, she thought as she hit the button marked L and the doors closed.

When they opened again, she stepped into the lobby. She paused a moment and looked around. The place was gorgeous. The ceiling soared thirty feet overhead, and was painted to look like outer space. Stars literally twinkled with tiny lights, forming recognizable constellations. Models of planets were suspended on invisible wires, seeming to float in the air. The floor of the lobby was made from black marble shot through with milky streaks of white, and as Six walked across it to the reception desk, she felt like she was walking across the sky.

"Welcome to the Saturn," a smiling young man said when she reached the desk. "I'm Mike. How can I be of service?"

"I need a phone," Six replied.

"Certainly," Mike said. "There's a courtesy phone right through there." He indicated a doorway to the right of the reception area.

Six thanked him and walked over to the alcove where a phone was attached to the wall. Picking it up, she dialed. Lexa picked up on the second ring.

"Hey, you'll never guess where I am."

CHAPTER TWO

MAX

POINT REYES, CALIFORNIA

"WHAT DO YOU MEAN, YOU'RE NOT GOING TO TAKE it out?"

Max stared at Nine. They were in the infirmary at the Human Garde Academy, where they had returned the previous night after escaping from the bunker in Utah using the bathysphere Nine had found. Ever since getting back, Max had been the focus of tests to figure out what was in his head. Scientists at the school had also been studying the creature that Nemo had brought in a jar. Max hadn't slept at all, and was exhausted. Now, finding out that they weren't going to remove the parasite that was inside him, he got even more frightened.

"Am I going to die?"

"No!" Nine said, coming and sitting on the edge of Max's

bed. "In fact, that's why they want to leave it in you. At least for now."

"I don't understand."

"Your body seems to be forming antibodies to the parasite," Nine explained. "It's fighting back on its own."

"Is that why I've been feeling better?" Max asked.

"Do something for me," Nine said. "Try to move the glass on your tray using your telekinesis."

Max looked at the tray sitting on the table beside his bed. It held the dishes left over from his breakfast. He focused his attention on the cup that a short time ago had been filled with orange juice. He pictured it flying across the room. Nothing happened. He lifted his hands and, feeling a little silly, pretended to push the glass while simultaneously trying to shove it with his mind. The glass moved a few inches, then toppled over.

"Well, that sucked," Max said glumly.

"Not at all," said Nine. "Last night, you couldn't do anything."

Max grinned. "True," he said. "So, they think I'm getting better?"

Nine nodded. "They think you're going to be fine. Even better, they think they can use your blood to make an antiserum that will help Six and Sam."

"Really?" Max said. "I guess that makes me a kind of superhero, huh?"

"You already were, bud," said Nine.

"Do we know where Six and Sam are?" Max asked.

"Not yet," said Nine. "But we're working on it."

"Actually, we do," said Lexa, walking in.

Nine and Max looked at her.

"Six called me," Lexa explained. "A couple of minutes ago."

"Where is she?" said Nine.

"Las Vegas," Lexa answered. "A place called the Saturn Hotel."

"Is she okay?" Max asked anxiously.

Lexa nodded. "She's fine. For now, anyway. But the Mogs took Sam somewhere else, and she doesn't know where yet. She's working on it."

"The Saturn Hotel," Nine said. "Why does that name sound familiar? Wait. Isn't that the place where they're doing that circus thing based on us?"

"Cirque des Étoiles," Lexa said. *"Battle for Earth."*

"That's it," said Nine. "They contacted me a while ago and asked if I wanted to be a special guest on opening night. Even offered me a free suite. I said no."

"Afraid they're going to get it all wrong?" said Lexa.

"Holding out for the penthouse," said Nine.

"Can we get back to Six and Sam?" Max said impatiently. "We're going to go help them, right?"

"Of course we are," said Nine.

Max started to get out of bed.

"Where do you think you're going?" Nine said, stopping him.

"You just said, we're going to go help them," said Max.

"Not so fast," Nine said. "First, Six is okay for now. Second, I told you, we need you to create an antiserum to that thing. That's going to take time."

"How long?"

"I don't know," said Nine. "But right now you need to stay here. Lexa and I have some planning to do."

"But—"

"I'll be back in a little while," Nine promised. "In the meantime, keep practicing your telekinesis. When I come back, I want to see you throw that thing across the room."

Nine and Lexa left, and Max leaned against the pillows. He stared at the glass. It moved a quarter of an inch. He lifted his hand and slapped it with the other hand.

"Did you just high-five yourself?" Nemo asked from the doorway.

"No," Max said, embarrassed. "Okay, yeah."

Nemo laughed. "You're something else," she said, walking over to the bed and sitting where Nine had been a moment before. "How are you feeling?"

"Good," Max said. "How about you?"

"Better," Nemo said. "I actually slept a couple of hours. It was nice to be in a real bed. But then I woke up and started thinking about everybody."

"Six and Sam?"

"Them," Nemo said. "But also Ghost and Lava and Bats. We don't know what happened to them. Or Seamus."

"Forget that guy," Max said angrily. "After everything he's done?"

"Yeah, I know," Nemo said. "Still. I saw his dad this morning. He looked upset."

Max grunted. He wasn't going to waste any time worrying about Seamus. But he was worried about the others. He'd been relieved to be out of the bunker, but he wondered if some of them were still trapped in there.

"They know where Six is," he told Nemo.

"I heard," Nemo said. "I ran into Nine and Lexa on my way up here. That's great. I also heard you've got magic blood."

"I'm a miracle of science," Max said.

"I'm really happy to not be carrying that thing around anymore," Nemo said. "I can't even imagine having one of those crawling around inside my head, eating pieces of my brain or sucking up my Legacies or whatever it is they do." She stopped talking and looked at Max, her eyes wide. "Sorry, I forgot you have one—"

"It's okay," Max said. "Anyway, I think it's dead, or at least it's not doing what it was doing anymore. I'm getting my telekinesis back. Watch."

He tried once again to move the glass. This time he succeeded in pushing it to the edge. He was concentrating on shoving it off and onto the floor, when a nurse appeared.

"Can I interrupt you for some blood?" he asked Max.

"More?" Max said. "How much do you need?"

"Only another gallon," the nurse said. "Maybe two."

Max groaned and held out his arm. "Just bleed me dry, leech man."

As the nurse tied the rubber tubing around Max's arm

and started looking for a vein he said, "Tell you what. After this, how'd you like to come down and see what we're doing with all this blood?"

Max shut his eyes and grimaced slightly as the nurse slid a needle into his arm. "Deal," he said.

Once the blood was drawn, Max got out of bed and he and Nemo followed the nurse out of the room, into the hall and into the elevator. This took them down to the level where the labs were. There they walked into an office filled with equipment. A woman was seated at one of the desks, looking at something through a microscope.

"Dr. Fenris," the nurse said. "This is Max and his friend Nemo."

The woman looked up. "What a pleasure," she said, standing and holding her hand out to Max. "I was just looking at your remarkable blood." She then shook Nemo's hand. "And thanks to you, we have a specimen of the parasite we're dealing with."

"Does Max's blood really kill it?" Nemo asked.

"Well, the antibodies his body produces in response to the parasite neutralize its effects," Dr. Fenris explained. "That in turn keeps it from feeding effectively on its host. So, yes, it will die. The important thing as far as we're concerned right now is that we think the antiserum we're working on will do the same to the parasite in another infected person." She looked at Max. "I understand some of your telekinesis has already returned."

Max nodded. "It's getting stronger and stronger," he said.

"That's excellent news," the doctor said.

"So, if we can get your antiserum to Six and Sam, they'll be back to normal?" Nemo asked.

"Hopefully," said Dr. Fenris. "Assuming the parasite hasn't developed too much."

"What do you mean?" Max asked her.

"The specimen Nemo brought back is a mature one," the doctor said. "The end-stage form. The one that was injected into you was microscopic. You didn't even know it was there. But once it gets as large as the one you retrieved from the bunker, it's likely too late to reverse the effects."

"How long does it take to get that big?" said Nemo.

"We don't know," the doctor admitted. "My guess is quite some time. Six and Sam have been infected for less than a week at this point, so I'm hopeful that the damage isn't irreversible. If we get the antidote into them soon."

"How soon?" asked Max.

"As soon as possible," said the doctor, without elaborating. But the expression on her face worried Max.

"Where did this thing come from, anyway?" Nemo asked. "Like, is it just out there in the world? Could it infect anyone with a Legacy?"

"I don't think so, no," said Dr. Fenris. "My guess is that it was created by the Mogs you had a run-in with. It's unlike any parasite I've ever seen before. Here. Take a look."

She beckoned them over to the microscope. Max leaned down, peering through the eyepiece. He saw something that looked like three big purple blobs. "What are those?"

"Those are the toxins created by the parasite," Dr. Fenris said. "Now watch what happens next."

She placed the tip of a thin pipette on the surface of the glass slide in the microscope. Max saw a thin stream of tiny red bubbles come out.

"What's that?" Max asked.

"Those are the antibodies from your blood," the doctor explained.

As if they sensed the antibodies, the toxins moved towards them, like monsters hunting their prey. Max felt his heartbeat quicken. For some reason, watching the toxins attack his blood terrified him. But then something interesting happened. The antibodies attacked, throwing themselves against the walls of the toxins until they broke through. Then they rushed in, filling up the purple blobs with red and consuming them.

"That's awesome," Max said, stepping aside so that Nemo could have a turn watching.

"That's science," Dr. Fenris said.

"So if Max's body can do this, why can't Six's and Sam's?" Nemo asked.

"Every body is different," Dr. Fenris said. "In medicine, we like to say that immune systems are built, not born. That means that your body develops defenses based on what it's exposed to over the course of your life. For some reason, Max's body has developed a way to fight the parasite. It could be because he was exposed to something similar in the past. Or his specific Legacy might have something to do with it, since his ability changes his brain function. Or his body could just be better at fighting invaders."

"In other words, you don't really know," said Nemo.

Dr. Fenris smiled. "The important thing is that it seems to work."

Listening to her talk, Max had a thought. "But it might *not* work in Sam and Six, then, right? I mean, if their bodies are different from mine."

"We're hopeful that it will," Dr. Fenris said.

The excitement that had been building in Max suddenly lessened. If the antiserum didn't work, that meant that Six and Sam would die.

"There's every reason to think it *will* work, Max," the doctor said, placing her hand on his shoulder.

Max nodded, but inside he was still worried.

"When will you take the thing out of Max's head?" Nemo asked.

"Soon," said Dr. Fenris. "If we take it out, his body might stop producing antibodies, and we need him to keep making those for now."

A dinging sound rang out, and Dr. Fenris pulled a phone from her pocket and looked at it. "Nine would like the two of you to come to his office," she said.

Max looked at Nemo. Something was up. "Let's go," he said.

When they arrived, they found Nine with Lexa, Dr. Goode and Peter McKenna. There was also a surprise visitor.

"Bats!" Max exclaimed when he saw the teen from Utah

sitting in a chair. She stood up, smiling, and Max went and hugged her. "How did you get here?"

"Nine sent a team to secure the bunker," Bats said. "They got me out. I just got here a little while ago."

Max's happiness evaporated. "I'm sorry we left you," he said. "Everything happened so quickly and I didn't know where you were."

"It's okay," Bats said, hugging him again. "I know. When everything went wrong, I found a place to hide and waited there until I thought it was safe to come out. Of course, I hadn't counted on Magdalena's little pets."

Max shuddered, remembering the dragon-like monsters that had chased him and Nemo through the halls of the bunker.

"The important thing is, she's here now," Nine said.

"What about Lava?" Max asked.

Bats shook her head. "I'm the only one who was left behind," she said. "As far as I know, anyway."

"Nobody else was in the bunker," Nine confirmed. "But we do know Six and Sam are in Vegas."

"We don't know that Sam is still there," Dr. Goode said, sounding concerned about his son. "The Mogs might have moved him again after separating him from Six."

"Until we have other information, let's assume he's there," Nine said. "Which is why we're going there."

"We?" Max said. "As in all of us?"

"Not *all* of us," Nine said. "But me and you and Nemo are."

"I thought I had to stay here," said Max.

"Do you *want* to stay here?" said Nine.

"No," Max said quickly. "I just thought you needed my blood here."

"And maybe we'll need it there, too," Nine said.

"I still don't like this," McKenna said tersely.

"I know you don't," Nine replied, giving him a dark look. "But you're not in charge here. I am."

"Why not call in Earth Garde to handle it?" McKenna suggested.

Nine sighed, as if this was a ridiculous suggestion. "Six is fine," he reminded McKenna. "And there are only a handful of Mogs left."

"Dangerous Mogs," McKenna said. "And they have Sam."

"They won't for long," Nine said. "I don't think calling in Earth Garde and making a big deal about this is going to help anyone. We can handle it."

Max glanced at McKenna. He looked exhausted. Max suspected the man was thinking about his son and what he'd done. Seamus had betrayed all of them, and that couldn't be sitting well with his father, particularly as he had kind of been Sam and Six's boss and had gotten them involved in all of this in the first place.

Nine nodded at Max and Nemo. "Go get ready," he said. "We leave in twenty minutes."

Max and Nemo hurried out. Once they were in the corridor, Max whispered, "Is it just me, or was it really tense in there?"

"Totally tense," Nemo said. "Something's up between Nine and Seamus's dad."

Max shook his head. "I wouldn't want to be Seamus right now," he said.

Nemo grunted in reply. Max knew she was as angry with their former friend as he was. He wondered what she would do if she came face-to-face with Seamus in Vegas. He wondered what *he* would do.

He had a feeling they were going to find out.

CHAPTER THREE

SAM
LAS VEGAS, NEVADA

ELENI WAS IN A RAGE.

Sam, seated on a chair with his wrists shackled to its back supports, watched as she stormed around the room she had dragged him to. Outside the windows he could see the sparkling lights of what he now realized was Las Vegas. The room he was in was very high up, and he had a sweeping view. He recognized a number of the hotel names that flashed in neon colors against the night sky, a number of the faces that appeared on billboards announcing concerts and shows.

He also knew that he was inside the Saturn Hotel. The hotel's logo was everywhere: on the stationery that sat on the nearby desk, on the pocket of the bathrobe that sat folded on the end of the bed, worked into the pattern of the wallpaper and carpet. He remembered reading about the building of the place in a travel magazine he'd looked at during a flight he and Six had taken from Paris to Venice. It was the Strip's newest, biggest and most opulent hotel. As he recalled it had only recently opened.

The question was, why was he there, and what connection did the Mogs have to it? They obviously had one, as Eleni knew her way around the place and had used an elevator clearly meant for internal staff to get him up to the room unnoticed. But why were they even in a hotel at all? Why not someplace more secretive and secure? It didn't make any sense to him.

Not that that was his primary concern at the moment. The thing in his head was. Whatever it was doing, it was getting worse. His whole body hurt, and he knew he was getting weaker. He'd of course tried to use his Legacies to help in some way—any way—and nothing was working. Not his telekinesis. Not his technopathy. He couldn't so much as change the channel on the enormous television that was mounted to the wall.

"Why are you not here yet?" Eleni shouted into the phone in her hand. She was pacing back and forth in front of the window, one hand on her hip. This was the third time she'd called the person, and the tone of her voice had grown increasingly impatient with each conversation.

The door to the room suddenly opened and in walked Magdalena, also on the phone. "I'm here now," she said.

Eleni practically threw her phone down on the bed. "What took you so long?"

"There was a lot to get ready for the—" Magdalena began, then looked at Sam. "For tonight."

Eleni grunted impatiently. "Well, now you can play babysitter with this human. I need to see to the other one."

"You left her alone?" Magdalena said.

"Did I have a choice?" Eleni snapped. "Besides, she's weak from that thing you put into her. She can't do anything. I'll go get her and be back in ten minutes." She left the room, slamming the door behind her.

"She's so dramatic," Magdalena said, sitting on the bed and looking at Sam. "She could have left you here by yourself for a few minutes. It's not like you'd be able to use your powers or anything, right?"

Sam didn't respond. Magdalena made a pouty face. "Don't be mad at me," she said. "I promise, I'll take my little pet out of you soon enough."

Hearing this, Sam felt fear stir inside of him. If he was right about how the parasite worked, taking it out meant that he would probably die. But if Magdalena was trying to provoke a response from him, he wasn't going to give her one. Instead, he stared out the window.

Magdalena patted a small bag that she had carried in with her. "Anyway, Eleni should be happy. I brought her a surprise. If you swear not to spoil it, I'll tell you what it is. Do you promise?"

Sam still didn't respond. The Mog was irritating him. What he wanted to do was blast her across the room with his telekinesis. Instead, he could only try his best to ignore her. But she wasn't going to make that easy. She stood up and walked into his line of vision, waving at him as if she had just spotted him and was delighted to see him there.

"I'll tell you anyway," she said as he turned his head and looked at the wall. "It's a new batch of serum. I harvested one of the creatures."

Sam couldn't help himself. "Harvested it from who?" he said.

Magdalena clapped her hands. "Oh, you *are* interested!" she said. "Don't worry. It was no one you know. At least I don't think so. Just some human boy with a pyro Legacy. We have a *lot* of those, so he wasn't anything special."

"He was a person," Sam snarled.

Magdalena rolled her eyes. "Yeah, well, and a hamburger is a cow before it's a meal. I don't see you getting all upset about that."

"You killed someone," Sam said. "For your experiment."

Magdalena sighed. "You know, I haven't brought this up before because I thought maybe we could be friends. But your people killed a whole lot of mine not that long ago. You might have killed a couple yourself, am I right?"

Sam shook his head. "You invaded our planet," he said. "It was war."

"This is why I hate discussing politics," Magdalena replied. "Nobody ever wants to consider the other side. They *say* they do, but they really don't."

"You're crazy," Sam said.

"Or maybe I'm a genius," Magdalena said. "See, there you

go again, only seeing things your way."

Before Sam could say anything else, the door opened again and Eleni stormed in, looking even angrier than she had when she'd left. "She's gone," she said.

"Who's gone?" Magdalena said.

Eleni didn't answer, but Sam knew exactly who she meant. Six had escaped. Magdalena too must have realized what Eleni was saying. "Well, she must be here somewhere."

"Of course she's here somewhere!" Eleni thundered. "And she's probably contacted help."

Magdalena looked at her watch. "The show starts in half an hour," she said. "And she has no idea what we're planning."

"That's more than enough time to cause trouble," said Eleni.

"You worry too much," Magdalena told her. "Like you said, she's weakened. Her Legacies are all but gone."

"And yet she still managed to escape," said Eleni.

Sam laughed despite himself. Eleni walked over and slapped him hard across the face. Sam laughed again, knowing it would anger her. It did. Once more her hand crashed into his cheek with the force of a freight train. His head rocked to the side, and he tasted blood. He looked up at Eleni. Her face was a maelstrom of emotions, none of them pleasant.

"She'll find you," Sam said in a clear voice. "She'll find you, and she'll kill you."

Eleni went to strike him again, but Magdalena caught her

arm. "I have something for you," she said. She held up a vial.

"What is it?" Eleni asked.

"Serum," said Magdalena. "A new batch."

The hint of a smile appeared on Eleni's face. "And it's ready?"

Magdalena nodded.

"Give it to me," Eleni said. "Now."

"Before the show has started?" Magdalena asked.

"What better time is there?" said Eleni.

As Eleni rolled up one sleeve, Magdalena retrieved a syringe from the bag on the bed. She uncapped it, inserted the needle into the vial of serum and drew some out. Eleni presented her arm, and Magdalena deftly slid the needle into a vein. As she depressed the plunger on the syringe, Eleni closed her eyes.

"It burns," she said dreamily. "I can feel it."

Sam watched with interest to see what would happen. He thought about the last time he'd seen someone attempt to create Legacies artificially. It was when the drug lord Bray had done it. That had ended with his gruesome death. Was Eleni about to suffer the same fate?

He watched for signs that she was reacting badly to the serum. But none came. Instead, she took several deep breaths and opened her eyes. "Something has changed," she said. "What was the power of the person this came from?"

"Fire manipulation," Magdalena said. "But that doesn't necessarily mean—"

Eleni raised her hands, and Magdalena stopped talking.

Eleni focused on the space between her palms. A moment later, a spark crackled and disappeared. Eleni tried again, and this time a small ball of flame formed. It remained intact, no larger than a gumball. Eleni grinned, and it flickered out.

"It works," Magdalena said breathlessly.

Eleni conjured the fire again. This time, the ball grew in size and strength. The Mog moved it back and forth between her palms, like a child playing with a ball. "It doesn't burn my skin," she said. "I feel its warmth, but I am not hurt."

"Careful," Magdalena said. "You don't want to set off the sprinklers, or start a fire."

"Not yet, anyway," said Eleni, making the fireball wink out, and they both laughed. Then Eleni looked at Sam and smirked. "Now I am like you," she said. "Or like you once were."

"We'll see," Sam said.

"Yes," said Eleni. "We will. Speaking of seeing, I believe it's almost time." She picked up a remote that was sitting on a nearby table and used it to turn on the television. On the screen, a male news reporter was standing outside the entrance to the Saturn Hotel, where a limousine was disgorging its passengers, a trio of gorgeous young women all dressed in glamorous outfits. Sam recognized the three immediately. They were sisters from a popular reality television series.

The girls, seeing a camera, immediately gravitated to it, flashing dazzling smiles and posing. The reporter, fawning, said, "We're here at the stunning Saturn Hotel for the grand opening of Cirque des Étoiles's latest extravaganza. Ladies, are you looking forward to the show?"

They nodded and beamed. One of the them said, "I *adore* the circus."

"Except for clowns," another of them added. "There are no clowns in this one, are there?"

The reporter laughed as if she'd said the funniest thing he'd ever heard. "I don't think there are clowns," he said. "But I hear the show is chock-full of surprises. And it's starting in just a little while, so you'd better get inside."

The sisters walked off, and the reporter turned to the at-home audience. "We can't take you inside tonight's premiere," he said, frowning sadly. "No cameras allowed. The only way you're going to see what takes place inside the Saturn Hotel arena is if you've got one of these." He held up a metallic silver ticket and waved it around. "Which I do! So I'm going to head inside and I'll report back later tonight. This is Trek Masters for KVAS, and I'll talk at you later."

"He's wrong about one thing," Eleni said. "You don't need a ticket to see the show. At least not if you're in one of the VIP suites." She changed the channel, and the picture on the TV switched to a scene of an arena, presumably the one attached to the Saturn Hotel. A stage was set up in the center, with seats all around it. A dark blue curtain patterned with stars and planets surrounded the stage, hiding it from view.

"Is everything in place?" Eleni asked Magdalena.

Magdalena took out her phone and tapped on it. "Everything's ready," she confirmed. "The trucks are in position."

"And the cargo?"

Magdalena grinned. "Hungry," she said.

"I'm going down there now," Eleni said. She reached into her pocket and pulled out a silver foil ticket like the one the reporter had shown. "I want to be there in person when those stupid women see what's coming for them."

She exited the room, leaving the television on. Magdalena sat down on the bed and continued to text on her phone as Sam watched the feed from inside the hotel's arena. Questions swirled around in his head, and when he couldn't stand hearing them buzzing in his brain any longer he said, "What is it you're doing?"

"Finally," Magdalena said, putting her phone down. "I can't believe you waited so long to ask."

She walked over to the desk and picked something up. Coming back over to Sam, she held a brochure out so that he could see it. "'Cirque des Étoiles presents the Battle for Earth,'" he read. "'A celebration of human triumph.' That's the show they're doing. I get it. But what does that have to do with you?"

"Everything," Magdalena said. "How do you think it feels seeing the worst moment in your people's history turned into a spectacle to entertain audiences? Especially so soon after it occurred."

Sam looked at the arena filled with people. "It's no different than having a parade," he said. "Like the Fourth of July."

"It's very different," Magdalena said. "But since you're on the so-called winning side, I don't imagine you can really understand."

"So much for wanting to be friends," Sam said.

"I didn't say I blame you," Magdalena told him. "I understand it was a war. And in every war there's a winner and loser. I also know what part you and your friends played in that fight. Everybody does, of course." She paused and looked at the TV. "But maybe the war isn't quite over yet."

"What do you mean?" Sam asked. "What's this about?"

"Haven't you wondered why you're here?" Magdalena said, indicating the hotel room. "And not somewhere more, you know, not here?"

Sam of course had been wondering that very thing, so didn't bother answering.

"This is what it's all been leading up to," Magdalena said.

This Sam didn't understand. "All what?"

"Everything," said Magdalena. "The drugs. The experiments. The camps for the runaway kids. All of it." She waited for a reaction, then said, "You still don't get it, do you?"

"Maybe your parasite ate the part of my brain that figures out riddles," Sam said.

Magdalena rolled her eyes like a bored teenager. "It's all part of 'the plan,'" she said, making air quotes around the final two words. "First, we got humans hooked on that drug that makes them think they have Legacies. Honestly, that was mostly just for fun, but it had the added bonus of making people suspicious of Legacies themselves, and particularly of the people who have them. You know, because people started hurting themselves trying to be like you. That's bad PR. Then we figured out how to make a serum to actually give *us* Legacies. I think it's obvious why we would do that. And tonight, well, tonight we're going to remind humans why it is they should fear us."

"How?" said Sam.

In the arena, the lights went dark. The crowd murmured excitedly.

"Shh," Magdalena said. "It's beginning."

All Sam could do was watch and listen. After a moment, the curtain surrounding the arena stage fell. The audience gasped as a giant spaceship was revealed, suspended in the air and all lit up with blue and purple lights. Fog swirled around it, and projections of comets flew by, making it look as if the ship was flying through space.

"They came from the darkest reaches of the universe," a woman's voice intoned. "Looking for revenge."

Ominous music filled the air, throbbing with bass that sounded like engines pulsing. The spaceship moved, turning from side to side on hidden hydraulics.

"Our planet had no warning of what was about to befall us," the voice continued. "They arrived in darkness."

Magdalena sighed. "That's a little dramatic," she said. "Space is dark, after all."

The spaceship descended to the stage. Then it split open, the two halves pulling apart. A dozen costumed characters emerged, their faces painted in reds and yellows, their bodies covered in what looked like iridescent scales.

"Well, that's just insulting," Magdalena said. "They made us look like devils."

Sam watched as the performers moved through a complicated choreography that involved tumbling and leaping. The movements were jerky, violent, primitive. They were accompanied by flashes of red and yellow lights and the sound of beating drums.

"They did not come alone," the narrator's voice said.

"Okay," Magdalena said. "Pay attention. This is the good part."

"They brought with them monsters," said the voice. "Creatures made to hunt and kill."

The spaceship transformed again, this time breaking into pieces as something else rose from beneath the stage. It was an egg, massive and pulsing with greenish-yellow light. The performers representing the Mogs swirled around it, almost as if they were worshipping it. They held out their hands to it. Then cracks appeared in the surface and the light inside shot out in thin beams.

Sam looked over at Magdalena. Her face was bathed in the glow from the television. Her eyes were wide, and a smile played at the corners of her mouth. She held her hands clasped in front of her as she stared at the screen. For some reason, Sam found himself frightened.

The egg broke open, revealing a huge creature inside of it. Easily twenty feet tall, it resembled a prehistoric lizard, with a spiked tail and armored hide. Its eyes glowed with yellow light. When it opened its mouth, it revealed wickedly pointed teeth.

"It's like a piken," Sam said, an involuntary shudder rippling through him.

"Only bigger," Magdalena said. "Faster. And meaner."

The creature opened its mouth and let out a ferocious screech. That was when Sam noticed something peculiar. The actors were all looking at one another and backing away. Some pointed at the beast standing on the stage, then turned and fled.

"What's going on?" Sam said. "Why would they be afraid? They're acting like it's—"

Magdalena turned to him, grinning. "Real," she said.

CHAPTER FOUR

SIX
LAS VEGAS, NEVADA

"WHAT THE HELL?"

Six stood beneath the massive stage, looking up through the opening the performers used to make their way on and off. Now many of them were pushing their way inside. From the arena came the sounds of people screaming.

After phoning Lexa, she had looked for Sam, but found no clues to his whereabouts, so since her Legacies were still not working and she was feeling worse and worse, Six had decided to wait for Nine to arrive with backup. In the meantime, she had used her resemblance to the understudy for the show to look around. She knew there was some reason the Mogs had brought her and Sam to the hotel instead of to some more secure location, and she had a feeling it had something to do with the show that was being put on. Once inside the floors that housed the Cirque des Étoiles performers, it had been easy enough to remain out of sight for a couple of hours. Nearly everyone was dressed in strange costumes, and she was one of the least interesting people walking around. Several times she had been pegged as Camilla's understudy, but she had always made an excuse that she was needed somewhere else, and had managed to avoid participating in the show.

"Get out of the way!" a woman screamed as she pushed past Six, nearly knocking her down in her rush.

Six glanced at the monitors that showed what was happening onstage and in the arena. She'd seen the giant egg crack open to reveal a monster. Almost immediately, a stagehand next to her had said, "That's not what's supposed to be inside there."

Six's mind raced as she evaluated the situation. She knew the thing terrorizing the arena was something the Mogs were responsible for. What it was, exactly, she didn't have a clue. That didn't really matter, though. It had to be stopped.

But how? She had no Legacies to use against it. No weapons apart from her makeshift knife.

And yet she was still probably the only person in the place qualified to try.

"You!"

Six turned. That assistant, Allison, was standing behind her with a clipboard in one hand.

"You are *not* Camilla's understudy," she said firmly.

"I'm not sure that's important at the moment," Six said as a roar pierced the air.

"That costume is Cirque property."

"Again, maybe not the real issue here," said Six. "What are you doing about *that*?" She pointed to the stage.

"Not my problem," Allison said. "Security can handle it."

Six stared at her. The woman's presence of mind was impressive, but she didn't seem to understand that what was going on above them was more than a technical glitch. But then she realized that Allison had completely shut down. She was staring at the monitor with a blank-eyed expression. The clipboard in her hand trembled.

"Stay here," Six said. "Don't move. I'll be back."

She ran up the steps and onto the stage. It was a disaster area. The massive sets had been smashed into pieces. The few performers left were wandering around, dazed and bloodied. Six saw two bodies lying motionless amid the clutter of the broken scenery.

The monster had turned its attention to the arena filled with spectators. It had left the stage and was rampaging through the rows of seats, tearing at them with its claws. Because the audience had at first believed the creature to be part of the show, most had not gotten up and run away until it had leaped onto the arena floor and begun its assault. By then it had been too late for some of them.

Now they pushed and clawed at one another in their race for the exits. Six watched as the monster knocked half a dozen of them aside with one sweep of its claw. A small blond woman swatted at it with her designer handbag, and the beast struck her down with its tail. Two other women ran to her aid, trying to pull her to her feet. The creature roared at them, sending them screaming away in terror.

Six knew she had to do something. She was exhausted and growing weaker, but she was still a Garde, and she still had plenty of fight left in her.

She ran to the edge of the stage and jumped off, running towards the monster. It was heading for one of the exits.

When Six caught up with the thing, she leaped up onto its tail and climbed the ridge of its back. Sensing her presence, the beast stopped and tried to shake her off. But Six dug her fingers in between the scales that covered its massive body, lying flat against the thick plates and holding on as the monster attempted to dislodge her.

When it couldn't shake her off, the monster decided to keep going. It headed for a doorway. Now several security guards had appeared, pointing pistols at the creature. Six heard the sound of shots. But the bullets did no damage, burying themselves in the heavy scales. The beast lumbered forward with barely a pause, crushing one guard beneath its feet and sending the other two scrambling to get out of its way. It pushed its head through the doorway; then with its massive shoulders tore a hole in the wall large enough to fit through. Six felt plaster and pieces of wood fall around her as she was carried out on the monster's back.

The creature made its way inside the long tunnel that connected the arena to the hotel. It moved rapidly on all fours, its back nearly brushing the ceiling. Every so often it let out a piercing cry, as if it was calling to someone. Then Six heard an answering cry, and her heart froze. There was more than one.

She continued to move along the beast's back, working her way up to its head and what she hoped was the most vulnerable part of its body, the eyes. The thing seemed to have forgotten she was there, and she hoped she could still catch it off guard and stop it—or at least slow it down—before it remembered her.

She reached the head and, holding on to the scales just behind the neck with her left hand, she used her right to draw out the knife she had fashioned from the shard of broken glass. She was inching forward, searching for a good angle from which to attack, when she heard the roar of the other creature. It was closer. The beast she was on paused, listening, and echoed it. Then it began tearing at the wall of the tunnel, making a hole. It was going outside.

Six couldn't wait. Lifting the knife, she brought it down in the direction of the monster's eye. She felt it connect with something, pause and then keep going. Warm fluid covered her hand. The creature screamed in pain and shook its head. Six felt herself slipping off, and let go of the knife so that she could push both hands into the scales and try to hang on.

The beast reared up, its head hitting the roof of the tunnel. It continued to thrash back and forth. Six was dangerously close to being crushed against the ceiling. She clung to the monster as best she could, but she felt her strength ebbing away with the effort. She made an attempt to claw her way to the head and retrieve her knife, but it would be impossible to move without being thrown off.

Then she heard the sound of something tearing at the wall beside her. A section of the tunnel tore away, and she saw a second monster looking in. Sitting on its back was Eleni. When the Mog saw her, she snarled. Then she raised her hand. Six saw a ball of fire appear. Then it flew at her like a small comet, a burning tail stretched out behind it.

Six rolled away, and the ball of flame struck the side of the monster she was on. Its scales seemed to protect it from the worst of the heat, yet it shied away and gave an irritated shriek. Then a second one came, and a third. The last one struck Six in the shoulder. Searing pain bit into her as it ate through the leather of her costume and licked at her skin, and she cried out. Her grip faltered, and she felt herself falling. She scrabbled at the creature's scales, trying to hang on.

The monster Eleni was riding pushed its way in, nosing the first one out of the way. From her position astride its back, Eleni looked at Six, clinging to the other creature, and smiled cruelly.

"Magdalena has outdone herself, don't you think?" she said, lifting her hand and showing Six the fireball that was swirling there.

So, Six thought, they had succeeded in giving Eleni a Legacy after all. Meanwhile, she had none to fight back with. Six's stomach burned with fury and pain as she slowly pulled herself up the back of her monster. Eleni watched, obviously amused.

"It seems unfair to kill you when you have no way of defending yourself," the Mog said. "Plus, Magdalena needs you alive to harvest the parasite inside of you so she can give your Legacies to me." She cocked her head. "But that doesn't mean I can't hurt you a little."

She hurled another fireball at Six. Drawing on the last of her strength, Six dug her fingertips into the scales of the creature's back and dragged herself up to its shoulder. Her burned arm screaming in agony, she grabbed for the end of her knife, still embedded in the beast's eye, and jerked it to the side.

The monster whirled, turning to face Eleni as it sought to wrench the knife free. Six pulled back on the hilt, treating it like a steering mechanism and using the pain it inflicted to make the beast go where she wanted it to. She gave it another pull and the creature turned again, then started moving quickly back to the arena.

Eleni gave chase, following Six as her monster reentered the arena and headed towards the stage. Six still didn't know what she was going to do, but she felt better not being trapped in the tunnel. Here there was more space, more options.

Eleni was attempting to hit Six with fireballs, but she succeeded only in striking the monster, annoying it and causing it to run more quickly. Several of her throws struck the debris scattered over the floor, starting small fires that immediately began to spread. This seemed to confuse and frighten the creatures, who darted away from the flames.

When her beast neared the stage, Six jumped. She landed on her feet, rolling to get out of the way as the creature, now enraged from the pain and its fear of the fire, turned its head and tried to bite her with a mouth full of sharp teeth. Six wished she'd been able to pull the knife from its eye, as she now had no weapon at all.

Then she spied something on the floor. It was one of the staffs that had been part of the costumes for the show. About six feet long, it was made of metal and had been intended for use during one of the acts in which six acrobats performed stunts using the poles to launch themselves into the air. Six picked it up.

Her injured shoulder burned, but she fought the pain as she crouched, gauging the distance between Eleni and herself. The Mog was urging her monster forward, screaming at it in her language. Fireballs shot from her hand as quickly as she could form them. Six swatted them away with the staff, shattering them into bursts of sparks.

She swayed on her feet, suddenly too exhausted to move. As if sensing her weakness, the parasite in her head seemed to grow stronger. She felt her thoughts begin to break apart, and she had trouble concentrating on what she needed to do. It felt like the best idea in the world to just give up, to set down the staff and let Eleni run her over.

Then she pictured Sam's face. She wasn't going to give up a chance to see him again. Not for a Mog. Not for anyone.

And she was damn sure going to take Eleni out first.

Six reached deep, pushing down through the pain in her head, in her shoulder, in the rest of her body. She crouched, looking Eleni right in the eyes. Then she sprinted. Her legs pumped with the last of the strength in her. She held the steel staff out. When she was a dozen feet from Eleni and the charging monster, she planted the pole and swung herself up and into the air.

The monster opened its jaws to catch her, but she sailed past it and connected with the Mog. Her feet hit Eleni in the chest, knocking her backwards. Eleni fell, landing on the arena floor. Six fell beside her, the wind knocked out of her.

Neither of them moved for a moment. Then Eleni was on her feet. She called to the retreating monster, which turned and came towards them. Then she brought her attention back to Six and kicked her in the side. Six grabbed the Mog's leg and pulled, throwing Eleni off-balance. Eleni stumbled and fell again. Six rolled on top of her, pinning her down. She gripped Eleni's wrists and held her arms down.

"Try to make a fireball now," she said.

Eleni thrust her hips up, trying to throw Six off. Six dug her knees into the Mog's sides as hard as she could. She leaned forward, using her weight to press Eleni into the floor.

"You'll have to try harder than that," Six said.

Eleni turned her head and shouted something to the approaching beast. It opened its mouth and screeched.

"If it runs over us, it'll kill you, too," Six said.

"Then we die together," said Eleni.

The enormous creature was bearing down on them. Six stared into Eleni's face, deciding what to do. She knew she was too weak to fight her much longer, especially now that the Mog had a Legacy. If she was going to die anyway, maybe it was better to do it taking Eleni with her. At least then there would be one less thing for Nine and the others to worry about when they showed up.

She could feel Eleni struggling to throw her off. The Mog was scared. This made Six even more determined not to let her up. *Let her feel what it's like to stare death down,* she thought.

The monster was almost on them. Six could feel each thunderous step it took. The smoke from the growing fires stung her eyes, and the heat was increasing around them.

When there were just seconds left, Eleni screamed and tried one last time to get out from under Six and save herself. Six almost relented. Then she felt a powerful push, like a great gust of wind. Smoke and flames streaked around her. The charging beast was shoved sideways, rolling over on itself with a grunt of surprise, its limbs flailing. Caught up in the blast of air, Six was tugged from atop the Mog and pulled along the floor.

When she came to a stop, she was on her back. She sat up, looking for the source of the force. The monster still lay on its side, unmoving but bellowing in pain. Six realized then that one of the metal staffs was sticking out of its chest. She looked for the second creature, but couldn't see much through the smoke and flames. She also couldn't see where

Eleni was. She had disappeared.

Then a figure emerged from the inferno.

"I see you got some new pets," Nine said.

"They followed me home," Six said. "Can we keep them?"

"Okay," said Nine, kneeling down beside her. "But you're responsible for their litter boxes."

Six laughed. It hurt. She coughed.

"I thought you told Lexa you were fine," said Nine.

"I didn't want you to worry," Six said. She tried to turn her head. "Where's the Mog?"

Nine looked around. "Gone," he said. "Probably ran off when she saw me coming."

"Don't flatter yourself," Six said, coughing again.

"We need to get you out of here," Nine said, sliding his hands under her and lifting her up.

"You don't have to carry me," Six said. "I can walk."

But she couldn't. Now that she was no longer alone, her body finally demanded rest. She gave in, closing her eyes and letting exhaustion sweep over her. All her worries—Eleni, the monsters, Sam, the parasite—retreated as she shut down. It felt as if she was falling into thick blackness. She surrendered, her head falling against Nine's chest, and the world went dark.

CHAPTER FIVE

NEMO

LAS VEGAS, NEVADA

NEMO HEARD THE FLIES BEFORE SHE SAW THEM.

She and Max were standing in the lobby of the Saturn Hotel, where Nine had told them to wait while he investigated what was happening in the tunnel connecting the hotel to the adjacent arena. Judging from the throngs of panicked people running through the lobby from that direction, Nemo guessed that whatever it was, it was bad. Several people had stumbled through covered in blood, and she'd heard the word "monster" used more than a few times.

The hotel staff didn't seem to know what to do. A couple of security guards had come through, heading in the direction of the screaming, but hadn't returned. The desk clerks were huddled behind the counter, looking at one another with dazed expressions as frenzied guests demanded answers.

"Looks like we got here just at the right time," Nemo remarked.

"Or the wrong one," said Max. "Do you hear those roars?"

Of course Nemo heard them. They seemed a lot like the roars of the monsters Magdalena had let loose in the bunker. Nemo had no doubt these sounds were coming from something even worse. Part of her wanted to go see for herself, but another part—she liked to think it was the more cautious part, and not the more fearful part—told her to stay where she was and wait for Nine to come back.

That's when the buzzing became impossible to ignore. At first, she had thought the sound had something to do with all the commotion in the tunnel. Now she realized that it was coming from inside the hotel. And it was getting louder.

"What is that?" she asked, looking around.

The elevator doors at one end of the lobby opened and the swarm blasted into the room, a black cloud that seemed to explode, filling the air with the incessant hum of wings. Walking out of the elevator after the flies was Seamus. He strode into the lobby with his hands held up, magician-like, an expression of sadistic joy on his face as he watched people trying to swat away the insects he'd called together to form his army.

When he saw Nemo and Max standing there, his expression changed. He scowled. Then he moved his hands, pointing them at his former friends. The flies coalesced into a smaller ball and barreled towards Nemo and Max like a cannonball. Instinctively, Max and Nemo raised their hands and formed a telekinetic barrier. The flies struck it, many of them falling to the floor dead. The rest broke apart, swirling off to regroup under Seamus's orders.

"I'm getting better at this," Max said, grinning.

Seamus attacked again, this time forcing the flies to make several different balls. Nemo and Max turned in circles, trying to deflect all of them, but there were too many to fight simultaneously. Within seconds Nemo found herself at the center of a buzzing cyclone, with flies crawling over her face. Their tiny wings and legs scratched at her lips and eyes. She swatted at them, feeling them crush beneath her fingers. The sensation was almost worse than the actual attack, and yet the awfulness of it was enough to make her want to run from the hotel.

Which was exactly what Seamus wanted. Only when Nemo was able to get close to the lobby doors could she see that something worse awaited her if she left, as many of the guests had discovered. Outside, the real monsters were waiting. Three huge dinosaur-like creatures were in the street in front of the Saturn Hotel. People who had run out there trying to get away from one horror were now confronted with a worse one, as the things were blocking their escape. Dozens of people stood in frightened knots as the monsters circled them, seeming to herd them.

Nemo didn't know what to do. Wiping more flies away from her eyes, she turned back to see what Max was doing. Seconds later, the flies lifted away from her face and disappeared. Nemo shuddered, wiping the few remaining ones off her. She didn't know why the flies had given up, but she was relieved that they had. She scanned the lobby, looking for Max.

She spied him on the floor, on top of Seamus. They were fighting. Max appeared to have the upper hand, as he was straddling Seamus's chest and punching him in the face. Seamus was blocking the blows with his hands and attempting to throw Max off. At first Nemo wondered why Max had resorted to fighting Seamus physically. Then she realized that the surprise and distraction were likely what had stopped Seamus from using his insect telepathy, at least temporarily.

She ran over to where the boys were fighting, determined to help Max subdue Seamus. But before she could get there, something hit the ground nearby and exploded, startling her. She stopped and looked around. On the other side of the lobby, near the check-in desk, stood one of the boys she'd encountered in Utah. Boomer. He was dressed in the same black clothes, and watched her with the same peculiar expression of disinterest that she remembered from before.

Boomer picked something up from the counter, a glass paperweight shaped like the planet Saturn. Hefting it in his hand, he held it out in front of him as it began to glow, first a pale yellow and then a fiery orange. He had turned it into an explosive device.

He threw it. But this time Nemo was ready. She reached out with her telepathy, grabbing the orb and hurling it back at Boomer. His expression changed from one of bored indifference to one of fear as he saw his own missile coming at him. Just in time, he ducked, and it hit the wall behind him, exploding in a shower of sparks that sent Boomer falling to the ground, his arms over his head.

Nemo used the distraction to cover the distance between her and the boys. The momentum of that skirmish had changed. Seamus, bigger than Max, had managed to get out from underneath him. Now they were grappling like wrestlers, Seamus's arms around Max's middle. Then Max threw his head back, slamming it into Seamus's nose. Blood spurted and Seamus let go, bringing his hands to his face and swearing forcefully.

Max whirled around and kicked Seamus in the stomach, pushing him backwards so that he fell down. He advanced on Seamus, fists raised. Nemo had never seen his stony face before. He was seriously angry, and wasn't going to back down.

Blood soaked the front of Seamus's shirt as he prepared to meet Max. Nemo saw him ball his hands into fists, and when the sound of buzzing increased, she knew he was going to try once more to use his Legacy against them.

At the same time, another glowing item struck the floor by Max's feet. He yelped as whatever it was exploded, dancing away from the flames that licked his jeans. Nemo ran to him and grabbed his hand.

"Come on," she said, dragging him towards the elevators.

"But—" Max objected.

"You can kick his ass later," Nemo said. "I promise."

The doors of one of the elevators were open. Nemo pulled

Max inside and hit a button at random, aiming for a high floor. As the doors slid shut, something crashed against them. One of Boomer's little bombs, Nemo thought as the elevator started up.

"Where are we going?" Max asked. "And why? I almost had Seamus."

"Yeah," Nemo agreed. "You did. But what were you going to do with him?"

Max looked at her. "Pay him back for being a traitor," he said, as if this was the stupidest question she could ask.

"And *after* that?"

Max shrugged. "I hadn't gotten that far," he said.

"Exactly," said Nemo. "Think about it. We don't have anywhere to stick him. We don't have anyone to help us. Everyone who works here is freaking out."

"For good reason," Max said.

"For very good reason," Nemo agreed. "My point is, we're on our own, at least until Nine shows up again. And we have more important things to do than beat the crap out of Seamus and Boomer. Besides, if those two are here, there are probably more of them. Like Freakshow."

Max made a face. "That girl is bad news," he said.

"Right," Nemo said. "So let's try to stay away from her and do something useful, like find Sam."

"We don't have any idea where he is," Max reminded her. "He might not even be here."

"I think he is," said Nemo. "All of this is happening *here* for a reason. I think Sam is here, too."

"Okay," Max said. "But there are like two thousand rooms in this place. He could be anywhere. And I'm guessing he's not by himself."

"Probably not," Nemo admitted.

"And right now Seamus and Boomer are probably warning whoever *is* with him that—"

"I get it," Nemo interrupted. "We're still going to go look for him." She patted her pocket, where she had stored two syringes containing the parasite antiserum. Nine had two as well, and whichever of them found Sam or Six first was supposed to administer it to them.

"I'm not saying your plan is *bad*," Max said. "But like I said, there are more than two thousand rooms here and only two of us."

"Housekeeping," Nemo said.

"You mean like maids?" said Max.

"I hate that word," Nemo said. "It sounds like they're servants or something. But yeah, them."

"How are they going to help us find Sam?"

"The housekeeping staff know *everything*," Nemo said. "They're in and out of these rooms all day long. And trust me, if they see anything weird, they remember it. My cousin Ha worked in a hotel last summer, and she had some crazy stories about what went on there."

The elevator stopped and the doors opened. Nemo stepped out. They were on the sixty-third floor. It was deserted. But at one end she could see a room door propped open with a housekeeping cart.

"I'm surprised anyone is still working," Max remarked as they walked towards the room.

"News probably hasn't reached up here yet," said Nemo. "This place is huge, and it's not like the hotel is on fire—yet—so anyone who hasn't been downstairs might not have any clue about what's going on."

They reached the room. From inside the sound of water running spilled out into the hall. Nemo stepped in and peered into the bathroom. A young woman knelt next to the tub, scrubbing it and humming along to a popular song that was just audible. She wore headphones. Max, looking around Nemo, said, "No wonder she has no clue the place is under attack."

Nemo wasn't sure how to get the girl's attention without startling her, so she knocked on the bathroom door. The girl turned around and frowned.

"Hi," Nemo said, trying to sound as friendly as possible. "I was wondering if you could help us find our friend. He—"

"What?" the girl said, removing the earphones.

"We're looking for someone," Max said impatiently. "Our friend Sam."

"If he's a guest here, you can ask at the front desk," the girl said. "They'll connect you."

"Yeah, that might be a problem," Max said. "See, there are these things attack—"

"The thing is, we're not entirely sure he's here," Nemo said. "We're hoping you might have seen him, though."

The girl laughed. "Do you know how many people are

staying in this hotel?" she said. "Thousands." She sighed and glanced at the tub she was scrubbing. "And I think I've pulled their hair out of every drain in the place."

"Gross," Max said.

Nemo looked at the girl's name tag, which was affixed to the front of her shirt. "Basia," she said. "Um, this is kind of embarrassing. But Sam is actually my boyfriend."

Max snorted, and Nemo shot him a dirty look. "*Was* my boyfriend," she said. "See, he kind of ran off with this girl. And I think he brought her here."

Basia was shaking her head, obviously about to tell them that there was nothing she could do to help. Before she could, Nemo burst into tears. "And it's *my* birthday and he's supposed to be here with *me*," she wailed.

Basia's face softened. "I'm sorry," she said. "I know what that's like. It's terrible."

"It is," Nemo said, forcing tears from her eyes. "And all I want to do is tell him that I don't need him because I've got somebody way better."

"Me?" Max said hopefully.

"Chad," Nemo said. "My ex's best friend."

Basia laughed. "You go, girl," she said. "But I don't know the names of anyone in these rooms. Maybe if you have a picture of this guy. Sam, right?"

Nemo nodded. "I don't," she said. "I could describe him, but he looks like a lot of other guys."

"But maybe you've seen the girl," Max said. "She's kind of hard to miss. Thin. Pink hair. A little on the weird side."

"Room 7192," Basia said instantly. "I don't know if the guy you're looking for is with her. She wouldn't let me in to clean, so I don't know who's in there. But she ordered a ton of room service, and I had to cart all the dishes away." She frowned. "You don't forget people when they do stuff like that."

"7192," Nemo repeated. "Thanks. Oh, and you might want to see about leaving early. But be careful when you go downstairs, okay? Don't go outside until you know it's all right."

"What's going on?" Basia asked, suddenly looking worried. Her eyes went wide. "Is it a terrorist attack?"

"No," Nemo said quickly. "There's just a lot of . . . commotion . . . going on in front of the hotel. Some kind of accident, I think. It's just safer for you to avoid it if you can. Is there another way out?"

"There's an exit in the basement," Basia said.

"Use that," Nemo said. "On second thought, maybe stay up here until you know it's safe. Okay?"

Basia nodded. She was already taking out her cell phone and dialing someone.

"Come on," Nemo said to Max as she left the bedroom.

"Shouldn't we tell her exactly what's going on?" Max said. "You probably scared her to death."

"She should be scared," Nemo said. "And we warned her."

Outside the room, she took hold of the cleaning cart and wheeled it in front of them.

"What do we need that for?" Max asked.

"You ever heard of the Trojan horse?" Nemo said.

"Sure," said Max. "Supposedly, a million years ago the Greeks tricked somebody into letting them into their city by building a giant wooden horse and hiding soldiers inside of it. The people thought it was a gift, brought it into the city and, bam, soldiers everywhere."

"It wasn't a million years ago, and the city was Troy, but yes, that's basically it," Nemo said.

"What does a wooden horse have to do with this cart?" said Max.

"This cart is a lot like a wooden horse," said Nemo as she stopped at the elevators and pressed a button.

"Except it's not wooden and it's not a horse," Max pointed out.

Nemo lifted the top of the cart, which held things like little bottles of shampoo and tiny wrapped soaps. Underneath was an area partially filled with wadded-up sheets and towels. There was more than enough room for two people to hide inside.

The elevator came and they got in.

"Okay, but how are we going to get Magdalena, or whoever is in there, to bring the cart inside?"

By the time the doors opened on the seventy-first floor, Nemo had thought of an idea. She just needed a little bit of good luck to make it work.

She got it when she saw some dishes sitting on the floor outside of a room. She pushed the cart over and swept the toiletries from the top of it onto the floor.

"Get in," she said to Max.

"What about you?" Max said.

"Someone has to push this thing," Nemo explained. "I'm going to take it to the door of 7192 and tell them room service is there."

"What if they didn't order any room service?" Max argued. "I mean, this is kind of a weird time to be doing that, what with those monsters running around. I think they have bigger things to worry about than scarfing down some burgers and fries."

"Have you got a better idea?" Nemo asked.

Max thought for a moment. "No."

"Then get in."

Max did. Nemo shut the top and arranged some dishes over it. They had metal cloches on them, so it wouldn't be immediately obvious that there was no food. And the room's occupants had left enough food on the plates that they at least smelled like a meal.

"If they open the door, I'm ramming this cart into whoever is standing there," Nemo told Max as she wheeled him down the hall. "And if they tell me to leave it, you wait until they bring it inside. Then jump out and—"

"And what?" Max said.

Nemo thought. "And keep them busy until I can get in there and help you," Nemo finished.

"This is the worst plan you have ever had," Max said as Nemo turned a corner and headed for the part of the hall where room 7192 was. "You're going to get us killed."

Nemo ignored him, mostly because she was afraid he was

right. But she was also right—it was the only chance they had to get into that room and see if Sam was in there.

She reached the door of 7192 and hesitated a moment. Then she knocked. A moment later a girl's voice said, "Who is it?" It wasn't Magdalena.

"Room service," Nemo said, keeping her voice steady.

There was a pause. "Did one of you idiots order room service?"

Nemo heard several male voices answer her, all of them denying ordering anything. Nemo thought quickly. "It's complimentary pizza," she said.

It was a ridiculous ploy, and she was tempted to turn the cart around and get out of there before either a stranger opened the door and she had to make up something about having the wrong room or one of her enemies answered the door and she and Max would be in for the fight of their lives.

There was more conversation from behind the door. Then it swung open. Freakshow looked out at Nemo. Behind her, Nemo caught glimpses of Ghost and Spike.

It took Freakshow a few seconds to recognize Nemo. "What the—"

Nemo shoved the cart into the girl, using her telekinesis to give it extra momentum. Freakshow flew backwards, knocking into Spike. They fell to the ground, and Nemo wheeled the cart into the room and slammed the door behind her.

She flung up the top of the cart, sending dishes flying.

"Now!" she shouted.

CHAPTER SIX

SIX
LAS VEGAS, NEVADA

SIX COULDN'T SEE THE THING THAT HAD WRAPPED its tentacles around her and was squeezing the life from her, but she fought against it with everything she had. She was somewhere dark, and cold, and every cell in her body screamed out in torment. It was as if she was on fire from the inside, like some terrible poison had suffused her veins and was pumping through her with every beat of her heart. She tried to breathe, but no air entered her lungs.

"Fight it!"

She heard the voice calling to her through the dark. It was familiar, but the pain racking her head made it impossible to think. She could only feel.

"Fight, Six!"

Whatever monster was trying to kill her redoubled its efforts. Only now she realized that it wasn't anything outside her body. It was inside, and it was trying to claw its way out. It wanted to be free of her. But it also wanted to take her life with it, leaving her an empty shell.

She wasn't going to let that happen. Whatever it was attempting to kill her, it was going to have to try harder than that. Even if she couldn't see it or touch it, even if she had no idea what it was, she was going to be victorious.

"Come on." The familiar voice sounded again in her ear. She felt something touch her arm. The prick of metal. Something thick and syrupy flooded her veins.

Then it was as if an electrical connection had been made. Somewhere in her brain, sparks fired. She felt the thing that was trying to control her pull away. It was afraid. Running. But there was nowhere for it to go. More connections formed. More sparks flew. It was as if a switch had been flipped and the machinery of her mind had come back to life.

Lights flickered behind her eyes. The tentacles binding her slid away. She could breathe. Then she felt the familiar sensation of her Legacy returning, suffusing her with power like warmth spreading throughout her body. She focused her energy, picturing it as a ball of swirling light the color of flames. Then she sent it throughout her body, chasing the darkness and filling her with dazzling brilliance.

She opened her eyes.

She was lying on the floor. Nine was kneeling beside her. He held a syringe in his hand, and he was looking down at her with an expression of concern that quickly turned to a grin of triumph.

"All right, then," he said. "I guess we can tell the doc her antiserum works."

"What did you do?" Six asked. She felt tingly all over, a little light-headed, but better than she remembered feeling in days.

"I think we killed the thing in your head," Nine answered. "Or at least slowed it down long enough for you to come back. How do you feel?"

"Weird," Six said, sitting up. "But actually pretty good."

"Do something," Nine said. "You know, with your Legacies."

Six looked around. She had no idea where they were at first. Then she remembered—the show. They were backstage, surrounded by props and pieces of equipment. She focused on one of them, a wooden box about three feet high and just as wide. She lifted it up easily with her telekinesis, then set it down again. Then she tried going invisible. She barely had to even think about it before she blinked out. When she reappeared again she was smiling. "Looks like I'm back," she said.

Then she remembered other things. "What happened to Eleni?" she asked. "And that—whatever it was."

"Still out there somewhere," Nine said. "We can deal with her next. I was more concerned about you."

"Aww," Six said. "You care."

Nine snorted. "Hardly."

Six touched her head. "It's still in there," she said.

"They'll take it out back at HGA," Nine said. "The one in Sam, too."

"You have him?" Six said hopefully.

Nine shook his head. "Nemo and Max are looking into it," he said. "But I'm not sure he's even here. He could be anywhere."

Six's elation at having her Legacies back faded a little.

"Don't worry," Nine said. "We'll find him."

Six nodded. "What's going on here anyway? What are the Mogs doing? And how did they manage it? Those things weren't exactly tiny. Someone had to have helped them set this up."

"Lexa did some snooping after you called us," Nine said. "Turns out the Saturn Hotel is owned by one of Helena Armbruster's companies."

"Why am I not surprised?"

"My guess is they've been planning this for a while," Nine continued. "Maybe with the help of someone inside Cirque des Étoiles."

"But those things are huge," Six said. "Where have they been keeping them?"

Nine shook his head. "How about we ask them when we catch them?" he said. "Speaking of that, are you up for getting going?"

He stood and offered Six his hand. She allowed him to help her to her feet.

"How do you feel?"

"Are you going to ask me that every five minutes, Dad?" Six said.

"Keep that attitude and there'll be no ice cream for you, little lady," Nine said, shaking his finger at her.

"I feel fine," Six said. "Where to now?"

"We should probably follow the fire and the screaming," Nine said.

They walked back into the arena. In the time that they'd been backstage, the fire department had arrived and was putting out the dozen or more fires blazing around the place. Seeing Six and Nine, one of the firefighters trotted over.

"You can't be in here," she said. Then she looked again. "Hey—you're the Garde! What are you doing in here?"

"Same thing you are," Nine said. "Trying to get this under control."

"What the hell is going on?" the woman asked. "People are saying there are monsters running loose."

"Animatronics," Nine said. "Built for the show. Something went wrong."

The woman looked doubtful. She nodded at the dead beast lying by the ruins of the stage. The metal pole still jutted from its body. Sticky black blood oozed from the wound. "That looks pretty real," she said.

"Hydraulic fluid," Nine said smoothly. "And don't touch it. It could be corrosive."

The firefighter ignored the comment. "There are bodies," she said, indicating several telltale black bags lying off to one side.

Nine and Six looked at one another.

"Listen," Six said. "We're going to contain this. For now, all you know is that those things are robots built for the show. Something went wrong with them and some people got hurt. Okay?"

The woman looked doubtful. She started to say something.

"We'll take care of it," Six said quickly. "I promise."

The firefighter nodded. "Animatronic space monsters," she said. "You got it."

"Thank you," said Six.

"By the way, some of those injured people are pretty famous," the woman said. "It won't be long before someone tweets or posts about this to their millions of followers. So you should probably have a plan."

"I always do," Nine said, giving the woman his most charming grin.

The woman looked at Six, obviously not enraptured by Nine's personality.

"We'll take care of it," Six said again.

The woman went back to work, ordering the various crews around the arena. Six and Nine left her to do her job, walking into the tunnel connecting the arena to the hotel. It too was in ruins.

Nine took out a phone and started typing.

"What are you doing?" Six asked.

"Looking at Instagram," he said. "Just kidding. I'm letting Lexa know that she needs to start doing damage control. We can't have anyone knowing that a bunch of monsters are trying to destroy Las Vegas. And we don't want a mass panic about the Mogadorians."

"It's going to be kind of hard to cover this up," Six said as they reached the lobby. She pointed outside. "Those monsters aren't exactly tiny."

Nine looked. Three creatures were out there. A throng of people had gathered around, and lights from police cruisers flashed red and blue.

"Shit," Six said. "There's a news van."

They walked towards the doors and went outside. Six expected to find people in a panic, but was surprised to discover that many of them were actually doing things like taking video of the three creatures with their phones and snapping photos of themselves or their friends standing with the monsters in the backgrounds. The beasts themselves were oddly still. They looked around, occasionally roaring and rearing up on their back legs to claw at the sky, but they weren't attacking.

"This is weird," Six said.

"They're waiting," Nine said.

"For what?"

"I'm guessing a signal of some kind," Nine said. "It's like they're trying to draw as big a crowd as possible here before starting the next attack."

Six understood. "They want witnesses," she said. "An audience."

"Dude, those things are awesome," a young man standing

next to them said to his friend. "They look totally real."

"I heard it's part of a promo for the new *Revengers* movie," the friend said.

"You guys really need to get out of here," Six said.

The boys looked at her. Their faces lit up. "You're Six!" one of them said. His eyes shifted to Nine. "And you're . . . that other dude."

"Nine," his friend said. "They're Six and Nine. Hey, are you guys part of this movie?"

"Yes," Nine said as Six said, "No."

"I get it," the young man said. "You're not supposed to talk about it. Don't worry. We'll play along." He held up his phone. "Dude, get in there with them. I'll get a pic."

The second boy squeezed in between Six and Nine and gave a thumbs-up, his friend taking the photo before Six or Nine could stop him. They started to swap places for another photo, but Six said, "We've really got to go," and walked away.

Nine caught up with her. "That was rude," he said. "You should always be nice to the fans."

"That one didn't even know who you are, Other Dude."

"Not everyone is good with numbers," Nine said.

Six scanned the area. "Didn't you say you left Nemo and Max here?" she said.

Nine looked at his phone again. "They went looking for Sam," he said. "Oh, and they had a run-in with Seamus and Boomer."

"They *texted* you?"

"I was kind of busy saving you and everything," Nine said. "Besides, that's how kids communicate these days. When did you get so old?"

Six ignored him. She walked over to a group of police officers. "You need to get these people out of here," she said. "Those things are going to attack."

The officers laughed. Six stared at them. "I'm not joking around here. Those things are real."

"Sure they are," one of the officers said.

"Wait a minute," another one said. "You're the girl from the security footage. You were riding one of those things in the hotel."

"Yeah," Six said. "I was. And you saw the damage they did in there. The fires. The injured people. The goddamn *bodies*."

The officers stared at her, saying nothing.

"Are you hearing anything I'm saying?" Six said, her voice rising.

"I think you should come with me."

Six turned. Another officer was standing behind her.

"Finally," Six said. "Look. Those things are going to—"

The officer reached for his belt and unhooked a pair of handcuffs. "Maybe you didn't hear me the first time," he said.

Six realized what was happening. "You want to arrest *me*?"

"According to the Cirque des Étoiles folks, you pretended to be one of their cast members, stole one of their animatronic critters and caused a whole lot of trouble," the officer said. "And like Officer Herren said, there's video to back it up."

"I was trying to *stop* them," Six objected. "Nine? Tell him—"

She looked around, but Nine was nowhere to be seen.

"Where the hell did he go?" Six said to herself.

"All right," the officer said, reaching for her arm. "Let's just go down to the station and—"

Six shoved him. He flew backwards. Behind her, she heard the sound of guns being drawn, followed by three voices saying, "Hands up!"

She went invisible. The officers shouted. One reached out to touch where she'd last seen Six standing. Six darted out of her way. She didn't have time to deal with this latest problem. Whoever was helping the Mogs was obviously orchestrating a setup of some kind, distracting anyone who could actually help from doing so.

Well, Six was going to do something. At least she was if she could figure out where the hell Nine had gone. She was scanning the crowd for him, when she heard an excited roar go up. She turned around.

Eleni had appeared, floating over the crowd on some kind of hovering platform. She looked like something out of a science fiction movie, dressed all in black with her platinum-blond hair streaming around her. In one hand she held a staff tipped with a glowing blue orb. In her other, a fireball swirled.

She maneuvered so that she was just above the heads of

the three monsters, who stood beneath her swaying from side to side, as if they were in a trance. All around the plaza, cameras flashed. The news crew turned their attention to her, a reporter talking excitedly as the camera operator filmed the proceedings.

"This isn't good," Six said to herself. "Come on, Nine. Where are you?"

Eleni raised her staff. The orb changed from blue to an ugly yellowish-green. At the same time, the three beasts' eyes also began to glow. They opened their mouths and roared. One of them took a step forward, its huge foot crushing the hood of a police car. The crowd cheered.

Six saw the police officers who had been so anxious to take her in approach the monsters. One of them shouted something at Eleni. Eleni responded by throwing the fireball in her hand at them. One of the officers caught fire, spinning around as he attempted to put out the flames. The crowd gasped.

Another of the officers aimed a gun at Eleni. She formed another fireball and launched it. The officer fired, missing her. Eleni pointed her staff. The nearest monster leaned down, its jaws opening, and took the man in its mouth. A moment later, the lower half of his body tumbled to the pavement.

"Oh my God," someone said. "She wasn't kidding. Those things are real."

Six turned her head and saw the two young men she and Nine had interacted with earlier. They stared in horror at

Eleni and her trio of monsters.

"Dude," one said. "We've got to go."

As if hearing him, the crowd began to scatter. Shots rang out. And the three beasts began their attack.

CHAPTER SEVEN

SAM
LAS VEGAS, NEVADA

SAM HAD BEEN IN A KIND OF HALF SLEEP, FADING in and out of wakefulness. He didn't know how long it had been since Magdalena had left the room, leaving him with the others. They were supposed to be watching him, but they'd taken his chair into the bedroom and left him there while they hung out in the living room. The door was shut halfway, and voices from the television mingled with their own, so he couldn't tell them apart. They were watching some kind of sci-fi movie, and that had run together with the thoughts in his head, so that he couldn't quite remember where he was or what was happening. He was sure that he knew the people who were talking—at least some of them—but he couldn't recall their names. His memory was getting worse. He was so tired. All he wanted to do was close his eyes and have everything fade away.

He was about to pass out when he heard shouting. Something was happening in the other room. He heard a series of crashes. More yelling. Then someone burst into the room and the door slammed shut.

"Keep them out!" a girl's voice said.

"How?" a boy answered. "There are three of them."

"Just try," said the girl.

Then someone was touching his face. "Sam?" It was the girl.

Sam opened his eyes and looked at her. Something about her was familiar, but he couldn't remember why.

"It's Nemo," she said as she dug something out of her pocket. "I've got something that will help you. At least, I hope it will."

She moved behind him. Sam felt something like a bee sting, then a burning sensation.

"Is it working?" the boy called out as someone pounded on the door from the other side.

"I can't tell," the girl said.

She moved away from Sam, joining the boy by the door. Sam didn't know what they were doing, and now he was distracted by the intense pain that had ripped through his head. He cried out.

"What's wrong with him?" the boy said.

"I don't know," said the girl. "I don't know how this is supposed to work."

The room grew suddenly cold. Sam shivered and moaned

as a fresh wave of pain broke over him.

"It's Spike," the girl's voice said. "He's trying to freeze us out."

Sam's body spasmed. His teeth chattered. It felt as if a giant hand was squeezing his head. Then someone was beside him, putting a hand on his face. Sam's vision blurred, but when he looked up he saw a girl standing in front of him. Not the first girl, but a new one. She regarded him with a sad expression.

"Get away from him, Ghost!" the boy shouted.

"I'm sorry," the girl whispered to Sam.

He felt the world dissolve around him. For a moment he had no body. His atoms had been pulled apart, and he existed only as pure thought. It felt wonderful to be free of his tormented body, and he experienced several seconds of joy before he was slammed back into the prison of flesh and bone.

He was outside. It was night. The moon seemed to hang just overhead, fat and white. When Sam looked out, it appeared he was floating in a sea of stars. Then he realized that they were electric lights. He was somewhere high up.

"We're on the roof of the hotel," a voice said. "Magdalena told me to get you out of there if anyone came for you."

Sam saw the girl from before standing a little way away. His mind was rapidly clearing. He was starting to remember.

"Ghost," he said.

The girl nodded, smiling a little.

"And Nemo," Sam said, recalling the name of the other girl. "Nemo was there."

Ghost's smile faded. "I wish they hadn't come," she said. "I wish she and Max had stayed away. There's nothing they can do."

But they *had* done something. Sam felt different. Better. More and more memories flooded his head: the Mogs, the parasite, the bunker, Six. Then he recalled the sting on his arm. Had Nemo injected him with something? Is that why he was remembering?

Ghost walked closer. She turned and looked out over the city, pushing her hair behind her ear with a small gesture that made her seem younger than she was, like a little girl. "I want to go home," she said softly. "But I don't know where that is anymore."

Sam recalled the first time he'd seen the girl, the details coming to him with surprising ease. New Orleans. Only a few months before. She'd seemed weak then, unsure of herself and her Legacy. He remembered seeing her lying on the street in a puddle of blood after being shot by Dennings. Dennings, who was dead now. So much had happened to this girl. So many terrible things. She had become someone different.

And yet, standing in the moonlight, her face was once more that of the frightened little girl Sam had first encountered. She was still in there somewhere.

With every minute that passed, Sam was feeling more himself. He was still very, very tired. But his head was clear and he could think again. Whatever Nemo had injected him with, it was working. He decided it would be a mistake to show Ghost that the parasite's control had been broken, so he continued to sit with his head bowed as he quietly tested his Legacies. He first tried to see if he could levitate the chair at all. He succeeded in lifting it a quarter of an inch, then set it back down. The effort exhausted him, but at least he knew he could do it.

"I know how you feel," he said, keeping his words mumbled.

Ghost turned her face to him. Her cheeks were wet with tears. "What do you mean?"

"I know what it's like to feel like you don't belong anywhere," Sam said slowly. "Remember, I was one of the first humans to develop a Legacy. I had no idea what that made me, or what it meant."

"But you had Six and Nine and the others," Ghost said.

"And you have them, too," said Sam. "And Nemo and Max. They understand you better than anybody."

Ghost didn't respond. She looked away. Sam wondered what the Mogs had done to make her so loyal to them, to make her feel like they cared more about her than her real friends did. He wondered if she was beyond saving, if the girl he'd caught a glimpse of earlier was too far gone to come back.

He tried using his telekinesis to work the locking mechanism on the handcuffs. He pushed the pins with his mind, sliding them in different directions until he felt them open up. Carefully, so as not to alert Ghost to what he was doing, he slid a hand free, then used it to pull the cuff from the other wrist. His arms ached from being in the same position for so long, but he forced himself to keep them there so that it looked like he was still attached to the chair.

"You know you're always welcome at the Academy," he said, trying to keep Ghost talking.

Ghost made a sound halfway between a laugh and a cry. "They don't want me," she said. "It's too late for that."

She walked a few steps, until she was standing on the edge of the roof, the tips of her boots hanging over the edge. Seeing her there made Sam's heart beat faster and his palms sweat. He wanted to call her back, but resisted the impulse.

"I wonder what would happen if I fell," Ghost said, seeming to speak to herself as much as to him. "Would I be able to let myself fall all the way? Or would my Legacy kick in at the last second and teleport me somewhere safe?"

"Let's not find out," a voice said from behind Sam.

He turned his head, and for the first time noticed something huge perched on top of the hotel. It was an enormous metal statue of the planet Saturn, complete with rings circling it. It stood atop a pole, seeming to float in the air above the building. Lights inside of the central globe were visible through small holes in the surface of the planet, making it radiate light.

Magdalena walked out of the shadows that pooled beneath the statue. Sam kept his hands behind him, hoping she wouldn't look too closely and see that the handcuffs were loose. But she seemed more interested in twirling around with her arms stretched out.

"Isn't it a beautiful night?" she said.

Neither Ghost nor Sam answered her. Sam kept his head low, reminding himself that he was supposed to be incapacitated by the parasite. Ghost stepped away from the edge of the roof and folded her arms over her chest.

Magdalena skipped to the edge of the building and looked over the edge. "You should see what's going on down there," she said. "My babies are having quite a time." She sighed. "Of course Eleni is making herself the star of the show. I probably shouldn't have given her that Legacy."

Sam looked at her, forgetting that he was supposed to be out of it. *What had she said? She'd given Eleni a Legacy?*

Magdalena giggled. "Just imagine what I can do with what my little friend is collecting in *your* head," she said, walking over to Sam. "I can't wait to take him out." She frowned. "That means you'll be dead, which isn't great for you. But you probably don't really know what's going on at this point anyway."

"What's happening in the room?" Ghost asked.

Magdalena shrugged. "I don't know," she said. "I heard a lot of banging and figured you'd left. I was right."

"You didn't even check on the others?" Ghost said.

"Why should I?" said Magdalena. "The only one I need is right here."

She tapped Sam on the head, as if petting him. Sam, watching Ghost, saw her expression harden. If Magdalena noticed, she didn't say anything. Rather, she said, "We might as well transport him out of here. Back to the lab. It's about time I remove the parasite."

"What about Eleni and those . . . things?" said Ghost.

Magdalena waved a hand. "That's her problem," she said. "She's the one who wanted to make a big production. Now she's got it. She doesn't need me to help her control the grindles. She's got the staff."

Grindles. Is that what she calls them? Sam thought. He hadn't seen one yet, so he could only imagine what they looked like. He pictured mouths full of teeth. He wondered what the rest of them looked like. And what was this staff Magdalena was talking about?

"All right," Magdalena said. "Let's get moving. Come over here and whoosh us back to the lab."

Ghost hesitated a moment, as if she might say something. Then she walked over to where Sam and Magdalena were standing. She reached out her hand to touch Sam's shoulder.

Sam jumped to his feet. The chair toppled backwards. Magdalena, startled, took a few steps back. Sam grabbed Ghost and, lifting her, ran to the edge of the roof. He hesitated only a moment, then jumped with Ghost in his arms.

The night raced by them as they fell. Sam wrapped his arms around Ghost, holding tightly and thinking about their earlier conversation. What would she choose? He thought he knew—hoped he was right. But what if he wasn't? What if she decided to just let them both fall? He prayed she wouldn't, but even if she did, at least the Mogs wouldn't have his Legacies.

The ground was rushing up at them. Sam saw lights

flashing blue and red. He saw tiny specks moving, then realized that they were people running. And he saw, finally, the grindles. They were monstrous, lumbering around in the street, smashing things with their claws.

Then they were gone. Everything was gone, and he once again felt as if he'd left his body. Ghost had chosen.

When he reappeared, the first thing he heard was someone yelling, "Jackpot!" This was followed by the ringing of a bell and the sound of coins falling into a metal tray. Then he realized that he was lying on the floor, still hugging Ghost, and that several people were bent over staring at them from their seats on stools that were pulled up in front of slot machines.

"Must be part of that magic show," a woman said, taking a sip from the drink in her hand and turning her attention back to the machine she was playing.

Sam let go of Ghost, who sat up. "It was the first place I thought of," Ghost said.

Sam sat up too, then got to his feet and pulled Ghost up beside him. "I'm just glad you picked someplace," he said.

Ghost was looking at him intently. "How long have you been back to normal?"

"Not long," Sam said. "Nemo gave me a shot of something. I don't know what it is, but it seems to have worked."

Ghost sighed. "I've got to go back to her," she said. "Magdalena, I mean. Not Nemo."

"Why?" Sam asked.

Ghost shrugged. "I just do," she said. "That's all. But

you should go help Nemo and Max. They're right down the street. I'd teleport you there, but I'll be in enough trouble for losing you."

"You don't have to go," Sam said.

But Ghost was already gone.

"How does she do that?" the woman playing slots nearby asked. "Is there a trapdoor or something under there?"

Sam ignored her, turning and making his way across the casino. The place was packed, and he wondered why everybody wasn't in the streets, given the commotion going on outside the Saturn Hotel. When he neared the casino doors, however, he saw that there were police there, keeping people from leaving. Also, several casino employees were handing out vouchers for free game play and the buffet.

"All-you-can-eat crab legs!" a smiling woman said, waving a piece of paper at Sam. "And a chocolate fountain?"

Sam pressed by her and tried to leave, but a policeman stopped him. "You need to stay inside, sir," he said. "There's a downed power line, and it's not safe to walk out there quite yet. But the crew is working on it, and it should be fixed shortly."

"That's not true, dude," a young man nearby said. "There are freaking *monsters* out there. We saw them. Here. Look."

He dragged Sam away from the doors and held out his phone. Sam looked at the photo. It was of Six. Behind her was one of the grindles.

"We were *right there*, man. Right. There. Don't believe

what the cops are saying. They just don't want anyone to know."

Sam wasn't listening. He was staring at Six. She was all right. He had to get to her.

He turned and ran back through the casino, looking for another exit. He found several, but all of them were blocked by guards and a phalanx of nervous-looking casino workers armed with buffet passes. Looking at them, Sam got an idea.

He closed his eyes, focusing his concentration on the room full of slot machines. Their internal machinery whirred and clicked as levers were pulled and buttons were pressed. He reached out to the closest one, telling the gears to settle into a winning position. A moment later, the sound of a payoff alarm jangled and someone shouted in delight as tokens poured out.

Sam kept going. Around the room, machines began to clatter and ring as everyone playing them became a winner. Sam opened his eyes and smiled at the sight of people greedily catching tokens in their hands and in the big plastic cups designed to hold the payouts. But their excitement quickly turned to chaos as the machines kept spitting out tokens and they began to fall to the floor, where other players knelt to scoop them up.

"Hey!" a man shouted, shoving aside another man who was busily cramming tokens into his pockets. "Those are mine!"

The men began to wrestle. Similar skirmishes erupted

throughout the room as more and more of the little metal coins flew out. The police guarding the doors abandoned their posts to break up the worst of the fights.

Sam took advantage of the disruption to run to one of the now-unguarded doors. He pushed it open and looked around. He was at the rear of the casino, in an alley built for delivery trucks and trash cans rather than the feet of tourists. There were no cops to stop him from leaving.

He walked to the street. Looking to his right, he saw the towering form of the Saturn Hotel. Flashing lights surrounded it. Helicopters buzzed nearby. And in the middle of the lights he saw the forms of the grindles.

He started running.

CHAPTER EIGHT

MAX AND NEMO
LAS VEGAS, NEVADA

MAX STARED AT THE SPOT WHERE SAM HAD BEEN.

The temperature in the room had dropped considerably thanks to Spike, and Max's breath fogged the air. Beside him, Nemo continued to use her telekinesis to keep the door shut, while on the other side, Freakshow was working just as hard to open it.

"Max!" Nemo said, trying to get his attention.

"She took him," Max said. "He's gone."

Nemo glanced over. In the moment that her attention was diverted, her telekinesis faltered. The door burst open and Freakshow stood there, a triumphant grin on her face. Spike, beside her, shook his hands as if they were worn out from using his Legacy.

"You could have just opened it," Freakshow said.

Max faced her, his hands balled at his sides. "Where did she take Sam?" he said, his voice tight with anger.

"Don't know and don't care," Freakshow said. "He's not my problem now. You are."

Max raised his hands.

"Look at you, getting all forceful," Freakshow said, laughing. "What's your Legacy again? Oh, right. *Translating*. Not exactly a great offense." She looked at Nemo. "And I don't see any water here."

"I don't need water to kick your ass," Nemo said, holding her hands palms out and sending a telekinetic blast at the girl.

Freakshow put her own hands up, blocking the attack. The girls were evenly matched, and neither was doing much in the way of hurting the other. Spike and Max were likewise cancelling one another out. The only difference was that Max and Nemo were trapped inside the room, and the only way out was through Freakshow and Spike.

Max looked at Nemo. As much as it pained him to admit it, she was stronger than he was telekinetically. Also, she was faster. If one of them was going to have a better chance than the other of getting out and getting help, it was Nemo. He could help her, but it meant doing something he was afraid to do.

He took a deep breath and charged at Freakshow. Thinking that neither of them would dare get within touching distance of her, this took her by surprise. Max tackled her, shoving her into Spike. The three of them went down to the floor.

"Run!" Max shouted as Freakshow grabbed his wrist.

Immediately, Max saw himself on the street in New Orleans. Ghost lay on the ground nearby, bleeding. A little way off, a man had his arm around Nemo's neck. In his other hand was a gun.

"Help Ghost!" Nemo yelled.

Max stepped towards his friend.

"Do it and I'll kill her!" the man holding Nemo said.

Max looked at Ghost. Her chest was rising and falling irregularly. He knew she was dying.

"Do it, Max!" Nemo said.

Max looked from one friend to the other. If he helped Ghost, Nemo would die. If he did nothing, Ghost would die and the man might kill Nemo anyway. He felt powerless, hopeless, useless. He didn't even know how to use his Legacies to help.

Ghost turned her head, looking at him with eyes that were quickly dimming. "Max," she whispered. "Help me." She lifted her hand, holding it out to him.

Max cried out in frustration and rage. He took a step forward. There was a shot. He started to turn his head, but then the vision vanished. He was lying on the floor in the hotel, looking up at the ceiling. Beside him, Freakshow was standing up.

"Knock it off," she said to him.

Behind her, Spike was rubbing his face.

"Why didn't you stop her?" Freakshow said accusingly.

"She caught me by surprise," Spike said. He looked at his fingers. Blood covered the tips, and more dribbled from his split lip. "And she kicked me in the mouth jumping over us. Should we go after her?"

Freakshow took a phone from her pocket. "Nah," she said. "I'll text Seamus and Boomer. Let them take care of her. It's not like she can do much of anything. Her Legacy is useless here. We'll wait here for Magdalena. That was the plan. Then Ghost can teleport us all out of this place."

"I wish we could see what's going on out there," Spike said. "How'd we get stuck with babysitting anyway?"

"Just tie him up," Freakshow said. She looked down at Max. "And don't even think of trying to be a big hero again. Whatever it was you saw, I'll make you see it over and over until your mind can't take it anymore and it breaks."

Spike bent down and roughly pulled Max to his feet. Pushing him over to a chair, he forced him into it. "Stay there," he warned, then went and took the belt from a bathrobe hanging on the back of the door. He used it to tie Max's hands behind his back.

"I don't get it," Max said. "What do you guys think the Mogs are going to give you for being their sidekicks?"

"I'm nobody's sidekick," Freakshow said.

Max snorted. "Whatever you say, sidekick."

Freakshow stormed over, holding out her hands. "Sounds

like you want to be back in nightmare land," she said. "What's your worst fear, anyway? Finding yourself in your underwear in front of the whole school?"

"What's yours?" Max shot back. "Everyone finding out that without your Legacy you're a scared little bully who's pretty much afraid of *everything*?"

Freakshow's face turned red, and she started to come towards Max. Spike grabbed her arm. "Let it go," he said.

Freakshow shook Spike's hand off. She pointed a finger at Max. "Once they tell me they don't need you anymore, you're *dead*. That is, if the operation to get that thing crawling around in your head out doesn't kill you first." She laughed meanly.

Max didn't say anything. He didn't want to give away the fact that the parasite was dead and couldn't hurt him anymore. But Spike was looking at him with a peculiar expression. Max caught his eye for a moment, then looked down.

"How come you're not sick?" Spike said. "Like Sam is. If you've got a parasite in you, you should be all messed up, and you're not."

Max shrugged. "I don't know," he said. "Maybe I don't really have one in me. Maybe Magdalena just wanted me to think I did."

Spike shook his head. "Uh-uh," he said. "She made a big deal about it. You've got one, all right."

"Then maybe it's not working," Max said. "I don't know."

He hoped Spike would let it go. He didn't.

"Or maybe someone figured out a way to stop it," Spike said.

He was looking around on the floor. Now he bent down and picked something up. It was a hypodermic needle.

"What's that?" Freakshow said.

"Looks like somebody got injected with something," Spike said. He waved the syringe back and forth. "Any idea what was in this?" he asked Max.

Max thought about denying knowing anything. But he knew they wouldn't believe him anyway, so he took another tack. "It's supposed to be something to slow it down," he said. "Until we can get him back to HGA."

"Did they give it to you too?" Spike asked.

Max nodded.

"Well, it seems to be working," Spike said. "So it will probably work on Sam, too." He looked at Freakshow. "We need to let Magdalena know. If Sam is back to normal, he's dangerous."

"And if they got it into Six, she's even more of a problem," Freakshow added, taking out her phone and texting furiously.

Max looked at the floor. He'd tried to help, but now things were even worse. He hoped Nemo was having better luck.

Nemo ran down the corridor of the hotel. She was almost to the elevators, when she realized that she had no idea where she was going. She stopped and looked behind her.

Spike and Freakshow weren't following her. This was more a worry than it was a relief. It meant that they didn't think they needed to.

She almost went back. Leaving Max alone with the two of them didn't sit right with her. But she needed to get help. As much as she hated to admit it, her and Max's Legacies were no match for Spike's. And even though Freakshow's Legacy wasn't something that could flat-out hurt them, it was even more terrifying. She knew the girl had used it on Max, and it killed her to think of what he might have seen, might even be seeing right now. He'd put himself at great risk creating an opportunity for Nemo to get away. She was determined not to waste it.

She took her phone out. Now she regretted not sending Nine a text letting him know what she and Max were doing. But she would fix that now. When she saw that she had one from him, her heart leaped.

I HAVE 6. ON OUR WAY. WHERE R U?

Even though she was worried, she laughed at his use of textspeak. She started to reply, when the elevator doors dinged. She looked up just in time to see Seamus and Boomer coming out.

"Going somewhere?" Seamus asked.

Nemo turned and ran. Her phone slipped from her hand and fell to the carpet, where she accidentally kicked it and sent it sliding even farther out of reach. There was no time to bend and retrieve it, so she left it behind, cursing her clumsiness as she tried to outrun the two boys, who were hot on her heels. She swore as she saw Seamus pause to pick her phone up and slip it into his pocket.

She had no idea where to go, and so she just ran, turning when she came to a corner and continuing down another hallway. When she spied a red sign at the end saying *EMERGENCY EXIT*, she doubled her efforts. Reaching the door, she glanced at the warning there saying *ALARM WILL SOUND* and hit the push bar hard. True to the sign's word, a loud buzzing sound began ringing.

Behind the door was a set of stairs going both up and down. Nemo considered going down, then decided that was the way Seamus and Boomer would expect her to go, and so she chose to go up. She hoped that maybe she could open the door on the next floor and retrace her steps back to the elevators.

When she reached the next landing, however, she discovered that it was a dead end. The door in front of her said *ROOF ACCESS ONLY.* She was about to turn around, when she heard footsteps coming behind her.

She opened the door. A cool breeze hit her in the face as she stepped out onto the roof of the Saturn Hotel. She paused, trying to figure out where she could go, but the sound of the boys' voices behind her forced her forward. She ran blindly, heading for the center of the roof, where she saw a huge statue of the planet Saturn rising up into the night sky. She hoped she could find someplace there to hide.

Seamus and Boomer were not far behind.

"There she is!" Boomer called.

Nemo reached the base of the statue, where she discovered a ladder set into one side. She put her hand on it and started to climb. As she did, Magdalena appeared from around the other side. When she saw Nemo, she clapped her hands.

"Oh! I love surprises!" she said.

Nemo ignored her and climbed. Magdalena didn't have any Legacies, and right now she was the least of Nemo's worries. She kept going, reaching the top of the platform, where she paused and looked down. Seamus and Boomer were standing beside Magdalena, looking up at her.

"There's nothing to turn into a bomb," Boomer said, sounding irritated.

"We don't need one of your bombs," Seamus said. "I'll just call some of my friends."

Nemo didn't wait around to see what kind of bugs he was going to summon. She went to the large pole that the statue of Saturn stood on. It too had a ladder affixed to it. She started climbing. She had no idea how going even higher up was going to help her, but she figured it was better than being on the roof in a three-against-one battle.

When she reached the bottom of the planet, she discovered that it was hollow, and that she could crawl inside. She did, finding herself inside a globe about twenty feet wide. It was filled with lights that twinkled on and off. The ladder kept going up, ending in a platform that had a small door in it. Nemo ignored it for the moment, trying to catch her breath and think.

She didn't have long. A moment later, she heard buzzing.

Not more flies, she thought.

But it wasn't flies. It was bees. They began pouring into the globe through the cracks in the planet's surface. They immediately surrounded Nemo, stinging. She swatted at them with her hands, but it did little good. For every one she killed, there was another to take its place. Soon they were stinging her all over.

Out of desperation, she climbed again, going up to the little platform. She shoved open the door she found there and crawled out onto a narrow platform that extended out about ten feet before connecting with a wider, curved ledge. It was supposed to be the ring around Saturn, she realized.

The bees had followed her, and continued to sting. Her body burned as their venom coursed through her. She tried using her telekinesis to push them away, but it didn't work. The constant pain made it impossible to sustain a field for very long, and whenever she faltered, the bees slipped through and resumed their assault.

Out of desperation, she crawled along the platform and onto the metal ring. Looking down, she saw that she was now actually extended over the edge of the room. The ground seemed miles away, and she felt her heart freeze in her chest as vertigo overwhelmed her. She flattened herself against the metal and closed her eyes.

"Not afraid of heights, are you?"

Boomer's voice came from behind her. Her eyes, swelling shut from the bee stings, refused to open. She forced them, blinking through tears, and saw Boomer in the doorway. He held something in his hand. Something glowing.

"You should have gone down," he said.

Nemo started to crawl. She could barely see, but she could feel the metal beneath her hands. The buzzing bees kept up a disorienting cacophony that filled her head. She almost didn't feel the stings anymore, there were so many of them.

She felt a burning pain sear through her leg. Boomer had thrown whatever was in his hand at her. She screamed, instinctively rolling onto her side. Then she realized that her shoulder and head were not touching anything solid. She had almost fallen over the edge of the ring.

"Magdalena says she doesn't have any use for you," Boomer called out. "She says I can do what I want with you."

Nemo, on her back, forced her eyes open. Boomer was standing on the ring, staring at her from a dozen feet away. He had another glowing object in his hand.

"Guess I don't have a fear of heights," he said.

Nemo anticipated the hit, but it still felt like being shot when the burning thing struck her stomach. She screamed and rolled. She felt herself sliding over the edge and clutched at the surface of the ring. She managed to hang on, but she knew she was close to falling.

Boomer laughed. "This is too easy," he said.

The bees buzzed in Nemo's ears, taunting her.

"Hey!" Boomer shouted. "Call off your bugs!"

A moment later, the bees left just as they'd come, lifting away from Nemo and disappearing into the night. Her body still burned from their stings, and she gasped for breath as the venom did its work. She could feel her throat closing up.

"Come on," Boomer said. "At least *try.*"

Nemo looked up at him through narrow slits, barely able to see him. He held up his hand, showing her another glowing object.

"Last chance," he said.

Rage surged through Nemo, pushing the pain back enough for her to get onto her knees. She breathed in ragged gasps as she forced herself to her feet to face Boomer. She swayed unsteadily, and thought she might fall over if she tried to take even one step. But she stood her ground. She held up her hands, willing her Legacy to work.

Boomer laughed as he threw his bomb at her.

Nemo saw the air between them shimmer. Then Ghost appeared. She was facing Nemo, and didn't see Boomer behind her. When Boomer's missile hit her in the back, she stumbled forward, her mouth open in a scream. Nemo opened her arms and caught her. The force almost pushed both of them over the edge of the ring, but Nemo fought to stay still.

Ghost was lying limp against her. Nemo fell to her knees and laid her friend on the ring. When she pulled her hands away, they were covered in blood. Nemo looked at Boomer. He no longer had anything in his hands. Nemo realized that he was out of weapons.

She summoned the last of her fading strength. Holding her hands up, she focused her telekinesis and pushed as hard as she could. She watched as Boomer flew backwards, off the ring and out over the edge of the hotel. He didn't even scream as he fell.

Nemo looked down at Ghost. Her eyes were open, and she was smiling a sad smile.

"You're going to be okay," Nemo said. "Can you get us out of here?"

Ghost shut her eyes. She winced in pain as she tried. "No," she said. "I don't think I can."

Nemo gathered her into her arms. "It's okay," she said.

"I'm sorry," Ghost said.

"Me too," said Nemo.

Ghost started to say something else, then coughed.

"Shh," Nemo said, stroking Ghost's hair. "It's okay."

Ghost said nothing. Nemo felt tears slip from her eyes. "It's okay," she whispered again. "It's okay."

CHAPTER NINE

SIX

LAS VEGAS, NEVADA

SIX HAD NEVER IN HER LIFE WISHED SHE COULD fly more than she did standing on the ground looking up at Eleni hovering overhead, conducting the movements of the three monsters as if she was some kind of orchestra leader.

The towering beasts roared and clawed at the air. Where their feet fell, cars crumpled and street signs fell like sticks. People scattered, screaming and running away from the destruction now that they realized that what was happening was real. Watching them, Eleni laughed.

"Hey! Why don't you pick on someone your own size?!" Six shouted. "Metaphorically speaking," she added under her breath. She looked at Nine. "What's that thing she's riding, anyway?"

"I don't know," Nine said, eyeing the floating platform. "But I want one."

Eleni turned her attention to Six and Nine, noticing them for the first time. She scowled. Then she waved her staff. The three monsters turned their heads, each looking a different direction. Two of them started off in opposite directions, their bulky bodies filling the street as they went deeper into the city.

"She's trying to divide our attention," Six said angrily.

"Well, it's working," said Nine. "Do you want to go after those two or deal with her and the third one?"

"Leave her to me," Six said. "This has been a long time coming."

Nine grinned. "Have fun," he said, then took off after one of the retreating beasts.

Six focused her attention on Eleni and the remaining monster. It loomed over her, the stench of its foul breath filling the air as it roared.

"Here goes nothing," Six said, and ran towards it.

She leaped up, getting a purchase on its scaly hide and climbing its leg until she was on its shoulder. Eleni still hovered above it on her platform, out of reach. Six attempted to hit the platform with a wave of telekinesis, but Eleni was expecting it and rose up and away.

Six considered conjuring a storm. Something to knock Eleni off. But since she was getting reacquainted with her Legacies, Six knew she had to be careful about collateral damage with the crowd below. Police were attempting to herd bystanders out of the way, but people were too interested in what was happening to leave.

She decided to risk it.

Concentrating on the air above Eleni, she summoned lightning. The air crackled with electricity. Eleni, hearing it, looked up just as a bolt burst towards her. She managed to maneuver out of the way at the last second, and the lightning hit one of the police cars.

"She's attacking us!" an officer shouted, pointing at Six as two more bolts rained down.

"I'm trying to stop the psychopath!" Six shouted back.

He ignored her, pulling his pistol as several of the other officers did the same thing. Half pointed them at Six, while the other half pointed them at Eleni. Six braced herself to deflect the bullets if they fired, and quickly quelled the lightning storm, not wanting to antagonize the police any further.

Before she could figure out another way to get to Eleni, the Mog's staff started to glow. Then she raised it, and the beast Six was standing on tried to shake her off. Six fell into a crouch, hanging on as she had the first time she'd ridden one. She was used to their movements now, and knew where to stick her fingers between the scales to keep from falling off. The monsters were huge, but they were also slow, so she was able to adjust to the thing's attempts to dislodge her.

Eleni called up a fireball and launched it at Six. Six deflected it easily with a burst of telekinesis, rendering it harmless. Then she went invisible. Eleni shouted in rage and frustration, sending out a volley of smaller fireballs towards the place where she thought Six was. But Six had moved, climbing onto the beast's head. Eleni was just above her now, scanning for signs of Six.

Six crouched and jumped, propelling herself into the air. She reached for the edge of the hovering platform, managing to grip it with the fingertips of one hand. But it was her injured arm, and her shoulder burned fiercely as she tried to maintain her hold. The platform rocked under the added weight, tipping to the side. Six swung her body, trying to knock Eleni off her balance.

Eleni countered by bringing the end of her staff down hard on where she thought Six's fingers must be based on the tilt of the platform. Unfortunately, she guessed correctly. Six felt her fingers break. The intense pain caused her focus to falter. She flickered into view. Eleni kicked her in the face, hard, and Six flew backwards, falling onto the monster's back and rolling. She dug in with her ruined fingers, screaming as they were torn even more out of joint but managing to just hang on. She went invisible again, and this time stayed hidden.

She needed a new plan of attack. Eleni could easily stay out of her reach, and with no immediate weapon at her disposal, and nothing around her to turn into one, Six had no way of knocking her off the platform. *I need to bring her to me*, she thought. But how? What could she do that would make Eleni come closer?

She decided to attack the creature. Maybe if Eleni thought it was in danger, she would risk coming down from the platform to help it. First, Six attempted to set her broken fingers, gripping them with her good hand and pulling them back into place. The pain was horrific, and it only partly worked, but at least she could move a couple of her fingers now. She turned onto her stomach and began crawling up the thing's neck, going towards its head. Stabbing the thing in the eye had worked once. Maybe something similar would work again. The only problem was, she had no weapon now.

She reached the spot just behind the creature's head, but still had no idea what she was going to do. Then she had an idea. She materialized, allowing Eleni to see her. At the same time, she pretended to collapse on the beast's back, letting her body slump to the side. It took all of her willpower to hang on as pain tore through her hand and shoulder, but she did it. Her head lolled as if she had passed out from pain, her legs dangling along the side of the monster as it rocked back and forth.

Eleni took the bait. Thinking that Six was incapacitated, she formed a huge fireball in her hand. When it was glowing red, she hurled it at Six. Six, watching from between eyelids open only a slit, waited until it was almost upon her, then let go and slid down a few feet, thrusting both hands between a row of scales to stop herself from falling off completely.

The fireball struck the beast. Despite its scales, it felt the searing pain of the resulting explosion, and it whirled. Six hung on, her body flying out sideways as the monster turned towards Eleni and slashed at her with its claws. It struck the platform, tipping it, and Eleni tumbled off. She scrabbled to hang on, but with the staff still in one hand she wasn't able to grab on, and fell.

She bounced off the monster's side and tumbled to the ground. Six was about to let go of the creature and go after her, when Eleni surprised her by climbing on the beast herself. She drove the staff in between its scales, enraging it even more. Then the orb at the end started to glow again.

Six had only a moment to wonder what the Mog was up to before the monster turned and began scaling the side of the hotel. Its claws easily punctured the glass and steel, crunching loudly as it moved far more quickly than Six thought possible for such a huge animal. It was four stories up before she could even think about getting off. Now it was too late.

The thing climbed. Six held on as best she could, keeping an eye on Eleni, who was slowly making her way up towards Six. The surrounding buildings quickly retreated as the monster ascended the side of the Saturn, the flashing lights streaking by, making Six dizzy.

Six's only advantage was that because Eleni was still holding on to the staff, she only had one hand for maneuvering on the monster's back. The higher and faster it climbed, the more Eleni struggled, until finally she was forced to stay in one place, glaring up at Six with an expression of pure hatred, waiting for her chance.

Six too was barely hanging on. With each thud of the creature's claws, she was shaken again. Her shoulder had gone past the point of hurting to become a throbbing knot of pure pain. The broken bones in her hand ground together with each thrust of the beast's body, and she expected at any moment to simply fall from its back. If she did, she planned to take the Mog with her.

But that didn't happen. Instead, the two of them clung to the monster as it climbed to the very top of the hotel, hundreds of feet above the Strip. Six waited for it to reach the top and settle on the roof. When it was within a few floors of the top, though, it stopped, clinging to the side. Six could feel it breathing, its sides moving in and out. She waited for it to start moving again, but it remained in place.

She looked down at Eleni. The Mog's blond hair streamed in the wind that whipped around the hotel, hiding her face. Six wondered if she had somehow commanded the monster to stop or if it had done it of its own accord. The orb in Eleni's staff wasn't glowing, so Six didn't know.

She turned her attention to the monster itself. Above her, the wound created by Eleni's fireball oozed a sticky black substance. Then Six noticed something protruding from the hole in the scales. At first she thought it was bone, but moonlight glinted off it as it would off metal.

She planted the toe of her boot between some scales and pushed herself up a few inches. Her injured hand throbbed, but she ignored it, jamming it between more scales and using it to pin herself to the monster's body as she climbed a little bit at a time. She hoped it wouldn't start climbing again, and it didn't. Still, the wind tried to tear her away from the thing's back, and it was slow going.

When she got to the wound, she reached for the thing sticking out of the monster's back. It was cold, metallic. She ran her hand down it, feeling the ends of wires. They were frayed, and when her fingertips touched them, she got a slight shock. The creature bellowed. Six dipped her fingers into what she'd thought was blood, then brought them to her nose. She did smell the iron scent of blood, but also something else. Something oily, with a chemical odor.

It's part machine, she thought. *Some kind of biomechanical creature.*

Now she understood the role the orb played. It was some kind of transmitter. And since Eleni had injured the thing, it wasn't working exactly the way it was supposed to.

This might or might not be a good thing. They were stuck on the side of the hotel, and the creature wasn't moving. If it stayed where it was, Six didn't know how they would get off. And she wasn't sure how long she could hang on.

She heard a sound and looked down. Eleni was climbing up. She was grunting with each step she took, exclaiming in her own language in a way that Six understood clearly was the Mog equivalent of cursing. She had apparently realized what was going on with the beast, and had decided to act.

Six turned her attention back to the creature's wound. Sticking her hand inside again, she found the wires she'd located before. There were several of them, all torn and exposed. She took the raw ends and tried touching them to one another. The monster shrieked and lifted one front leg.

Its weight shifted to the other arm and it swung to the left. Six barely managed to hang on by gripping the protruding metal rod.

She let go of the wires and the monster steadied itself, although its right arm now flailed against the side of the building, as if it couldn't help itself. The glass of the windows broke, raining down on Six and Eleni. Six didn't want to risk making it let go completely, so she abandoned the mechanical innards. Eleni was only a few feet behind her, and moving more quickly. Six decided to climb.

She moved past the wounded area and onto the creature's neck. The only way for her to go was up its head, and so that's where she went. The scales of the neck gave way to the larger, smoother plates of its head. These were slipperier, with fewer places to hold on. Plus, the animal was moving its head back and forth, screaming.

Six crested the top of the thing's head. On either side, its huge eyes glowed like moons, the irises round and black. It blinked, trying to look at her. Then it threw its head back, attempting to dislodge her. She gripped the bony ridges around its eye sockets until it stopped, then kept going, inching down the bridge of its snout. Behind her, Eleni perched between the thing's shoulders, using her legs to hang on. She raised her hand, a fireball forming in her palm.

"Do it and this thing will let go!" Six called back to her. "We'll both die."

Eleni faltered. Six knew the Mog was weighing both the likelihood of the creature letting go and the value of her own death against taking Six's life. Six counted on Eleni's vanity winning out over her desire for revenge.

Eleni threw the fireball out into the night, where it streamed like a meteor through the dark, slamming against the wall of a building across the street. Six breathed a little easier, but only for a moment. She still had to figure out what to do next.

She looked up, past the thing's open mouth, to the side of the hotel. Each floor had a ledge running around it. Between the floors, the walls of the hotel had a brick-like texture. It might be possible to climb them, if she could hold on. And if she could get past the monster's mouth.

She had no choice. She inched forward. The monster was moving its head around, twisting its neck as it felt her crawling. Six swung away from the building, then back again. She didn't look down.

When the creature moved its head back towards the building, she jumped. She landed on a ledge. Her heels stuck out over the narrow strip of metal, and there was nothing to hold on to, so she pressed against the glass. The monster's head swung within inches of her back, its breath hot on her skin. She heard its teeth clack together.

Slowly, she inched her way to the left, until the glass ended and the wall began. The beast's claws were embedded in the wall above her, and she skirted the curved talons as she began to pull herself up. She didn't dare look to see what Eleni was doing, concentrating on moving up the wall one painful step at a time.

It felt like hours passed as she rose slowly up the remaining distance to the top of the hotel, although she knew it was only minutes. Several times she had to stop as the monster's head came within inches of knocking her off, but she kept going. She didn't think about how high up she was, or what would happen if her broken hand refused to hang on just one more time. She only thought about taking the next step, keeping her eyes on the edge of the roof as it grew closer and closer.

Finally, she reached it. She threw one hand over the edge and started to pull herself up the final stretch. Then someone grabbed her wrist. Six looked up.

"It's about time," Magdalena said. "I thought you would never get here."

CHAPTER TEN

SAM
LAS VEGAS, NEVADA

NINE WAS COVERED IN WHAT LOOKED LIKE BLOOD and oil.

"It's not mine," he reassured Sam, who was staring at him with concern. "Well, not all of it. Turns out, those things are part machine. But only part. The other part is real bitey."

Sam had encountered him while racing towards the Saturn Hotel. Actually, he'd had to stop because a dead grindle was blocking the street. Then Nine had appeared, climbing over the side of it, looking like the victim of a hit-and-run.

"They're called grindles," Sam said.

Nine turned and looked at the scaly-hided monster lying behind him. "Grindles? That's actually kind of cute. Too bad they have such shitty attitudes." He turned his attention back to Sam. "Also, how do you know that?"

"Magdalena told me," Sam answered.

"Oh?" said Nine. "You two been chatting?"

"It's a long story."

"Well, you look like you feel better," Nine said. "Which I assume means Nemo and Max found you."

Sam nodded. "But then Ghost showed up and teleported me away. Like I said, long story."

"Well, it worked on Six, too," Nine said. "So yay for science."

"Where is she?" Sam asked.

Nine glanced towards the Saturn Hotel, where a grindle was clinging to the side. He pointed. "I'm guessing on about the sixty-eighth floor, give or take."

Sam followed his gaze. "We have to get up there," he said. "Magdalena's on the roof. And Eleni has a Legacy now."

"That part I knew," Nine said. "And that's super great for everybody. But you're going to have to handle that one on your own, at least for the moment. There's another one of these things a couple of streets away. I should probably go kill it. Stop it? Whatever you do to something that's part animal and part robot."

Sam nodded. "Go."

"I'll get there as soon as I take care of Mr. Grindle," Nine said.

He ran off, leaving Sam to scale the dead grindle to get to the other side. When he did, he saw the gaping wound in its side and the mechanical innards visible through the gore. He hesitated a moment, then focused on the machinery. He told it to move. When one of the grindle's claws twitched, he jumped back, surprised. But it gave him an idea, and as he turned and ran the rest of the way to the Saturn Hotel, a plan formed in his head.

At the hotel, he slipped through the crowd of police and clueless gawkers and raced through the lobby to the elevators. As he rode up to the roof, he prepared himself for whatever he might find. He was feeling like his old self, but part of him feared that it wouldn't last and his Legacies would falter at the worst possible moment.

When he reached the top floor, he dashed down the hallway to the exit, surrounded by the sound of an emergency alarm clanging a warning. The door to the roof was open, and when he stepped outside he found himself in the middle of a battle.

On one side were Eleni, Seamus and Spike, who had formed a ring around Six, who stood in the middle using her telekinesis to fend off their attacks. Magdalena was kneeling on the rooftop not far off, cradling one arm in the other. Sam suspected Six was somehow responsible for her wounded arm, although there was no time to wonder too much about it. Something was obviously wrong with one of Six's arms as well. It hung limply at her side, and she was using her other one to shield herself.

Sam kept to the shadows, trying to remain unnoticed for as long as possible and maintain some element of surprise. He went for Spike first, using his telekinesis to shove the boy aside. Spike, unprepared for the attack, skidded across the roof, shouting. Before he could right himself, Sam hit him again, lifting him into the air.

Then he stopped. What was he going to do with Spike now? He couldn't kill him. But what else could he do to take him out of the game?

He lifted Spike and slammed him into the side of the statue of Saturn. "Sorry, dude," he said as Spike's limp body fell to the roof, unconscious.

Next, he looked for Seamus. But Seamus had disappeared. Sam knew this was bad news, and his worry was confirmed a moment later when he found himself surrounded by a cloud of flies and bees. Unable to see, and instinctively shying away from the bees' stings. As he was stumbling around, trying unsuccessfully to get the insects off his face, he was hit with a blast of telekinesis, and fell. He thrust his hands out, and his palms scraped against the rough surface of the roof, cutting them open and adding fresh pain to the torment of the stings.

"I'm getting *so* good at this," Seamus said, his voice cutting through the hum of the insects.

Sam struck out blindly with his telekinesis. The bugs dispersed, and he saw Seamus clearly for a moment. He pushed with his mind, and Seamus faltered. But he righted himself again and resumed his own attack, so that Sam found himself once again surrounded by bees and flies.

Anger flooded him like poison from the bees' stingers, giving him the strength to get to his feet. He still couldn't see Seamus, but he struck out with everything he had. He heard a shout of pain, and once more the attacking insects left him alone. Seamus was picking himself up, and now he attacked, abandoning the bugs for pure telekinetic force.

Sam met him head-on, and for a moment they remained deadlocked, each pushing with equal strength. But Sam was more experienced, and Seamus's frustration became his undoing when he attempted to summon the bees and flies again and couldn't maintain his assault. Sam used the opening to hit Seamus with a blast that spun him around. Then he ran at him, tackling him and throwing him to the rooftop.

Seamus bucked, trying to throw him off. Again, Sam had to decide what to do with him. Part of him felt like tossing the guy over the edge of the roof for all of the trouble he'd made for the rest of them. But he knew he couldn't bring himself to do that. Underneath everything, Seamus was still just a kid trying to figure out who he was. Besides, Sam knew that Peter McKenna would be able to reach him with enough time and help. Or at least he liked to believe that he could.

For now, though, he needed to do something to get Seamus out of the way. As he was trying to figure out what that was, something struck him in the back of the head. Not hard enough to knock him out, but he saw stars as he rolled off Seamus and onto his back.

Magdalena stood over him, still holding one arm with the other. She had kicked him.

"Your girlfriend broke my wrist," she said. "And I was just trying to *help her up.*"

"Somehow I doubt that's all you were trying to do," Sam said.

Magdalena stamped her foot. With her pink hair and an outfit that should be on a little girl, she looked like some kind of child playing dress-up. Sam had to remind himself that she was actually insanely dangerous. She somehow created the parasites and the grindles; who knew what else she had up her sleeve.

"Get up!" Magdalena shouted, not at Sam but at Seamus, who already was struggling to his feet.

The monster on the side of the hotel bellowed again. Sam reached out to it as he had to the dead grindle in the street. Because this one was still alive, it wasn't quite the same as interacting with only the mechanical parts. This time, the creature's living brain was part of the equation. He hoped that whatever control center operated the nonbiological parts could override it.

He told the monster to move. Because he couldn't see it, he wasn't sure if it was working. Then he heard the sound of claws piercing metal, and of glass shattering. The grindle was responding.

Hurry up, he urged as Seamus stood and prepared to attack him, the sound of buzzing insects filling the night air. Then there was another crunching sound, and Magdalena turned her head. Her expression changed to one of delight, and she clapped her hands.

Don't get too excited, Sam thought as he sent more instructions to the beast. The grindle heaved itself over the edge of the roof, slowly pulling itself up. Sam saw that it was injured, and moving awkwardly. But it was moving, and that was all he needed.

"Tell it to attack!" Eleni shouted to Magdalena, pausing in her battle with Six long enough to move away from the grindle's snapping jaws.

Magdalena let go of her injured arm and pulled something from the pocket of her dress. It was an ordinary phone. Sam watched her tap at the screen. *Don't tell me she's got an app for it*, he thought incredulously as he focused again on the monster, which was standing in one spot, leaning to one side and roaring.

He looked again at Magdalena's phone. Within seconds, he had connected with it, taking over the app. He ordered the grindle to move. It took a step towards them, looking as confused as a giant creature could that its body was doing something its brain hadn't told it to. It opened its mouth and bellowed in distress, but kept coming.

"That's not what I told you to do!" Magdalena yelled.

The grindle ignored her. Eleni, back to fighting with Six, dodged out of the way of its claws. Seamus, watching the beast approach, seemed to forget all about controlling the flies and bees, which Sam now swatted away easily.

The grindle was growing angrier as its injured body was forced to move. It lurched to the side, falling on one shoulder as its organic muscles failed. But Sam told the hydraulic parts to take over, and they did. The monster stood again. It turned its yellow eyes on Magdalena.

To Sam's surprise, she walked towards it, shaking her good hand angrily as she repeatedly pressed something on her phone. She was acting as if it was a dog disobeying her commands, and not some giant beast capable of tearing her to shreds with one swipe of its claws.

Now she was right underneath it, screaming at it to do as she said. She turned and pointed at Sam.

Sam told the grindle what to do. It bent down and picked Magdalena up in its mouth. She kicked and punched at it as it rose into the sky, standing up on its rear legs until it towered over everyone watching. Then it kept going, tumbling backwards over the edge of the roof. Sam closed his eyes as it disappeared, hating that he'd had to do it. But both Magdalena and her creations were too dangerous. He'd made the right choice.

When he opened his eyes again, Seamus was staring at him. But for some reason the defiant look was gone from his face and he looked frightened instead. "You did that," he said. "You made it take her."

Sam nodded. "I did," he said.

Seamus turned and ran, heading for the open door to the stairways. Sam started to go after him, but stopped when Six called his name. He turned around.

"Let him go!" she shouted. "Nemo and Ghost are on the statue, and they're hurt. Help them."

Sam didn't understand what she meant at first. Then he realized she meant the statue of Saturn. But he couldn't see where Nemo and Ghost might be. His eyes scanned the enormous structure, still finding nothing.

"The ring!" Six yelled.

Now he understood. He ran over to the base of the statue and started to climb the ladder affixed to its side. Eleni threw fireballs at him, which Six pushed aside. Then he was inside the giant sphere, and all he could hear was the sounds of Six and Eleni continuing to fight. The lights inside the planet were dazzling, almost blinding as they twinkled merrily, oblivious to the battle raging around it.

He found the little door that opened to the ring and pushed himself through it. Then he inched onto the ring itself, staying on his hands and knees as he circled Saturn, looking for the girls. He found them a quarter of the way around, huddled against one another.

"Nemo!" he called.

There was no response. Sam crawled faster. When he reached them, he saw that Ghost was badly injured. Nemo's face was swollen from what appeared to be dozens of bee stings, and she seemed unconscious. He shook her gently. To his relief, she opened her eyes.

"Hey," Sam said.

"I killed Boomer," Nemo said, her voice hoarse. "He was attacking us, and . . ." Her voice trailed off as she gasped, trying to draw in breath.

"Don't talk," Sam said.

"Ghost," Nemo said, ignoring him. "Is she . . ."

"She's alive," Sam reassured her. *But not for long*, he thought. He had to get them out of there.

All of a sudden, the statue shuddered. Then something hit it again. Sam turned and crawled around the ring, trying to see what had happened. When he saw what it was, his heart dropped. Eleni had launched a fireball onto the base of the statue. It was melting the pole on which the model of Saturn rested. Now Six and Eleni were engaged in an exchange of punches.

Sam returned to where Nemo and Ghost were seated on the ring. As he crawled, he felt the statue shake again. Then it lurched, leaning farther out over the edge of the hotel. Sam saw Nemo and Ghost start to slide.

"Nemo!" he shouted.

Nemo stirred. When she saw what was happening, she suddenly became alert. She grabbed Ghost, holding on tightly with one hand as she gripped the edge of Saturn's ring with her other, trying to prevent herself and Ghost from sliding off and into thin air.

The planet continued to fall, and Sam realized that there was no way he was going to get to the girls in time. Even if he did, he had no way of getting them off the statue and onto the roof. He *might* be able to save himself, but only if he abandoned them. And he wasn't going to do that.

He thought fast. "Nemo, try to use your telekinesis to push the statue back towards the building," he said.

He did the same, attempting to create a force strong enough to counteract the weight of the statue. He felt the giant sphere resist, and for a moment he thought it might work.

"Keep pushing!" he encouraged Nemo.

But the weight was too much. The planet continued to fall as the pole holding it up came apart. Sam saw Nemo lose her grip. She and Ghost slid to the edge of the ring, then over it. Sam wanted to shut his eyes, but couldn't. He could only watch as the girls, still holding on to one another, fell.

Only they didn't. They hovered in the air, the planet looming behind them. Something was holding them suspended in place. Sam, clinging to the ring, looked to see what might be going on.

"A little help would be nice," said Nine's voice. "This thing is heavy."

Sam couldn't see him, but the voice was coming from somewhere below him. With no time to ask questions, he once more used his telekinesis to try to move the statue. And this time, it worked. Slowly, Saturn returned to an upright position. Once he was no longer in danger of falling, Sam crawled to Nemo and Ghost. Then Nine finally appeared, riding on a floating platform.

"This thing is awesome," Nine said. "I can see why Eleni liked it."

"We have to help Six," Sam said. "But take these two. Then help me push this thing over."

Nemo was able to climb onto the platform with Nine, holding the still-unconscious Ghost. Sam remained standing on the ring. "Showtime," he said to Nine. "Give it all you've got."

Nine grinned. He backed the floating platform away from

the building and lifted his hands. Sam felt the planet begin to tilt the other way. He turned and faced the hotel, and as Saturn began to topple over, he ran across its surface, looking down at the roof below him. Eleni and Six were still fighting, and didn't notice what was happening.

"Six!" Sam called.

Six looked up. She looked exhausted. But she nodded.

She sent out a telekinetic burst that knocked Eleni over, then collapsed onto her knees. The Mog looked up, saw the statue as it came down and tried to roll out of the way.

She didn't make it. Saturn crashed into the roof of the hotel, breaking through and coming to rest half in and half out of the structure. Sam jumped, landing on the roof beside Six.

"Show-off," Six said as Sam helped her to her feet and wrapped his arms around her. Six hugged him back. "I could have taken her, you know."

"I know," Sam said. "But I was getting tired of sitting around on Saturn without you."

Nine alighted on the roof next to them. "We need to get these two to a hospital," he said.

"We're not leaving without Max. No more splitting up," Nemo said.

"I'm right here," Max said, emerging from the darkness. "Although you almost killed me with that," he added, pointing to the collapsed statue.

"How'd you get away from Freakshow?" Nemo asked him.

"I'd like to say I kicked her ass and got away," Max said.

"But the truth is, Seamus came back to the room, and the two of them took off. I don't know where they went."

"We'll find them," Nine said. "With Magdalena and Eleni out of the picture, they're probably running scared." He looked at Sam. "By the way, there's quite a mess in the plaza down there."

Sam grinned. "I'll be sure to leave the cleaning staff a big tip when I check out."

EPILOGUE

GHOST AND NEMO
POINT REYES, CALIFORNIA

GHOST OPENED HER EYES.

"How do you feel?"

Ghost looked at the girl standing beside her bed. "Edwige?"

Edwige smiled and nodded.

"I feel okay," Ghost said. "Did you do this?"

"Dr. Fenris did the surgery," Edwige said. "I healed you afterwards."

Ghost looked around. "Where am I?"

"Human Garde Academy," a voice said from the doorway.

Ghost looked over and saw Nemo standing there. For a moment, she felt panic flicker in her chest.

"It's okay," Nemo said. "You're safe."

"I should go," Edwige said. She squeezed Ghost's hand. "I'm glad you're okay."

Edwige left, and Nemo came and sat down on the edge of Ghost's bed. There was an uncomfortable silence as neither really looked at the other.

"So," Nemo said.

"What happened?" Ghost asked. "On the roof of the hotel, I mean. All I remember is looking at you. Then everything hurt."

Nemo hesitated, as if she didn't want to tell the story. "You got hit by one of Boomer's explosives," she said. "He was trying for me, but you kind of got in the way."

"Oh," Ghost said, not sure what to say. "Is he . . ."

"Yeah," Nemo said, nodding. She looked like she might cry. Then she did. "It's all my fault."

Instinctively, Ghost reached out and took her friend's hand. Nemo startled, then relaxed. "Sorry," she said, almost laughing while she wiped her eyes with her free hand. "I thought you were going to teleport us somewhere else."

"Not this time," Ghost said. "Unless you want to go to Disneyland or something."

Now Nemo did laugh. "Maybe later," she said. Then she turned serious. "We've been through some tough shit."

"Yeah, we have," Ghost agreed. "And nobody is . . . mad at me?"

"Well, *I'm* not," Nemo assured her. "And I don't think Max is. You know he can't stay mad at anyone for very long. Especially you."

"What about, you know, the others?"

"Nine will definitely have some questions for you," Nemo

said. "And they'll probably want you to talk to someone about what happened. You know, to make sure you're really okay."

"In the head, you mean," said Ghost.

"Well, yeah," Nemo said.

"I kind of went off the deep end," Ghost admitted. She waited for Nemo to comfort her, to say again that everything was going to be fine. When her friend didn't respond, Ghost said, "Are we okay?"

"We will be," Nemo said, adding, "You're not going to disappear on me again, are you? That Legacy of yours can be really annoying, you know."

Ghost shook her head. "No more disappearing," she said. "I promise."

Another uneasy silence settled over them. Ghost knew it was going to take time before things were back to the way they were before. There was nothing she could do about that. And it was okay. She still didn't entirely understand why she had done the things she did either, so how could Nemo understand them?

"You should get some rest," Nemo said.

"Yeah," Ghost agreed. "Thanks for coming."

"I'll be back later," Nemo promised her, letting go of her hand and standing up. "I mean, you saved my life. The least I can do is bring you some chocolate, right? And I'll bring Max with me."

Nemo left, giving her a wave from the doorway. When she was gone, Ghost felt herself start to be afraid again.

She'd done some things that seemed unforgivable. She was especially nervous about seeing Max. She knew he must be disappointed in her. For a moment she considered breaking her promise and teleporting away. Then she forced herself to calm down. Maybe Nemo was right, and everything would be okay. Not easy, but okay.

She looked out the window and saw a blue sky. For the first time in a long time, she felt hopeful. For now, that was enough.

SEAMUS

UNDISCLOSED LOCATION

"What did you do to me?"

Seamus glared at his father, trying to summon something—anything—to attack him. It wasn't the first time he'd tried to use his Legacy since waking up and finding himself in a cell that morning.

"We've implanted you with an Inhibitor," Peter McKenna said. "It'll help us keep your abilities under control."

Seamus snorted. "So, if I don't do what you want, you'll just control me like a robot?"

His father's expression remained impassive. "You know why this had to be done. You're dangerous."

"Wow," Seamus said, clapping his hands together. "Congratulations. You finally got what you always wanted—complete control."

"I never wanted to control you, son" his father said.

Seamus ignored him. He thought back to the night before. He remembered running from the fight on the roof, going back to the room. He remembered telling Freakshow and Spike that they needed to leave, and them slipping past the crowd in front of the hotel.

Then things got a little hazy. He'd argued with Freakshow and Spike about where to go. With Eleni and Magdalena gone, he knew things would fall apart. They were better off sticking together. But Freakshow and Spike wanted to return to their new hideout and wait for orders, so he headed off alone.

He remembered stealing a car, but there was a roadblock on the freeway. Then a voice telling him to step out of the vehicle.

"You're lucky Watchtower got involved and they didn't shoot you when you tried to attack them."

"I wish they had," Seamus said. "At least then maybe I'd be back with Catriona."

At the mention of Seamus's sister's name, he finally saw some emotion on his father's face. It was there only for a moment, but he could tell he'd struck a nerve. He pushed. "Then you'd have killed off both your kids. Isn't there some kind of merit badge for that?"

His father seemed about to speak. Then, abruptly, he turned and walked out of the cell, the door sliding open and then shut behind him.

Seamus lay back on his cot and wondered if he should have stuck with Freakshow and Spike. Surely they weren't worse off than he was, trapped here with no way out.

Except that there was always a way out. He just had to find it. And when he did, a lot of people were going to be very sorry. Especially his father.

MAX

POINT REYES, CALIFORNIA

"Do it again!" Max cried.

"Okay," Kalea said. "Hang on."

The ground beneath their feet rumbled. Max fell down, laughing. Rena, holding on to a tree trunk for balance, shook her head. "That is one dangerous Legacy."

"It's not as bad as Kona's," Kalea said, pointing to her brother. "At least I don't turn things into liquid fire."

"I don't know," said Bats, seated at a picnic table nearby, watching her friends show off. "I think Rena's Legacy might be the coolest."

Rena walked over and sat down across from her. "We *all* have great Legacies," she said as the others joined her and Bats.

Max could tell by the expression on Kalea's face that she still wasn't entirely comfortable with them. He couldn't blame her. After all, until recently she'd kind of been playing for the opposite team.

"You guys are all going to love it here," he said enthusiastically.

"I already do," said Bats.

Kona put his arm around his sister. "I'm just happy to have my sister back."

Looking at Kona and Kalea, Max couldn't help but think about Ghost. Nemo had invited him to come with her to visit, but he'd said no. The weird thing was, he *wanted* to see her more than anything in the world. But he wasn't ready.

He knew that every time he looked at her he was going to think about what she'd done, and he wasn't sure he could ever trust her again, not completely.

Then again, if Kona could forgive his sister, maybe Max could forgive his friend. After all, he cared about her. A lot. They'd been through so much together even before meeting Six and Sam. And he'd made mistakes himself, and nobody was bringing that up. Didn't Ghost deserve the same chance?

"You okay?" Rena whispered in his ear, bringing him back to the moment.

"Yeah," Max said brightly. "I was just thinking about how tomorrow it's back to classes. It's like we've been on Christmas break and now it's over."

"I don't know about you," Bats said, "but *my* Christmas breaks never involved fighting giant dinobots on top of a hotel in Sin City."

Everybody, including Kalea, laughed as Max nodded. "Okay, well, maybe it wasn't *quite* like Christmas," he said. "And maybe this school isn't exactly like my old one. But we still have classes tomorrow."

He tried to imagine life going back to normal. Was there even such a thing now?

"I haven't been in school in a long time," Bats remarked. "Not a real one, anyway."

"Don't worry," Max said. "At least here you'll always get to sit with the cool kids at lunch."

Bats turned to him. "Really?" she said. "Are you going to introduce me to them?"

The table erupted in laughter again as Bats put her arm around Max, hugging him.

Yeah, he thought. *Everything is going to be fine.*

SIX AND SAM

NEW YORK, NEW YORK

Sam placed a folded-up T-shirt on top of the other clothes in his suitcase, then closed the top.

"That should be enough for two weeks, don't you think?"

Six held up a bathing suit. "This is all I need," she said. "I don't plan on leaving the beach."

"Then I say Operation Bye-Bye Parasites is officially underway," Sam said.

They'd been given the all clear by Dr. Fenris only hours earlier. And thanks to Edwige, all of their other injuries were healed as well. It was as if Vegas had never happened.

"And Nine said he'd take care of cleanup, right?" Six said.

Sam nodded. "McKenna used his connections with

the Vegas police to squash any further investigations, and they've done damage control with the press. As far as anyone knows, what happened was simply a publicity stunt gone wrong."

"Publicity stunt," Six said. "People will believe anything."

Sam shrugged. "You know what they say, what happens in Vegas stays in Vegas. Anyway, they picked up Freakshow and Spike, and they're in custody. Now they just have to round up what's left of the Mogs."

Six picked up her bag. "In that case, let's get out of here before somebody finds another monster for us to fight."

"I'm afraid Bali will have to wait," said a voice with an accent Six couldn't quite place.

An older man with slicked-back brown hair and a tailored suit had walked into the room. Six didn't recognize him, but he looked like someone who didn't want to be noticed or remembered.

"Who are you?" she asked.

Two more men entered the room. They were wearing light body armor and Six eyed the weapons holstered at their sides. This apparently wasn't a casual visit. The man, ignoring Six's question, reached into his pocket and took out a tablet, which he held up so that Sam and Six could see the screen. A video began to play. It showed Six riding the grindle up the side of the Saturn Hotel.

"And?" Six said.

"That video made it onto YouTube," the man said. "Briefly,

but long enough for certain people to see it and become very interested in what a member of the Garde was doing involved in, shall we say, unsanctioned interaction with Mogadorian rebels."

"In case you can't tell, I was *stopping* her," Six retorted.

The man touched the screen of the tablet and another video played. This one showed Sam standing in the middle of the casino while the machines around him spit out rivers of coins.

"This one came from a security camera," the man said. "The casino owner isn't too happy about paying out all those jackpots."

"Like Six said, we were fighting the Mogs," Sam argued. "Surely you can explain to—"

"You're missing the point," the man said. "The fact that the two of you went rogue after you left Watchtower and didn't let them or the Earth Garde handle this isn't sitting well with some people."

"What people?" Sam asked.

"People who make decisions about the future of the Garde," the man said. "People whose job it is to enforce the Accord, and make sure the public believes it's working. And you're starting to give them the wrong impression."

"Which is?" asked Six.

"That maybe the Garde aren't as harmless as we've been led to believe."

Sam laughed. "This is ridiculous," he said. "We were *helping*. If anything, we prevented an even bigger disaster from occurring."

The man slipped the tablet back into his pocket. "That's not the way everyone sees it. Your activities have just raised too much concern."

"Then tell us who we need to talk to," Six said. "Who needs to understand what really happened."

The man fixed her with a steely expression. "I'm afraid it's the two of you who don't understand," he said as the men behind him stepped forward with their weapons now raised. "You're under arrest."